More than three centuries after the Cataclysm, Krynn still bears scars from the wrath of angry gods. In this land where fear prevails, magic is as mysterious and mighty as the legendary dragons. The Defenders of Magic trilogy is the story of powerful mages who daily defend their beloved Art against those who would corrupt it or see it abolished.

**Guerrand**—his responsibilities as Bastion's high defender place him at odds with an old friend and in conflict with his family, which is afflicted by a mysterious and deadly plague.

**Bram**—nephew of Guerrand DiThon, he feels a lord's responsibility for the suffering of his villagers, and sets off to find a cure—and his long-lost mage-uncle.

**Lyim**—the mage of the Red Robes has traveled the world in search of a remedy for his cursed hand, but his quest has led him to Bastion, a place he is forbidden to enter.

DragonLance® Saga

# DEFENDERS
# OF MAGIC

*Night of the Eye*
Volume One

*The Medusa Plague*
Volume Two

*The Seventh Sentinel*
Volume Three
(Spring 1995)

**DRAGONLANCE books by Mary Kirchoff**

*Kendermore*

*Flint, the King*
(with Douglas Niles)

*Wanderlust*
(with Steve Winter)

*The Black Wing*

**DragonLance** ®  Saga

**Defenders of Magic
Volume Two**

# The Medusa
Plague

**Mary Kirchoff**

DRAGONLANCE® Saga
*Defenders of Magic*
Volume Two

THE MEDUSA PLAGUE
©1994 TSR, Inc.
All Rights Reserved.

First Printing: October 1994
Printed in the United States of America.
Library of Congress Catalog Card Number: 94-60104
9 8 7 6 5 4 3 2 1

ISBN: 1-56076-905-X

TSR, Inc.
P.O. Box 756
Lake Geneva, WI 53147
U.S.A.

TSR Ltd.
120 Church End, Cherry Hinton
Cambridge CB1 3LB
United Kingdom

To John Porter Arnold,
wherever he may be . . .

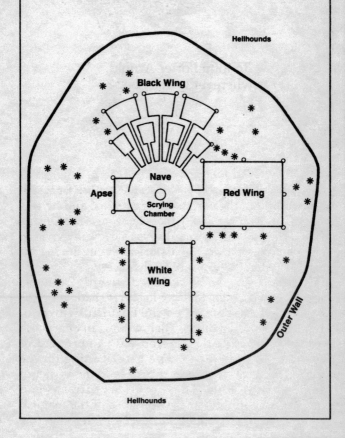

# Prologue

The memory that had haunted Guerrand DiThon for months came to him in the eerie way of dreams, and he was both main character and witness to events. The Dream, as he'd come to call it, was always as painfully vivid as when he'd reenacted the historical event during his magical Test in the Tower of High Sorcery.

Guerrand was the black-robed wizard, Rannoch. He watched himself standing in secret shadow on the Death Walk that encircled the beautiful Tower of High Sorcery at Palanthas. Below him, an angry and avaricious mob had gathered with the regent of Palanthas outside the tower's gate, waiting for the Council of Mages to turn over the key to this center of magical knowledge. These ordinary citizens had come, anticipating their first glimpse of the magical wonders inside. None had foreseen witnessing one mage's desperate act of love for the Art, a love all wizards shared.

As a gesture of his beneficence, the Kingpriest had promised all users of magic sanctuary from persecution at Wayreth, the last and most remote of the original five towers of sorcery. But Rannoch had no intention of retreating to the wilds of Wayreth, no faith in the charlatan's oath of safety there.

The Conclave should never have given in to the zealots' demands. In doing so, they damned magic, the current of Rannoch's life. Like blood to the body. Like water to the earth. What will feed my soul when the magic is gone?

The answer was, simply, nothing.

The Head of the Conclave, a wizard of the White Robes, used a silver key to close the gates of the tower for the last time. As Rannoch, Guerrand could see the eyes of the regent, who would take the key, linger on the tower greedily. The sight of the Conclave's most powerful mage standing shoulder to shoulder with an agent of their greatest enemy made Rannoch's blood boil. The regent reached out his hand, eager for the key.

Rannoch's voice rang clear and cold from atop the Death Walk and echoed across the tower's courtyard, to the Great Library itself.

"The gates will remain closed and the halls empty until the day when the master of both the past and the present returns with power!"

In the body of Rannoch of the Black Robes, Guerrand raised his arms like the wings of some great raven and let himself plummet from the walk. The spikes atop the silver and gold gates spun dizzily toward him, like talons eager to tear at his chest. . . .

\* \* \* \* \*

Esme woke Guerrand with a kiss to his fevered brow. "The Dream again?" she asked, honey-colored eyes filled with concern. She brushed his damp, dark bangs to the side. "I came back from the construction site and found you mumbling, with your arms spread."

Guerrand's eyes were wide with fear until he recognized the small room he shared with Esme in the temporary housing built by the Conclave of Wizards. Guerrand breathed his relief in a huge puff of air and pushed himself up onto his elbows. "Yes, the Dream again."

Esme shook her auburn head. "I don't know why you've let just one aspect of the Test bother you so," she said, sorting through the tangle of his clothing on a nearby chair. She handed him a rumpled tunic and trousers. "Here, put these on. Justarius intends to finish the last granite wall in the Red Order's wing today. He needs all six of his representatives to accomplish the task."

"We're starting early," muttered Guerrand. With the heels of his hands, he rubbed the seeds of restless sleep from his eyes.

"The Council of Three are anxious to get Bastion in place." The young woman chuckled. "If you ask me, I think there's an unspoken competition between them to complete their wings first."

Guerrand nodded absently. Dipping his hands into a basin of cold water, he splashed his face and reflected on how much had changed in the year since the destruction of Stonecliff's magical pillars. Solinari, Lunitari, and Nuitari had made it known to the Council of Three that they were most displeased, furious even. Belize's actions had been a flagrant violation of the gods' decree that no mortals attempt to enter the Lost Citadel. To appease the gods and prevent future attempts to enter this most sacred of magical places,

Par-Salian, Justarius, and LaDonna had agreed that the Conclave of Wizards would construct a fortress to stand between the mortals on Krynn and the storehouse of all magical knowledge that was the Citadel. The Council gathered the members of the Conclave and drew up plans for an impenetrable fortress that would serve as the final line of defense before the Lost Citadel.

But the death of the Master of the Red Order and the promotion of Justarius to Belize's position had left the Conclave of Wizards two members short. In appreciation for their courageous and skillful efforts at Stonecliff, Justarius had offered Guerrand and Esme positions on the Conclave during the building of Bastion. The two had just passed their magical tests at Wayreth and were eager to participate in such a historic event.

Guerrand's gaze wandered out the window of their room to the construction site. Bastion was teeming with activity, mages and monsters working side by side to create history. Even months of backbreaking labor had not inured him to the majesty of the panorama.

Bastion was being constructed in a remote area of the Kharolis Mountains, hidden by the lushness of summer trees. When the Conclave had first arrived at the site, the only remarkable thing about it was the smooth gray rock that pierced the valley floor. The stone was taller than Guerrand—taller even than the elves now working around it. Clearly it had not always been there, because the ground was torn and churned as if the stone had just recently erupted through the turf.

Inscribed upon it in the language of magic was this message: "Whoever accepts the power must bear the responsibility." The Council of Three had made it known that the gods of magic had left the missive as both inspiration and threat. Some of the mages debated the precise interpretation of the stone's inscription, but all agreed that further angering the gods would carry grave consequences.

Towering behind the stone and dominating the flat, green valley were three enormous architectural wings, incongruously designed by the magical orders to reflect their differing temperaments. Modeled after the cathedral-like Palace of Palanthas, the porcelain white wing comprised the right side of the structure. Par-Salian's design was all intricate spires and flying buttresses fired with a glaze that gave the section a seamless appearance, one ornate joint flowing into the next. White-robed wizards, elves, and humans directed the efforts on the white wing.

Guerrand watched as earth elementals, enormous creatures of dirt and precious stones, called forth the finest clays from the soil. Water imbued with the essence of magic was added to the purest of this clay, then spun at terrific speed until the mixture resembled a towering tornado of mud. When the whirlwind ceased, a wet section of porcelain wall stood. Fire elementals, tall sheets of living flame, then set to work baking the wall to an unearthly hardness.

Summoning and controlling such powerful elementals was exhausting work for the white mages, but the grace and beauty of their wing was proof that the effort was worthwhile.

In contrast, the black wing seemed an odd, artificial-looking endeavor. The onyx edifice felt as cold and imposing as LaDonna herself. More concerned with secrecy than practicality, the members of the black council had designed seven separate, unadorned rooms that couldn't be reached through each other. Splayed out in a semicircle to the left of the white section, the black wing resembled the spokes of a double-rimmed wheel.

Onyx from rich veins of chalcedony mined in the Kharolis Mountains were carried night and day by stone golems, who were themselves made by dwarven masons of the evil, magic-wielding Theiwar race. Next, rock-fleshed xorns, which always reminded Guerrand of six-limbed fish heads, painstakingly polished the onyx to a high gloss.

As Guerrand looked on, stone golems were making slabs of the lustrous onyx for the wing's final room. Working tirelessly under the enchantment of the black wizards, the monstrous golems were silent save for the steady thudding of their feet.

Guerrand shifted his gaze back to the center of the site. A smile of pride lit his face. Without a doubt, he mused, Bastion's red wing was the most distinctive for its expert craftsmanship and its simple but practical design. The wing jutted back between the white and black wings, a simple rectangle made of red granite blocks mined by stone giants summoned from the Khalkists. A battalion of these smooth, gray giants, three times the height of a human, were under the direction of stalwart Daewar dwarves. The behemoths carried blocks of granite on their backs or slung between two of them on tremendous tree trunks borne on their shoulders. More Daewar stonemasons, using precision tools, fashioned burnished red blocks that were then put into place upon magical mortar by the stone giants. The wing was a vision of simple elegance, reminding Guerrand of Justarius's villa in Palanthas.

The massive blocks of granite and porcelain and onyx would have stood on their own for centuries. But Bastion was an extraordinary edifice, with an extraordinary purpose. To symbolize the cooperative effort of the magical orders, as well as make the structure impervious to time and nature, Bastion's mortar was being imbued with a portion of the essence of every wizard-in-good-standing on Krynn. But the process of adding the magical contributions of a thousand wizards was time-consuming. Guerrand had lost count of the hours he alone had spent over the slurry of mortar, endlessly repeating the phrases and gestures of the incantation. It was spellcasting that left a mage's body exhausted, but the discipline had sharpened Guerrand's mind.

Accelerated by the magic of twenty-one wizards, the project had gone amazingly well, considering the diversity of temperaments of those working on it and the participation of monsters. After six months of planning and three months of construction, the stronghold was only days away from completion. Soon all but the Council of Three would be magically dispatched from the site.

Par-Salian, LaDonna, and Justarius would then combine their considerable magical abilities to etch the final magic onto the building itself and send the shell of Bastion to a place between Krynn and the Lost Citadel. Only those three venerable mages would know the secret of Bastion's final location.

Guerrand turned his back on the spectacle outside and rested against the windowsill. "I'll be sorry when Bastion's finished," he said. The wizard colored slightly when he realized how selfish he might sound. "Don't get me wrong," he continued hastily. "I understand it's crucial that we prevent anyone from stepping foot inside the Lost Citadel. I'm as afraid as every other mage is of what the gods of magic would do if we allowed it to happen again."

"You know what would happen," said Esme. "All the mages on Krynn have dedicated a portion of their own magical essence to Bastion. That energy binds the mortar to the blocks, as we wizards have bound ourselves to the Art. The Council of Three warned us that if Bastion fails, the energy will be forfeit to Lunitari, Solinari, and Nuitari."

Guerrand dropped onto the bed. "We're a part of history, Esme, of the greatest cooperative magical effort in nearly three hundred fifty years! This is what the builders of the towers of sorcery must have felt. Is it so wrong of me not to want it to end?"

"I've had the same thought," confessed Esme, coloring. "Being a part of this melting pot of skills, this suppression of arrogance and alignment in the defense of our common Art . . ." Esme shook her head. "We'll not see it again in our lifetime."

Guerrand nodded, thinking that the last time the Conclave had joined together to save their artifacts—their lives—was from the wrath of the Kingpriest. The realization brought to mind again the black wizard Rannoch.

"I'll tell you why the Dream bothers me," Guerrand said, abruptly breaking the gentle spell their musings had wrought. He searched through his clothespress for his best red robe. "I've been trying to figure out why the final segment of my Test put me in the body of the *black* wizard who cursed the tower in Palanthas. I'm a *red* wizard," he said, his hands on his hips. "I don't understand what that means."

"I can't answer that either," said Esme. "I can only remind you that the Test exists to weed out those wizards who might be harmful to themselves, to the order, or to innocents. Remember, too, that the Test is meant to teach the mage something about himself." Esme raised a silky brow. "What did Justarius say when you asked him about this after you passed?"

Guerrand wrinkled his lips in distaste. "He told me that the Council designed all three segments of my Test with two goals in mind. First, they wanted to measure the limits of my magical skills. Second, they wanted to

demonstrate that no one is all good or bad or even perfectly neutral at all times. Justarius in particular
wanted me to see that each new day, each new situation, brings with it choices.

"Historically," Guerrand continued, "the black wizard Rannoch chose to throw himself from the Tower of
High Sorcery and curse the place, acts considered in
keeping with an evil wizard. I, on the other hand,
chose neither to jump nor curse the tower. That particularly day, I followed the path of Good and joined the
majority of white and red mages who left peacefully.
But in the first two segments of my Test, my solutions
were inclined toward Evil and Neutrality, respectively."

"There you have it!" Esme exclaimed, pulling the
robe he sought from under a pile of carelessly dis-
carded clothing.

Frowning his distraction, Guerrand slipped an arm
into the sleeve she held out to him. "But in today's
dream, I threw myself—as Rannoch—from the tower!"

"That merely validates Justarius's explanation,"
Esme returned. "Today you chose the path of Evil. In
tomorrow's dream, you might follow the white and red
wizards again. The point is, your choices balance out
and thus follow the ways of the red order."

Guerrand still looked disturbed, skeptical. Esme's
brows drew together with concern. "You're beginning
to sound obsessed, and that worries me."

"You think I *like* dreading sleep, for fear I'll dream?"
he demanded hotly.

She gave him a frank but compassionate look, one
hand on a slender hip. "I think you worry too much
about events you can't affect. Things usually happen
for a reason," she said, recalling a line Justarius liked to
use, "even if we never learn that reason."

Guerrand frowned. "Then this is one time when I've

got to learn the reason for the memory. I'm certain there's some additional lesson I'm supposed to take from it. What if I miss it?"

"You'll miss the rest of your life," returned Esme, "if you keep agonizing over this." She strapped her pouch on over her red robe and sensible trousers, preparing to leave.

Nodding in concession, Guerrand followed the young woman out the door, to where giants and golems worked among mages to make history.

# Chapter One

Harrowdown-on-the-Schallsea
Five years later . . .

Gritting his teeth, Guerrand stretched out his left arm, straining until he thought his shoulder would pop from the socket. It was no use; the juiciest, orange-red rose hips were still a handspan beyond his reach. He would simply have to plow his way through the thorny wild rose-bushes that grew on the banks of the Straits of Schallsea. Resigning himself to ruining his homespun red robe, yet thankful for the protection it offered, he held high his small wooden gathering basket and plunged ahead. His sights were locked on his quarry, highlighted against the bright blue of the nearby straits.

Guerrand stopped abruptly and asked himself, What am I thinking? He shook his head, graying now at the temples because of his Test at the tower, though he was still shy of thirty years. Stealing a glance around, the mage assured himself he was alone on this stretch of heath several rods west of Harrowdown. It was not fear of persecution that made him think twice about casting the simple cantrip that would pluck and carry to him the nutrient-rich fruit from which wild rose petals bloomed. Quite the contrary. The villagers had grown used to—almost complacent about—his magical abilities.

He had grown five years older since the day he and Esme had stopped for the night at the Settle Inn in the small, run-down village of Harrowdown, between Hamlton and Restglen in Southlund, the southernmost province of Solamnia. They had chosen it simply because the inn was nearby at the precise moment their legs would move no farther.

The couple had been wandering northward from the forests near Skullcap without real purpose for more than a fortnight after the building of Bastion was completed, vaguely intending to make their way to mage-friendly Palanthas. Their wanderings had taken them through Abanasinia, a territory decidedly unfriendly toward mages, which was why they were so exhausted. The struggle to keep from getting lynched by barbarian plainsmen or pirates had taken its toll, just as life had taken its toll on his relationship with Esme.

Guerrand chased the unexpected and unpleasant memory of lost love from his thoughts, as always. There were too many happy moments with her to recall. He focused his thoughts on the task at hand. The rose hips that he would use and sell for a soothing tea were steadily filling his basket when Guerrand heard the loud squawk of his familiar.

"Kyeow!" Zagarus's white wings lowered him from the cerulean sky to a dark branch of a spreading cypress tree. *There you are, Rand! I have a message for you from Dorigar.*

Guerrand looked up from the thorny bushes to the large sea gull. Guerrand had conjured his familiar more than a decade before, in what was perhaps his first successful attempt to wield magic. Zag's head was brown-black in a diagonal from the base of his small skull to his throat. His entire underside was yellow-white. Edged with a sliver of white, his wings and back were once as black as onyx. There was no doubt about it; Zag was getting old. The intense coloration of his feathers was duller than it once was; and his yellow legs shambled more than walked now.

"You were no more than three rods away, near enough to speak with me," Guerrand remarked, referring to the mental link that allowed masters and familiars to communicate even over distance. "I'm surprised you left the comfort of your nest at the cottage," he gibed gently. Settling into the late autumn of his life, the gull was less inclined to fly these days.

Zagarus looked at him with one eye closed. *I thought I might find some food while I was about.*

Guerrand snorted. "I should have guessed. What's the message?"

*Message? Oh, yes. There's some creature Dorigar calls a sylph waiting for you with a scroll from Justarius. She won't give it to anyone but you. An odd-looking little thing, if you ask me. Wings like spiderwebs. I don't know how she can handle a head wind with them.*

"Justarius!" cried Guerrand, extricating himself from the tangle of rosebushes. "Why didn't you say so?" He hooked the handle of the basket over his shoulder, hiked up the hem of his robes, and broke into a run.

Watching him flee, Zagarus muttered, *I thought I did say so.* Despite clouding vision, the wily old bird spied a fish leaping in the nearby straits and closed on it,

Guerrand forgotten.

Instead of following the curving dirt path along the shore, the mage took a shortcut on the balk, the turf left unplowed between the rows of Jeb Sanbreeden's field of maize. The rich green leaves rifled Guerrand's shoulders and fluttered like a wave on the sea breeze of the late-Sirrimont day. Strange, he thought, that after five years he still thought in terms of the Ergothian calendar, instead of the Solamnic one the locals used.

Five years . . . Guerrand could scarcely believe so much time had passed since his and Esme's first night in Harrowdown, when Seth, the outgoing innkeeper, had recognized their calling and offered to hire the two mages for short-term work. Though Guerrand had found the man a bit unsettling, Esme had thought the respite the small village offered would do them good while they determined a direction for their lives.

They settled into a cottage on the edge of the village. Initially fearful of displaying their calling, little by little Guerrand and Esme let their skills be known. The people of Harrowdown immediately saw the good that could come from magic. The village and its people flourished. Months turned into two idyllic years for Guerrand.

He was not even aware that Esme had begun to find their life mundane until news reached them that Esme's father, farther north in Fangoth, was ill. Guerrand was equally surprised to hear that she was ready to return to her father and face the shadows of her past.

"You're hiding out here in Harrowdown," she accused him when he'd declined the offer to join her. "This was supposed to be a transition in our lives, not our final destination."

"I'm needed here now," Guerrand remembered responding defensively, "but I don't intend to live in Harrowdown forever."

"Your family in Ergoth, this dream you have of your Test and jumping from the tower as Rannoch . . ." She'd shook her head sadly. "You'll be here until you stop letting your past haunt you," she'd pronounced. Then, kissing him tenderly, bittersweetly, she'd wished him luck and exited his life with the same independent and determined spirit she'd exhibited on the day she'd entered it, in the hills surrounding Palanthas. He'd spent the last three years trying to fill the emptiness she'd left in him by helping the villagers of Harrowdown. Some days were better than others.

The field gave way to the first of the small buildings in Harrowdown, and Guerrand was reminded again how much the village had changed since their arrival. Timber-framed and of wattle-and-daub construction, the homes and businesses of the small village were neat, clean, and newly thatched. Guerrand remembered how run-down they'd looked when he'd first arrived; many had half rotted away, offering little more than a windbreak in winter and a place for rats and other vermin to find food in the warmth of summer. Life in Harrowdown-on-the-Schallsea had certainly changed since a wizard had come to town.

" 'Scuze me, Your Honor," said a stout woman in a well-patched apron, rosy jowls bouncing as she tried to match Guerrand's stride. "Just wanted to tell you them herbs you give me for Cowslip done brought the milk down again."

"Yes, well, I'm glad, Agnus. If you or your cow need anything else, just stop by the shop." Guerrand remembered the woman and her cow's malady, and he knew that if he allowed her to engage him in conversation for even a moment, he would be trapped for hours. The mage forced the pace of his stride until he left the woman panting before the huge, slowly turning waterwheel that marked the miller's shop.

Rounding the corner, Guerrand's glance fell upon two children on the green playing a placid game of mumblety-peg with dull trowels. He smiled and waved at their mother who was nearby, shooing chickens from the lettuce and onions in the small, burgeoning croft next to their house; she waved happily back. Wilery had come to him a fortnight before, haggard and pale, complaining that her children's wayward behavior was more than she could bear. A pinch of marjoram added to their daily milk had apparently calmed them considerably and put color in their mother's cheeks again.

Guerrand hastened past the Settle Inn. Seth, the scrawny innkeeper, spotted him through the open door and hurried out to the steps. "Stuffed that white chicken with wild onion and boiled him for soup," said Seth. "My luck turned around, just as you said it would!"

"I'll bet it made a delicious broth, too," Guerrand said kindly without stopping. A corner of his mouth turned up in a slight smile. Seth was an odd one, all right. Somewhere he'd come up with the notion that the lone, snow-white hen in his coop glared at him every time he came to collect eggs. Stranger still, Seth was certain the hen was angry at him for taking her eggs. Guerrand knew that he wouldn't change the man's mind, so he gave Seth the idea to stuff the bird. A chicken's life was short in the best of times.

The mage reached the eastern edge of town at last. His eyes fell upon his own modest, thatched home with a sense of pride many would have found surprising had they known he was raised in a castle. In fairness, he had to credit Esme and Dorigar for its simple beauty. She had insisted on the window boxes that adorned every opening, and he had faithfully replanted them every spring since she'd left. He'd long since given up hope of her return. Still, to leave them fallow would have reminded him too painfully of the void she had left in his heart.

The garden of annuals and perennials was the domain of Dorigar and the envy of every woman in Harrowdown. Hardier crops like parsley and carrots, protected by thick piles of dried oak leaves, were harvested even in the dead of winter. In summer, the garden had a tumbledown, overgrown look that was at once inviting and overwhelming. Bees buzzed around the fist-sized clumps of crimson bee balm, then flew back to their hive, where he and Dorigar regularly extracted the fruit of their labor.

Chickens scattered, and one of Guerrand's two pigs skittered from his path and into Dorigar's garden. The mage surveyed the grounds from the stoop of his small home to the smaller drying shed, but saw no sign of a waiting sylph. He hastened through the heavy wooden door and into the house. Guerrand squinted while his eyes adjusted. A small fire smoldered in the hearth, the smoke rising through a hole cut in the thatched roof. A kettle of water whistled softly. His assistant was nowhere to be seen on the first floor.

Guerrand knew that Dorigar's love of naps was second only to his love of gardening. The mage set his basket of rose hips on the plank table and scrambled up the narrow, makeshift ladder to the sleeping loft. The feather tick lay upon new hay just as he'd left it this morning. Frowning, he pressed his feet to the outside rails of the ladder and slipped back to the dirt floor.

"Where could Dorigar and this sylph be?" he muttered aloud. Standing stock-still, he cocked his head toward an open window and could vaguely hear his assistant's prattle coming from behind the cottage. Guerrand bounded out the door again, blinking against the bright sunlight as he raced around the house.

He found Dorigar in the sunlit herb garden, chattering wildly at a most unusual-looking creature.

"Youreallyshouldnteatchervilyouknow. Wereshortonit. BesidesImnotquitesurewhatitwilldotoasylph. CouldgrowwartsforallIknow."

Dorigar, being a gnome, was more than a little unusual-looking himself, thought Guerrand. His skin was as brown as aged wood. Vibrant violet eyes, a bulbous nose, and strong white teeth poked through the mussed and curling hair that otherwise obscured his face. His clothing sense made Guerrand's coarse red robe seem like the height of fashion. His favorite, and current, ensemble consisted of an orange-and-green pair of trousers woven with the stripes running horizontally and worn with the pockets pulled out, and a soiled yellow tunic under a hot, brown leather vest, heavily stained with vegetable dyes. Tools and notebooks and other gizmos dangled from all manner of straps and handles attached to his stocky three-foot frame.

Guerrand chuckled at the odd little gnome, then turned his attention to the reason for his return to the cottage. His breath instantly caught in his throat at the sylph's fragile beauty. She appeared as a small, extremely slender and sinuous human woman in a diaphanous gown through which jutted enormous dragonfly wings. They were the most vibrant iridescent purple-green, and veined like a dried leaf. Her hair reminded him of vaguely ordered seaweed, woven with delicate meadow flowers and variegated vines.

Guerrand stepped forward. "Thank you, Dorigar. I'm here now and can take the message myself."

"Wellitsabouttime," huffed Dorigar. "Ithoughtshemighteatmyentirecropbeforeyouarrived."

As the annoyed and colorful gnome stomped past Guerrand, the mage patted his assistant on the back good-naturedly. "Don't forget to take your medicine," he advised.

"AllrightbutIdontseethatitchangesanything," said Dorigar, blowing out an exasperated breath that fanned his frizzy hair, briefly exposing his frowning face. "Ifyouaskmeyoushouldtaketheherbstospeedupyourears." Dorigar continued to mutter to himself as he rounded the corner and disappeared from sight.

The sylph calmly continued to pluck the soft green chervil leaves, either unable or unwilling to understand the fast-speaking gnome. Guerrand had to clear his throat several times before the enchanting creature looked up, strings of chervil hanging from her mouth. "You have a message for me?" he asked.

Wings fluttering to lift her several feet above the garden, the sylph approached Guerrand. She looked him over, then shrugged, as if she found him wanting. The sylph reached delicate, marble-pale fingers into her revealing little robe, extracted a delicate parchment scroll bound with a pressed dollop of beeswax, and held it toward him.

Guerrand turned the scroll over and recognized the crescent-moon-in-a-cup imprint in the wax from a ring Justarius wore. "How did you come by this?"

Her voice was as lilting and evanescent as the wind. "I am returning a favor to Justarius." With that, she lifted her wings, as fine as spiderwebs, and slipped away like mist into the thick canopy of trees beyond the rectangular herb garden.

"Wait!" Guerrand cried, knowing as he did that the elusive creature would wait for no one. He looked again at the scroll, tapping it thoughtfully as he went back inside the homey cottage. Now that he had the missive in his hands, Guerrand was more puzzled than ever. What did Justarius want with him after so many silent years?

He set the scroll on the table. Dropping a handful of the rose hips into a mug, the mage covered them with hot water from the simmering kettle in the hearth. He sipped the brew unsteeped, staring at the scroll pensively.

*Aren't you going to open it?*

Guerrand's head shot up, and his gaze went to the open window. He hadn't even heard Zagarus's return. He set the mug down and looked into the flames. "Eventually."

*You're afraid.*

Scowling, Guerrand snatched up the scroll and broke the wax seal with a flick of his thumbnail. The curled parchment tumbled open. Guerrand blinked in confusion when he saw only an intricate, symmetrical pattern inked there. He had been expecting words, not magical symbols. These symbols meant nothing to him, although they stirred a distant memory.

The star-shaped mosaic pattern in the summer dining room of Villa Rosad . . . These symbols reminded Guerrand of the configurations of colorful tiles Justarius required all of his apprentices to memorize through visualization to heighten their awareness of magical patterns.

*What does Justarius have to say?* asked Zagarus.

"That's going to take me a few minutes to figure out." Guerrand moved the clutter of spellbooks, notes, and pots of dried and fermented components to the floor. He lit his biggest tallow candle, as thick and long as his forearm, and used it to pin the top of the curling scroll to the coarsely planed table. Staring at the odd symbols, he racked his brain to recall the key to Justarius's tile exercise. He'd conjured few spells more complicated than cantrips for a long time, and he'd had no need to create his own as Justarius had taught him. He was simply out of practice.

Guerrand's eyes were dry and red from smoke, and the candle had burned by half before he began to make sense of the missive. The spiral pattern was far more complex than it had appeared at first, consisting of not one but eight intertwined paths. Woven through the spirals was a series of recurring symbols, elongated ovoids, that repeated an intricate pattern.

He leaned back in the stool and rubbed his eyes with the heels of his hands. Outside the open window was darkness. Guerrand wrapped a hand around the mug of his long-forgotten tea; it was well past cold.

*If it's proving so difficult, why don't you just get rid of the note?* The gull was settled in his nest in the far corner of the room, his small eyes closed.

Guerrand sat motionless for several moments. Abruptly he jumped to his feet and kicked back his stool, sending it crashing to the dirt floor. "Perhaps you're right, Zag." With that, Guerrand snatched up the scroll on his way to the open hearth and tossed the odd message into the flames.

Zagarus's beady orbs popped open in surprise as his master then jumped back behind the meager protection of the table and watched the missive burn. Smoke from the scroll roiled out of the hearth and formed the face of the Master of the Red Robes, Justarius, in a wavering, gray image. Excited, Guerrand came around the table to face the foggy image.

*Ah, Guerrand. If you're hearing this, you were able to recognize that fire would release the magical bonds. I must apologize for putting you through yet another test so long after your apprenticeship, but I had to be sure that you alone received the details of this missive. I also had to be sure that years of life among the simple folk hadn't robbed you of your wits.*

Guerrand ground his teeth against the presumption, particularly since it was so close to the truth. "How could you be sure that someone else didn't just toss it in the fire?" he demanded of the smoke, but the image didn't respond to his question. The mage had to remind himself that Justarius wasn't really here, just his magically recorded message.

*Random placement in a fire wouldn't have released the message,* Justarius's image was saying. The archmage had obviously anticipated his former apprentice's question. Guerrand vowed to keep his mouth shut and listen before he missed any more of Justarius's words.

*The purpose of this missive is to inform you that the Council of Three requests your presence at Wayreth immediately. We wish to discuss with you a most urgent situation. Use your mirror to speed travel. All questions will be answered when you arrive.* With that, the smokey visage of Justarius broke into wavering tendrils and stretched toward the hole in the thatch.

Guerrand jumped when the door behind him abruptly banged open. Dorigar stomped into the small house, slamming the door closed. "I don't suppose you've made anything to eat."

"No." Guerrand noted vaguely that the gnome had remembered to take the magical concoction the wizard prepared each morning to slow his assistant's speech to an understandable rate.

Dorigar marched up to a butcher's block and retrieved a device from beneath it. Several gleaming blades extended at divergent angles, mounted alongside measuring rods and depth gauges and mesh hand guards. With this doodad, Dorigar commenced slicing leeks into a kettle. Adding carrots and other herbs, he filled the pot with water. Last, Dorigar used an iron poker to hang the pot from a ring above the fire, stoked to furnace proportions.

Mary Kirchoff

Guerrand quickly grew annoyed by the gnome's happy scurrying. The cottage seemed to grow a degree hotter with each beat of the wizard's heart. He jumped to his feet and rushed out into the night to lean against a linden tree. Drawing gulps of cool summer air, Guerrand listened to the distant lowing of cows, the ringing of bells calling men in from moonlit fields. The familiar sounds calmed him.

*What's bothering you?* asked Zagarus, settling upon a branch of the tree above his master. *I haven't seen you so shaken since Esme left.*

Guerrand slid down the tree into a crouch and dug his fists into his eyes. "I don't know. Maybe I'm just tired from concentrating all afternoon on deciphering Justarius's message."

*What do you think the Council wants?*

"I'm sure I don't know that either." Guerrand crossed his arms tightly before him. "I do know that I'm not too keen on going back to Wayreth."

*You'll have to check your handbook, of course,* said Zagarus with exaggerated stuffiness, *but I believe you gave up the right of refusal when you vowed loyalty to the Red Robes.*

Guerrand scowled up at his familiar. "I know that, as well as you know there's no handbook. I merely said I don't *want* to go, not that I wouldn't."

The dull-black feathers on Zagarus's wings lifted in a shrug. *So what's the problem?*

Guerrand absently touched the scar along his cheek that had never healed completely in five years.

*Is that still bothering you?*

"No!" Guerrand snapped a little too quickly. He wasn't sure whether Zag meant the external or internal scars left by the third and final segment of his Test. A week never went by without him waking up in a sweat from the Dream. Though he had passed the Test, he felt certain the Dream meant he was supposed to take

23

something else from the lesson. But he had no clearer idea of what that was now than he'd had when he walked away from the dreamlike tower in Palanthas and Justarius had told him he'd passed.

Guerrand glided up the tree to his feet. "I have no interest in leaving Harrowdown, even briefly, to stand around and compare spellbooks with a bunch of high-powered mages. I'm needed here." He began to pace. "To the villagers, my work is important. Harrowdown is prosperous compared to what it was when I arrived. Life as a mage may not be exactly what I dreamed back in Castle DiThon, but it isn't bad, either."

*This is what you and Esme fought about, isn't it?*

Guerrand's hand sliced the air like a scythe. "You know I won't talk about that."

Zagarus was silent for some time. *You don't even know why Justarius has summoned you. Aren't you the least bit curious? Maybe he just wants to say hello.*

Guerrand chuckled without humor. "That's so like Justarius." He sighed his resignation. "But I guess we'll find out the truth soon enough." Heading back for the cottage door, he announced over his shoulder, "I'm going to take a few moments to eat some of Dorigar's delicious-smelling stew. Then I'll pack a few things, and we'll leave for Wayreth through the mirror."

*Do you even have that piece of glass anymore?* asked Zagarus. *I haven't seen it for years.*

"I packed it away in a safe place after the confrontation with Belize," explained Guerrand, referring to the magical looking glass the archmage Belize had given Guerrand before they'd left Castle DiThon. It allowed the bearer to magically travel far distances via a mirror world by mentally picturing a mirror where you wished to reenter the real world. Guerrand had used it only once since the Night of the Eye upon Stonecliff, and that had been to transport Esme, himself, and Zagarus away from the site of the destroyed pagan pillars to Palanthas.

*Is it wise to use it after so long?* asked the gull. *I mean, you need a familiar destination point, and we've been away from Wayreth for a long time. Even there, things must change.*

Guerrand waved away the concern. "Justarius himself recommended we use it. He must have removed any magical wards on Wayreth that would prevent us from entering."

Guerrand returned some time later from the cottage with his old leather pack filled and strung from shoulder to hip. Digging around in the bag, he pulled from it a familiar, hand-sized fragment of dusty glass and set it on the dirt path. The mage smiled ruefully up at his familiar and extended his arm as a perch for the gull. "Justarius awaits us."

With the heavy old gull on his arm, Guerrand felt a long-forgotten sense of déjà vu as he stepped upon the surface of the magical glass and slipped into the extradimensional mirror world.

\* \* \* \* \*

As Guerrand suspected, Justarius had left a glowing trail in the mirror world that bypassed any protective wards and led them directly to a man-sized looking glass right inside the Hall of Mages. The room had not changed one jot since Guerrand's first audience here. It was a vast, round chamber carved of obsidian; the far walls and ceiling were beyond his sight, obscured in shadow. As usual, there were no torches or candles, yet the room was lit by a pale white light, cold, cheerless, without warmth.

Shivering in the dampness, Guerrand remembered with a bittersweet twinge his friend and fellow apprentice Lyim Rhistadt's first bit of advice to him, when they both were waiting outside in the foretower to be assigned masters: "It's a snap." He had been so afraid then. Now he felt only cold.

This time Guerrand was not surprised by the sudden appearance of the heavy oaken chair behind him in the otherwise empty room. He slipped into it and waited, fingers drumming the intricately carved armrests, anxiously at first, then with growing impatience.

"Be at ease, Guerrand," he heard at long last. He still could not see a face, but he recognized the slight quiver of age in Par-Salian's voice.

"We're delighted you responded to Justarius's missive." The years had not dulled LaDonna's sultry voice.

The members of the Council of Three chose that moment to reveal themselves. The light had not increased or crept farther into the shadows, and yet Guerrand could now see the semicircle of twenty-one seats, all but three empty. He had sat in one of those seats briefly, during the Conclave to discuss the building of Bastion.

Seated in the very center, in a great chair of carved stone, was the extremely distinguished, though frail-looking, head of the Conclave of Wizards. Age had not dulled Par-Salian's piercing blue eyes; the long, gray-white hair, beard, and mustache that nearly matched his white robe had not grown an inch.

LaDonna, too, looked as if not a day had passed since Guerrand's first audience. The Mistress of the Black Robes was seated to her superior's right. She was a striking woman whose iron-gray hair was woven into an intricate braid coiled about her patrician head. Her beauty and age still defied definition.

"You're looking well, Guerrand."

Guerrand's eyes shifted at last to the speaker whose voice, robust with unspoken humor, he knew so well.

Justarius alone seemed to have aged. There was more salt than pepper now in the mustache and the shoulder-length hair that was simply parted down the middle. New, tiny lines pulled at the corners of his mouth and the narrows between his dark eyes. His usual neck ruff was a crisp and clean white, in contrast to the red linen robe below it.

"I *am* well," the former apprentice said stiffly.

The three revered mages exchanged surprised looks. Par-Salian brushed a wisp of white hair from his watery old eyes. "The Council has summoned you, Guerrand, to offer you a position of some importance."

"I'm happy enough where I am."

Justarius's eyebrows narrowed in a familiar gesture of irritation. "I see you've compounded your impertinent tendency to jump to conclusions. You would do well to listen and not waste our time."

Though words welled in his throat, Guerrand had the wits to press his lips into a tight line.

"Let us not mince words, Guerrand," began Par-Salian. "Bastion's representative from the Red Robes has abruptly resigned, and we are in need of an immediate replacement. The Council has raised your name as a possibility to fill that position."

Guerrand could not keep the shock from registering on his face. His mouth dropped open. None of his musings regarding the nature of the summons had included Bastion. He couldn't speak, which was fortunate, because there was still more to hear.

"Since its completion," continued Par-Salian, "Bastion has been run democratically by three occupants, a representative from each order, but that doesn't seem to have worked. Somehow even the most trivial issues degenerate into a two-against-one brawl. These conflicts divert the mages' attention from their real purpose in the stronghold: to be ever vigilant against intruders seeking the Lost Citadel."

Par-Salian leaned forward on his chair, elbow propped on the right armrest. "To prevent this from continuing, the Council has voted to create the position of high defender. The model is this very Council. I am the head of the Council of Three, as would the high defender be to the occupants of Bastion."

Par-Salian paused for effect. "Justarius has recommended you for that position."

"So I would be in charge of two mages who've been there for some time?" Guerrand asked.

Par-Salian nodded, but held up a blue-veined hand for Guerrand to allow him to finish. "You must also know that the work is lonely and tedious, requiring constant vigilance for something that is likely never to happen."

Guerrand squinted one eye suspiciously. "Why did the previous mage resign?"

"Vilar . . . was unstable," Justarius said, picking his words carefully. "Bastion is very isolated, particularly if you don't get along with its other occupants." The red mage sighed. "He was not the first, but the second to resign; Ezius of the White Robes is the only original representative. You will be the fifth sentinel and the first high defender . . . should you accept the position."

Overwhelmed, Guerrand ran a hand through his mop of dark hair. "I-I can't give you an answer right now. I need time to go home and think, and—"

"There isn't time for a trip," interrupted LaDonna a bit peevishly. "Surely you can understand the need to fill this position immediately. You have until sunrise to decide."

"Your old room in the north tower has been prepared for your comfort," Justarius added more kindly. "Of course, Zagarus is welcome. I'll take you there now."

Guerrand stood weakly, holding fast to the arm of

the chair. He nodded briskly to Par-Salian and LaDonna, then walked from the Hall of Mages at Justarius's side. The red archmage seemed to be limping more than Guerrand remembered, favoring the leg that had been twisted by his own Test. Their footsteps, Justarius's irregular, echoed against the cold, circular walls. The two mages crossed the small foretower where once Guerrand had waited with other hopeful apprentices, then entered the north tower.

Both men knew there was no need for Justarius to show Guerrand the way to the sleeping chamber some five levels above Par-Salian's study. He'd stayed there for several days before and after his Test, then during the planning of Bastion. Guerrand couldn't decide if Justarius was acting as jailor or host now. Neither spoke as they climbed the narrow flights of stairs to the sixth level. The exercise brought warmth to feet that had grown cold in the foreboding ceremonial hall.

Guerrand automatically took a sharp left at the top of the stairs, passed the first room, and turned the marble knob on the second. Squeezing through the door to the triangular room, he mumbled, "Thank you," and made to shut the door behind him.

Justarius's good leg shot out to place his foot between the door and its frame. "I know you well enough to see when something is troubling you, Guerrand. Do you care to tell me what it is?"

Guerrand looked at his feet. "I don't know what you mean."

"You don't do coy at all well," Justarius remarked. "That was always Esme's specialty."

Guerrand's head jerked up at the mention of Esme's name, as Justarius had obviously intended.

"She's doing well, by the way," Justarius said conversationally. "She's still living in Fangoth." The archmage managed to steer them into the small, triangular room. Thin light filtered through a tiny window, more an arrow loop, on the far wall. "Her father died several years back, and she's working toward restoring the locals' faith in magic after her father's reign of terror. But you would know about that."

"I-I knew her father died, but not the rest," confessed Guerrand. "I haven't heard from her in years."

With pursed lips that raised his mustache, Justarius acknowledged the admission. "I meant, you would know about raising the morale of a village with your magic. From what I've observed, you've accomplished near miracles in Harrowdown-on-the-Schallsea."

" 'From what you've observed?' You mean you've been watching me?"

"I make it a point to follow the progress of all my students." Justarius's eyes alone held the warmth of the confession.

Guerrand sank with a sigh into the deep chair by the hearth on the curved, outside wall. "I didn't know."

Justarius let out a breath as he closed the door. "Why do you think I recommended you for the position at Bastion?"

"Frankly," chuckled Guerrand, "I haven't had time to consider your reasoning. Your missive revealed nothing about the nature of the meeting."

"What made you answer the summons?"

Guerrand considered the question honestly. "Mainly curiosity," he admitted at last. "Besides, I wasn't sure I had the option of ignoring a summons by the Council."

Justarius raised one brow. "I believe I told you once, when you wanted to return to Thonvil to help your family, that you always have a choice."

Guerrand acknowledged the memory with a small nod.

Justarius moved by the fire and crossed his arms expectantly. "So now that you've had your curiosity satisfied, are you interested in the position?"

"I . . . don't know," Guerrand admitted. "There's just so much to consider. The people of Harrowdown depend on me, and—"

"They'll survive without you," Justarius broke in. "Every master must let his students fly or fall one day. You've given them the tools to succeed on their own."

Guerrand gave a self-deprecating chuckle. "But will I survive without them? What if I'm no more suited to the job at Bastion than the previous red mage?"

"I have not succeeded at a great many things," Justarius said soberly. "The only thing I have not failed at is trying. Failure is an integral part of the life cycle."

"But I am a rousing success in Harrowdown," said Guerrand. "There's a great deal of comfort in knowing that."

Justarius cocked his head in question. "Is comfort the achievement that you seek?"

Guerrand frowned, discomfited with the introspection, but unable to deny Justarius his answers. "At one time, I didn't think so. After the battle at Stonecliff with Belize, then the creation of Bastion, I believed I was destined to follow in your footsteps to becoming an archmage. But when that didn't happen, I began to suspect I wasn't suited to more than I had in Harrowdown."

"If you feel shorted of opportunities," Justarius observed, "it's because you haven't sought them out." He gave an ironic chuckle. "Just how many times did you expect to save the world, anyway? You've already been given more opportunities than most. Life is tedious, life is dirty, life is stimulating, life is ordinary for all of us. There are good days and bad days, and there will be no less of each at Bastion if you accept the position."

Guerrand set his chin firmly. "But I've resigned myself to my small success in Harrowdown. That's enough for me now."

"Now, today, perhaps, but will it be sufficient three years hence? Or fifteen?" demanded Justarius. He tapped a finger to his chin as he seemed to recall something. "This conflict of expectations, exacerbated by fear of failure, was the source of your conflict with Esme, wasn't it?"

Guerrand winced, nodding. It still hurt to think of it, let alone speak of his separation from the young woman. She had never understood his conflicting emotions. "Be happy with what you are, whatever it is, and you'll be a success," she'd say. He understood now that she had been right, but it didn't erase the conflict from his mind. That conflict had been the springboard of their friendship, since she, too, had suffered from confused expectations. The difference was, she had conquered her demons sufficiently to return to help her taskmaster father, while Guerrand had never been able to return to Thonvil, even for a visit.

Justarius watched the interplay of Guerrand's emotions on the young man's face. Shaking his head sadly, the archmage turned to leave. "I have things I must attend to while I'm here at Wayreth." He eased his crippled leg to the door and placed his hand on the knob. "Let me just say this, Guerrand. If public adoration or the trappings of comfort represent success to you, then turn down the job. But if you seek the opportunity to use your skill for something important, you'll jump at this chance." The archmage squinted through one eye at his former apprentice. "You'll probably never get another." Justarius wrapped his cloak more tightly about himself and stepped from the room.

Guerrand was staring, unseeing, at the closed door when he became aware of something moving about on the small, thick window ledge. Turning, he spied Zagarus. He'd not even heard the bird arrive. Zagarus merely stood staring expectantly at his master.

"What? Why are you looking at me like that?" Guerrand demanded. "Let me guess. You heard our conversation, and you think Justarius is right?"

*It doesn't matter what I think. I'm just a bird,* Zag shot back. *Don't expect me to solve all your problems. What do you think?*

Guerrand already knew the answer to that. Both Esme and Justarius, the two people who unquestionably knew him best, had so easily recognized in him what he had refused to believe until now. He *had* been hiding out in Harrowdown, at least for the last few years. He had already lost Esme because of it. Justarius would not recommend him twice for the position of high defender. He had to accept the offer, or he would always wonder what his life might have been. Besides, if he failed, he could always return to Harrowdown, couldn't he?

Guerrand yanked open the door and stepped out of the room. Justarius stood a dozen paces away, conversing with another red-robed mage. Both looked up as Guerrand entered the hallway.

"I wouldn't miss this opportunity for the world, Justarius," Guerrand announced. "I'm your man."

# Chapter Two

"There it is!" breathed the old fisherman, pointing a knobby finger to the churning water off the New Coast peninsula. "The Boil above Itzan Klertal."

Lyim Rhistadt looked over the bow of the small fishing boat to where a swath of sea appeared to boil in a wide, dark, frothing circle. Dead fish and other sea creatures bubbled to the top as if in a stewpot. Since its birth more than three hundred fifty years before, New Sea had roiled here, like an eternal flame, to mark the spot where the evil city once known as Klertal had stood. Lyim had never seen anything like this angry black water, and it fascinated him.

"Take me closer," he ordered the fishermen he'd paid handsomely to ferry him to this locally feared triangle of sea. Lyim's eyes never left the spot where angry black water boiled and churned.

"This is near enough," hissed the sailor's son, a thin lad with a wispy mustache and fly-away hair the color of mouse fur. His eyes grew wide as he saw bloody bits of fish float nearer their small boat. His lips trembled. "We'd best turn back, Pa."

Lyim's left hand stopped the old man as he leaned into the oars to turn the small craft. "I paid you a year's wages to take me to the Boil."

"And that we have done," said the old fisherman, beads of sweat forming on his upper lip. "Any closer, and we'll surely be pulled into the maelstrom."

"If it's a closer look he wants, I say push him in and let him swim," grumbled the man's other son, a surly, suspicious lad with thick, veined forearms. He had strongly opposed his father accepting the job from the first, when the strange, secretive man had approached them on the dock back in the tiny fishing village of Balnakyle.

Lyim's coal-dark eyes pierced the burly son's, saying what his lips did not. I have not searched five long years to let your pitiful fear stop me now. The surly lad drew back to the farthest corner of the dinghy, and still it was not far enough from the shrouded man who hid his right hand.

"You'll take me wherever I say." Lyim turned his back on all three of the fishermen dismissively, mentally measuring the distance to the angrily boiling waters. He could easily swim the distance, and yet it was the principle of the thing. He had paid these fainthearts well.

The boat shifted abruptly. It was too silent behind him. Lyim whirled around to find father and sons, hands outstretched, closing in on him slowly. They froze in the dark shadow of Lyim's gaze.

The mage's left hand reached into his dark shroud and withdrew a small, wrapped cocoon. He didn't hesitate for a heartbeat before locking his eyes on the surly son and mumbling the words to the spell that had come to mind. There came one short, high-pitched scream, then a hideous slurping and popping sound. Where once stood a dark-haired human was now a flapping mass of tentacles trying desperately to support a heavy, soft body with bulging eyes. The squid fell against the side of the dinghy, then slipped overboard into the sea.

"Maginus?" yelped the father, leaning overboard with his other son. Both desperately searched the surface of the rippling sea. When Maginus didn't answer, his family drew back from the edge in horror and looked to Lyim's face. The mage sat and calmly crossed his legs.

Lyim derived great pleasure from watching them realize his profession. The sailors looked fearfully from him to the seething water and back, as if trying to decide which was more dangerous, a mage or the angry boiling sea. They decided to take their chances with the sea, because both men wordlessly snatched up the oars and paddled the dinghy closer to the roiling water.

Satisfied at last, Lyim stood carefully once more and shrugged the simple shroud he wore down from his shoulders, letting it dangle from his forearms. He was naked from the waist up and oblivious to the quaking fishermen. The mage closed his eyes and concentrated on the remembered pattern of the spell he sought; its only component was verbal, so it was more important than ever to be precise. At last Lyim opened his eyes and let the shroud slip to the bottom of the dinghy. He saw the men's eyes shift from his nakedness, searching for the source of the odd hissing sound. Both gasped aloud when they found it at the end of Lyim's right arm.

The appendage that was no longer an arm.

The limb was a writhing thing covered not with flesh, but with scales of brown, red, and gold, patterned symmetrically in rings and swirls. At the end of the limb, where a hand should have been, thrashed the head of a snake, its eyes inky black and malevolent. Sighting the two frightened fishermen, the hideous creature hissed and flicked its tongue.

The younger man backpedaled in undisguised horror. The father had to grab his son's arm to keep him from falling overboard and joining Maginus.

Lyim had never grown used to the looks of revulsion his snake arm drew. He had a difficult time not recoiling from it himself. Nearly six years had passed since his own master, Belize, had viciously thrust Lyim's right arm into a magical portal at Stonecliff. When then-apprentice Lyim had been allowed to withdraw his arm from the extradimensional bridge, he found his limb had been replaced by a living snake.

Soon, Lyim reminded himself, people would no longer draw back from him in horror. Below, in Itzan Klertal, he would learn the secret for removing, once and for all, the hideous thing his arm had become.

The thought propelled the mage on, made him mumble the words that would polymorph him into a sea creature. The sensation was an odd, painless stretching that sounded worse than it felt, with all manner of pops and crackles. Lyim grew to tower nearly twice the height of the witless men in the little dinghy. He gingerly passed his thick, insensitive tongue over hundreds of needle-sharp teeth. Though he could feel nothing through his thick, green-scaled hide, he knew the luxurious mane of hair of which he was so proud was now like limp seaweed. His left arm had lengthened as if made of hot taffy; he could touch his wide, webbed feet, so useful for swimming, without even bending.

But no amount of research had prepared the mage for what it would feel like to be a scrag, a water troll. Despite years of living with his repulsive limb, Lyim was still vain enough to be glad he couldn't see how grotesque he must look now. Yet the water troll was the safest form to adopt to explore the ruins of Itzan Klertal in search of the Coral Oracle.

The boat was pitching dangerously with the added weight of Lyim's new, ten-foot-tall form, not to mention the fishermen's frantic scrabbling to get away from him. Lyim threw himself overboard, heedless of the huge wave he left in his wake. The men were as good as dead anyway.

The mage-turned-scrag instinctively reached out his long, green arm toward the swirling maelstrom and drew powerful downward strokes, kicking his wide, webbed feet. Lyim wasn't surprised to see that even as a scrag, his snake arm remained. Nothing he had tried in nearly six years had removed it for more than a day. He had starved himself, but while he withered, the limb flourished. He had chopped off the snake, even doused it in oil and burned it in his desperation, willing to live with only one arm. But the grotesque limb always regenerated. Illusionary spells to disguise it simply misfired, even when cast by the most powerful mages he could bribe. He had journeyed far and wide looking for anyone who might know how to fix his magically mutated limb. Each fruitless trip left him more bitter and frustrated. He hoped fervently that this trip to the sunken city would end that pattern.

Strangely, the failure that had left him the most bitter was the first. Oh, the Council of Three had been kind enough when he'd agreed to return to Wayreth with Justarius after the fiasco that had caused the mutation at Stonecliff. They'd taken him under their wing, so to speak. Par-Salian, LaDonna, and Justarius had given him lodging for more than a month while they searched their books and their collective memories for some way to banish the snake from his limb. Justarius had even encouraged him to take his Test while they searched. Despite the handicap of his right arm during spellcasting, Lyim's natural ability had helped him to struggle successfully through the arduous trial of magic taken by all mages who wished to progress beyond rudimentary spells. He saw it as vindication for all that he had suffered, and somehow he connected that positive sign with the belief that the Council of Three would find some way to cure him.

That was why Lyim had been stunned—beyond stunned—when they called him into the Hall of Mages to inform him that they had been stymied in all efforts to discover a cure for his hand. The problem was, they said, none of them knew what Belize had done, what spell had caused the mutation. Though Justarius specialized in rearranging magical patterns to create new spells, he needed to see the old pattern, which was known only by Belize, who had been tried in a tribunal and put to death.

Justarius had concluded the meeting by encouraging Lyim to overlook the handicap and get on with his life; obviously it had hindered Lyim little in his Test. The newly appointed Master of the Red Robes had even pointed to his own crippled leg and said, "We've all given up things for the magic."

Justarius knew nothing about Lyim, if he didn't realize how much the mutation had altered his life. How could anyone compare a game leg with the monstrosity that was Lyim's hand? Night and day the thing hissed and thrashed, until he could hear nothing else, until he thought he would go mad. Nodding numbly, Lyim had backed out of the Hall of Mages and left Wayreth without another word exchanged.

Lyim believed they had spoken honestly, that Par-Salian, LaDonna, and Justarius had tried. What he could neither understand nor forgive was that the three most powerful mages on Ansalon were unable to find a solution to his problem. It confirmed what he had always suspected: You had only yourself. For the umpteenth time in his life, Lyim had set off alone to alter the cards the cruel fates had dealt him. That day had been the first of the five-and-a-half-year search that led Lyim to a city sunk by the Cataclysm.

A whispered conversation in a dark Nerakan inn had brought him here. There had he met Ardn Amurchin, an evil mage who resided in the corrupt city dominated by volcanoes. Amurchin was a sinister and hideously wizened old dark elf who told Lyim at their first meeting that he knew of one who had an answer to every question. At a second meeting, Amurchin divulged the secret of an oracle who was trapped in the submerged city of Itzan Klertal. Of course, he revealed this only after Lyim handed over three of his best magical scrolls. Eager for any lead that might cure him, Lyim had readily paid the mage.

He was eager, but not hasty. Lyim had first traveled back to Palanthas, to the Great Library. He found pre-Cataclysm encyclopedic entries written by the city leaders to be unrevealing whitewash, though he did learn that before the gods' wrath had reshaped the world, the city he sought had been known only as Klertal. The prefix Itzan, meaning 'submerged' in old Kharolian, was added to the name of the ruins after the Cataclysm, as well as to all nearby cities that suffered a similar fate.

Lyim's most fruitful research came from recovered journals written by traveling clerics and merchants. By all those accounts, Klertal had been an old, highly developed inland city, a cynical place of cutthroats and thieves. It had been the primary city along a busy trade route between Xak Tsaroth and Tarsis. One account referred to Klertal as a "blasphemous place, without morals or redemption." Obscene wealth abutted rank poverty. As a rule, everyone, including city officials, cheated and lied.

Including the potentates. Unlike kings, who were born to their stations, the leaders of Klertal apparently bought, bartered, or beheaded their way into the position. Each remained ruler as long as he staved off his enemies. The last potentate, Sullento the Profane, was evidently exceptionally good at squashing rebellions; he held the position for nearly ten years.

Lyim found one entry, written by a merchant who had dealt directly with Sullento, particularly interesting. Although there was no mention of an official oracle in Klertal, the merchant recalled having had the rare honor of meeting one of Sullento's concubines. Reported to be the potentate's favorite, she claimed to be something of a seeress. The merchant recalled the meeting clearly, primarily because the woman had accurately predicted that a world-shaking cataclysm was imminent. Of course, no one had believed the dire predictions of a concubine. Luckily, the merchant had traveled on, thus living to tell his tale.

Lyim stroked the chilling water with his strong, elongated arm, kicking with his webbed feet. He looked for the city ahead in the dim, murky light of the sea. Bubbles from his own many-toothed mouth swirled about his head, obscuring his view. He turned his head to release breaths, and at last got a view of the city of Klertal.

Even if the citizens of Klertal had believed the concubine's prediction, it wouldn't have prevented their city from becoming the rolling expanse of kelp-covered rubble Lyim was now seeing. Former streets were distinguishable only as the clear spaces where debris had fallen three centuries before. Seaweed waved and bowed in patchy forests scattered across the tumbled city. Schools of fish, undaunted by the area's sinister reputation, darted above the sunken city like madly dashing clouds. Aside from them, the ruins were unnaturally quiet and dark, save for a soft glow that radiated from a spongy green moss that crawled across the surface of every crumbled stone. There was no sign of the source of the churning water on the surface of New Sea.

Lyim realized now that he had seen a miniature version of the sunken city in the wizened mage's home in Neraka. Amurchin had built a glass-sided water tank in his laboratory, filled it with exotic fish (for spell components, he said), and constructed shipwrecks and buildings for them to swim through. Lyim had thought it an odd hobby at the time, but for reasons of his own, the old mage had apparently recreated the sunken city in his home. It was a minor thing, but it spoke volumes about the significance Amurchin placed on the underwater ruins.

Lyim paused in his descent to orient himself above the ruins. There were very few two-story structures; most buildings of any size had long ago crumbled under their own weight and the debilitating effect of the sea. What remained of the city was obviously very old. The architecture was an ancient, classical style, not unlike that used in Palanthas. Given the journal entry that cited tumbledown shacks surrounding great opulence, Lyim realized he must be seeing the ruins of the wealthier homes and official city buildings; the shacks would have long ago been swept away by the sea.

Off in the distance, Lyim spotted the broken remains of an open-ended oval-shaped colonnade. It led to a lone structure that rose above the others, reminding him of the pre-Cataclysm woodcut print of the potentate's palace he'd found at the Great Library. Though greatly reduced by both the earthquakes and the years underwater, the palace retained a suggestion of its former opulence. A double-sided central staircase led to a small balcony, where potentates had undoubtedly once addressed the citizens of Klertal. Behind the balcony, seven narrow archways still rose three stories above the courtyard encircled by the colonnade. Lyim was too far away to discern more, but he was determined to make his way through the endless debris to reach the palace.

Where the streets were not littered with rubble, Lyim spotted many skeletons of humans, elves, and dwarves. The mage assumed them to be the original inhabitants who ran in panic into the streets as the city submerged. But there had been no escape from the city's doom. Even large ships would have been dragged below in the massive wake, as evidenced by the many rotting hulks scattered incongruously across the empty streets and rooftops.

Movement caught Lyim's eye as he surveyed the scene. Several blocks from where he floated, a large body of creatures was swimming slowly, following the path of an old street. He swam toward the group until he could see that these, too, were original inhabitants of the city. But these had not been not lucky enough to die in the Cataclysm. Somehow they had gained a state of unlife, and now lurched down the avenue as zombies. The bloated and discolored beings ranged in age from the very young to the very old, but all had empty eye sockets, and most had twisted or missing limbs, injuries suffered during the Cataclysm that caused their deaths.

Around and above them swam a dozen or more sahuagin, herding the zombies toward an unknown destination. Lyim had never seen these legendary fish-men before, but had heard tales of their rapacious attacks on coastal towns and their utter brutality. He also knew they had a paralyzing fear of magic, and so he drifted in for a closer look.

Their backs were blackish green, shading to white on their bellies. A dorsal-like fin, black at the base and shading outward to red at the spiny tips, marked each of their spines. Webbed fingers and toes made them fast swimmers; mouths filled with sharp fangs made them dangerous. That, and the assortment of cross-bows, daggers, and spears they carried. Though in the body of a scrag, Lyim drew back instinctively behind some kelp-covered rubble.

He didn't see the shark until it was nearly too late. The mage could feel something part the water behind him. Spinning about slowly, he spied the frighteningly sleek and speedy creature rushing toward him, jaws spread wide. The polymorphed mage twisted aside, narrowly avoiding the razorlike teeth in that gigantic maw. His own huge claws raked across the shark's flank as it sped past. Now spewing a thick plume of crimson, the shark turned and attacked again. But even its speed and power were no match for the brutal strength of the scrag. As it closed again, Lyim's claws slipped beneath the creature's belly and tore it open with one long slash. Thrashing wildly, the monster dis-appeared in a churning red cloud that sank slowly to the buildings below.

Unfortunately, the brief fight had drawn the atten-tion of the sahuagin guards. Immediately they aban-doned their mindless zombie captives and rushed to attack the scrag, one of their most hated enemies. Half a dozen maneuvered to the left, another half a dozen to the right, with the rest coming straight on.

Normally, this would have been a titanic struggle,

given a scrag's ability to regenerate itself almost instantly. The sahuagin, even with the advantage of numbers, would be hard-pressed to actually kill the sea troll. But Lyim was not in fact a scrag; he only had the form and strength of that monster. Without its regenerative power, he would quickly be overcome by small wounds.

But the last thing the sahuagin expected from this foe was magic. Among the few things Lyim knew about sahuagin was that they detested light almost as much as they feared magic. Lyim's claws raked out. He snatched up a handful of the faintly glowing moss that grew all over the ruins, then he muttered a single magical word. A ball of light erupted within the front ranks of onrushing fish-men. It was a simple light spell, one of the first that any apprentice learned. On land, it cast a pale blue light. Here, where light had not shone for hundreds of years, it seemed as if the sun had just risen in their midst.

With hideous shrieks and guttural curses, the sahuagin scattered away from the hated brightness—all except the one on whom Lyim had actually cast the spell. Unable to escape, blinded, nearly insane with rage, it thrashed and writhed like a hooked fish.

Another band of sahuagin now burst from the ruins to Lyim's right and approached warily. Their foe was obviously no normal scrag. They appeared to be considering how best to attack when a bolt of lightning ripped into their ranks as a ball of flame, boiling the water around them. Five charred and stewed sahuagin sank slowly while the rest scattered toward cover.

Lyim knew that, underwater, the usual bolt of lightning became a fiery ball and would not harm him if he cast it to form at least ten paces away from himself. He didn't know that behind him, a third group rushed on unabated, perhaps thinking that speed was their only salvation. Before Lyim was even aware that they were within striking distance, a heavy net of woven kelp was drawn tightly around him. Both his snake and long scrag arms were pinned to his sides, despite the scrag's great strength. He could not break free. Without freedom to move, Lyim could not cast spells. His struggles increased until the sharp claws on his webbed feet shredded the lower portion of the net, but still he remained tightly wrapped. His snake arm's wild hissing erupted as bubbles. The sahuagin, true to their reputation, watched his plight with cruel amusement while anxiously fingering their wickedly barbed spears and tridents.

*Let the human pass.*

Lyim was startled to hear another creature's voice inside his head. He was certain he'd not heard it with his ears, and yet it conveyed a direction, as if it were coming from behind him. He struggled to paddle himself around inside the net. Lyim's sharp scrag eyes fell on the remains of the palace through the broken colonnade.

Apparently the sahuagin heard the voice as well, because they immediately released their net lines and paddled away from Lyim and into the shadows of the rubble.

*Come to me*, the voice commanded. This time it clearly came from the palace. Lyim freed himself from the slackened net and paddled through the broken sections of columns, swimming toward the palace. Rubble filled the courtyard within the colonnade, but Lyim floated above it unaware, eyes and thoughts focused on his destination. He set his long flat feet upon the right side of the crumbling staircase, stopping upon the balcony. Just beyond the seven archways was a towering central double door. He approached it slowly, walking instead of swimming across the undulating mosaic floor. Lyim was mildly surprised when the

mossy doors swung open smoothly though slowly
with only a light push.

The room beyond was round, not unlike the rotunda
of Lyim's villa in Palanthas, which he appropriated
after Belize's death. In the center of the vast room was a
dais, and upon it a throne, its carved marble back to
Lyim. He kicked his scrag legs and swam around the
dais. What he saw upon the seat of majesty made him
gasp, bubbles hissing in a torrent through his razor-
sharp teeth.

Seated in the throne was a woman—assuming she
had once been human—pinned to the marble seat-back
by a harpoon through her chest. Hundreds of slender
tendrils of living orange coral wrapped around the
entire throne, as if the stuff had been dripped over the
oracle like candle wax. Her head was unfettered, but it
was as pale as death and bloated like the zombies. Her
hair looked to be made of barnacles. Amurchin had
dubbed her the Coral Oracle.

"I thank you for your aid," Lyim said smoothly,
"though I could have managed the situation myself."

*I think not,* said the vaporous voice inside his head.
*That form severely hampers your magical abilities, Lyim
Rhistadt.* Though she resembled a zombie, the oracle's
eyes shifted with a light the undead did not possess as
she evaluated the scrag.

Her familiarity startled him. "How do you know my
name?" Though she spoke telepathically to him, his
words came out in bubbles. When the woman didn't
respond, only continued to stare, Lyim realized the
answer himself and was encouraged. A legitimate seer
would know who he was, and much more.

"I've come," he said, "to ask you to reveal the cure
for my mutated hand."

*I know.* The oracle slowly blinked. *Hold the limb in question to my cheek,* she instructed. *I must draw a sense of it.*

Reluctantly, the mage-turned-scrag swept his color-ful snake hand up to one of her belly-white cheeks. To his surprise, the snake, though usually driven into a frenzy by others, was uncharacteristically calm and content. Lyim derived no sensation through the snake's flesh, but he had a good imagination; she must feel like a bloated corpse.

The woman's expression softened slightly, as if the contact were pleasant for her as well. Abruptly she blinked again. *I have the answer you seek.*

Lyim glided backward to a four-foot remove from the oracle and waited anxiously for her to continue, his bulbous scrag eyes searching her bloated face. "Tell me, please!"

*First you must do something for me.*

Lyim dropped back still farther, his fist clenching at his side. He had done more "favors" for self-serving informants and doddering mages over the last five years than he could remember, all in exchange for vague, often useless, snippets of information. "What is it you ask me to do?"

*A human must remove the harpoon from my chest to lift the curse that holds me here.*

Lyim paddled around to get a closer look at the en-crusted weapon. "This"—Lyim indicated her predica-ment with a graceful sweep of his elongated left arm—"was the result of a curse?"

*My entrapment here was, yes. My ability as a seer came to me naturally and was, in fact, partially the cause of the curse. It is a long tale—the story of my entire life—but I will tell it to you simply. I was Potentate Sullento's favorite con-cubine, for more than the usual reasons.*

"I read about you!" exclaimed Lyim.

She continued as if uninterrupted. *From the start Sullento believed in and relied heavily on my skills as a seer-ess to manage the city. However, I was not his first or only mistress, but his fifth. The other four, old and fat shrews, grew more and more jealous as he turned all his attention away from them and entirely upon me. For a time I alone satisfied his every need. Not maliciously to deny them, I will tell you, but because it was my duty and my honor.*

*But they, of course, did not see the diminishment of their power that way. Together, they whispered in his ear, whenever they were near enough, that I was no prophetess at all. They told him I was betraying him with a mage who made my predictions come true.* The prophetess shrugged away a span of time and truthlessness with a blink of her eerie eyes. *It was only a matter of time before Sullento, who for all his power was no more confident than any man, came to believe their lies, instead of my truthful denials.*

"You tried also to warn them of an approaching cataclysm," interjected Lyim.

She blinked again as if nodding. *By then, Sullento no longer believed in me. To punish me and warn all others that no one was beyond his wrath, he bade his court wizard cast the curse whose first step imprisoned me thus. In a public ceremony Sullento himself inflicted the harpoon that sealed the curse. You see, he could not bring himself to kill me outright, and yet he knew no human would dare remove the harpoon and free me while he was ruler, for fear of retribution. And then the cataclysm struck, as I predicted, and there were no humans left alive to free me.*

"Surely I'm not the first to come seeking answers?"

*The first to seek me, no. Many have arrived over the centuries, but Itzan Klertal's underwater inhabitants are even more inhospitable than the surface dwellers of Klertal were. Only two survived to reach me before you. One was a clever little dark-skinned elf named Amurchin, and the other was a denizen of the Abyss in the service of a human mage master. Neither could lift the curse. But you can; the curse will recognize your true human form.*

Lyim could certainly appreciate her desire to have

the curse lifted, but he was reminded again of the useless leads for which he'd paid dearly. "Give me my answer first, and if it is adequate, I will gladly do as you ask."

*I will not,* she said firmly, the first true inflection in her voice.

Lyim's lips pulled back in a scowl that exposed his needlelike teeth. "I could destroy you with one spell!"

*That would be punishment for you and liberation of a kind for me,* she said without guile.

"What if I refuse?" he demanded, feeling backed into a corner.

*Then I will remain here, and you will still have no hand.*

Lyim heaved an inward sigh and briefly pondered his options, which were slim to none. He would never willingly leave without his answer. He consoled himself for giving in with the thought that he could always obliterate her afterward, if her words proved pointless.

Planting his webbed feet at the base of the slick, kelp-covered throne, he wrapped the long green fingers of his left hand around the smooth harpoon shaft and tugged. It didn't budge. Surprised at the difficulty, Lyim tucked the pole under his arm more firmly and pulled with all his might. The lance shifted. Summoning even more strength, Lyim was rewarded for his efforts when he felt the weapon shudder slightly. Probably a barb breaking off, he thought. And then it slid back, slowly at first but gaining speed. At last he wrenched the harpoon from the oracle's chest. The effort sent Lyim spinning away from the dais. He dropped the harpoon and righted himself so that his eyes locked on the oracle in the throne.

The vivid coral that crawled across her pale form, pinning her, cracked like glass and sank to the dais at her feet; the bloated woman broke free of the throne. Whatever dress she had once worn had disintegrated during more than three hundred years in salt water. Her hideous, blue-white body spun away, circling the room with a slow, jerky motion.

*I had forgot what it felt like to move,* she breathed softly, examining every nook and cranny of the room with a child's delight. The oracle paddled slowly, stiffly toward the wide-open door that led out to the sunken city, eager to see what was beyond.

"Wait!" cried Lyim, swimming after her. "I freed you. Now pay me what you owe me!"

The oracle paddled halfway about and regarded him over the hardness of her barnacle locks. *You have been searching for a cure without knowing the true cause of your malady. The answer, and your arm, still lie within the dimensional bridge where it was lost. Seek the builder of the bridge.*

"Belize?" cried Lyim. "But he's dead!"

*The dead are not beyond the reach of those who wield magic.* The oracle's eyes were focused over Lyim's shoulder, at the world that lay beyond this room. *No one knows that better than I, who have waited more than three centuries to punish the spirits of four shrews. Fare-thee-well, Lyim Rhistadt.*

Lyim's dark scrag eyes watched her vaguely as she slithered out the door and disappeared into the murky city. The answer that had eluded him for so long had been under his nose from the start. Strangely, the realization left him with more questions than he'd had before coming to blasphemous Itzan Klertal.

# Chapter Three

Dear Maladorigar,

I am writing this without knowing if I will ever be allowed to send it. The rules regarding communicating with people outside Bastion are unclear. Perhaps this will help me sort through my thoughts, at any rate, and then I won't feel so lonely.

Zagarus and I arrived five months ago, although you would be able to calculate that better than I. Time is an odd thing here. There's neither sun nor moons to mark the passing days. I am estimating time by the growth of my hair: one index finger joint every two months. With nowhere to go, it matters very little anyway.

The Council of Three teleported Zag and me to the courtyard, or inner bailey, my bags in hand. It was as dark as ink, for there were no stars above. I felt dizzy, and it took several minutes for my eyes to adjust—to the darkness, I thought first. The immense building before me looked flat and seemed to waver as if in a summer heat wave. I closed my eyes and willed my body to stop swaying, as Justarius had instructed me. I opened them again when I could stand still for at least three heartbeats.

The sight took me back five years, to a mountain valley in the morning shadows of Skullcap. I couldn't help thinking of Esme and the time we had spent helping to build this marvel. I still miss her.

Bastion's outline fit the pattern in my memory: a short, flat-faced facade leading the way to the disparate designs of the three wings behind it. The facade is made of a mosaic of fired white porcelain, red granite, and black onyx to symbolize the working harmony of the three orders of magic. I could see that gargoyles—real, live ones—had been added to every ledge and arch on all three sections. Topiary trees and odd statues, carefully designed to cast realistic and frightening shadows in the odd, angled light, were also new to my eyes.

One other new feature that I must comment on was almost imperceptible in the wan light until I got very close to Bastion. The entire edifice is covered, top to bottom and front to back, with runes, sigils, and mystic etchings of every variety. I've since spent much of my free time studying their design and have them nearly unraveled. The challenge of it kept me interested and active when I otherwise might have begun seriously missing my home and familiar sights.

Seeing Bastion again after so long brought to mind something unexpected and long forgotten. Many years before the building of the stronghold, while I was an apprentice in Justarius's house, Esme had talked me into watching my first theatrical production. I had not even heard of such things before coming to the big city of Palanthas. What impressed me most was not the story, or even the players, for I can remember nothing of either, but the backdrop that had been created for the stage. It was a street scene, with false shop fronts and homes that looked quite real in the odd green-white glow provided by the bowls of powdered lime and water that served as footlights.

I realize this seems a long digression, but I tell you because if you have ever seen such a sight, you will understand how the exterior of Bastion looks now. Not dark, exactly, but very dimly lit from the bottom up. I felt as if I stood upon a stage, though I knew the building before me was not false-fronted, nor the darkness beyond the edges of my vision merely stage wings hidden by heavy curtains.

I knew, too, that the frightening sounds around me did not come from actors in the wings, waiting to play the parts of hounds. Plaintive baying echoed from beyond the lacy wrought-iron fence that surrounds the stronghold. I could see red eyes glowing at an unknown distance, oddly shaped and placed; one here, three there, not like any wolves I had ever seen.

Zagarus was pressed against my leg, for once speechless. To our mutual great relief, the enormous, arched door before us swung open on creaky hinges, flooding the courtyard at our feet with yellow light. I remember it only because I had not felt like such a rube since I arrived as an apprentice at Justarius's villa those many years ago. My mouth hung agape, I am sure.

"You're here. Come in. I have too much to do to be standing in the doorway." The voice was brisk, yet unmistakably female, and had the hint of an accent I still have been unable to place. Her face was entirely in shadow.

There was no question of not complying with that voice, however. I could feel Zag paddling up the slick, porcelain steps next to me and can only imagine how incongruous he must have looked to her, a sea gull with no sea in sight. The silhouetted woman pointedly ignored him.

We stopped next to her in the doorway, and I squinted, still unable to see her features. "I'm Guerrand DiThon," I said, knowing as I did how foolish I must have sounded.

She looked meaningfully at my red robes. "Do you think I

open the door for just anyone who happens by?"

I looked toward the red eyes beyond the fence. "Has anyone just happened by?"

"Not yet."

"And your name is—?"

"My business." She waved us through the door impatiently. "Dagamier." The bright light fell across her face, and at last I could see her. She looked young, perhaps of an age with my little sister Kirah, except around the eyes. Though her skin was unlined, there was a depth of experience, a cynical sadness, even, in orbs the dark blue of an angry, storm-tossed sea.

Dagamier was—is—a study in contrasts. Skin as white and unblemished as unveined marble, more polished than pale. Straight, shoulder-length hair the same midnight black as the silk robe she always wears. She's one of those people who looks good, sensuous even, in black, with her sharp, compact angles and a woman's soft, graceful moves. She's smart as a whip, with a tongue to match. I am ever on eggshells with her. Frankly, I haven't figured her out yet, and I'm not sure a lifetime of study would help that. But I'm getting ahead of myself.

"I will show you the nave area that is common to us all and to the red wing," Dagamier said, leading us into the apse. "Ezius will likely give you a tour of the white wing when he has completed his shift in the scrying sphere. You will have no need to see the black wing."

"I have seen it," I said abruptly, involuntarily. "I've seen them all, at least from the outside."

She looked over her shoulder, one brow arched skeptically.

"Didn't the Council tell you?" I felt compelled to ask. "I was among the twenty-one mages who helped build Bastion before it was moved here from the Prime Material Plane."

Honestly, Maladorigar, I don't know what made me tell her all that. I should have known it would annoy her.

Dagamier's firm-lipped silence confirmed that it had.

"Then you will not be requiring a tour." She took a step to leave, and I instinctively reached out a hand to her forearm. I thought I had touched fire.

"Oh, but I do need one," I assured her quickly, pulling my hand away. "Nothing inside looks as I remember it. My involvement in the construction ended with the raising of the walls. The interior was completed by the Council of Three after they sent the other eighteen representatives from the site. Even the gargoyles, the fence, the creatures beyond it, the runes that surround it, are all new to me."

"The runes were drawn upon Bastion by the Council of Three to send Bastion here. The creatures are hell hounds, other-dimensional flame-belching monstrosities with fangs and claws, brought here by LaDonna as the black order's contribution to security. They patrol outside the fence." She continued in her bored voice, as if reading the information from a handbill. "The gargoyles were conjured by Justarius for the red wing; they watch the forecourt for unwanted visitors."

Catching the pattern here, I asked, "And the fence was Par-Salian's doing?"

She stared at me for long moments in a most disconcerting manner. "No."

Dagamier walked through the apse to the soaring central nave. It, too, was new to me, and seemed to serve no other purpose than to connect the three wings that join it at equidistant points from the towering front door. Actually, nine doors lead away from this area: one each to the white and red wings respectively, seven into the black wing, seven separate and distinct rooms that can only be entered from the nave.

In the center of the room is a wide, round column that stretches from floor to ceiling. A support pillar, I supposed, not recalling it from the construction. The column is ringed by a narrow, fish-filled gurgling stream, like a miniature moat, whose source is a mystery.

"That column houses the scrying diorama, Par-Salian's

56

*contribution to defense," Dagamier said pointedly. "Each of us takes a shift inside, watching Bastion and this entire demiplane for signs of intrusion."*

*"Of course," I said lamely, wishing I sounded more like the new high defender than some sheepish apprentice. Glancing around, I was struck by the whiteness of the walls, the natural-looking brightness that seems to filter down from the ceiling, as if it's a glass pane that faces the sun. Par-Salian's influence here is obvious, as is Justarius's. The snowy whiteness is broken only by man-sized lush, tropical plants. There is little evidence of LaDonna's hand here, except, perhaps, in the shadows.*

*Dagamier must have seen me looking at the greenery, because she said, "The plants and fish have always been the responsibility of the red representative. They'd all be dead if it were up to me." She looked at Zagarus for the first time. "Naturally, your gull and its mess is also your responsibility."*

*Zag's wing feathers gathered up like a bird in the cold. Does she think I can't hear her?* he griped. Imagine talking about me like I'm some wild animal.

*"Of course—" I barely managed to mutter to Dagamier.*

*"We can discuss other duties, like the scrying sphere, after you've settled in your rooms."*

Uh-oh, *sang Zagarus.* She obviously doesn't know you're the boss!

*"Did they . . . the Council, that is . . . tell you about my position?" I gulped.*

*Dagamier looked up with one dark eye. "The top guard thing?"*

*"High defender," I corrected her gently. This was not going well. Since I was to be her superior, I decided to take the bull, so to speak, by the horns. "You don't like me much. Or is it the idea of me?"*

*"Frankly, I haven't thought of either," she said with a dismissive wave of her hand. "If it makes you feel any better,*

*though, I don't like anyone much. That's why I sought out this position. I prefer solitude."*

And the world is better for it, *snorted Zag.*

*I swallowed a smile with a cough.* "Uh, how long have you been here?"

*"Long enough." She pierced me with narrowed eyes. "I hope you won't be inclined to change procedures and routines you know nothing about."*

Do you want me to peck the harridan? *Zag said to me.* I think I'll call her Harry, for short.

*I almost laughed despite my growing irritation, so unexpected and apt was Zag's evaluation. I can handle her, I ensured my familiar silently.*

*Actually, Zagarus's genuine but ridiculous offer helped knock the insecurity right out of me. I sensed that if I didn't demand Dagamier's respect in that instant, if only for the position I hold, I would never get it. I silently invoked a quick protective magic and quite literally but gently poked her once in her mannish lapels.*

*"Look," I said fiercely, "I can understand your irritation at being passed up for promotion, but I won't tolerate your insolence. I'm in charge here, whether you like it or not. The Council of Three obviously wants me to be high defender. I would hate to have to report to them that there is another position to fill." I spoke without heat, but lowered my eyes briefly to the pattern on the floor. "Dependable black wizards are hard to find."*

*Dagamier pushed herself away with surprising strength for someone of her size. She met my eyes fully for the first time, and there was neither anger nor distaste there. I wouldn't call it respect, but a weary acceptance. It was more than I expected.*

*The short tour went better after that. Dagamier was at least civil, if not pleasant.*

*"Did the Council tell you where Bastion is, in the scheme of the cosmos, that is?" she asked while we walked slowly*

*about the nave.*

" 'Beyond the circles of the universe,' I believe they said. They didn't want to tell me more specifically for fear that I might let the secret slip."

"Believe it or not," she said, beginning to steer me in the direction of the red wing, "Bastion is visible from Krynn, if only you know where to look." She must have seen the disbelief on my face, because she stopped to look me. "It's true. Have you ever noticed the dark line on the horizon, where earth and sea meet sky? That's the side of Bastion, like the rim of a steel piece."

I nodded slowly in understanding, thinking it somehow fitting that I should end up here, when I had spent so much of my youth staring wistfully at the horizon from the heath near Castle DiThon.

Contemplating that line, I said aloud, "That would mean Bastion's plane is two-dimensional."

Dagamier looked impressed. "You probably noticed a sense of disorientation, of flatness, when you arrived in the courtyard."

I nodded again. "It went away so fast I thought it was a side effect of teleportation."

"Most people's senses adjust to the change pretty quickly and everything begins to look normal."

"Does that mean I have only two dimensions now?" The thought worried me for some reason.

Dagamier's glossy head shook as she pondered. "Let me think of a way to explain it. You, me, this place"—she gave an inclusive wave of her arm—"were created in the three dimensions of the Prime Material Plane, then transported here. We didn't lose any of our definition by coming to a place that only recognizes two dimensions."

She snapped her fingers when another thought came clear. "It's like visual acuity. You and I may both look at a statue that's fifty feet away. If my eyesight is better, I will see more detail in the statue than you, but that doesn't mean the detail isn't there when you look at it." She held up both hands in an expressively questioning gesture. "Does that make sense?"

"I think so," I muttered, trying to piece it all together. "Does it follow, then, that anything created here and sent to the Prime Material would have only two dimensions?"

Dagamier nodded.

"Then that's why the Council decided to build Bastion on Krynn and bring it here," I realized at last. "I'd thought it was only for convenience or secrecy."

"Probably all three." She dismissed the subject with a shrug. "The nave," she said, redirecting my attention, "is the only space we share, aside from the entry apse."

Dagamier pointed to the column. "Each of us spends a third of our time, in rotating shifts, monitoring Bastion's perimeter through a magical replica of the plane." She blinked. "At least, that is how we have divided the task previously."

I was surprised that so much of my time would be spent staring at a model. "It sounds as fair a system as any," I assured her.

Just then, a hidden door-sized panel slid back in the column, and a sparkling footbridge of glass spread like a rainbow across the moat. Out stepped a funny little man who reminded me strongly of the wizened old chamberlain at Castle DiThon. He wore an ill-fitting white robe edged in gold thread. His long, frizzy hair, the color of sunlight on a dull day, was askew, as if he'd just stepped out of a fierce wind. Seeing me with Dagamier, he blinked with eyes that were small black dots behind very thick spectacles. He crossed the small magical bridge and stood among the greenery.

"Nothing to report today," he said to my black-robed guide, ignoring me. "Your hell hounds became excited with the new arrival, and the gargoyles grew edgy, but they all seem to have quieted now. Is he ready for his first watch?" the man asked with a slight jerk of his head toward me. "Or will you be taking the next one?"

Before I could say I would be happy to take my turn,

*Dagamier stepped across the bridge and paused under the sliding panel. "He hasn't even been to his rooms yet." The bridge retracted like a fan and disappeared. Dagamier withdrew into the column, and the panel closed behind her, leaving no seam.*

*I stood with Ezius, feeling uncomfortable and vaguely irritated. No one had warned me that they both had stunted social skills. If he was as abrasive and resentful as Dagamier, I was going to have quite a time of managing things here.*

*"Yes, well, that won't do," Ezius muttered to himself. "The only way to fix that is to let him look at his rooms. There's no point in delaying that. None at all." The white-robed mage meandered toward the door to his wing.*

*"Say, uh, Ezius, is it?" I called after him awkwardly.*

*The man stopped his mumbling and his steps to look vaguely over his shoulder. "Yes? Yes, well?"*

*"I-I thought we might at least introduce ourselves."*

*"Haven't we?" He shrugged. "I guess not. I don't know your name."*

*"It's Guerrand. My friends call me Rand."*

*"Rand. . . . Yes, well, that's a nice name, isn't it? I once knew a man named Rind, an excellent cobbler from Blodehelm. He could resole a pair of boots in two winks of an eye, and always used the best quality thread and leather. Although there are those who think that catgut made from twisting the dried intestines of sheep is superior." He blinked at me through those thick lenses. "Rind was his name. I don't suppose you know him?"*

*I looked at him closely to see if he was jesting, but his face was guileless. "No, I'm sorry I don't."*

*What plane is he on? Zagarus snorted.*

*I breathed a sigh of relief so loud even Ezius would have noticed if he hadn't already departed through an arched, immense white doorway to the right of the nave. I'd realized the mumbling mage wasn't being intentionally abrasive, he was simply befuddled.*

Reading over his master's shoulder, Zagarus pecked gently at Guerrand's hand until he set his quill down upon the desk in the library of the red wing.

"What is it, Zag?"

*Make sure you tell Maladorigar that Ezius isn't just befuddled, he's a real stick-in-the-mud.*

Guerrand didn't entirely agree with the gull's assessment, so he ignored it and picked up the quill again. But the bird wasn't ready to be silent yet.

*Is it just me, or does Dagamier remind you of LaDonna?*

Guerrand screwed up his face in thought as he tried to envision both women side by side. "I suppose I see a little resemblance," he agreed at last, "but I'm not sure it isn't just because they're both women and both mages."

*Esme was a woman and a mage,* Zagarus pointed out, *and Dagamier doesn't remind me the least bit of her.*

Guerrand felt himself tense at the mention of Esme. Would it ever stop hurting? And why was Zagarus, who knew how much the subject pained his master, poking a wing in the wound? Guerrand closed his eyes tightly and willed patience. "What I meant was, LaDonna and Dagamier are both dark-haired women who wear the black robes."

*I suppose.* With that, Zagarus closed his beady eyes in reluctant concession, ruffled his wings into a comfortable position, and dropped off to sleep on the desk next to Guerrand.

The mage gratefully returned to the safety of his letter to the gnome back in Harrowdown.

*With the introductions out of the way, there was nothing keeping me from exploring the red wing.*

*Maladorigar, I can't begin to describe how comfortable and carefully considered the red wing is. There is a sense of Justarius's own subtle dignity to the magic that maintains my apartments—no talking teapots or crazed brooms and their ridiculous like here.*

*The wing's six rooms are set in a rectangle, all of them more warmly inviting than the last. Just one is large enough to make our house in Harrowdown look like a shack. I'm sorry, that was less than thoughtful, since you're still living there.*

*Anyway, the first room on the right off the circular nave is a large, practical storeroom. All I have to do is set whatever I wish stored just inside the doorway, and the next time I return it's been put in its proper place upon the shelves.*

*Across the hall from the storeroom is the daily living area, where I cook and eat my meals. It's stocked with enough pans and platters and is of sufficient size to feed a visiting troop of nobles and all their retainers. There's a huge fireplace that burns constantly and is far larger than I need to prepare the simple gruels I am capable of cooking. I surely miss your herbal stews.*

*Next to this area is my sleeping chamber. I spend little time upon the soft feather tick, yet enough to know that I far prefer it to my straw bed in Harrowdown.*

*The sleeping chamber leads directly into a room that I suspect was modified by Justarius for my benefit. Or should I say Zagarus's? I don't remember it from the original floor plan. All of nature that is absent from Bastion is painted here in murals that cover the floor, walls, and ceiling. Blue sea to the left, green fields to the right, and in the middle is an elaborate pool someone (which is why I suspect Justarius) went to a great deal of trouble to make look like the seashore near Thonvil. Live heather and pampas grass abound. Real water abuts the blue sea mural on the left edge, giving the scene the infinite look of the horizon line between water and sea. Zagarus in particular feels quite at home here.*

*My favorite room, though, is the laboratory. It's by far the biggest, taking up the entire short end of the rectangle farthest from the nave. I was concerned about being unable to collect my own components of the quality you grow in*

Harrowdown, but I needn't have been. Oh, I didn't mean that the way it sounded. It's just that the lab came stocked with things I've never even heard of, all perfectly catalogued and stored in the highest quality green glass. I don't know if I have Justarius or my predecessor to thank. I suspect the former, since the jars magically refill themselves. No more plucking posies in a hot field while angry bees sting my head!

Or maybe my favorite room is the library. I have not seen one its size since my father's at Castle DiThon. But instead of containing only the occasional tome about magic, this one holds floor-to-ceiling spellbooks, with softly cushioned benches on which to read them. New books appear on the shelf now and then. I even found an entry about Rannoch, the black wizard from my dreams, that I hadn't read before. Unfortunately, it added nothing new to my understanding of him.

I've had the Dream with great regularity here, Mal. I thought it might go away, once I took charge of my life again and came to Bastion, but it hasn't. If anything, it comes more frequently and fervently to me here. I confess, Bastion has inspired moments when I could understand Rannoch's sacrifice. I feel I am a part of something bigger than myself, something worth dying for. . . .

Still, I can't shake the thought that there's something else I'm supposed to learn from that part of my Test, some lesson I've not yet been able to understand. I've been trying to screw up the courage to ask Dagamier if there is something about Rannoch in her library. He was, after all, a wizard of the Black Robes, which is what continues to disturb me. We don't enter each other's areas without invitation here, and neither Dagamier nor Ezius have been forthcoming with one. It is my right as high defender to demand entrance, but I don't want to lose whatever goodwill I have engendered by doing so without good reason.

The Dream aside, I am wanting for nothing here, except

*companionship. Ezius is pleasant enough when he's lucid. But it seems that he's always either scurrying off, muttering about some obscure and unintelligible thing, or stopping to lecture me about some obscure and boring thing. Sometimes, I confess, I'm lonely enough to feign interest.*

*Dagamier is another story. While she is no longer insolent, there is a darkness in her soul that permeates everything she says and does. Conversations with her frequently leave me lonely and depressed. I have no doubt why she chose to wear the black robes.*

Guerrand stopped again briefly to make sure Zagarus was no longer reading over his shoulder. He watched the slow rise and fall of the bird's breast, heard the slight whistle-wheeze of Zagarus at sleep. Reassured, he picked up the quill once more and dipped it into the pot of black ink.

*You may be wondering why I'm so lonely with Zagarus here. I can tell you, Mal, that Zagarus is not doing well. I don't know if it's old age, or being away from the sea and other birds, or both. His color is bad, feathers and eyes dull. He scarcely talks to me anymore, especially after I reprimanded him for fishing in the moat around the scrying column.*

*I must also confess to occasional restlessness. Am I one of those people who is never satisfied with where he is or what he is doing?*

Guerrand's head shot up from the page at the distant sound of wild baying. He set the quill down, cocked his head, and listened.

Zagarus's eyes popped open. *Sounds like the hell hounds*, he observed.

The mage nodded. "But how can they be so close that we can hear them? Unless . . ." Guerrand let the word trail as his mind finished the horrifying thought. "Stay here," he commanded as he jumped to his feet. The chair flew back and crashed to the floor of the library. Guerrand was through the doorway and down the long hallway to the nave in a matter of heartbeats.

Ezius stood by the column, his pale face etched with concern. "I've never heard the hounds from inside Bastion," he remarked soberly.

Just then the panel in the central column opened. Dagamier poked her dark head out anxiously. "The hell hounds and gargoyles appear to be poised for a fight."

"How is that possible?" demanded Ezius. "Control of the hounds is your responsibility, Dagamier!" He looked at Guerrand. "Can't you maintain the enchantment on your gargoyles?"

Ezius's accusations brought a scowl to Dagamier's white face. "Not all of Bastion's magical defenses are entirely predictable, Ezius. Gargoyles, if you haven't heard, are chaotic evil creatures. I think it's remarkable that this hasn't happened before in five years."

"I still say the Council should have anticipated such problems."

"They did," cut in Guerrand. "That's why we're here. If Bastion functioned automatically, there'd be no need for guardians." Guerrand was already running for the apse and Bastion's entrance when he said, "Ezius, man the sphere. I'm going out to see what's happening."

Dashing after him, Dagamier caught Guerrand by the arm and spun him around. "You can't go charging out there. Maybe you trust the gargoyles to attack only intruders, but the hell hounds will kill anything they can sink their teeth into."

Dagamier had pulled him into one of the black wing's seven doorways before he was even aware of moving. "Let's use the observation tower above the black wing," she said, tapping the wall inside the door. A doorway slid open, revealing a long, narrow flight of stairs.

Another door flew open and they emerged into the windless, dark air above the courtyard on a narrow walkway hidden by the facade. The sounds of snarling, shrieking animals cut them both to the core. The mages clapped hands over their ears to hush the sound, but it did little good. The noise seemed to slice through the flesh and bones of their hands like a sharp pick on its way to their brains.

Apprehension made Dagamier's voice sound like a whisper, though she shouted above the din, "The gargoyles are gone."

Guerrand did a swift scan of the nearby pointed gables of the white wing. He searched the smooth, flat ledges of the red and black wings. The hideous, winged creatures who posed as downspouts on a stronghold that never saw rain were indeed gone.

"There!" yelled Dagamier, pointing. Guerrand followed her finger and the sounds to the left, to an area in darkest shadow beyond the fence. Bursts of flame and red-hot eyes revealed the presence, if not the outlines, of the hell hounds. Squinting in the perpetual dimness, Guerrand could make out bent bars in that section of fence, and through them constant but undefined movement. Occasionally the area was lit up by a flash of fire from a hell hound, but this did little to illuminate the situation.

By the time Guerrand realized that Dagamier was casting a spell, she was already done. It was a simple light spell, suspended over the battle. All six of the gargoyles appeared to be battling four to six hell hounds. The entire scene was such a chaotic swirl of limbs, dirt, and fire that it was hard to tell which side, if either, was winning. The stony gray hide of the gargoyles was largely impervious to the fangs and claws of the hell hounds, and if a gargoyle did get into serious trouble its enormous wings could easily carry it out of danger. But the dark red hell hounds were vicious fighters who would gang together to overwhelm one foe at a time, or disappear into the shadows if hard pressed.

At the corner of his sight, Guerrand saw Dagamier's eyes sink shut. "What are you planning to do?" he asked.

Her hands began to rise in a swirling motion. "Slay them before they completely destroy the fence. We'll replace them with a new batch."

"That would solve the immediate problem, as would putting them to sleep," agreed Guerrand, "but it would also leave us with no inner guardians for some time. I have a better idea," he said. "Follow my lead."

"Do I have a choice?" asked Dagamier, but there was no malice in her husky voice. "We'd better hurry before the light spell goes out."

Guerrand dashed to the opposite side of the overlook. Below in the courtyard were many of the strangely sculpted topiary plants he had seen on his arrival. When viewed directly, the plant shapes were unidentifiable. But in the oddly angled light of Bastion, they cast very distinct, disturbing shadows against the edifice. While none of these shadows was recognizable, all of them had an eery familiarity, like shapes remembered from nightmares.

Guerrand spread his arms and extended them forward in a sweeping motion. As he did so, the shadows moved away from the trees and lumbered forward. Their motion was graceful and fluid, and they advanced steadily toward the gashed fence.

Dagamier was unsure what Guerrand had in mind, but she did as he had ordered and animated the shadows from the other side of the main entrance. Shortly, several dozen shadows were flowing toward the fight.

As the first shadows slipped into the melee, the gargoyles and hell hounds paused momentarily, unsure what was happening. Then one of the hell hounds unleashed a blast of fiery breath at the shapes, but it crackled harmlessly through the darkness. Guerrand was ready on the roof and immediately loosed a sleeping spell at the attacking hell hound, which crumpled soundlessly to the ground. Startled by the apparent demise of one of their own, two other hounds tore into the shadows and fell prey to Guerrand's spell. Both lay motionless on the ground.

The remaining hell hounds and gargoyles slowly backed away from the advancing shadows. In the brief respite, Guerrand and Dagamier quickly reestablished their charm spells that usually controlled the guardian beasts.

The gargoyles returned to their perches, chittering softly, their sights anchored on the shadows in the courtyard. The hounds whimpered briefly behind the fence, then fell silent, red eyes watching.

Guerrand lowered arms that felt as heavy as if a bag of coins hung from each.

Dagamier's head tilted to regard him. "What made you think of using the shadows?"

Guerrand shrugged. "My brother and sister and I used to play a game when we were kids. Back when the garden was more than weeds, we'd wait until dark and then tell each other stories about what all the shadow-shapes really were. Rosemary shrubs became child-eating ogres under moonlight, and the like. Then we'd dare each other to go farther and farther into the garden. I tell you it was frightening, even though we *knew* they were only shrubs." He shrugged. "Everything looks different in darkness.

"It's hard to predict how long it will take gargoyles and hell hounds to catch on," continued Guerrand. "They're really more brawn than brain. Still, as long as they think the shadows will intervene, neither side is likely to cross the darkness of the courtyard."

Tired to his bones, the mage took several steps toward the staircase. "This episode has taught me two things, though," he confessed. "We must be even more vigilant about maintaining the enchantments over such creatures—take nothing for granted. And, starting tomorrow, while one of us remains in the scrying sphere at all times, the others will begin practice drills for battle readiness. We'll have no more scrambling for the doorway like scared rabbits."

Dagamier held the door open for Guerrand. On her face was an unmistakable look of respect. It was a look the high defender of Bastion had long waited to see.

# Chapter Four

Standing in the underground laboratory that had once been Belize's, Lyim continued to ponder the oracle's message. She'd said that Lyim's former master had the answer to curing the snake mutation. It was not a new thought. It wasn't idle curiosity that had prompted Belize to thrust his apprentice's arm into the portal that night on Stonecliff. The archmage had known full well the consequences of the action. He alone knew the exact cause of the mutation, so it was only logical Belize could have fathomed a cure, if he were alive.

The oracle told Lyim to look beyond the grave for his answer, to seek it from Belize's spirit. However, what she was suggesting was not usually in the realm of a wizard's power. Still, Lyim had never paid much heed to the distinctions between schools of magic. If ever a mage had broken the bounds, it was Belize. Lyim had

once seen the master conjure a denizen of the Abyss—
was Belize's spirit really so different from that?

The spellbooks and other texts not used at Stonecliff
by the former Master of the Red Robes still lined the
shelves in the underground laboratory. The Council of
Three had reviewed them after Belize's execution, having burned those he'd used, but found nothing else
related to Belize's attempt to reach the Lost Citadel.
They had then turned their attention to removing the
ghastly remains of Belize's gating experiments.

Lyim rolled up the left sleeve of his red robe and
began pulling books down to the table. He held one
open with his scaly right elbow and thumbed through
the parchment pages with his left hand, looking for ref-
erences to conjuring the dead.

The snake bobbed back and forth for a short time,
eyeing the paraphernalia on the table. Then it suddenly
lunged at a candlestick, knocking over the metal stand
and the burning taper. Lyim snatched up the candle
before it could scorch any of the potentially valuable
papers spread before him. In the meantime, the snake's
thrashing also knocked an empty glass beaker to the
stone floor and scattered several quills. Lyim yanked
the cursed arm back and held it well away from the
disruption while he struggled one-handed to put
everything back in its place.

It was tough, even after nearly six years, using his
left hand for tasks. He still couldn't write legibly with
it, so he avoided writing whenever possible, or used a
minor cantrip to make notes. Eating was a one-handed
embarrassment—food simply refused to stay on his
fork. He had resorted to drinking most of his meals,
since he could hold a mug well enough.

The real shame of it was, he rarely indulged in his
favorite mug-holding event: partaking of ale at the
many inns of Palanthas. His face, though thin and

drawn, was still perfectly handsome. Women continued to follow him with their eyes and their bodies. Until they saw the snake. Their horrified stares as they drew back convinced him that even solitude was better than their disgust, or worse still, their pity.

Books, scrolls, parchments, it took Lyim days to sort through all that Belize had acquired or written. He lit a third thick beeswax candle in the windowless laboratory, letting his tired eyes linger on the soothing yellow flame. Was he grasping at straws by trying to conjure some flicker of Belize's essence? Was he just prolonging the moment when he would have to admit to himself that there was no cure for his hand? He had long ago decided that that day would be his last.

Lyim looked away from the candle, eyes burning from the sweet-smelling smoke. Wearily he pulled down one of the last books on the shelf, a smallish, homemade thing, bound together with a brittle leather lace. It looked more like a collection of vegetable recipes than a spellbook of any import. The words had worn off the cheap leather cover, but an intriguing, tooled illustration remained. The picture was crude, unlike the finely rendered designs Belize had done. It showed a skull inside two nested triangles, a symbol Lyim had never encountered elsewhere in any of Belize's writings.

The book crackled with age as Lyim opened it. The pages inside were apparently much older than the cover. The first page repeated the double triangle symbol, but also bore the book's title: *Achnaskin's Guide to Summoning the Dead.*

Excitement sparked to life in Lyim's chest. His left fingertips lingered upon the title while he willed himself to remain calm and focused. Only when his pulse had slowed did he allow himself to turn to the next page. At a glance the page had no illustrations and looked black with crowded but carefully inked text, topped by a larger heading.

*Tips before spellcasting*

*When speaking with the dead, the spellcaster would be wise to remember the following unchangeable facts:*

1. *The dead respond best to simple questions, so phrase yours accordingly.*

2. *The dead tire and bore easily. Although they would seem to have nothing but time, their attention spans are extremely limited. Do not waste time with pointless questions.*

3. *The dead conjured from the Abyss (those of an evil disposition before their dissolution) are usually in great torment and may be difficult to comprehend.*

4. *Understandably, the disposition of most deceased creatures has been soured by death. Many are extremely bad tempered.*

Lyim shrugged, thinking the advice only common sense. Still, he took it to heart before eagerly turning the page once more. There began the anticipated entry containing the incantation, under the large heading: *The Spell to Summon the Dead.* He began reading with an intensity he'd not felt in many years.

But before long, beads of perspiration joined the streaks that already flowed down Lyim's temples, pooling in the short whiskers above his lips. He read and reread the entry, pushing back the anxiousness that made it difficult to concentrate and really digest the words. The spell's magical patterns were in an unusually complicated order. Lyim could find no shortcut to memorizing them, no distinguishing marks or pauses to aid in his usual rote memorization. Hours or days could have passed while he studied the patterns. Five thick candles and a dusty stub found in a drawer had burned away before Lyim began to feel he understood and had memorized the spell.

Lyim looked up abruptly from the fragile book. A horrifying thought began to blossom behind his eyes. What if, after all this study, he hadn't the components to carry out the spell? He would forget the pattern if he had to stop for even an hour to locate some obscure ingredient.

Lyim had inherited surprisingly few of Belize's components. He'd returned to Villa Nova after his Test to find the laboratory a frightful pile of broken beakers, hopelessly mixed and moistened powders, and dried-up pickled components, none of it salvageable. He had swept it all outside the villa into a magical fire that had lit the sky above Palanthas like fireworks for two days and nights.

Lyim spun about and carried Achnaskin's small book to the shelves containing the components he'd purchased from street vendors near the Great Library. Most mages insisted upon drying and storing their own things, but Lyim had never had the time for such tediousness. Propping the book open with a heavy marble mortar bowl, he traced a finger down the short list. The first three were easy enough; every mage had lye, sulfur, and goat's hoof on his shelves. The fourth item was trickier. He didn't remember ever having used mace. Lyim's eyes quickly surveyed the shelf, but he couldn't find the spice. He reread the spell list and noticed a little star inked next to the word "mace." He found a similar mark at the bottom of the page and read:

*A double dose of nutmeg may be substituted for this item.*

A sigh of relief escaped Lyim's lips, and he licked away the sweat there. He had a whole jar full of dark, spicy nutmeg.

Lyim turned the page and continued reading the instructions.

> *Mix the components thoroughly. Place mixture in two flaming braziers set near the body and burn until smoke—*

The body? The instructions so far had said nothing about having a body. The Council of Three and the gods alone knew what had happened to Belize's corpse. Lyim was stymied. He reread the passage, and again he found a small star, this time inked next to the word "body." His eyes jumped to the bottom of the page.

> *In the event that the body is not available, due to immolation, devouring, disintegration, or any other factor, a small bit of skin, hair, nail, or bone can be substituted. The duration of the spell will be halved.*

Lyim scowled. Where was he going to get a piece of a dead man? Lyim blinked, recalling the one door in the villa that he had never opened. Snatching up a hand broom and small pan, he lifted the hem of his red robes and sprinted up the staircase two steps at a time. The mage emerged in the large rotunda through an archway that appeared to be a floor-length mirror. Lyim pounded across the inlaid marble floor and down the long hallway that led to the kitchens . . . and Belize's sleeping chamber.

Lyim paused outside the door before placing his hand on the faceted diamond knob. He had kept the room he'd had as an apprentice upon returning from Wayreth those many years ago. He'd had no need for, or curiosity about, the archmage's sleeping chamber. He'd actually tried hard to forget Belize had ever lived here, blaming his former mentor for the mutation whose removal had become his obsession. Lyim stayed at the villa only because it was practical and convenient.

Was the door trapped? Lyim doubted it, since the archmage had frequently mentioned he preferred marking his possessions so that he could track down thieves. Still, Lyim would not take foolish chances this close to a solution. A simple divining spell assured him he would not be harmed by opening the door.

The door creaked loudly from disuse when Lyim pushed it open. He peered cautiously around it, feeling foolish as he did. Who was he expecting to find, Belize himself? The mage stepped in boldly and looked around.

The room was small, even smaller than Lyim's own. A layer of dust as thick as his little finger covered everything: the granite floor, the narrow spartan bed, the night stand. Lyim's heart sank. He'd been hoping to sweep the room for any trace of Belize. But how would he be able to separate a lock of hair or petrified fingernail from the dust?

Then his eyes fell upon it. The small corked jar on the night stand. It was half filled with red-tipped nail clippings. He snatched it up and hugged it to his chest, relieved laughter bubbling from his throat. Belize wasn't vain; he must have had some magical purpose for saving his garishly painted nail clippings. If Lyim hadn't hated the archmage so, he might have blessed the soul he was about to conjure.

Lyim took the nails to the laboratory and continued reading where he'd left off. Hunger gnawed, and he felt his energy flagging. He would have to cast the spell soon.

*Speak the words of the spell. Next, place your pre-
pared mixture in two flaming braziers set near the
body and burn until smoke forms.*

Lyim reached under the central table and withdrew
the requisite braziers, placing them on the table near
the open jar of nails.

*Inhale smoke deeply. Exhale by calling forth the full
name and suspected realm of containment for the
soul in question. If a successful conjuration is
attained, the caster is advised to recall the recommen-
dations for speaking with the dead.*

"Yeah, yeah, yeah," muttered Lyim impatiently. His
left hand, on the bowl of mixed components, was shaking. Using his teeth, the mage removed the cork from a
seldom-used bottle of snowberry wine and took a long
pull, waiting for it to burn a trail to the pit of his empty
stomach.

After carefully speaking the words that would acti-
vate the spell, Lyim took up the bowl again and divided
it evenly between the two small flames. The flames
roared up from both braziers, singeing Lyim's eyebrows on the way to the ceiling. Slowly the flames
flickered back down and in their wake left beautiful
plumes of purple smoke. Lyim exhaled harshly, then
thrust his head into the smoke and sucked in the acrid
fumes until his lungs could hold no more.

"I call from the Abyss the essence of Belize of Palanthas!" Lyim cried in a rush. The smoke that blew from
his mouth now was as black as the air in that fetid realm
of the dead. While Lyim watched, the smoke began
forming into the familiar profile of the archmage Belize.
The image, which wavered like the smoke from which
it was made, lacked detail, but the stubble-ringed pate

and goateed chin were unmistakable.

A tide of conflicting emotions swept over Lyim: relief, fear, reverence, hatred. But hatred was the strongest. "Belize."

The apparition looked up at the sound of its name. There was neither recognition nor confusion in Belize's expression, only an expectant stare.

"You bastard." Lyim was tempted to go on, but remembered that because of substitutions he would get only half the spell's usual brief duration. "Tell me what you did to cause my hand to be changed to a snake." Lyim viciously shoved the overlong cuff of his right sleeve back and held the hissing snake up to the apparition.

As if looking beyond Lyim's mutation, Belize seemed not to see the limb. "Your arm was the first living thing to enter the dimensional portal to the Lost Citadel in untold years." Belize's unearthly voice reminded Lyim of the wavering, ghoulish timbre he'd used as a child to frighten his friends.

"Yes? So?"

"Waiting within the unused bridge were starving extradimensional creatures. One was feasting on your flesh when your arm was withdrawn from the portal." The apparition's face contorted as if it were in pain. Its head spun about, and it appeared to bite at something behind it that only it could see.

"The extradimensional snakelike creature was forced to meld with you to survive the transplantation to the Prime Material Plane."

It made a certain sense. "How do I remove the creature?" Lyim asked.

"Recreate the events and reverse the process."

"But that's impossible!" Lyim heard himself cry for the second time in recent days. "Thanks to you, no one can create a portal to the Lost Citadel!"

Suddenly the image of Belize began to break up. "Don't go yet!" Lyim didn't know if the spell was expiring, or Belize was angered by his verbal attack. Frustrated, he continued to ignore the advice about dealing with the dead. "I conjured you, and I demand that you stay! I'm not finished with you yet!"

But the fires in the braziers choked out simultaneously as if doused with water, and the smoke became purple and featureless again.

Lyim collapsed onto a small wooden stool and rubbed his face wearily with one hand. He hadn't been this exhausted since the conclusion of his Test. Then he'd felt good, proud. Now he just felt empty.

Things had changed in the world of magic since Belize's departure for the Abyss. Big things. One thing in particular, as he'd started to tell Belize's apparition. No one would ever again be able to create a portal directly to the Lost Citadel. Just after Lyim had passed his Test and returned to Palanthas he had heard through magical circles that the Conclave of Wizards, in a rare moment of cooperation, had begun to build a stronghold to protect the entrance to the storehouse of godly magic. Those same sources mentioned that the location of the redoubt, called Bastion, would be a secret place beyond the circles of the universe and guarded by a representative of each of the orders.

Five years ago Lyim had given the story little more than passing attention, consumed as he was with finding a cure for his arm. Now he wished he'd listened more closely to the gossip. Wherever it was, Bastion stood between Lyim and the Lost Citadel, between Lyim and his arm.

Suddenly Lyim saw a glimmer of light flicker through the crack in what he'd thought was his last door of hope. Could he recreate the portal to the citadel at Bastion? It only made sense that, if creating the portal was still possible at all, Bastion was the only place to do it. Hope spread like magical fire in his heart. Each time Lyim had found himself at a dead end, a secret and unexpected door seemed to open for him.

But where was the door to Bastion? Beyond the circles of the universe . . . that could be almost anywhere! The Abyss alone had six hundred sixty-six levels. Lyim considered it safe to rule out the realm of the dead, considering that the Council would not have sent their creation to such an evil place.

Still, Lyim was undaunted. All he had to do was find the way to Bastion, and then bribe the jailor with the keys. The magical world was a small one. Tapping his chin in thought, he wondered if, perhaps, he even knew one of the representatives stationed there.

# Chapter Five

He'd been told the manor house he sought was at the end of the narrow lane, behind a tall and obscuring copse of trees. The mage trudged the muddy track between cropped hedges of bright green dogwood. The light but steady rain continued, piercing the fog that clung like cotton batting to everything it touched, including the mage's mood.

Cinching the hood of his cloak closed beneath his chin, Lyim hoped this miserable trek would prove worth the effort. Lightning flashed overhead, and he hastened his steps. The path abruptly opened up around a curve in the road, giving view of a large beige stone-and-timber manor, windows and shake roof overgrown with curling tendrils of ivy. Lyim stood in the rain for a few long moments, staring up at the manor; he was not looking forward to again witnessing the pity he'd seen in her honey-colored eyes that night on Stonecliff. But there was no way around it, if he was to get what he'd come all this way to retrieve. Not even a pretty girl and her pity would keep him from reaching the goal of a half decade.

Lyim rolled down the last fold of his right cuff and secured beneath it the fingerless leather glove he'd had specially made for this trip. The mage came to the gateroom, a three-quartered cylinder fit against a corner of the manor. Standing under a small overhang, Lyim pounded first with his fist, then banged the lion-faced wrought-iron knocker repeatedly against the thick wooden door. Before long, he could sense someone regarding him through a small peephole. Lyim stood up straight, deliberately looking away from the door to present a casual profile.

The door creaked open on unoiled hinges. Lyim spun about with a warm smile of greeting on his face, expecting a servant to answer. His lip trembled slightly at the sight of the woman herself. Lovelier than he remembered, statuesque and still slim, Esme's face had taken on a depth of wisdom with age. The soft, round cheeks were now attractively hollowed and burnished with a healthy red glow. Shiny tendrils of curly golden-brown hair ringed her face and draped her shoulders like a thick cloak. Lyim preferred it loose to the tight bun he remembered her wearing at the nape of her neck. Her gown, a rosy whisper of a thing, draped and clung to her best advantage.

"Lyim Rhistadt."

"Hello, Esme." Lyim took note that her smile held genuine warmth. He gave a courtly bow from the waist. "You look as exquisite as ever."

"And you are ever the charmer," she said, clearly pleased despite her cynicism.

"It makes my words no less true," he said smoothly,

calling upon skills dusty with disuse.

Esme colored ever so slightly. "What brings you to Fangoth?"

"You, of course," he said, his eyes sparkling directly into hers. He held his left hand out from under the stoop to catch the drops of rain that pelted his back. "May I come in?"

"I'm sorry," she mumbled, coloring a becoming shade of red. "Of course, please come in." Esme swept wide the heavy door and waved Lyim into the gate-room.

"I don't know what's the matter with me," she said, leading him over the polished slate floor in the small, circular room. "I've had so few visitors since my father died."

They entered a long hallway, dark and draped with thick tapestries. Esme turned left, into a small, cozy sitting room. Three large, arched windows, adorned with heavy mauve chintz, let in the rainy afternoon's meager light. The room was overfilled, for Lyim's taste, with flowery throw pillows and dark, heavy furniture, and tables covered with lace doilies and odd bric-a-brac. It was a very feminine place, and Esme slid into it like a hand into a well-worn glove.

The young woman lowered herself gracefully into an enveloping chair by the unlit hearth. "This room was always kept closed when my father was alive," she explained. "The furniture was here, though badly water-damaged from some long-ago flood. The first thing I did when I returned here to tend Melar during his illness was to clean the place up and redecorate to my own taste. It's my haven within the manor house. Most of my time is spent here—when I'm not in the laboratory."

Lyim spied a black-framed silhouette of a man with Esme's patrician nose and chin, but distinguished from her by a curling mustache. "Was your father ill very long?" he asked, settling into the second heavily padded chair. Lyim crossed his legs and arranged the folds of his red robe about his knees.

"No." Water dripped loudly and steadily from the windowsills outside.

In the awkward silence that followed, Lyim spied a spellbook, open and lying facedown, on the parquet table between the two armchairs. "I heard you passed your Test at the tower," he said.

"From the same person who told you I'd come back to Fangoth?" she quizzed.

"Yes, as a matter of fact I believe it was Justarius who told me both," Lyim said mildly.

"Justarius?" Esme looked surprised and a little disappointed at the mention of the Master of the Red Robes.

"Who else?" Lyim asked archly.

Esme stood and rubbed her arms as if chilled. "No one, of course," she said, fidgeting as she placed some tinder in the cold hearth. "I lead the quiet life of a mage in study here. Justarius is about the only other wizard with whom I ever communicate, and then only rarely." Esme stood and brushed off her hands, preparing to light the wood.

Lyim watched her profile as he artlessly asked, "What about Guerrand?"

The young woman went stiff. "What about him?"

Lyim shrugged his shoulders. "I thought you two were—"

"We were," she cut in abruptly, "but we aren't anymore." The fire leaped to life beneath Esme's fingers. She whirled around, amber eyes flashing, her composure totally fled. "Why don't you cut short this little fishing expedition and tell me why you're really here, Lyim?"

"Esme!" Lyim feigned shock, left palm pressed to his breastbone. "I merely came to see an old friend—"

Her laughter cut him off. "You traveled hundreds of leagues from Palanthas—"

"It's not that far."

"Just to see me and check on my social life after—what's it been, five, six years?" Esme chuckled again. "Lyim, Lyim," she intoned, "you might have been able to fool Guerrand, but I always saw through your slick act." She shook a tapered finger at him. "Mind you, I'm not overly angry, but neither am I stupid."

"No one would ever mistake you for that." Lyim matched her firm expression, but he was the first to look away, smiling sheepishly. "I'm no less sincere about seeing an old friend, just because I had a dual purpose to this visit," he said with exaggerated contrition in his tone.

Esme had the good grace to acknowledge the possibility with a polite nod. She leaned against the back of a chair, facing him, her arms crossed expectantly.

Lyim blurted, "I understand that you were among the mages who designed and built Bastion."

"That was quite some time ago," she replied cautiously, leaning forward. "How did you hear about it? I thought the identities of the designing members were supposed to be kept secret."

"What can I say? The magical rumor mill in Palanthas is a living thing. Besides," he said, shrugging, "it wouldn't have been a difficult thing to figure out. In addition to the Council of Three, who were the other eighteen members of the Conclave at the time of construction?"

Esme pursed her full lips. "Why the curiosity about a place none may enter?"

Lyim decided to speak boldly. "I want to become our order's guardian there. Frankly, Esme, my life hasn't turned out as I'd planned. I haven't been able to cure my . . . deformity." He drew his leather-gloved hand back when her eyes inevitably strayed to it.

"I'd welcome the isolation," Lyim went on in an enthusiastic rush. "There, only two other people would be subjected to seeing my hand."

"I'm sorry, Lyim," she said softly.

He tore his gaze from the pity he'd expected, and now found, in her eyes. "I don't want your sympathy," he said sharply. "I want your help. You know what Bastion is like. You were among those who designed and built it. Tell me what you know," he rushed on, leaning toward her, "and it will give me an advantage over other candidates the next time the position becomes available."

Lyim reached out with his hand for one of Esme's, then noticed the thick, silver bracelet in the shape of a snake encircling her right bicep. He remembered well the electrical shock the protective armband delivered. Lyim's hand curled into a desperate fist. "Please, Esme. I've never wanted anything so much in my life."

The young woman visibly paled. "Don't you know?"

For once, Lyim didn't have to pretend ignorance. "Know what?"

"That Guerrand took the position less than a year ago," she supplied. "And unless something has happened to him—"

"Guerrand DiThon is the Red Robes' guardian?" gulped Lyim, uncharacteristically surprised.

Esme nodded, her brow furrowed. "I can't believe that you spoke to Justarius recently and he didn't mention it."

"We didn't really discuss Bastion or Guerrand," muttered Lyim. That wasn't surprising, since he hadn't spoken to the Master of the Red Robes in years.

"I'm sorry to be the one to dash your hopes," Esme

said. "Frankly, I don't think I could have helped you very much anyway. Though I participated in the exterior design and construction of the stronghold, all but the Council of Three were dispatched from the site before the interior was complete and it was sent to the plane where it would block passage to the Lost Citadel."

"What plane is that?" Lyim asked.

Esme pondered the question. " 'Between earth and sky' was all Justarius would ever say about it."

"Bastion sounds like a wondrous place," sighed Lyim. "One I'm destined never to see."

Esme smiled distantly in fond memory. "It *is* a wondrous place, made of the most pure and perfect red granite mined from the Kharolis Mountains." She strode to a recessed shelf and took from a triangular pedestal a palm-sized red and creamy pink-veined ball from among the bric-a-brac there. "I pocketed this from among the scraps at the site as a souvenir. A local sculptor fashioned it to look like a miniature Lunitari."

Lyim laid his hand to the cold, polished stone. "It's flawless," he breathed in wonder. Abruptly, he set it back down and stood. "I'm sorry, Esme. It appears I've disturbed you for nothing."

"Oh, I wouldn't say that," Esme said generously. "I'd forgotten how . . . entertaining you could be, Lyim. Please stay long enough for me to offer you some repast."

Lyim hesitated, swallowing a pleased smile. "It *was* a long trip."

She headed for the door and placed her hand on the knob. "Just give me a few minutes to prepare something." Lyim nodded his consent, a smile still pulling up his lips as Esme slipped from the room.

The door clicked shut, and the mage nearly swooned with delight over his good fortune. He would get everything he'd come for *and* a meal with the beautiful woman he'd always desired.

He had to move quickly, though. Lyim began muttering an incantation. Wisps of dark material emerged from the air around him, which he plucked and gathered into a ball. As long as he chanted, the wisps appeared, until he had collected a lump of sufficient size. His refrain then changed, becoming less rhythmic. The ball of material hovered in the air as Lyim's hand wove around it, shaping it without touching it. Wisps separated from the ball to curl around Esme's moon globe, then dart back to their starting places. The orb pulsated as if alive as it shifted and formed itself.

And then it was done. The red globe of granite dropped into Lyim's hand, pleasantly small but weighty. He compared the two; the match was perfect. Lyim placed his creation in the triangular holder on the shelf and concealed the original among the thick folds of his robe. The facsimile would not last forever, but it would certainly endure long enough to get Lyim away from Fangoth with the real globe of granite that would help him locate Bastion, and that was all he wanted. For now, anyway.

* * * * *

Guerrand rubbed his eyes, which were red from staring, and glanced at the time glass on the small table behind him: only half the sand had sifted from the top to the bottom beaker. The mage let out a small sigh. He had half a shift to serve yet in the scrying sphere. Why was the time passing so slowly today?

The muscles in Guerrand's shoulders were knotted into thick cords. His stomach growled unrelentingly. The high defender's temples throbbed from the strain of concentrating on the model of Bastion and its perimeter.

Usually a patient man, Guerrand could hardly wait until Dagamier came to replace him in the sphere. He knew exactly what he would do then: pour an entire flask of restorative rosemary oil into the warmed wading pool in the seascape room. While the hot water covered him to the waist, cool air would fan his chest soothingly. Then he would open a bottle of green Ergothian wine, his own brew aptly named for both its color and flavor. Nibbling sweet biscuits, Guerrand would drink just enough wine to ease the stress from his back.

Imagining it erased one furrow from Guerrand's brow. He blinked; his sight wavered briefly before settling again upon the model on the table beneath him. It really was a marvel, this magically imbued diorama of Bastion. It resembled an architect's rendering of a city. Guerrand had seen such a diagram back in Thonvil, a rotting and dusty wood-and-stone model made by Castle DiThon's original architect.

The similarity ended there, however. Bastion's diorama was aglow with minerals and magic. In the middle of a curved table covered by clear glass, the stronghold's three wings were represented in the model by resonating crystal that continuously hummed softly. The wings were surrounded by the courtyard, whose topiaries and statues were carved of emerald. Beyond the small fence that enclosed the model's courtyard was a ring of crystalline sulfur attuned to the area patrolled by the hell hounds. Encircling the sulfur was a wide band of quicksilver, a literal representation of the vast mercury moat that was the final border of this demiplane of shadow. The outermost edges of the diorama were shrouded in ever-roiling gray mists that represented the Ethereal Plane, which abutted Bastion's demiplane.

Though the defender who watched the diorama was

unable to see into the Ethereal, any disturbances in this demiplane of shadow would be evidenced on the model in the scrying room. Trouble in the courtyard would make the emerald topiaries wink light and dark; disturbances among the hell hounds would illuminate the yellow sulfur. Guerrand, Dagamier, and Ezius watched in neverending rotation for such an event.

Though time in the usual sense had no meaning at Bastion, a defender's turn in the scrying sphere was kept to a short period predetermined by a sand-filled glass. The defender sat on a hard, wooden chair, intentionally uncomfortable to discourage dozing in the column's silence. The only source of light was the diorama itself, which naturally drew the occupant's attention in the otherwise dark sphere.

As a rule, Guerrand looked slightly beyond the model, letting his gaze take in the whole image, rather than study one specific area at a time. The advantage was that any change in the replica would immediately catch his attention. The technique also lent itself to vacant staring.

A faint, popping splash sounded in the small column. Guerrand watched the model intently. He heard splashing again, and a flicker of motion caught the mage's eye. Guerrand spotted the disturbance on the farthest edge of the outer ring of mercury. A bubble formed out of the shiny liquid, growing slowly until it popped. Then a series of bubbles appeared and burst in rapid succession. Each time the rings left by the bubble receded rapidly into the Ethereal. Something was trying unsuccessfully to enter the quicksilver.

In the year Guerrand had stood watch no intruder had entered Bastion's demiplane. He could scarcely credit the bubbling mercury, but he swallowed his disbelief and set about his duty as high defender. Guerrand drew a crystal lens from a cupboard beneath the model table and peered at the bubbles. The sole purpose of the lens was to reveal glitches in the magical diorama. The bubbling mercury was clearly seen through the lens.

There could be no question now—someone or something was trespassing upon the demiplane's boundary. The intrusion could be caused by anything, from a real attack against Bastion to a wayward xorn that had lost its direction in the interstices between the planes.

Following the established but never-used routine for such an occurrence, Guerrand consulted a schematic of the planes that bordered Bastion's demiplane. In the ether that abutted the mercury moat, a powerful magical creature known as a ki-rin watched for intruders. The Council of Three had employed the ki-rin for this purpose because of the creature's lawful nature and ability to read the mind of any living thing through telepathy.

Guerrand unstoppered a beaker of clear alcohol and poured the liquid into a very shallow bowl carved into the lower right corner of the model table. The bitter smell of the volatile liquid filled the room. As the surface ripples died away, an image of the ki-rin appeared.

Vaguely horselike in appearance though bulkier, the ki-rin's forehead was adorned with a unicorn's horn. Luminous golden scales covered its torso, though its tail and mane were hair. The ki-rin had eyes the oddest shade of violet. Despite its disturbing appearance, the ki-rin radiated an aura of beneficence.

*A human wanders the Ethereal,* announced the ki-rin, its melodious voice echoing inside Guerrand's head.

"A human," Guerrand repeated. "What does this person look like?"

*The Ethereal is vast, and even I cannot see everywhere at once. However, I have read the creature's mind.* The ki-rin paused, head tilted. *This human seeks Bastion and you,*

*Guerrand DiThon.*

Guerrand started. Who but Maladorigar and the Council of Three knew he was here? The gnome couldn't possibly have found his way to the outer edges of Bastion. Only a mage could have made that journey. Could Justarius have told Esme of his position?

*My instructions are to slay intruders,* said the ki-rin.

"Wait," Guerrand commanded. "Continue monitoring the person's movements," he told the ki-rin. "Prevent the intruder from penetrating the demiplane, but do nothing else without my direction."

Guerrand spun away from the diorama and searched the shelves that surrounded the sphere's door. They contained components for spells, as well as other magical devices that allowed passage through each of the uninhabitable protective spheres around Bastion. Guerrand sought the oil that would permit him to travel through mercury and observe the intruder at a safe distance.

He spotted the appropriate label on a cobalt-blue bottle. Pouring the oil into his palm, he spread it over his skin and clothing like lotion. He felt his consciousness separate from his physical body, like the yoke from the white of an egg. He could think and see as usual, but he felt weightless. Guerrand looked down at his arms and hands and saw both his body and its dark reflection. His physical self would remain in the scrying sphere, while his conscious shadow would explore the lightless ring of mercury.

Guerrand rested dark, flat palms upon the lefthand portion of the diorama's mercury border and intoned the magical words, *"Illethessius umbra intentradolum."*

Guerrand slipped like fog into a sea of warm, dark quicksilver. It enveloped him, rolled over his shadow form in thick, heavy waves. He was as buoyant as a bubble, though without its delicate nature. As shadow, he saw in the darkness of the mercury as people see in light. He stretched his dark, shadow-flat arms and swam toward the distant grayness of the Ethereal Plane.

Guerrand was stopped at the farthest edge of the mercury moat by the defenses of the demiplane and could not see into the Ethereal.

*Ki-rin*, he called telepathically, bobbing in the sea of mercury.

*Yes, high defender*, the guardian creature responded.

*Open a window to your plane so that I can see who seeks me.*

As instructed, a curtain of gray slowly parted.

Standing in the mists of the Ethereal Plane was a red-robed mage Guerrand knew well. "Lyim Rhistadt," he hissed.

* * * * *

Lyim heard his old friend's voice, and he spun around to face the wall of black mercury. His snake arm hissed at the sudden movement. Lyim unconsciously cursed the vile creature.

Squinting into the darkness of the quicksilver he said, "Rand, is that you? I've been sending message after magical message to you, but I was beginning to think I'd never draw your notice."

"You drew it," Guerrand said grimly. "You must have stepped briefly from the Ethereal into the mercury, because you set off the alarms in Bastion. What are you doing here?"

"Looking for you, of course," said Lyim, trying to sound jocular. "You might at least say hello, after my extraordinary efforts to find you."

When Guerrand said nothing, Lyim frowned. "Can't you make yourself visible? I feel foolish talking to a black sea."

Consisting now only of shadow, Guerrand could not rise above the mercury. So instead he formed the mercury to himself and pressed upward slightly against the surface, forming a slight, three-dimensional image of his face on the smooth, silvery stream.

"How did you determine the location of Bastion's plane?" Guerrand demanded. "It's a well-guarded secret."

"I had a piece of the exact red granite used for its walls and a visual memory of you to home in on. That spell brought me as far as this border, but I've been unable to get any closer."

"Bastion's defenses are far too powerful," said Guerrand proudly. "A ki-rin was moments from slaying you as it was." His mercury-delineated eyes squinted suspiciously. "Where did you find the granite?"

"Come on, Rand," Lyim said evasively, "you know I'm a resourceful guy."

"I also know you're not one to go through all this trouble just to chat with an old friend," Guerrand said evenly.

Despite his annoyed tone, Guerrand's silvery face showed conflicting emotions. Lyim believed he also saw a measure of warmth.

"You know me too well, Rand, so I'll not mince words," said Lyim. "I need a favor that only you can grant me. I've learned through painstaking research that in order to restore my hand I must recreate the portal to the Lost Citadel Belize constructed on Stonecliff. Bastion is the only place left where that's possible." Lyim paused for effect. "Bring me into Bastion, Rand, and we can work together to restore my hand."

"I can't do that," Guerrand responded softly, but without hesitation. "I can't let anyone into Bastion."

"Don't answer so quickly," said Lyim. "Just think about it."

"I'm sorry, Lyim," said Guerrand, "but there's nothing to think about. I took an oath to prevent anyone from entering Bastion."

"I don't ask this lightly," growled Lyim. "Believe me when I say that I've literally been to the ends of Krynn trying to get my hand back."

"And I don't refuse you lightly," said Guerrand. "No one would like to help you more. But you of all people understand what it is to be a mage, to pledge your life to magic and magic alone. I strengthened that pledge when I took the position of high defender. To violate that vow, here at the final stronghold before the Lost Citadel, would betray all magic and all mages—everything that I stand for. I can't do it, even for you, Lyim."

Lyim regarded the profile in the gray-black wall with an uncontrollable sneer. "You were my last remaining hope, Rand."

"Have you petitioned the Council for entrance?"

"Those three help no one but themselves," snapped Lyim. "Your master promised to find a cure for my hand." He held up his mutated right limb; the snake sputtered and hissed above his head. "You can see the result of his promise at the end of my arm. Justarius knew there was only one cure for my hand. If he had been willing to let me recreate the portal to the Lost Citadel, he would have suggested it himself."

"Perhaps they'll make an exception to their rule, considering your heroism at Stonecliff," Guerrand suggested. "I'd be willing to petition them on your behalf."

Lyim could see the pity in Guerrand's silvery face, could hear it in his tone. It angered him more than Guerrand's refusal to let him into the stronghold. "A supreme sacrifice, I'm sure, from the man whose life and family I saved."

Lyim exploded in helpless, caustic laughter. "It occurs to me that once again I play the fool in this friendship. I thought you were the one person who wouldn't let me down, if only out of a guilty sense of debt." Lyim's hysterical laughter hiccuped to an angry sob. "Seems your ambition is greater than your guilt these days."

"This isn't about such transitory things," Guerrand said coldly. "My position has taught me that Bastion's purpose is far more important than one man's guilt— or another's hand. It's about the survival of magic, of life. I won't make a choice that puts that in jeopardy."

"Everything is a question of choice."

"Petition the Council," Guerrand urged more strongly.

But Lyim scarcely heard him. Once again, he realized that he was the only one he could rely on.

"I'll help you any other way I can, Lyim."

Lyim vaguely heard Guerrand's voice through the fog of his bitterness. "There *is* no other way," he responded, low and threatening.

"Then I'm truly sorry." Guerrand's rubbery profile disappeared from the surface of the mercury wall.

"Not as sorry as you will be." In a vessel-bursting fury, Lyim dispatched himself from the Ethereal Plane with a magical wave of his left arm. Guerrand DiThon might be safely back in the confines of his precious Bastion, but Lyim Rhistadt was far from through with him.

# Chapter Six

Bram DiThon picked his way carefully between the potholes and ice patches on the road to Thonvil, wishing the soles of his boots were not four years thin. The usual freeze-and-thaw cycle was in full swing, dawn ice turning to afternoon mud. Sometimes Bram wondered if spring would ever truly come to Ergoth's moors. The dark-haired young nobleman drew his winter cloak, heavy as a sack of coins, closer as he headed for old Nahamkin's cottage for some promised seeds.

Bram had been hoping the eighteenth day of Misha-mont, his twenty-first birthday, would find him with new boots. He was not terribly surprised when they didn't appear. His mother Rietta was too busy struggling to maintain the image of the lady of the manor. His father—well, Cormac was someone Bram didn't like to think about. Besides, not receiving a present from his family was a small price to pay for the freedom of neglect.

In fact, Cormac's neglect of all of his responsibilities had given Bram's life purpose. It was his ambition—his obsession, even—to restore Castle Thonvil to the productivity and prosperity of his grandfather's time. Due to lack of coin, Bram's mother had been forced to abandon her aspiration for him to become a Knight of Solamnia, so he had been free, at sixteen, to inconspicuously assume the day-to-day duties of a castle's steward.

Unsurprisingly, Cormac's overtaxed tenants had long ago fled. It had taken Bram almost five years of working alone from dawn to dusk to resuscitate Castle DiThon's demesne and get the family's personal lands producing food again. That had been no small feat, considering he hadn't horse or ox to plow with.

Bram had not yet had time to attend to the castle itself, which looked run-down enough to be abandoned. Besides, crumbling stone walls just weren't as interesting to him as the perennials that would be popping up soon: lady's mantle, foxglove. He'd already seen hopeful lavender poking through the last crusts of snow. Bram supplied many of the villagers with dried herbs, but the winter had been a bad one for minor influenzas, and he was running low on the more common medicinals. Fortunately, the end of the season of sickness coincided with the beginning of the herb season.

Bram's eyes were on the small village ahead when he caught movement in the grass to his right. Startled, he looked over, then let out a slow sigh. A snake. He'd seen at least two handfuls of them already in the gardens. Their exodus from the cold earth seemed to have come a little early this year. He watched the long, black creature with the golden diamond pattern on its head slither swiftly through the still-brown roadside grasses. What's your hurry? Bram thought. The snake fell stock-still briefly, then sprang on an unsuspecting mole and gobbled it down in one gulp. The nobleman's shiver had nothing to do with the cold.

Bram hastened toward the village, which boasted no gates or other symbols to mark its entrance. It was too small, too unassuming, too poor. No neighboring lord in his right mind would care to storm Thonvil now. These days the village was no more than an unimpressive collection of dilapidated houses and small shops grouped together out of apathy and convenience. Anyone of youth or ambition had run off to the capital city of Gwynned in the last five years, when the economy had turned sour alongside the lord's fortunes.

The exodus had included members of Cormac's own family. Most recent to leave was Bram's sister Honora, who had married beneath her station to the seneschal of a small estate in Coastlund. The family had neither seen nor heard from her since, which was no burden for Bram, who found he had just enough tolerance for haughtiness to deal with their mother.

The first to leave, of course, had been Uncle Rand. Bram frequently pondered the shadowy memory of the man. Cormac had forbidden anyone to even speak Guerrand's name in Castle DiThon for more than a half decade. Was he still alive? Not even Kirah knew, or at least his aunt wouldn't say.

The notion that the spindly little blonde was his aunt always made Bram laugh. She was two years younger than he. But then, the branches of his family tree were as tangled as the limbs of a hagberry bush and just as susceptible to wind damage. And what a wind had blown through the DiThon family seven years before, when Guerrand had defied Cormac and left to pursue the study of magic.

Bram came to the long, half-timbered building whose ground floor housed the baker's shop on the right half and the only remaining carpenter in Thonvil on the left side. A narrow flight of wooden steps hugged the area between the baker's front door and the right wall, and led to the room let by his Aunt Kirah.

She had been the second member of the DiThon family to leave for Gwynned. Bolted, in fact, when Rietta had tried to marry her off to a toothless old man thirty years her senior. To everyone's surprise, Kirah had slouched back into town but seven months later, a different person, and not the better for it. While it was true she had already changed from the carefree, outspoken scamp she'd been before Rand's leaving, this was different. Worse somehow. She was skittish and withdrawn, like a reclusive old woman, though barely possessed of nineteen years. Something awful must have happened to her, but she refused to talk about it.

Bram had no notion of how Kirah paid for the room she let from the baker, or why she'd returned to a village she'd always professed to hate. She had explained to him once that it was not the village but the castle she hated. Rietta would never have welcomed her back at the castle anyway.

Nevertheless, Bram stopped by to see her whenever he came to the village. He took the stairs two at a time and knocked on his aunt's door. When no answer came, he pushed the door back gingerly, calling, "Kirah? It's me, Bram."

He stepped full into the spartan room and saw that the rope bed was made, feather tick fluffed into place, but he was alone. Some objects on the wooden table under the small, street-side window caught his eye. A quill and ink pot were next to a note with his name neatly lettered on the front. He picked up the parchment and caught his bottom lip between his teeth; behind the note was a pair of boots quite obviously too large for his diminutive aunt.

*Bram,*

> *The boots, of course, are for you. Don't insult my resourcefulness by protesting the expense. Besides, we can't have the local lord's son walking about like a beggar, can we? What will people say? But then, you know how concerned I've always been about that sort of thing. . . .*

> *Sorry to have missed you, but I felt the need for a walk and the peace it provides. Have a most merry day, dear nephew.*

*—K—*

Bram shook his head, touched and sad at the same time at the thought of her solitary walk. The village rumor mill had it that Kirah went daily, no matter the weather, to a cove along the coast to wait for a lover who would never return. Frankly, Bram suspected his aunt had never had a lover, could not see when or where she'd had the opportunity, except, perhaps, during the time she'd spent in Gwynned. So what if she sat looking out to sea, seeking solitude?

Bram slipped on the new boots, and his eyes sank shut languorously. The fit was perfect, the soles double-thick. He no longer dreaded treading on the half-frozen dirt road.

Bram spied the quill. Taking it up, he dipped it in the ink pot and scratched a brief, *Thank you,* —B— at the bottom of Kirah's own note. He rolled his old, soft boots into a floppy log, tucking them under his arm as he pulled Kirah's door shut behind him. Bram checked the position of the sun in the grayish sky. Nahamkin would be wondering where he was.

A freckle-faced young woman was leaving the bakery with a coarse loaf of bread stuffed in her flour-sack apron when Bram bounded back down the stairs. Blushing, she bobbed the courtesy due the lord's son and hastened down the street, past Roxtin the carpenter's shop. Bram found himself reflecting that, although he was very friendly, he had few friends. Perhaps it wasn't possible for the villagers to be more than distantly polite with anyone named DiThon, he decided.

Bram had one true friend, a funny old man, Nahamkin. A farmer all his life, the man rose before the sun and set before it as well. Too old to make a living at farming anymore, Nahamkin was a cotter now, a tenant of a village cottage that held just enough land for him to sustain himself on the small plantings. His sons struggled on with the larger potato, barley malt, and maize fields that surrounded the village as part of the DiThon estate. Nahamkin puttered with the flowers and vegetables that had not been profitable enough for him to bother with as a farmer.

Rounding a corner at the far edge of town, Bram came into sight of the hovel in which Nahamkin happily lived. During the growing season the cottage's seediness was obscured by tall, wild gardens and flowering trees. Unfortunately there was nothing to cover it now. The thatch was rotted to black all over. The walls were not the wattle and daub of the rest of the village, but old, rocky mud, crumbling in places. And yet there was a sweet and comfortable look about the place, for the sun seemed to shine more strongly here, bringing the yellow-green of spring to the chaos of Nahamkin's gardens earlier than to the rest of Thonvil.

Bram knocked at the oddly tilting door. He could hear the old man shuffling behind it. The door flew open, revealing the stoop-backed, wrinkle-faced codger Bram had grown so fond of. Nahamkin waved him inside with a work-weathered hand.

"Come in, come in," Nahamkin said in his hardy, toothless lisp.

Bram dipped his head to keep from smacking it on

the low door frame, having done it too many times to his own discomfort and the old man's amusement. Pots and tins and wooden pails were scattered everywhere, catching the drips of melting snow that pounded a steady, irregular rhythm with the sound of a crackling fire. It was an oddly welcoming clamor. Or perhaps it was Nahamkin's wide, toothless smile that made Bram feel welcome. The old farmer had taken the nobleman under his wing when Bram was very young and shared everything he knew about sowing the earth.

Nahamkin wiped suet from his wrinkled hands onto his stiff, much-stained leather jerkin. "You're just in time to help with the candle makin'," he announced, then returned to the dry sink to slice beef tallow into a dull, green-stained copper pot.

Evidence of the cotter's work hung from the beams overhead. Butter-colored candles-in-the-making dangled from a branch in pairs by cotton wicks soaked in a lime water and vinegar solution.

"Take the thinner ones and give them another coating in that pot over there." Nahamkin bobbed his head toward a tall tin by the fire. "That one's got the alum and saltpeter that makes 'em burn longer and cleaner. Dip them in the pot of cold well water to speed up the cooling between layers."

Bram did as he was told and withdrew the thinnest pair of candles from the branch. "How do you know so much about making candles?" he asked more for conversation than curiosity.

"My wife, rest her soul, used to make and peddle them," said Nahamkin, moving his pot of suet scraps to the fire. "I'm afraid mine don't come close to the perfection of hers, but I've got to see, haven't I?" Watching Bram, Nahamkin shook a knobby-knuckled digit at him. "Here, now, you'll have to roll those on some parchment, or they'll be as crooked as my old fingers."

Chuckling, Bram quickly complied. They worked quietly, companionably, Bram dipping, rolling, cooling the candles, Nahamkin inspecting his work and cutting new wicks. It took thirty to forty dips to make a candle of sufficient size.

At last the old man rocked back on his heels and regarded the day's work with a satisfied sigh. "That ought to hold me until this time next year, provided I live that long." Nahamkin made a reverent gesture for luck.

"I don't know why you need so many candles," jibed Bram, wiping waxy residue from his hands. "You're always on the straw, eyelids drawn, before darkness falls."

"Those of us who rise with the chickens need to see, too," Nahamkin shot back. He smirked as he added, "But you wouldn't know about early rising, being a lord's son."

Bram threw his head back and laughed. "We both know how much good that's done me."

The old man nodded kindly, fondly watching his young friend put away the candle-making supplies. No one knew better than Nahamkin that Bram's life was not typical of a lord's only son. The two had talked of it often enough. The old man secretly thought Bram *was* the lord of Castle DiThon, for all practical purposes, considering the work he alone did there. No one had to look very close to see that the responsible young man was nothing like his parents and sister. Over the years, Bram's comments had drawn Cormac as an oddly distant father at his closest moments, and Rietta as a mother who'd been domineering until life had forced her to consider only herself.

Bram was still chuckling as he put away the last of the wicks. He held up a new boot for Nahamkin's inspection. "Yes, the lord's son is so prosperous that his poor, crazy, penniless aunt had to buy him boots for his birthday!" Bram frowned suddenly, sorry he'd dog-eared the day.

Nahamkin's gnarled hand came up to pat Bram's head. "Ah, yes. That's why I asked you here today. Twenty-one, isn't it?" He steered the young man toward the door, pushing Bram's head down to avoid the low archway. "And here you are, spending your birthday dipping candles with an old man."

"I-I enjoyed it, really, Nahamkin," Bram assured him. "It was better than plowing a field without an ox. I don't have much opportunity to do things like this."

"Not since you took over your father's duties, anyway." Nahamkin couldn't hide his scorn.

As usual whenever criticism of Cormac came up, Bram was torn between defending his father and acknowledging the truth. "He does the best he can," the nobleman said.

"Well," said Nahamkin, anxious to change a subject he hadn't meant to bring up, "just wait until you can plant these seeds I've been saving for you."

The old man took Bram's arm and guided him outside and around to the back of the cottage, beating back a path through the brambles that leaned against the structure. He looked down at a long, rectangular box built against the house, nestled in the last snow and frozen leaves. "I've been wanting to show you my newest invention for getting a jump on the weather."

Following his gaze, Bram looked down, then quickly away as a hot glint of reflected sunlight caught him square in the eyes. "What is that?" he howled.

Nahamkin knelt stiffly on one knee and lifted from the top of the box a large, expensive pane of good-quality glass. "I call it a hot box," he explained, setting the pane carefully to the side.

Bram dared another glance. The box was filled to its last inch with clay pots, and in each were tender little sprouts reaching for the sunlight. He recognized fuzzy, hand-high tomato plants, among many others. Bram was stunned. The earliest he'd ever seen annuals break seed and germinate was during the last days of Chislmont, and then only after an unusually warm winter.

"Got the idea at the Red Goose Inn last month. I was sitting by the one window, and the afternoon sun came pouring in. If it was hot enough to cook me through glass, I reasoned it could cause a seed to sprout. Picked the glass up from Jessup Lidiger's wife, after the weaver ran off for the city," explained Nahamkin. He cupped a willowy tomato seedling in his tough palm, sending up a cloud of fresh, acidic scent. "I'll have tomatoes ripe on the vine by Argon, mark my words."

Bram ran a hand lovingly around the box's frame. "I've got to make one of these at the castle," he breathed. "Do you realize I could grow herbs year round with this hot box of yours?"

Nahamkin half nodded. "Maybe not year round. I'll wager Aelmont and Rannmont are a touch too cold and dark to generate enough heat even through the glass, but you could certainly extend your growing season." He held up a hand expectantly, and Bram pulled the farmer to his feet, old knees popping and cracking.

"You can draw up some plans if you like while I sort through my seeds for your birthday present." Nahamkin leaned heavily on the young man's arm as they headed back through the brambles to the cottage's front door. Bram looped an arm over his friend's sloping shoulders. "A man's twenty-first birthday used to mean something, a coming of age."

Bram stopped before the door and looked over his shoulder at the dilapidated village. "Nowadays people are more concerned with surviving than marking the passage of time."

"That's so," Nahamkin grudgingly agreed.

The sound of dripping snow water inside the cottage had slowed with a late afternoon drop in temperature. The room had grown dark, except for the faintly glowing fire. The old man slit the loop that connected two new candles and held one wick to the smoldering coals. Shuffling over to an old chest, he rummaged around in it and extracted a seldom-used quill and ink pot, as well as a slip of curling, golden parchment.

"The size of your box should be determined by the glass you have," he said, placing the items, including the lit candle, on a lap desk before Bram.

The nobleman nodded. "I know where pieces have been salvaged from some of the castle's more neglected wings." He wasted no time dipping the quill to scratch an illustration of the support bars and spacers.

Nahamkin lit another candle and, for lack of a better holder, put it in the top of an empty, narrow-necked bottle. He set the light on a cabinet that he kept farthest from the fire, then pulled the handle of a long, narrow drawer. Inside were neatly catalogued parchment packages containing seeds saved from last year's crops. He flipped through them, withdrawing some well-marked favorites to divide and share with his young friend. They worked in happy, companionable silence, Bram sketching, Nahamkin sorting.

The old man was about to suggest Bram stay for some of yesterday's soup and bread, when both men heard frantic footsteps and labored breathing on the path outside. A knock came, quick and demanding.

"Bram DiThon, are you still in there?" a voice rasped through the drafty door. "I saw you walking through the town earlier."

Surprised, the young nobleman flew to his feet and

opened the door. Young Wilton Sivesten, the miller's son, stood wheezing in the doorway.

"Thank my lucky stars you're still here," he said, still struggling to catch his breath. "Ma sent me to find you, what with Herus attending a death in Lusid."

Bram recognized the name of the coroner, a cavalier by training who doubled as the village physicker. "Is your mother ill?" he asked.

Wilton shook his sweat-drenched head. "It's my father. Yesterday he had the fever real bad, and today he's even worse."

"It's probably just the mild influenza that's been going around," Bram suggested in a kinder tone. "I can give you some herbs—"

"That's what Ma thought, until today." The boy's slight frame shuddered. "Today he started scratching and thrashing, and whole patches of skin are coming off." Wilton trembled again. "You just gotta come and see for yourself."

Bram was shaken by the boy's news. He'd never heard of the influenza causing someone to lose skin. Maybe it was a new strain. "I'm no physicker," he thought, surprised to hear himself saying it aloud. "I don't even have any herbs with me."

"You're the best we got with Herus gone," the boy said, pulling desperately at Bram's hand. "My ma's about to lose her mind. You gotta come, or she'll wallop me and say I never bothered to find you."

"What will you need for fever, Bram?" Nahamkin asked, his face creased with concern.

"If it's just a fever . . ." the nobleman mumbled, his mind a jumble. "Uh, I don't know. Elderflower, or maybe some yarrow."

Nahamkin snapped his fingers and shuffled off to the dry sink. He offered up a cork-stoppered crock to Bram. "Dried yarrow I have." Helping Bram into his cloak, the old farmer clapped his young friend on the shoulder.

Smiling his thanks, Bram raced out the door in the tow of the miller's anxious son. He shook off the boy's desperate hand after they both stumbled over unseen rocks and roots in the dusky path. The air felt cold enough to snow, and yet none fell. They arrived at the mill before many moments had passed.

"This way," Wilton panted, snatching at Bram's arm again to lead him toward a small door on the far side of the mill. The nobleman had been to the mill many times, brought his own grain here for grinding. The storehouses, the strong scent of the donkeys who powered the massive wheel, the creaking and grinding were all familiar to Bram, but he'd never even wondered where the family lived.

He paused in the doorway of their quarters, feeling uneasy. Already he could smell wood smoke and heat . . . and sickness beyond fever. Why did people always seal the sick into dark, sweltering boxes, as if fetid air could cure them? Steeling himself, Bram stepped inside.

"Leave the door open," he instructed Wilton briskly, "and stop stoking the fire for a while." The boy's eyes widened in surprise, but he kicked a block into place to prop open the door. A man's husky voice howled in the next room; the two young men exchanged alarmed glances. Wilton bounded around Bram and waved him through the small front room and into the smaller one behind it.

Bram could not keep from gasping when he saw the miller. Hoark Sivesten lay on a narrow cot, naked save for a thin sheet draped over his groin. The skin of one leg and two arms was as raw-red as flayed flesh; his torso was still lily white. A large man, he'd obviously enjoyed the bread made from the mill he ground, but his limbs looked swollen beyond their normal size. Hoark was feverishly thrashing and scraping the one leg that was not that hideous vermilion against the bedclothes, his head lolling from side to side as he muttered and moaned.

"Tell me everything that's happened," Bram said, reaching out to feel the man's forehead. The miller was thrashing so furiously that it was impossible to hold a hand to him.

"It started with the fever yesterday," said Hoark's wife, Sedrette, wringing work-reddened hands against her apron. The stout woman's flour-flecked apple cheeks were streaked with tears. "I thought he got better. He was even talking this morning. Then he started rubbing his legs and arms so fast and steady, like a cricket, that I was afraid he might start a fire with the bedding. We ripped his clothes off after he shed the first leg of skin."

Bram looked up in wonderment at the odd phrase. "Say again?"

For an answer the woman reached down to the floor on her side of the cot and held up a collapsed, crystal-colored membrane as thin as a soap bubble. Her eyes dared Bram to believe. It looked for all the world like the abandoned snake skins Bram had found in fields and meadows since his youth.

"Hoark rubbed and rubbed until this came off his leg," Sedrette explained hoarsely.

Bram looked quickly away from the sheaf of flesh and to the man on the cot. "Maybe we should tie him down so he can't rub off any more skin."

"We tried that," Sedrette said. "He's sick, but it seems only to have made him stronger. No one could hold him still long enough to fasten him down."

Still and all, Bram whispered for Wilton to fetch some twine. Next he told the woman to put some water on to boil, and to bring a kettle of it and a cup. Both scurried off, obviously relieved to have something useful to do elsewhere. Bram stood alone in the sickroom with Hoark Sivesten. Within moments the walls began to close on him, the sound of the man's frantic scraping and moaning all Bram could hear. Where were those people with the rope and the water? How long could it take to find twine in a mill, anyway?

Bram looked at the man on the cot. Hoark's thrashing had removed not only the sheet, but it had loosened the skin of his other leg as well. Bram bit his lip until it hurt as he watched a jagged split in the miller's skin race, like cracking ice, from groin to ankle. The flesh beneath it rushed up like red sausage released from a too-tight casing. The top layers of skin peeled back with the dry, crackling sound of old leaves. Finally, the man stopped thrashing and lay panting in a twisted mess of bedding and sweat and dead skin. Just as suddenly his breathing slowed. The young nobleman had to look closely to see the shallow rise and fall of the miller's sodden chest.

Bram jumped when the man's son dashed, breathless, through the doorway, trailing a length of coarse twine. "He's so still," Wilton observed almost distantly. "Is he dead?"

Bram shook his head. "No, but I don't think we'll be needing the rope anymore."

"I got that water," the miller's wife announced as she scraped her ample hips through the narrow doorway. Sedrette Sivesten gaped slack-jawed, all the stumps of her front teeth exposed when she saw that her husband was quiet. "What did you do to him?" It was not an accusation.

Bram shrugged helplessly. "I guess he got rid of all the skin he needed to." He looked to the pot and cup she held. "It probably wouldn't hurt to have him still drink some yarrow tea, what with all the water he's lost sweating."

The miller's wife handed the steaming pot and cup to Bram. "What is this, some kind of skin-shedding influenza?" she asked, moving quickly to reposition the filthy sheet that had slipped from her husband's torso. "Is Hoark going to be all right now?"

"I . . . don't know the answer to either question," Bram admitted. "It's like no influenza I've ever heard of, but I think he's through the worst of it, whatever it is." He pinched three fingersful of Nahamkin's dried yarrow bloom and dropped it into the mug, filling it only half full with warm water. It would be difficult enough to get the reclining, insensate man to drink without burning his chest.

Bram gave directions for the tea to the miller's wife. "Get him to drink as much of it as you can, Sedrette. It should help stave off the return of a fever. Keep him warm, but don't try to roast him again."

She nodded eagerly, relief evident on her chubby face as she walked Bram out of the sickroom. At the doorway that led outside, she pumped Bram's hand furiously, thanking him. "You come to the mill any time, day or night, Bram DiThon, and we'll work your grain without taking multure—not a ring, or even a single bushel—for payment."

Bram felt decidedly uncomfortable with the gratitude and the generous offer, but before he could point out that he had done little more than make tea, Sedrette Sivesten scampered on lighter feet back into the sickroom.

Bram's first lungful of fresh, cold night air blistered its way down his throat, making him cough until he was certain he'd expelled every particle of stagnant air inhaled in the sickroom. It was late, by sight of the risen moon, how late Bram couldn't tell. Snowflakes,

dry as potash, swirled about in the wan moonlight.
Bram was weary to the bone, and he headed straight
home. Passing through the edge of town, where gates
should have been but were not, he recalled the reason
for his trip to Thonvil this day, his birthday still. With a
start he had a memory of seed packets on the dry sink
in Nahamkin's cottage. Bram sighed. It had not been
the best of birthdays.

At least, he thought, the end of the miller's day had
taken a turn for the better.

# Chapter Seven

The following morning Bram received his second summons to help someone with the skin-shedding sickness.

He had been searching for panes of clear glass and planed wood to construct one of Nahamkin's hot boxes. The planks were no problem; he found all that he needed by dismantling several of the stanchions in the castle's nearly empty stable.

He was, however, having more difficulty with the glass than he'd anticipated. The windows in the abandoned solar were a complicated bit of tracery work, with ornamental ribs and bars breaking up the glass into sections that were too small for his purposes. Some of the decorative sections were missing entirely, which was at least half the reason the family no longer used the solar as a living room. The other reason, of course, was that the family no longer gathered *anywhere* for conversation or quiet moments by the fire.

Bram crept silently down the second-floor hallway, past the door to the study where his father spent most of his time in an irrational stupor caused by years of drunkenness. Bram was headed for the gallery, which sported windows that faced the afternoon sun across the Strait of Ergoth. The expensive glass had been added to the long, narrow, third-story balcony several generations before, in the time of Bram's great-grandfather, when the family had been able to afford more than carrots for the table and the village had supported craftsmen of quality.

Gildee the cook (one of the few servants who remained, primarily because she had nowhere else to go), found Bram on the staircase to the third floor. "Someone from the village came running for you, Master Bram." The matronly woman's solemn tone and distressed expression told him the disease had struck a second time. Her words stopped his heart. "It's Nahamkin. He's got the fever."

Bram blinked at her in disbelief for just one moment, then sprang down the steps two at a time, stopping neither for herbs nor cloak. He was racing across the worn floor of the foyer when his mother's voice stopped him.

"Where are you going in such a hurry, Bram?" Rietta's words were light, but her tone was high, clipped as she strode into the circular foyer. The ragged hem of her cheap brocatelle dress, more gray now than lavender from repeated washings with lye soap, whispered across the stone floor.

In her midforties, Rietta had aged with the grace of the nobly born. Her skin was still remarkably wrinkle-free, though her shape was thinner than ever, thanks to a scarcity of high-quality food, and the worry over it. As always, she wore her dark, thin hair in a tight chignon covered by a strong veil of lace netting, and a long gorget around her neck.

Bram's mother settled light fingers on his arm.

"Mother," he breathed turning away, "I-I've got to go to the village." His eyes were on the door that led out. Unconsciously he began to pull away from her.

"I have need of you here," she said stiffly, too quickly.

He whirled around. "For what? Retrieving winter squash from the root cellar?"

Rietta's green, feline eyes narrowed, and her thin lips pouted at the sarcasm. "I just don't see why you have to go to the village again."

"It's Nahamkin, Mother," Bram said with forced patience, feeling the weight of time passing in the strained muscles of his neck. "He's ill."

"That old farmer?" she scoffed. "Aren't there family members who can tend to him? What about Herus?"

"Perhaps they could," conceded Bram, "but Nahamkin has asked for me. I've got to try to help him." He had no tolerance for her haughty attitude at this moment, which was why he couldn't help adding slyly, "Just be thankful that the villagers no longer expect the lady of the manor to tend their ills, as in days past."

Oblivious to his derision, Rietta bit her bottom lip until it was white, her brows furrowed with concern. "Is it that dreadful fever the miller had? I've heard Herus has returned and is treating him still."

"I don't know," Bram said, lying outright to give his mother hope as much as to gain his freedom. "I won't know until I see Nahamkin." He tugged his arm back gently, then put one hand unceremoniously against the small of her back to propel her along. "I've got to go now, Mother. I may not be back for several days." Uncharacteristically, Rietta resisted only briefly before bowing her head and retreating down the hallway that led to the kitchens.

Bram bolted through the door and began the three-rod sprint to Nahamkin's tumbledown cottage.

\* \* \* \* \*

Bram crouched in the cold and drafty loft, next to the cot that held the friend he knew must surely be dying.

The fever had passed two nights before, because of, or despite, Bram's herbal tea. It seemed to comfort Nahamkin, and that was reason enough for Bram to climb the rickety ladder to the loft four times an hour, round the clock, to bring more heated water from the hearth.

The young nobleman had tried to remain optimistic, to pretend even, that Nahamkin had a simple fever. Superstition—or perhaps premonition—had made him change the herbal mixture he'd given the miller to one designed to encourage and not break fever. But Bram's hope had faded when the old farmer's sweats and chills ceased abruptly and unexplainably on the evening of the first day, as Hoark Sivesten's had. It was a bad sign.

Bram understood how bad it was when, later that same night, the village bells chimed, signaling the miller's death.

Knowing what was ahead, Bram had sent for Nahamkin's family the next morning. Delayed by farm chores, or so he said, the son had arrived alone much later. Bram peered briefly over the edge of the loft to see Nahamkin's son standing in the doorway, obviously reluctant to enter the cottage. His eyes had darted everywhere and nowhere, as if he were afraid of what he'd see if they settled.

Bram had neither the time nor the patience to leave the loft to coax Nahamkin's own flesh and blood to see him one last time. The old man was halfway through the skin-shedding stage of the disease, and Bram had to call on all his strength just to keep his friend on the cot. When the first skin split on his leg, Nahamkin had brayed, and Bram heard the door slam shut below.

The nobleman paused for a moment, eyes closed, and reflected that blood wasn't any thicker in families where it wasn't blue. If Nahamkin knew his son had run away, he didn't mention it. Bram suspected that, inside, Nahamkin had known at the onset of the fever that his son wouldn't stand by him, since he'd sent for Bram.

Following the pattern of the illness, Nahamkin was quiet, lucid even, on the evening of the second day after the skin shedding. Bram brought stew up to the loft, though neither of them did much more than push the potatoes around in their bowls. They talked about flowers, and slugs, and summer heat, anything but what was happening now.

For the second night Bram stayed by the old man's side. Nahamkin dozed fitfully, but sleep came nowhere near Bram. He spent most of the night with his feet dangling from the edge of the loft, swinging them back and forth in a hypnotic, numbing rhythm; they were the only part of the nobleman to fall asleep.

Bram saw the sun rise now through the rotted thatch and closed his eyes tightly to the light, as if he could stop the day.

"You're still here, lad." Nahamkin turned to Bram with the slowness of seasons revolving. His eyes held an odd clearness.

"Of course I am." Bram smiled encouragingly and squeezed Nahamkin's leathery hand.

Nahamkin laid a weary, raw-red arm to his forehead. "I'm so thirsty, I swear I could drink an entire bucket of water. Be a good lad and bring me some," the old man said.

"Must be from the fever," Bram remarked as he

slipped down the ladder. He took a wooden bucket outside to the well, blinking in the bright, cold sunshine. Should he tell Nahamkin that Hoark Sivesten had died of the disease? Was it more cruel to tell him or not? Bram slapped his face with frigid water to chase away the tumult in his head.

He had no answers as he carried the filled bucket back into the dimness of the cottage. The young nobleman nearly gagged at the foul stench of sickness that his nose had grown used to before the brief breath of fresh air. His eyes watered, and when they adjusted enough to see, his gaze came first upon the tallow candles they had made just days before. Four days of witnessing unexplainable sickness had nearly erased the memory.

Bram jumped when a knock rang out against the wooden door. He opened it slowly, half-expecting Nahamkin's son to have sheepishly returned. The face was Herus's, eyes sunken, face gray. Bram wondered fleetingly if he looked as bad as the physicker.

"I've . . . finished with my other patients," Herus announced wearily. "Two more have died. I'm sorry to have left Nahamkin to you. Is he—?"

"No." Bram looked up at the loft over his shoulder and held a finger to his lips. He left the door open and crossed the small room for the stairs, the bucket of water sloshing at his side. Taking the open door as invitation, the physicker stepped inside.

"Bram!" Nahamkin called plaintively from the loft. "Where is that water, son?"

"Coming!" Bram snatched up a mug, Nahamkin's best pewter one, and put a foot on the first rung.

The physicker's hand grasped Bram's calf, stopping him on the ladder. "He has a great thirst?"

Bram nodded. The physicker's expression worried him more.

"Kill him," Herus whispered. "It'll be merciful compared to what I have witnessed with the others."

Bram was so shocked by the pronouncement that he nearly dropped the bucket of water. "What have you seen? Tell me what you know about this sickness."

"It is always the same," sighed Herus. "First they have the fever, the next day they shed skin, then on the third day—"

Herus was interrupted by Nahamkin howling again for water. Jumping as if burned, Bram readjusted the bucket in his hand and took another anxious step up the ladder.

"You can't help him," Herus said softly behind him. "The sickness is caused by magic more powerful than any of your herbs."

Bram paused but did not turn around, his heart hammering. "How do you know that?"

The physicker visibly paled. "Just take my advice, young man," he said. "Kill him before he slakes his thirst and the real pain starts, or he *will* die a hideous death at sunset."

Fury at Herus's callousness drove away Bram's exhaustion. "Get out," the nobleman hissed. "I'd sooner kill *you*, you fraud." Bram gave a humorless laugh before continuing up the ladder, slopping water. "And to think I was worried about not being a real physicker." Herus muttered something a bit profane before stomping out the door. Bram dimly heard it, but didn't care.

Nahamkin saw Bram's head cresting the floor of the loft. "I thought you'd never come with that water," he panted. "Who was at the door?"

Bram was thankful Nahamkin showed no sign of having heard Herus's words. "Just someone asking me to give aid at their house," he said. The lie came out easily enough, though the hand that poured water into a mug shook.

Nahamkin gulped greedily, water spraying from his mouth in his haste. "You should go to them, Bram. You've stayed with me long enough."

Bram's dark head shook as he refilled the heavy mug. "There is no one I care about as much as you, Nahamkin," he said honestly, his voice breaking. "I'll stay with you until you're well again." The words stuck in his throat past Nahamkin's seventh mug of water.

Bram sat stiffly while the old farmer tried to quench his thirst. Every muscle was tensed with dread. The pewter mug fell from Nahamkin's aged hands midway through his ninth drink. It fell to the floor with a dull *ting* that sounded like a bell of doom in Bram's head. He fingered one of a handful of small flour sacks he'd fetched to mop up the water Nahamkin had spilled while he drank. Bram twisted the sack so tightly the flesh of his palms began to burn.

Nahamkin's body abruptly shuddered, and his arm began to twitch. The raw flesh of his forearm undulated with hideous, unnatural spasms. Nahamkin groaned, a small, dry sound in the back of his throat that abruptly changed to a full-fledged shriek. Both men watched in horror as the thrashing arm began to bend and twist in ways no human arm was ever meant to. Bram struggled to grab the limb and pin it to the bedding, but his effort netted him a punch in the nose that left him dazed and bloody. As his eyes refocused, he saw the arm, thrashing left and right like a whip being played across the ground. The first and second fingers closed together and fused into one mass of flesh, then the third and fourth did the same. The thumb folded back on itself, becoming shorter and thicker.

Bram covered his mouth as the arm began splitting open between the newly formed digits. No sooner did the flesh split apart than it resealed itself, forming three distinct appendages all the way up Nahamkin's forearm to his elbow. Like three eyeless worms, the limbs writhed across Nahamkin's pallet. Quickly the color and texture changed from pale, fleshy white to green-brown scales with a pattern of red and yellow stripes. Two bulges appeared near the end of each appendage and popped open, revealing pure black orbs. Three fully formed snakes writhed from the stump of Nahamkin's arm, their forked tongues flicking in and out as they scanned their new world with unblinking eyes.

Wiping his bloody nose on his sleeve, Bram stared in transfixed horror at the creatures that Nahamkin's arm had become. He was relieved to see that Nahamkin was unconscious. But the old man's eyes slowly opened under Bram's scrutiny. Dazed, Nahamkin searched for the cause of the pain in his arm. When he saw the snakes resting in a coil there, Nahamkin's screams shook the rotted thatch above their heads. The snakes jumped from their slumber and rose up to hiss into the frightened man's face.

Bram did the only thing that came to mind. Ignoring his own horror, he snatched up one of the sacks near Nahamkin's pallet and slid it over the transformed limb, then cinched it tightly above the elbow.

"I'm dying," the old man said hoarsely.

"I should have warned you!" moaned Bram. "Herus told me, but I already suspected—"

Nahamkin touched his good hand to Bram's face. "It wouldn't have mattered. It's probably best I didn't have time to ponder it too much."

"I should have been able to help you in some way!"

"You have."

"Nahamkin," Bram whispered, so softly it was like a reluctant confession. He could not meet the old man's eyes. "Do you want me to . . . I mean, I could spare you—"

"No."

Bram's eyes shot away from the tangled bedclothes.

"How could I face Chislev in the grand forest Zhan," Nahamkin asked, his eyes strangely serene, "knowing that I hadn't patience or strength enough to abide by her will?"

"Who's Chislev?" Bram asked.

Nahamkin closed his eyes to gather strength against the forces that were fighting within him. "My goddess. I know most people don't believe in the old gods any longer, but I have tilled the soil and planted seeds in her honor for nearly four score years."

"Why have I never heard of her?"

Nahamkin's rheumy eyes took on a faraway look. "I suspect you have not heard her name because she has been called one of the old gods since the Cataclysm. Most people think she abandoned her followers then, but I have only to look at the beauty of the land to know better. You have seen her with every passing season and just not known it," he said. "It is said that her fear brings the fall, her despair the winter, her hope the spring, and her joy the summer. Every blade of grass, every creature in the field, turns toward her as toward the sun."

He smiled at some distant vision. "They say she appears to her followers as a beautiful woman whose hair glows like golden sunlight, and her clothes are made from living plants. I will see for myself soon enough."

"How can you revere something that would allow this sickness to happen to you?" Bram asked.

"It is Chislev's plan for me." He gave Bram a look of masculine pity. "I have long suspected your spiritual side has been neglected, Bram." It was said kindly enough. "Life is a series of tests. Death is simply the final one. The difficulty of each is a measure of a person's faith. Chislev must have great faith in me to have handed me my most difficult test now. I will not fail by avoiding it, Bram." He bit his lip against the pain. "I can endure this. You'll find, my friend, that there are times when you simply have no alternative but to have faith."

Nahamkin's face contorted as his left leg began the transformation. He didn't scream this time, but tears rolled down his wrinkled cheeks and across his clenched jaw. The limb thrashed wildly before settling into a calm undulation. Using his horror and the last of his strength as tools, Bram slipped the second cloth bag over the limb, hoping to calm the three snakes that sprouted from the knee.

When Nahamkin recovered his breath, he said, "I would be happier if I could go with you at my side, but I will understand if you leave."

"Of course I'll stay," Bram said firmly.

He stayed to put flour sacks over the last two limbs to turn into writhing snakes. He stayed through the long, cruel afternoon, the stillness broken only by the muffled hissing of the snakes and Nahamkin's pain-racked gasps. It was increasingly difficult, then impossible, for Nahamkin to speak through the pain. Bram couldn't even hold the dying man's hand.

The light through the rotted thatch faded quickly. As darkness grew in the hut, Nahamkin began whimpering and mumbling softly. Bram leaned in close to hear. "I'm dying, Bram, and I can feel it. It's spreading, I can feel it moving up my legs. It's death."

Bram pulled back the thin cover from Nahamkin's legs. Instead of flesh, he saw gray stone. The snakes still moved listlessly, but as the grayness crept along the limbs, the snakes' movements slowed and finally stopped. Bram touched Nahamkin's leg; it was stone, hard and cold. Looking up, he saw that the change had advanced all the way up Nahamkin's torso to his neck and jaw. Numb, Bram watched without flinching as his friend's eyes slowly clouded over and turned black as coals. "Close your lids, Nahamkin," he said gently. The old man complied, for he could no longer see. Within moments, as Krynn's three moons rose and the last traces of sunlight slipped away, his face, too, transformed to ashen gray stone.

Bram scarcely breathed. The snakes were deathly still beneath their bags, so Bram risked removing the flour sacks. The snakes on Nahamkin's arms popped up like whips, snapping at Bram. He stumbled back and nearly fell from the loft. "Guerrrannnd," they hissed. In unison, they fell like limp rope back to the cot, turned gray, and were silent.

Heart hammering, Bram knew there could be no doubt now that the illness was magical.

\* \* \* \* \*

The light in the refectory was dim, coming from two listing, bad-smelling candles. The castle had not seen beeswax, or even good-quality tallow, in at least a year. It was just as well, because the room looked less shabby when so little of it was visible beyond the long table. Rietta had moved the last of the castle's finely crafted furniture from the large formal dining hall to this communal eating area because this room was smaller and more easily heated. Also, it was closer to the kitchen, important now that they had only one downstairs servant, Gildee the cook.

There were no tapestries here to prevent drafts, and no point in moving the rotted and faded ones from the formal hall. The bare limestone blocks radiated cold, even on the hottest summer day.

"I couldn't help noticing you have new boots, dear," Bram's mother was saying.

"Hmmm?" He turned unseeing eyes to his right,

where Rietta was seated at the head of the table. Her black hair was pulled back in a severe knot, and her gown was an old, dun-colored, high-necked affair with grease at the embroidered cuffs.

"Your boots," she prompted, delicately spooning up her carrot soup. "They're new. Where did you get them?"

"Kirah gave them to me for my birthday six days ago," he supplied absently.

"I wonder where the little lunatic got the coin for *that*," muttered Rietta. "Very likely she stole them."

"I doubt it." Bram knew better than to do much more to defend his aunt to his mother; both of them always came away believing what they would.

"Anyway," Rietta continued in her loud, authoritative voice, "I hope you're not considering going back to the village again to help any of those people."

"You mean your subjects?" Bram asked with a bite in his tone. He shrugged. "I hadn't thought that far, but I'll go if summoned again." Fiddling his spoon in his thin orange soup, he gave a self-deprecating snort. "Not that I'll be able to help any of them."

Gildee set a pot of mashed winter parsnips on the table between Bram and Rietta, then backed away. "There's been two more cases in the village since old Nahamkin passed on," she breathed, her fear evident.

"Who are—were they?" Bram asked quickly.

"That will be all, Gildee," Rietta snapped. The nervous cook continued backing through the door to the kitchen. Rietta turned dark eyes upon her son. "The DiThons have not sunk so low that we are now conversing with the servants at the table, Bram." Rietta gave a dismissive twitch of her lips. "You forget, there's a perfectly competent physicker in the village—"

"Competent?" howled Bram. "Herus's solution is to kill the victims."

"I hear he's ordered people to kill every snake they can find," Rietta remarked. "Still, people say it hasn't reduced the unusual number of them this spring."

Bram's expression was still troubled. "He's addressing the symptoms of the disease, not the cause of it."

Rietta leaned back in astonishment. "And what, may I ask, is wrong with that?"

Bram could only gape at her in disbelief.

Rietta's nose lifted in the air. "I don't care to speak further of such hideous things at the dinner table."

Bram laughed. "Which of us won't be at the dinner table tomorrow?" He shrugged carelessly and fell against the back of his chair. "It's impossible to predict."

Rietta gasped, a hand pressed to her lips. "We're all fine at Castle DiThon. The disease doesn't exist here."

"Yet."

She looked at her son with annoyance. "You've been moody and distracted since you returned from that cotter's."

Bram flushed, his gaze fastened to his soup bowl. Since Nahamkin's death the night before, he had thought of nothing but the snakes who had hissed his Uncle Guerrand's name.

"Why have you taken so much of the burden of this illness on yourself, Bram?" his mother pressed. "You aren't responsible for the cause or cure of this affliction."

"I'm not so sure of that." Still, Bram held in the secret. "I remember a day when a lord's primary responsibility was the welfare of his subjects."

"Is that what this is about?" she demanded. "You think I should expose myself to illness just to help some peasants? Well, I won't do it! Mark my words," Rietta continued, "this plague is heavenly retribution against the villagers for their lazy and dissolute ways. It can be no accident that it hasn't struck here yet."

Bram's temper exploded. "You've practically sealed

off the castle, that's why!"

Rietta's thin shoulders lifted dismissively. "We lead virtuous, worthwhile lives."

Bram laughed without humor. "Do you really believe we DiThons are anything but blue-blooded peasants?" He waved his hands at the squalor in the refectory. Bram couldn't help reflecting that, in many ways, Nahamkin's drafty hovel was more appealing. At least it had a surplus of straight candles.

Rietta frowned darkly at her son. "I didn't raise you to speak to me this way," she said. "You are not so old, nor have we sunk so far, that I'll allow it now." Her tone, meant more to inspire guilt than fear, had been rehearsed to perfection on Bram his entire lifetime.

"The cause of this curse is obvious."

Both Bram and Rietta turned in surprise to look at Cormac, alone in shadow at the far end of the long table. The tall man's head was slumped onto his barrel-shaped chest as usual. Even in the dark Bram could see his father's red-veined nose and that his clothing was way too small for his obese trunk. At least his words weren't slurred, which suggested Cormac had gone easier on the watered-down bottle he usually nursed.

"Who said anything about a curse?" demanded Rietta. "You haven't left the castle walls in four years, Cormac. What could you possibly know about this illness—or anything, for that matter?"

Bram had long since stopped wincing when his mother sliced into his father like this. When he was young, his parents had always bickered. Bram had accepted early on that there was no love lost between them, had seen it as the way of things. But all the bluster had been knocked out of Cormac. Rietta's spiteful remarks, or even Bram's own thoughtful comments, usually went unnoticed.

"Did you have something to add, Father?" Bram

prodded gently.

Cormac's glazed expression suggested he hadn't heard the words as much as their cadence. "We have not seen the likes of such upheaval since there was magic in this house. There is vile sorcery at work here, there can be no doubt."

Bram froze. Had Cormac heard a rumor about what the snakes hissed before death?

Rietta threw herself back in her chair. "It always comes back to magic with you, doesn't it, Cormac?"

"That was the start of it all," rumbled Cormac.

"Seven years, and you're still blaming him for your mistakes," she sighed, rolling her eyes. "Everyone knows there was no love lost between Guerrand and me, but—"

"Don't speak that traitor's name!" spat Cormac. "We were doing fine before he brought his sorcery into our lives."

"Fine?" Rietta shrieked. "You'd already spent us into poverty. Frankly, this whole situation is your fault, Cormac," she said. "Bram would be safely away in Solamnia if you hadn't squandered the money we needed to squire him to a true knight."

"Don't you understand, woman?" roared Cormac. "There would be no plague upon our heads if my brother hadn't brought magic into this village, this house. We would not be living in poverty if that bastard had done his familial duty as he'd promised. Instead he lost us the Berwick money and Stonecliff in one fell swoop." Cormac's hammy fist slammed the table. "Mark my words, when so many people die of mysterious causes, there's vile magic involved."

"Father is right." Bram's voice was barely above a whisper. "I've seen for myself that magic has caused this illness. And I fear Uncle Guerrand is somehow responsible." He recounted the last moments of

Nahamkin's life, concluding with the snakes hissing Guerrand's name.

"But why?" she asked. "Why would Guerrand do something so cruel to us after all this time?"

"I don't know," Bram confessed. "But I intend to find out."

"I'll tell you why," snarled Cormac. "Because Guerrand is a contemptible black-hearted wizard, like all his kindred. That's reason enough."

Rietta's head was shaking slowly in disbelief. "Surely Guerrand is dead after all these years," she breathed. But she had already seen in her son's eyes the interest her husband's words had stirred. Growing alarmed, she took up Bram's hand and squeezed it. "You know I am not the opponent of magic your father is, but you can't possibly be taking Cormac's ravings seriously now, Bram. He hasn't said anything worth listening to in years."

"Father only confirmed what I already knew," Bram said. "I've realized since Nahamkin's death that I would have to leave to find Guerrand. If I can't persuade him to use his magic to stop this sickness, we'll all die."

"You think he'll do it just because you ask him to?" Rietta scoffed. "You don't remember Guerrand as I do, Bram. He was not even willing to marry for the sake of the family! And if he's not to blame for spreading this sickness, I assure you he won't risk getting the plague to save any of us."

"Nevertheless," said Bram, standing, "I feel a lord's responsibility, even if you and father don't. It may have escaped your notice, but I have been working too hard for five years to restore Castle DiThon's productivity to sit by and do nothing while people suffer. I wouldn't care to look beyond DiThon's walls one day and find we're all alone."

"Sometimes I think that would not be such a bad thing," his mother mused distantly. She knew she had lost the argument. "When will you leave?"

"Soon. I need to talk to Kirah first. She might have some idea where Guerrand went."

"You know, of course, that once you leave, you'll not be welcome at Castle DiThon again," his mother said softly. "I cannot risk exposing everyone here to plague for some folly of yours."

Bram saw the manipulation for what it was. Rietta had done the same thing to Kirah when she refused to marry. It was not a typical mother's concern that drove her to these ultimatums. Rietta simply abhorred anyone disrupting the fabric of her life, however threadbare the weave, whatever the cost in others' lives. Like the briefest fluttering of wings, the last glowing coal of tolerant affection for her winked to black in his breast.

"Do what you must," Bram said coldly. He bowed his head formally and backed toward the door. He looked first to Cormac in the shadows. "Good-bye, Father." He locked his determined gaze on Rietta. "Good-bye, Mother. I wish you long life in this self-imposed prison." With that, he slipped from the refectory.

"Bram!" his mother cried, and her hand flew to her mouth. "I didn't mean—" She sprang to her feet, but instead of following her son, Rietta descended upon her husband at the far end of the table, fists flying. "Damn you, Cormac, for putting the notion in his head! You knew he would feel obligated to do whatever he could to help those miserable peasants!"

Bram couldn't hear his mother's ranting turn to sobs, or see the small, triumphant smile that pulled at his father's lips.

# Chapter Eight

Bram sat shivering within the circle of broken boulders known before their destruction as Stonecliff, drying his stockinged feet at the small fire he'd managed at length to start. Bram had never been so cold, nor so far from home before.

He had packed wisely enough for the trip to Wayreth, he thought, bringing flint, tinder, knife, a tightly rolled wool blanket, enough food for three days, and an extra pair of trousers and jerkin. But he hadn't anticipated the cold, driving rain that had dogged him all day as he walked on feet blistered by new boots. Nearly everything in the pack was soaked through, but especially the winter cloak, white jerkin, and brown trousers he wore. Fortunately, the healing herbs he'd brought in small glass vials remained dry.

The young nobleman pulled out a knife that was

neither very sharp nor strong, meant more for cutting the tender flesh of vegetables than people. Still, it sliced easily enough through the wrinkled flesh of an autumn apple. He munched the sweet fruit in weary distraction, wondering what the next day would bring.

With any luck he would be aboard a ship headed for distant Wayreth. Kirah had told him Guerrand had gone there first in his quest to become a mage. Though many years had since passed, Bram reasoned that even if Guerrand were no longer at the place where mages regularly gathered, the wizards there would know where he was.

Bram's trip to Thonvil to speak again with Kirah had made him only more determined than ever to find his uncle. Two more people had succumbed to the mysterious disease, their snake limbs heard to magically sigh Guerrand's name. There could be no doubt the wizard was somehow involved with the pestilence. The life of every villager depended on Bram's finding Guerrand. He felt the full weight of a lord's responsibility for them. More selfishly, he'd worked long and hard to bring a spark of life back to Castle DiThon's lands. If the plague wasn't stopped soon, there would be no village left to revive.

At first light, he would thread his way down the cliff, cross the River Durris to Hillfort, and offer himself up as a shiphand in exchange for passage on the first ship headed south. The nobleman wouldn't take no for an answer.

Bram snapped some twigs and tossed them on the fire. He stared, unblinking, into the flames until his eyes teared so that his darkened surroundings wavered and blurred as if he were looking through the steam of a boiling pot. Through the corner of his eyes, he thought he saw movement behind a boulder at the limit of the firelight's range. Bram blinked, then dug his fists into his eyes to clear them.

When he looked again, a cloud of light snowflakes whirled up and caught the firelight like a thousand tiny prisms. The flurry slowly settled, revealing three beings, as short as young children. Each had enormous blue eyes that glowed like the hottest flame. Three heads of feather-fine hair the color of waxed walnut furniture were covered with colorful, jaunty hats of wool. All manner of pouches hung from their shoulders, as well as waist belts with loopholes for tools and carving knives.

"I've heard of you," breathed Bram. "You're brownies, aren't you? I wasn't sure if you really existed."

All three creatures crossed their small arms stiffly. "If I'm not mistaken, that name is also used to describe chocolate cake," said the one wearing a slate-blue cap and mantle. "It makes us sound like a bit of fluff, not at all serious or worthwhile. We'd as soon you called us 'milk' or 'fruit,' if you insist upon naming us after foodstuffs."

Bram put up his hands defensively. "Tell me what *you* call yourselves, and I will never use that other word again."

"We call ourselves tuatha dundarael." The creature saw Bram's eyes open wide. "If that's too difficult for you, you may use the shortened form, tuatha—pronounced 'too-a-ha.' "

"Tuatha," Bram repeated deliberately, looking relieved. He stood and walked around the three tuatha, peering closely at the small, soft-featured beings. "Where are your wings?"

The blue-mantled tuatha man gave a slight sigh. "Those would be pixies. While also faerie folk, they wear silly, curly-toed shoes like court jesters and, as a rule, come out only at night."

Bram raised his eyebrows and took in the darkened

sky. "You can see why I was confused."

The tuatha regarded him through one slow, lazy blink. "Not really."

Bram coughed self-consciously. "I'm sorry, I didn't catch your names. I'm Bram," he said, extending a hand.

"Yes." The blue-capped being ignored Bram's hand and put a tiny palm to his chest. "I am called Thistledown."

He gestured to his companion in the snug red hat. "This is Burdock." The second diminutive creature bowed his head.

Thistledown waved to the last tuatha, a young female wearing a long yellow wool stocking cap and a decorative gold sash from one shoulder to the opposite hip. Her face was rosy and clean. "She is Milkweed." The blush in her cheeks darkened to wine, and she averted her eyes from Bram's.

"Why don't they talk?" the nobleman asked.

"Because I am the speaker in this troop," explained Thistledown matter-of-factly. "Burdock is the pathfinder. Milkweed is the enchantmentcrafter. King Weador assigned us three to you when he heard you speaking here."

"King Weador?" Bram repeated dully. "I don't understand what you mean, 'assigned you.'"

Thistledown turned to Milkweed, who turned to Burdock, who turned back to Thistledown. Three small sets of shoulders lifted in shrugs. "It's what we do, we tuatha. We attach ourselves, so to speak, to humans of high moral standards."

Bram leaned back and crossed his arms. "I have high moral standards, have I?"

"And a natural earth magical ability," said Thistledown, as if he hadn't been interrupted.

"I do have a way with plants," agreed Bram.

Thistledown's eyebrows were drawn down in annoyance. "Watch that pride, or we'll have to leave," he threatened, while Milkweed and Burdock settled their shoulders as if preparing to disappear behind their speaker.

"I'm sorry," Bram said quickly. "I didn't mean to . . ." His voice trailed off awkwardly. He dropped back down by the fire and folded large hands around his knees, preparing to listen rather than get further into trouble by speaking.

Thistledown seemed mollified. "We perform small services in exchange for a mug of milk, a little bread, that sort of thing."

The nobleman looked at his wet belongings by the fire and said, "I'd be happy to share my foodstuffs with you." He fished around in his small pack. "I've been eating snow for water, but I have plenty of apples, carrots, and peanuts, and a half-loaf of bread—"

"We're not here to eat your food," interrupted Thistledown. "We've long partaken of the bounty of your gardens."

Bram straightened up in surprise. "You know my fields?"

All three tuatha beamed. "We tuatha have been working at night to help you return those weed patches into workable plots."

Bram's face lit with sudden understanding. "I've wondered some mornings about finding gleaming pitchforks and shovels when I left dirty ones in the garden the night before," he breathed. Bram leaned back from the fire. "So how long have you been helping me?"

Thistledown leaned toward Burdock. "Time has no meaning for us," he announced at length. "We have aided you longer ago than yesterday, but less than we will have tomorrow. This is the first time Burdock, Milkweed and I have been sent as a troop to aid you."

Bram blinked. "How many tuatha are there?"

Thistledown turned again to his companions before speaking. "I daresay we tuatha outnumber you humans."

"I'm surprised, then, that I never saw even one of you before," observed Bram.

"We did not want you to see us until now," Thistledown said simply. "We live in the faerie realm, beyond human sight. In this place where earthly magic once flourished, your thoughts were particularly resonant in our realm. That is why King Weador sent us to give you aid."

Bram used the toe of a new boot to nudge the unburned ends of a log into the flames. "Unless you have a ship and a full crew," he said, "I can't see that you can do anything to help me get to Wayreth."

"You could be there in no time if you took the faerie road," suggested Thistledown.

Bram waited for the tuatha man to explain, but as usual, Thistledown stared at him expectantly. "What's a faerie road?" the nobleman asked at length.

Once again, Thistledown conferred with his colleagues. "Burdock reminds me that the faerie road is like time. It looks different to every human who traverses it, and decidedly different to you than it does to us tuatha. It will magically allow you to travel great distances in a matter of heartbeats."

Thistledown turned to Milkweed, who dug into a pouch and extracted a small object she then pressed into the speaker's waiting palm.

"Here's your coin," said Thistledown. A gold coin of unfamiliar design glinted brightly in the light of the white moon.

Bram stared at the gold piece in Thistledown's palm. "I don't understand. Why are you paying me?"

The tuatha man flipped the coin in his small, pale hand. "This is milled faerie gold, the coin of our realm," he explained. "Only those invited to Wayreth may find its twin towers; the coin will serve as invitation. In addition, it will offer you protection in the faerie land, but only if you keep the coin with you and never stray from the main road."

"What happens if I step from that path or lose the coin?"

"You'll either be struck dead or kept hostage in some horrible fashion," Thistledown responded promptly.

"What if I meet up with bandits along the way and it's stolen from me?"

"The bandit who touches it without your leave will be struck dead."

"Hmmm." Bram stroked his chin thoughtfully. "What if I choose to spend it along the way for food, or I simply lose it, or I give it up to save my life?"

"Dead, dead, and dead."

Bram pursed his lips in dismay. "I should risk my life on this road?"

Thistledown looked east toward the cliff that overlooked Hillfort. "Only you can decide which of your options is the greater risk to you or the villagers for whom you feel a duty. I *can* assure you that you will be perfectly safe on the faerie road *if* you bide my warnings."

Bram looked toward Hillfort and knew the answer he must give. "How do I get to this faerie road?" he asked. "Is it far?"

"As near as here." Thistledown reached over to touch a finger, light as a feather, cool as running water, to Bram's right temple. "You have but to take the coin and speak aloud the name of your destination. A road will appear before you."

Bram stood, collected his belt and small pouch, then reached for the golden coin in Thistledown's hand. To his surprise, the tuatha man drew his own hand back.

"Remember," he admonished, "neither stray from the main road, nor give away the coin while in the faerie realm. Only the third fork to the left will take you to Wayreth."

Milkweed abruptly pulled Thistledown's ear to her lips again. "We have been advised to also tell you that when you reach Wayreth, you're to give the coin to a man named Par-Salian, and Par-Salian only. It will prove you took the faerie road, for the only humans to possess such a coin in your world are those who have safely traveled that road in ours."

That said, Thistledown placed the coin in Bram's waiting palm. The minted gold felt unexpectedly warm and heavy and bore the symbol of a disk that was half sun, half moon. On the other side was an image that Bram assumed was that of King Weador. Bram clasped the coin tightly as he gave a warm smile that took in all three tuatha, even the ones who'd never spoken to him. "Will I see you again after I return from Wayreth?"

Bram saw Thistledown's lips move frantically for one brief second, but he could hear no sound coming from them. He blinked once, twice, before realizing he'd unwittingly uttered the name of his destination. In the third blink of the nobleman's eye, the chilly hillside in Northern Ergoth gave way to a lush, green forest.

Bram had entered the realm of the tuatha.

\* \* \* \* \*

Bram's first thought was to keep the faerie coin safe, so he slipped it into a small inner pocket just beneath the drawstring that held up his brown trousers. Only then did he let himself look at his surroundings.

The road beneath his feet, crafted of interlocking blocks of stone worn or carved flat, was the smoothest he'd ever felt. This was no Ergothian dirt path riddled with wagon ruts and potholes of frozen water. His eyes followed its flat, gently curving ways around broad, gnarled trees and protruding boulders.

Above the road the green canopy was thick and close on all sides, making the path resemble a dark tunnel. The trees were a variety he didn't recognize, with broad, flat, oval leaves, some variegated with whorls of white, the rest a solid, blackish green. The bark was smooth and gray like that of a young maple, broken only by huge gnarls where once branches had grown. The underbrush was thick with thorny holly and rosy barberry bushes and a host of common roadside weeds, though how any of them received enough light through the canopy was a puzzle to Bram. Occasional thin slivers of bright blue limned the uppermost leaves, suggesting that somewhere above a sky and a sun existed. Unlike Stonecliff, the air was as warm as Ergoth in the month of Corij.

Strangely, it was a cheery forest in a dark, well-manicured sort of way. It looked neither magical nor foreboding as Thistledown's description of a death-dealing place would suggest.

Bram's fingertips traveled to the hidden pocket in his trousers for reassurance. Through the fabric he could feel the small, round outline of the faerie coin. Bram flung the heavy lapels of his winter cloak over his shoulders, looped the strap of his pack from waist to opposite collar bone, then set off down the road at a brisk pace.

He had not walked very far before he noticed that the forest was strangely silent, so silent he began to hear only his own footsteps. No birds sang, no squirrels chittered or shook the underbrush at the sound of his approach. Bram found himself self-consciously stepping so lightly that his heels made no noise to break the unnatural silence.

The road cut through a copse of draping, willowlike trees when the strange whispering began. Bram spun around, looking for the source of a vague, distant mumbling.

"Hello?" There was no one in sight behind or ahead of him on the road, nor could he see anyone among the denseness of the trees. He thought it odd that while no breeze lifted his hair, the thin, golden vines of the surrounding trees wafted in some mysterious wind.

"Is anyone here?" he called again. His voice echoed back at him three times, but there came no answering call. Just the odd whispering. He looked more closely at the unfamiliar variety of tree that surrounded him. The leaves were long, pink-tinged, and slightly humped in the middle. Though they looked vaguely like willow leaves, what each resembled more aptly was a delicate pair of lips.

The strange muttering began to grate on Bram's nerves, and he hastened down the road, hoping to escape the irritating noise. He left the odd copse of trees behind, and the whispering gradually receded. Bram began to relax.

It was only a matter of moments, however, before he spotted a flock of flamingo-sized birds perched on a single, bowed branch to the right of the path. With bodies of pink feathers and heads of orange fur, they watched him pass as one, five sets of yellow eyes glowing like small suns. They seemed more disturbing than dangerous, yet Bram picked up his pace to pass them quickly.

He had not walked very much farther when he heard a child's voice, thin and reedy, up ahead. The child sounded frantic and in need of help, so Bram broke into a run. His eyes searched the shrubs, looking for the owner of the plaintive voice.

The road curved gently to the right, and a narrow

fork, obscured by tall brush, abruptly appeared on his left. Bram stopped at the turn and peered down the smaller path for the source of the voice. Several paces away was a small child, no more than ten years of age. The child wore a grubby, ripped, pink tunic that hung past its knobby knees and brushed the tops of the rags that wrapped its feet. Pale yellow hair dangled in limp, tangled ropes to the shoulders. Bram could not be certain if the child was a boy or a girl.

"Please!" the child cried. "You must help me. My mother is trapped beneath a log near our home, and I haven't the strength with my girlish arms to move it off her. She's been there for some time and near to blue, sir."

Bram hesitated, peering down the path behind the girl, then back to the main road Thistledown had instructed him to take.

Seeing his reluctance, the young girl dropped to her knees. "Please, sir," she begged, holding up clenched hands, "with your muscles, it will take but moments to move the log that traps my mother."

Bram squinted again over her shoulder, looking for a cottage or any other sign of life behind the girl, but all he saw was a path much narrower than the one on which he stood, as dark and confining as a tomb. "Where's your father?" he asked her.

"He's in the forest, beyond the sound of my voice," she said. "The forest is thick and dark near our cottage. He left to chop some holes to the sky."

Bram could make no sense of any of this. "How did your mother come to fall beneath a log?"

The girl had begun to wring her hands. "She wanted to help my father by trimming some trees near our cabin. I warned her not to, for fear a log would strike our little home, but she wouldn't listen." She looked frantically over her shoulder yet again. "It's not very far to our cabin, just around that first bend."

Torn with indecision, Bram ran a hand through his hair. He looked at the road beneath her feet, a path of sorts. He'd been warned to take the third fork to the left, not the first. Somehow he knew the reason Thistledown had not mentioned any exceptions to the rule was because there were none.

"Please, sir," the girl beseeched him, palms pressed together. "I fear this hesitation may have already made it too late to save her. We could not survive without my mother."

Bram looked into her pale golden eyes and found them strangely unmoved, considering her desperate words. "Have you any rope?" he asked suddenly.

The question surprised her. "I suppose that we do."

"You'll need a long piece, more than twice the length of the thickest branch nearest your mother," he said quickly. "Throw one end of the rope over the branch, then tie both ends around the log that pins her. Establish a good foothold, then tug the rope sideways with all your might. The log should lift enough for your mother to roll to safety."

"But I told you I'm not strong enough to lift the log!" Her eyes were narrowing in anger.

"The pulley will supply enough strength," Bram reassured her, "but if you still have trouble, hitch the rope to a farm animal and let it help you lift the log." Bram watched her closely. "It is all that I would be able to do, I'm afraid." He thought for a moment. "I could give you some herbs that would ease the soreness your mother will feel, if you'd like."

The young girl stomped a rag-covered foot peevishly, her helpless demeanor gone. "What I'd like is for you to come and help me!"

Startled by the change, Bram backed away. "I'm sorry, but I'm in a great hurry," he said. Hastily wishing her luck, he nodded his head politely. When he looked up again, he saw something that nearly froze his feet to the stone path.

On the dark and narrow branch to the left was an enormous, buglike creature with six legs that ended in razor-sharp hooks. Above its fearsome facial mandibles were eyes the color of shiny amber. The thing was at least twice Bram's size. Beneath its yellow shell, its belly was incongruously pink and soft-looking.

Bram turned and ran down the main path. He couldn't be sure if the pounding steps he heard in his head came from the monster in pursuit or his own pulse pumping in his ears. He wanted to look back but dared not. Rounding a curve around a thick tree, he stole a half glance over his right shoulder. The fork was again obscured by shrubs, and the enormous thing was no longer in sight.

Bram bent at the waist, grabbed his knees, and drew in great gulps of air to catch his breath and slow his heart. He had a stitch in his side, and beads of sweat ran from his forehead and puddled above his lip. He quickly reached for the coin in the pocket at his waist and sighed in relief to find it still in place.

Bram continued on for some time. The road seemed to go on forever. The next bend was always just a few dozen paces ahead, holding out the promise of a destination. But around each bend was another bend, in a pattern that soon became monotonous, then tedious, and finally, downright irksome.

Hunger began to rumble in Bram's stomach, then slice clean through to his backbone. Without stopping, he pushed up the flap on his pouch and withdrew a rubbery carrot. Using his trousers like a strop, he wiped the root to remove the fine gritty dirt that hid under bumps and defied even a water washing. Bram wrenched off a too-soft bite of the root. It was tasteless and did nothing to ease the gnawing pain in his gut.

He spit the mouthful into the shrubbery and tossed the rest of the carrot after it.

Rounding another gentle bend, he scrubbed a finger to his teeth, wishing he had even a swallow of water to wash the grit and small, tasteless pieces from between his teeth.

"Yoo-hoo!"

Bram's head snapped up, and he was instantly on his guard. He followed the voice to his right and blinked in surprise at the sight. A stout, apple-cheeked elderly couple sat on the stoop of a quaint little cottage. Their wrinkled and pleasantly weathered faces were ringed by long yellow hair that showed no signs of gray. Both wore simple but colorful homespun clothes, adorned with beautifully embroidered suspenders, waist belts, aprons, and stockings. The man appeared to be carving faces on the handle of a large serving spoon while the woman shelled peas.

Bram stood in stoop-shouldered weariness and could not keep a jealous sigh from escaping his lips as he looked upon the food and the handsome cottage of neatly tuck-pointed stone and plaster. The thatch atop it was clean and yellow-new, with gentle arches above curved, stained-glass dormers. Before it, the shrubs had been cleared away to make room for beautifully tended raised beds of vegetables and flowers, with all the variety of Nahamkin's garden and none of the chaos. Yellow and white moths fluttered above flowering sweet peas, lush, ripe tomatoes, and minty-green cabbages the size of small boulders. Climbing roses of every color scaled the walls to encircle the second-floor dormers. The air smelled strongly of sweet-burning cherry wood and meaty stew.

"Hello, stranger," said the couple in unison.

"You look near to dropping," the woman observed kindly. "We have plenty of stew, fresh-baked bread, and dark-brewed ale, though we are not blessed with children to share it. You would be most welcome to join us for a moment or an hour to ease your journey, wherever you may be headed."

"That's very kind," Bram said, "but—"

"They say I'm a pretty fair cook," the woman coaxed, a modest smile lifting her fleshy cheeks and crinkling shut her eyes.

"Fair?" boomed her husband, patting his round stomach. "There isn't a better one for leagues, I'll wager. Actually, there *isn't* another cook for leagues," he confided with a chuckle. "This is a lonely stretch of road, but my Gorsha would be the best cook even if the path was littered with a dozen cottages."

Bram suddenly felt as if he'd been traveling without food for days. He shook his head sadly. "I can't tell you how much you tempt me, but to be honest, I was told not to leave the path for any reason, and—"

The man waved his hand as if to dismiss the notion. "That's just a myth the brownies spread to frighten folks and make themselves laugh," he said. "People leave the trail all the time. Unlike the brownies, who are always taking a person's food, my wife and I ask for nothing but the pleasure of giving sustenance to weary travelers like yourself."

Bram was jarred by the man's use of the dreaded "brownie" word. Suspicious, he looked back to where he'd come from, remembering the bug creature. "Perhaps," he said slowly, so as not to offend the couple, "but I've had a close call myself, without even leaving the path."

"That's unfortunate," the husband said sympathetically, "but the world's a dangerous place wherever you are."

"Why do you stay here, so far from everyone, if you're lonely?" asked Bram.

The man raised his shoulders and spread his hands to take in his homestead. "Who could leave such beauty as this, and why would we want to? We've made it everything we've ever dreamed. It suits us, and if the price is a little loneliness, it is a small enough fee." The woman nodded silently by his side.

Bram was sorely tempted, and it took every ounce of discipline he had to recall Thistledown's words once more. He bit his bottom lip until it hurt, then forced the words from his throat, "Thank you again, but I must be moving on."

"As you will," said the man. He and his wife regarded Bram with pity, lifted their shoulders in resignation, and stepped back into their homey and inviting cottage.

No doubt to have some delicious stew, Bram thought, gritting his teeth as he continued down the path. They'd made no untoward move, neither mentioned his coin, nor turned into vile creatures when he refused them.

Bram spun around and looked at the beautiful cottage, his eyes seeking some sign of the couple. His orbs were drawn, instead, to a bright whiteness in the yard behind the small building, previously screened from his view by the cottage itself. He blinked and focused again. The whiteness came from a pile of bones—legs, arms, and skulls—piled as high as the cottage itself, and picked clean. Bram broke into a run again, thankful he had withstood another deadly temptation.

The young nobleman came to the second fork in the road just as a pack of unseen creatures, like enormous moles, burrowed under the path in lumpy waves. Instead of cracking apart, the brick path heaved up like a gently snapped rope, throwing Bram to his knees. He dug his fingers around the loose edges of a brick and clung to it to stay on the path. Breathless, Bram waited many moments after the rumbling and heaving stopped before he crawled back to his feet and hastened on.

At a distance, the third path to the left looked the same, a little wider, a little brighter, perhaps, than the first two. The sight instantly renewed his flagging energy, for he felt certain it couldn't be much farther to Wayreth after the fork. He approached the turn with lighter feet.

Bram heard rustling in the bushes in the right **V** of the fork and he jumped back, instinctively putting a hand to the coin at his waist. Up popped a man, waist-high in greenery. Eyes on Bram, the man pushed his way through the bushes toward the fork. When he emerged, the nobleman could see that the man was actually a centaur. The man's naked, muscular chest stretched back into the chestnut-brown body of a horse. Four hooves clattered on the cobblestones as the creature moved to plant himself in the middle of the fork. A sword was strapped across his back, and he held a staff before him defensively, his expression distrustful.

"Which way will you go, stranger?"

"Left," said Bram, trying to get a better look at the oddly beautiful being.

"You may not go to the left," the creature said.

Bram frowned at the centaur's tone. "But I was instructed to take this fork to the left."

"You can only go to the right at this fork," explained the centaur unhelpfully.

Bram shook his head. "I don't want to take the right fork. I was instructed to follow the left fork because it is the only one that leads to Wayreth."

"But you can't."

Bram's eyes narrowed. "I can't go to Wayreth, or I can't take this fork?"

A corner of the centaur's mouth drew up slightly. "It

appears for you they're one and the same."

"Look, Mr. Centaur," Bram said with thinly veiled sarcasm, "the tuatha gave me a coin and said that it would allow me to go anywhere I wanted in the faerie realm, including to Wayreth."

"You have a coin?" said the centaur. "Then the tuatha spoke truly to you. Give the coin to me and you can go anywhere you wish."

"If you know about faerie coins," Bram said evenly, "then you also know I can't give the coin to you and still get safely to Wayreth."

The centaur shrugged. "Then you can't go left."

Bram slammed his hands on his hips. "Who are you to tell me where I can and can't go?"

The centaur lifted a brow and looked over his shoulder to the weapon on his back. "I'm the centaur with the sword."

And I'm the man with the vegetable peeler, Bram thought ruefully, recalling his little knife. "Yes, I suppose you are," he said instead.

The centaur continued to look at Bram expectantly, rhythmically tapping his staff in his hand.

Bram turned and stared back down the path he had walked. It looked the same behind as it did ahead. In fact, the intersection looked nearly identical from any direction. He paused, momentarily confused. He had come down the path and tried to veer to the left, which was now behind him to his right. An idea came; it was not necessarily a good one, for it interfered with his original plans somewhat, but it might pacify the centaur.

"What if I go back the way I came and take the *right* fork?" Bram asked. "Would that be acceptable to you?"

"I don't care where you go," said the centaur in a bored voice, "as long as you don't take the left fork."

"Yes, I hear that's not allowed," Guerrand said as he turned around and set off down the path.

Behind him to his left, the centaur shouted, "Where do you think you're going now? That's not the way you came."

The exclamation was punctuated by clattering hooves and a great deal of crashing and scraping, as the centaur bounded through the thick brush that hemmed in the **Y** intersection.

"It's not?" Bram exclaimed innocently, looking over his shoulder to where he had come from. "I guess I got all turned around and confused by your rules."

"There's nothing confusing about any of this," snapped the centaur. "You're just simple-minded." The centaur extended its left arm and pointed behind Bram. "Now turn around and go right."

Bram quickly spun about and retraced his steps. "Turn right here?" he asked, standing at the intersection again. Straight ahead was the path he had already traveled, and to the right was the path he had wanted to take from the start.

"Yes, yes, yes!" exclaimed the centaur. "My, you humans are thick. I'm certain I explained all this to you clearly. You may turn right, just not left. Now do it and leave me in peace, before I have to get nasty." To emphasize its point, the creature reached behind its back and placed a hand on the hilt of the sword slung there.

"Try not to be so thick in the future!" the centaur called after him.

Bram bowed his head in mock deference, then proceeded. He was scarcely ten steps down the left fork when he felt his vision shift and blur in a vaguely familiar way. He blinked once, twice, thrice; the magical path beneath his feet disappeared and he stood before wondrous gates of gold and silver.

# Chapter Nine

Lyim looked out across the awakening hillsides that sloped gently toward Thonvil, and he sighed with satisfaction. He had teleported to the eastern dirt road to give himself this view of the sleepy little burg. Despite its current run-down state, Thonvil's half-timbered buildings with thatched roofs looked warm and inviting against a backdrop of greening grasses and cornflower-blue sky.

It must have been a wonderful setting in which to grow up, Lyim thought, and not for the first time. Any place would have been better than the ugly and unyielding village of mud huts in which he'd lived on the Plains of Dust. The unfairness of the dichotomy was another entry on the ever-growing list of reasons to hate Guerrand DiThon.

The first time he'd had such envious thoughts was when, as an apprentice to Belize, Lyim had traveled to

Thonvil on behalf of his friend Guerrand. That had ended in the disaster that was Lyim's hand. He'd come to Thonvil then to save Guerrand's family. Now he was here to destroy it. It seemed somehow fitting to Lyim, a closing of the circle.

Every hideous and pain-racked death occurring this spring in Thonvil was on Guerrand's head. Lyim had no doubt about that and felt no guilt. Death knells rang here two and three times a day because of Guerrand's unwillingness to bend the rules to help the friend who'd given his hand saving Guerrand's life.

Lyim adjusted the fingerless leather glove over his right hand and tucked it inside the overlong cuff on his coarse brown robe. It would not do, particularly considering the prevailing air of suspicion and fear, to advertise his profession by wearing his usual red mage's robe or allowing anyone to see his snake hand.

Lyim followed the road into the village. The mage kept his eyes averted and drew into himself so as not to attract notice as a stranger, a habit he had developed since the accident that had changed his hand. He could scarcely remember the days when he had sought the spotlight by both deed and dress. The man in the drab, dun robe had once worn the brightest, most flamboyant colors in the newest styles. He had once made it a goal to get to know the people in any small village he visited for more than a few days. Especially the ladies. Those days were far in Lyim's past.

Women still admired him, he had noticed with some small measure of pride. Lyim's handsome looks had changed little in nearly a decade, with no care paid to them. His hair was long, dark, and wavy, though he no longer took the time to fashion his signature top braid. The rigors of his life had kept his muscles toned and defined as only a strict regimen of exercise had before. Yes, women still looked at him with eager eyes, until they inevitably saw the snake that was his hand.

Lyim felt the creature shift annoyingly inside the thick leather glove. He gave an angry shake of his head and turned his stride toward the village green encircled by Thonvil's timbered buildings. Standing in the shadow of a tree, Lyim watched as two men dug a grave in the newly softened soil. He counted eleven fresh mounds of dirt in the square that until recent weeks had but two or three new additions each year. The plague was turning out to be as deadly as he'd hoped.

Lyim could scarcely believe the luck of overhearing the whispered conversation of a sailor who had recently returned to Palanthas from the Minotaur Islands. The sailor spoke with horror of fleeing Mithas when a new and vile pestilence had sprung up among the smattering of humans there. "The medusa plague," they were calling it, a disease whose arrival and spread they were blaming on the unclean living habits of the bovinelike minotaurs who inhabited the isles.

Lyim had been struck by the plague's similarity to his own situation, however different some of the symptoms. He had never shed skin, and he'd lived with the affliction for many years. But the snakes . . . it was too coincidental to ignore, and so he decided to travel to the islands northeast of the Blood Sea to see this disease for himself.

En route, he had briefly entertained the hope that unlocking the secret of the minotaur plague might provide some clue to curing his own affliction, but that died when he saw the first victim. The man's limbs had changed to three-headed snakes, not the single head that was his hand. What was more, the victims all turned to stone within three days and died, so Lyim realized there was no link to his own condition to be found here.

But he was a mage with a bitter grudge to settle, and

the random pestilence in Mithas gave him another idea. A more delicious idea, in that it would allow him to cure his hand *and* get the revenge that he had longed for in the handful of months since Guerrand had refused to grant him entrance to Bastion.

Lyim spent two months among the brutish minotaurs, living in the most squalid conditions he'd endured since leaving the Plains of Dust. Most of the buildings on Mithas were of either mud or rough planking, with nothing better than a dirt path between them, even in the capital city of Lacynos. Despite horrid living conditions, the minotaurs were among the most honor-bound creatures Lyim had met in all his travels. They thought he was examining the stone bodies to find a magical cure. If they had known he was actually collecting the pestilence from the dead bodies and storing it in a specially prepared magical gem, they might have killed him, or worse.

Lyim saw spreading the plague in Thonvil as the perfect, triple-edged sword to use against Guerrand DiThon. As if inflicting an epidemic upon Guerrand's people weren't revenge enough, Lyim had added a curse to the pestilence so that Guerrand himself would appear responsible for the magical sickness. But the most useful of all the repercussions of the plague was that the news of its spread in Thonvil might very likely draw Guerrand from Bastion. Lyim would then have the opportunity to breach the stronghold more easily, gain entrance, and seek to reverse the process that had mutated his hand.

It had been a simple matter, under cover of a dark night less than a fortnight ago, to add the collected pestilence in the magical gem to the water in the village well. While monitoring the plague's progress was enjoyable, Lyim had returned this day primarily to discover whether news of the sickness had reached Guerrand.

The mage left the gravediggers in the square and sought the one person who was the likeliest to know: Guerrand's younger sister, Kirah. If anyone here still communicated with Guerrand, it would be she.

Lyim hiked the quarter league through unplanted fields toward the black and imposing stone castle perched on the Strait of Ergoth. Not usually of a mind to notice that spring had truly arrived, even Lyim could see that all patches of snow had disappeared into the earth, and the pale beige of winter was slowly turning to olive-green. The progress of the plague had put Lyim in an uncommonly good mood, and he launched into the uplifting last refrain from "The Lark, the Rave, and the Owl," singing in an aggressive and undisciplined base:

> *Through night the seasons ride into the dark,*
> *The years surrender in the changing lights,*
> *The breath turns vacant on the dusk or dawn*
> *Between the abstract days and nights.*
> *For there is always corpselight in the fields*
> *And corposants above the slaughterhouse,*
> *And at deep noon the shadowy vallenwoods*
> *Are bright at the topmost boughs.*

Lyim hadn't found much to sing about in recent years, though singing had been a favorite pastime of his since his days at the feet of bards in the smokey, decadent inns of his youth.

The brown-shrouded mage came to the last green, gentle slope that led to the portcullis on Castle DiThon's northern curtain wall. Staring up at the castle, blatant symbol of elitism, Lyim was struck again by the inequity between Guerrand's upbringing and his own. Cormac and Rietta DiThon had served as Guerrand's parents. Though nobly born, he knew from his own brief encounter with them that they were of no more noble spirit than his own poor parents. It was difficult to say of which pair that was a greater indictment.

Ardem Rhistadt and Dinayda Valurin were considered trash by the worst trash of Rowley-on-Torath. Lyim's parents had never married, in fact had done no more than pass each other in the dark one night, as was common with Dinayda's profession. Lyim was the result. Ardem Rhistadt had done no more than allow the child to take his name. Dinayda always maintained that she did the best she could, which was to let Lyim run wild, with the understanding that he always had a place to rest his head if he wanted it. Lyim didn't want it after the age of six. When he was ten, Lyim heard that his mother had died of one of the unspecified diseases that commonly killed women of her occupation.

By that time, Lyim's father had long since moved away from Rowley. That as good as made Lyim an orphan, but practically speaking nothing had changed. He was earning a few coins and some scraps of food as a general errand and clean-up boy at the local inn. It was there, one night in Lyim's twelfth year, that he saw something that would forever change the direction of his life.

A traveling sleight-of-hand artist—a charlatan trickster, really—was passing through Rowley. The magician, a tall, lanky man with a dirty yellow cape and hair, was earning coin by doing tricks for the patrons, such as making coins appear in their ears or under their tankards. Lyim was mesmerized; he'd never seen anything like this magic before, nor seen the power it held over the viewer.

Staying to clean up the inn long after the patrons had left, Lyim had opportunity to watch the magician count the evening's take; it was more money than the youth expected to earn in a lifetime. For one night's work! By Lyim's standards the magician was wealthy, even after he gave Mowe the innkeeper his due. The young boy knew in that moment that he had earned his last turnips from sweeping floors.

Lyim begged the magician to take him along as an unpaid servant, in exchange for teaching all he knew about magic. He quickly learned that Fabulous Fendock saved all his charisma and good humor for his performances. Off stage, what lessons he offered Lyim were impromptu and enigmatic, and more often than not they left the young man disgruntled and frustrated. But sometimes, when ale softened Fendock's mood, he could change radically, becoming ebullient, almost (but not quite) genial, and he would bring precious gifts of insight to the information-starved boy.

Lyim learned two truly useful things from Fendock. First, he learned that the man was a prestidigitator who played at performing simple cantrips, because true magic was a far more complex and powerful thing and was well beyond Fabulous Fendock's ability. In many ways it was unfortunate that Lyim proved to be a quick study, for Fendock punished the young boy for outdoing him in subtle and obvious ways.

The harshest and most far-reaching punishment came as a result of the other thing of value Lyim learned from this odd "apprenticeship": the name of a true wizard both revered and resented by Fendock. That lauded wizard's name was Belize.

One night, after the magician had drunk too much during a particularly well-received performance in Lantern on the East Road, he had pridefully shown Lyim his most prized possession: a spellbook written by the great mage Belize. Fendock's good mood caused him to confess with arrogance that he'd stolen the small tome from a patron some years back. He was in such a good mood, in fact, that he let young Lyim open the book, confident that the contents would be beyond the urchin's understanding. But Lyim's natural magical abilities had allowed him to read one or two of the words in the magical books before Fendock had furiously slammed the book shut and told him to never touch it again.

Lyim had seen the jealous look in the man's eyes, and he quickly realized that the magician didn't have the skill to read the book himself. Fendock was like a man who could appreciate fine music but was totally without skill to play it. Lyim's punishment for demonstrating that he possessed the ability Fendock lacked was the cessation of even the pretense of magical lessons.

When, on one dark night after a year of intolerable servitude, Lyim slipped away from Fabulous Fendock's wagon, he took with him Belize's writings. The young man reasoned that the magician could never utilize Belize's work properly and that he had served Fendock beyond what he had received in magical training.

"Never explain, never defend," had become Lyim's motto ever after. It was why he'd lied without remorse to Guerrand about getting the book from some elves. He had no shame about lying, but plenty concerning his blood and magical heritage.

Lyim came to the Castle DiThon's portcullis and was surprised to see it closed, as well as the vast double door behind it. He had never seen it so, even when the residents should have been expecting an attack from the family whose land Cormac DiThon had confiscated.

Puzzled, Lyim looked up to his right, to the guard tower. "Hallo? Who defends Castle DiThon this day?"

After a time, Lyim heard a squeaky voice that sounded vaguely familiar coming from the ramparts above and to his right. "What is it? Yes? We're not having any merchants from the village."

Squinting skyward, Lyim recognized the befuddled chamberlain who'd thought to dispatch an entire army of Knights of Solamnia with the announcement that he hadn't the authority to recognize their siege. The old man's face was even thinner and creased with more worry lines than when last Lyim had seen him, his eyes more milky with cataracts.

"Good chamberlain, I am no merchant with wares for sale. I am an old friend looking for Kirah DiThon," Lyim called up to the man in his most persuasive tones. "I heard there is plague in the village and was concerned for her welfare."

"Kirah is well, as far as I know," said the chamberlain, his tone eased.

"As far as you know?" repeated Lyim, puzzled. "Have you not seen her in the castle with your own eyes?"

"How would I?" asked the chamberlain as if the answer were plain. "I see little enough with these eyes. Even still, Kirah has lived in the village since shortly after she refused to marry the husband of her mother's choosing."

"Where does she live?" he asked the chamberlain.

"Above the baker's, I've heard," said the old man. "He's just died of the sickness, if Gildee the cook has it right from the gossips."

But Lyim was already on his way back to the village.

* * * * *

When Kirah heard the knock at her door, she thought it must be Dilb with some wood for her fire. With Bram gone to parts unknown, the baker's son was the only one she would trust to enter her little room. Still taking no chances, Kirah opened the door slowly and slightly, then pressed her right eye to the crack. Her breath abruptly caught in her throat, and her heart skipped a painful beat.

It could not be him. After all these years, and all her

wishes, it could not be Lyim. The world was too big a place, her dreams too inconsequential, for Lyim to arrive to help her twice in a lifetime. And yet there he stood on her stoop, beyond the crack in her door.

"Hello, Kirah," the mage said. "Is this how you welcome an old friend, peering at him like he's a robber in the night?"

Kirah primmed her mouth in superior fashion, then spoiled the effect by laughing girlishly. "Yes—I mean no! I mean, hello and come in!" she managed at last, flustered beyond all reason. Kirah opened the door with one hand and pulled closed her ragged wrap with the other, suddenly self-conscious. It had been so long since she'd been expected to behave like anything but a crazy hermit.

As Lyim walked into her room, Kirah noticed that something about him was different, yet she couldn't quite put her finger on it. It wasn't just the simple, oversized brown robe that seemed to engulf him, or the odd leather mittens, although they were uncharacteristic. His face and hair were essentially unchanged, no early gray at the temples. Maybe it was the eyes, she thought, looking for the sparkle of humor she remembered there and not finding it. Perhaps it was the man's stride, slower and more contained. His was no longer the strut of a peacock proud of his plumes.

Unlike Lyim, Kirah had never cared what she looked like. Until this minute, anyway, when a recent memory of her visage in a street puddle made her shiver. Her unwashed hair was dull gray instead of blonde, and flat against her head, as if she wore a cap. Kirah felt well enough, but her eyes and cheeks were sunken so that she appeared far older than her nineteen years. She looked beyond bony in the sacklike dress and wrap the baker's robust wife had given her some months ago when her previous raggedy shift had disintegrated at the shoulders.

Kirah made herself as small as possible in a reed-backed chair by the hearth. "Have you come to save the village again?" she asked more caustically than she'd meant. "There's a plague here."

"I know." Lyim removed his left mit and set it on the small table by the door, as if he had done so for years. "That *is* why I've come. I was hoping you'd know where Guerrand is."

She looked up, mildly surprised. "You've come to the wrong place, then," she said. "Guerrand came to see me just after we prevented the Berwick siege, but I haven't heard from him since."

"You sound as though you're still angry with him after all these years," observed Lyim.

Kirah thought about that briefly. "No, I don't suppose I am," she said at last. "We made our peace, Guerrand and I. He had to leave Thonvil." Kirah leaned forward in the chair to add her last meager log to the coals. Brushing off her hands, Kirah stood and took two chipped pottery mugs from the narrow mantle. "I can offer you rainwater tea, but I'm afraid I have nothing else. I get my meals after the baker's family below, and they're not coming regularly now, what with Glammis's death."

"Did you know him well?"

"Glammis?" She shrugged thin shoulders. "You know everyone in a village the size of Thonvil, even if you don't live above them. Glammis was kindly enough, a hardworking man with a wife and young son to support. I don't know how they'll get along without him." She dropped a pinch of tea leaves into one of the cups. "If they don't catch the disease themselves, that is."

Kirah poured heated rainwater from a kettle onto the brittle green leaves in both mugs. She stopped abruptly, her head cocked as she regarded Lyim. "It's funny that you should be looking for Guerrand now. Have you heard the rumors, too?"

"Too?" he repeated, taking in his left hand the hot mug she held out to him. He settled his bulk into the chair Kirah had vacated and took a tentative sip. "Who else is looking for him?"

Kirah whipped back dirty strands of hair from her face. "My nephew Bram left Thonvil in search of Guerrand because he thinks Rand may know something about curing this plague. I'm afraid my brother helped stir up Bram's suspicions, since Cormac believes everything that is wrong in and around Thonvil is Guerrand's fault. In the stupor that is his conscious state," Kirah said with great deliberateness, "Cormac has rewritten history to exonerate himself."

Lyim fidgeted in the chair. "What made Bram think Guerrand knows anything about it?"

"I haven't seen the pestilence myself," Kirah confessed, "but my nephew described it to me just before he left. Bram said that he had heard with his own ears what the gossips had been whispering: Just before death, the victims' snake limbs whisper Guerrand's name."

"Do you think it's possible Guerrand is responsible for it?" Lyim asked cautiously.

Again Kirah shrugged, a gesture seemingly as involuntary as breathing to her. "A month or more ago I wouldn't have thought anyone I knew could even contract such a bizarre illness."

Lyim sipped, looking at her over the brim of his mug. "And what do you think now?"

Kirah moved to sit across from Lyim on the edge of her small bed. "This illness is odd enough to be magical in nature," she said slowly, "but I can't believe Guerrand had anything to do with it." Her face scrunched up pensively. "Why on Krynn would he want to do such a thing?"

Lyim set his empty cup down and wouldn't meet her

eyes. "Do you think this nephew of yours, Bram, has any chance of returning with Guerrand?"

"I don't know. Frankly, he has more determination than experience."

Lyim frowned darkly. "Where did your nephew go, and when did he leave?"

"I suggested he start by asking the wizards at Wayreth—" Kirah stopped suddenly. "Say, you're a mage, Lyim. If the pestilence is magical, can't you do something to stop it?" Her face brightened in hopeful understanding. "That's why you're here, isn't it?"

Lyim grimaced, wrestling with some decision. "I had hoped to spare you what I know about your brother, but—"

"What is it?" Kirah jumped to her feet and reached out imploringly for Lyim's arm, his right. The mage snatched away his gloved hand viciously before she could lay a finger to it. Stunned, she drew back and looked at him with pain in her pale eyes.

Lyim rubbed his face. "I believe Guerrand is responsible for this plague," he managed at last. "I knew it the second I stepped into the village and heard the details of the illness."

"But why?" gasped Kirah, shaking her head in disbelief.

Lyim's laugh was not kindly. "Guerrand and I have not been friends since—" he paused, considering, then pushed back his big right cuff and removed the tan leather mit from his hand. "Since this happened to my hand."

Not knowing what to expect, Kirah hung back apprehensively. She jumped in stunned horror when a long, single-headed snake with a gold diamond pattern on its head slithered forth where Lyim's hand should have been.

"I-I don't understand," she stuttered, unconsciously

averting her eyes. "Are you saying Guerrand did that to you?"

His face red with shame, Lyim tucked the hissing creature back into its glove. "Not exactly," he said. "In fairness, I'm forced to admit that my own master inflicted this upon me. But it was within Guerrand's power to help me cure it. He refused. I've been unable to cure it myself, but I did manage to find an antidote that enabled me to contain it to one hand."

Paler than death, Kirah dropped back onto the bed and shook her head with slow but unceasing regularity.

"If he has the power to cure it, Guerrand also has the power to create the disease," reasoned Lyim. When Kirah continued to shake her head mutely, he said, "I didn't want to believe it either."

"But why?" asked Kirah in a small voice. "Why would Guerrand want to inflict the same horrible pain on us?"

"Because he can?" Lyim postulated. "You don't know Guerrand anymore, Kirah. He's become a powerful and influential mage. Perhaps his impoverished roots are an embarrassment to him, I'm not really sure, but I fear his power has gone to his head. It happened to my master—the magic took him over." Lyim's dark, wavy hair brushed his shoulders as he shook his head sadly. "I tell you, you would not recognize your brother in the man who refused my simple request to cure my hand."

Kirah's eyes held a faraway look. "He promised me when he first left that if ever I needed help, he'd somehow know and come to me," she said numbly.

"Instead he sent me, rather than risk his position with his master," Lyim reminded her. "Apparently the seeds for his selfishness had already been planted."

Lyim saw the firm set to her mouth. "Look, Kirah, I don't like to say these things, let alone believe them. But don't you think all the coincidences are a bit odd? My hand? The similarity of the plague's symptoms to the affliction Guerrand refused to cure in me? Why else would the snakes hiss his name? What but guilt or design could keep him away?"

Kirah bristled. "He probably hasn't heard of our troubles yet."

Lyim shook his head sadly. "You don't understand the powers of a mage if you believe that."

Kirah shook her head mutely. "I . . . can't . . . believe it. But maybe I don't know Guerrand anymore." Overcome, she pressed her face into her hands.

Lyim knelt by her on one knee, his hair falling to gently curl around his face as he lifted her tear-streaked chin with his good hand. "*I've* come to help you, Kirah."

Kirah tried to break the bond that held his eyes to hers, but the power that gripped her was as old as sorcery and far stronger. She could only manage a nod.

"Together, we can make Guerrand come forward and face what he has done," Lyim said smoothly. "Together, we can end the suffering." He reached into his brown shroud and withdrew a flask. "This is the antidote I traveled to Mithas to secure. It prevents those with symptoms of the disease from dying, though it won't cure the mutations. And it keeps those without symptoms from contracting the illness. Guerrand will surely come forward when he realizes we've foiled his plot."

Still on one knee and holding Kirah's gaze, Lyim pressed the flask into her small hands. "I have just enough with me for you, Kirah," he intoned. "You must take it. For me."

## Chapter Ten

Lyim had forgotten how menacing Wayreth Forest looked. The trees and bushes were all hideously twisted, casting sinister shadows. The distant sounds of wolves and bears didn't make the forest feel any more inviting, either.

He noticed these things, but he wasn't frightened by the forest, never had been. Right now he could think only of how his calf muscles were starting to cramp. He'd been waiting behind the underbrush outside the gates of Wayreth for days, ever since he'd teleported here directly upon leaving Kirah. Growing annoyed with waiting, he shifted to relieve the pressure on his legs, never taking his eyes from the elaborate gateway to the stronghold of magic.

Lyim resolved to give Guerrand's nephew until sunset to make it to the tower; the Council would recess then until the next day. After that he'd place a magical sentinel to watch for the young man's arrival. *If* the country boy ever made it, thought Lyim, knowing he could not have missed him already. It would take a non-mage more than a week to reach Wayreth from Northern Ergoth. Still, the discomfort would be worth the wait to Lyim if Bram got into Wayreth and persuaded the Council to send him to Bastion. It was the best change Lyim had for entering the stronghold himself.

The wizard had taken the plague to Thonvil, hoping to draw Guerrand from Bastion. Lyim had reasoned that if he watched Thonvil closely and witnessed Guerrand's magical arrival, he might find a clue to entering the impenetrable stronghold. But Kirah's revelation about her nephew's departure for Wayreth to find Guerrand had given the wizard another idea. A far superior and more expedient idea.

Lyim still tingled when he recalled how his mind had raced to conceive a plan that would take him all the way into the forbidden stronghold and cure his hand. Or kill him trying. But Lyim was no more afraid of that than of the forest behind him.

It was all within Lyim's grasp, if only the nephew's quest was successful. The wizard waited and watched with patience borne of hope. A few would-be wizards came and went; half of the latter were dragged away by dwarves, Lyim knew, because they had failed their Test. None of them met Lyim's mental image of Guerrand's nephew; most were either younger than Bram would be, or of a different race.

The wizard wasn't even aware he'd slipped into a shallow slumber of boredom until he was jolted awake for seemingly no good reason. Nothing had touched him; no one else had appeared before the tower. And yet, some sense told him that the air around the tower was somehow different, charged. He was instantly alert.

Lyim blinked. When his eyes opened again—it was

that quick—a young man stood looking up with surprised awe at the gates of gold and silver. Though magical entrances were more common than not at Wayreth, this one seemed different, as if the young man himself were surprised to be here.

The man in the heavy cloak turned to look at the forest that hid Lyim, giving the wizard a good look at his profile. The resemblance to Guerrand in hair color and facial shape was remarkable.

Lyim smiled. He had only to wait and monitor the towers for significant external radiations of magical energy. He was as good as in Bastion already.

\* \* \* \* \*

The gates of gold and silver before Bram were so masterfully crafted they looked as thin as cobwebs. The gates adjoined a wall in the shape of an equilateral triangle, with a small guard tower at each point. Odd, unfamiliar symbols were carved upon the surface of the dark stone, symbols that suggested the strength of the earth even to those with no power to read them. There were no battlements on the smooth-topped obsidian walls. Bram presumed the wizards who gathered there had little use for such mundane protection.

Beyond the gated wall, twin towers of polished black obsidian pierced the forest roof. He turned to glance around, but the forest here looked and felt so oddly malevolent that he quickly returned his attention to the structure. The gates were open, so he strode slowly through them, eyes attempting to look everywhere at once. The courtyard was stark and barren, paved with cold gray flagstone. Though he could see no one, he had the vague feeling that he was not alone, as if the yard were teeming with people rushing to and fro. Turning quickly, he thought he saw a face and the upturned collar of a white robe, but then it was gone. He shook his head, knowing the vision was impossible. Other than himself, he could see no one in the flagstone courtyard.

Bram walked toward the only door in a small foretower between the twin columns. At his approach the door abruptly flew back. Though no one appeared, it was obvious he was expected to step inside, and so he did. Smokeless torches provided dim illumination inside the simple, circular room. Three doors led from the room at equidistant points in the circle. Opposite the door an empty row of chairs followed the curve of the wall. Inside his still-new boots, Bram's feet had begun to throb, so he slipped over to the row of chairs and lowered himself into one. Bram unconsciously tapped his foot while he waited for someone to arrive to direct him.

And waited. Had he overlooked some bell or buzzer new arrivals were expected to ring? Bram squinted in the dark, spotted a simple wooden stand in the shadows to the left of the door, but it held only a thick, much-used book from the look of the binding. He drummed his fingers on the armrests.

Many more anxious moments passed, and Bram began to debate whether he should pick a door and go looking for someone. Perhaps he should just leave.

He had just risen to do so when the door to his left opened abruptly with a noisy creak, and from it emerged a man in a white robe, pushing a broom, his head bent to the task. Actually, Bram only assumed it was a man, since all he could see was the top of the person's tilted head, hair slicked down and carefully arranged so that each toothmark of the comb was still visible.

"Pardon me, my good man," Bram tried to say, but his voice was phlegmy from lack of use this day. The words came out sounding like something a chicken might croak.

The man's head shot up. Spying Bram in the shadows, he whirled his broom about and held its handle like a spear. "Speak the common tongue or be sausage!" he threatened. The man was old, his skin ash-gray, as were the fingers that trembled upon his mock weapon.

Bram cleared his throat and summoned the words he had been rehearsing since Northern Ergoth. "I have traveled far to speak with the wizard named Par-Salian."

The man smacked his lips in thinly veiled impatience. "You've come too late in the day for Testing, or to declare an alignment. The Council of Three has recessed for the day." He continued to sweep, pausing expectantly when he came to the floor under Bram's feet.

The young man stepped from the broom's path. "I don't know anything about Testing or alignments," said Bram. "I need Par-Salian's help."

"Come back tomorrow," the man said, shooing Bram toward the exit with a wave of a blue-veined hand.

"But tomorrow may be too late," Bram cried. He refused to be put off so easily. "Can't you make an exception this once?" he pleaded, impulsively touching the man's arm.

Blue light crackled around the bent figure, gathered near his shoulder, and arced to Bram's hand. The young man yelped and yanked back his smoking fingers, as surprised as if a bucket of cold water had been splashed in his face. He had just suffered from what he was sure was a small demonstration of the mage's ability. If he wished to get any information here, he would have to use his wits.

A vision of the tuatha coin sprang to mind, and he fished about in the folds of his waistband to retrieve it. "I'm afraid I've started out on the wrong foot here," he began again in his most conciliatory tones. "I don't know if it matters, or warrants an exception to the rules, but I was given a faerie coin and instructed to hand it to Par-Salian by way of intro—"

"A faerie coin?" the man repeated over a hunched shoulder. "Why didn't you say so earlier?" He let the broom handle drop to the slate floor with a loud, ringing sound, while he stepped over to the book on the stand near the front door. Squinting in the dim light, the man flipped back the heavy cover, sending dust flying, and began leafing through pages. He came to one in particular and traced an ash-colored finger down a column of words. Abruptly he tapped the page and mumbled, "Ayup. Faerie coins are right here under, 'Reasons to disturb Par-Salian, Head of the Conclave, Master of the White Robes.' "

The man slammed the heavy book shut. When he looked at Bram again, the smile on his face made it obvious his attitude toward the young nobleman had changed. "The name's Delestrius, and I'm the warden on duty. Come along, then," he said, stepping over the broom on his way to the door through which Bram had seen him enter the foretower. Delighted with his new treatment, Bram hopped over the broom handle and followed the hastily retreating man through the door.

The old man in the white robe scurried like a mouse up a staircase immediately inside the door, allowing Bram not a glance about him as he hurried along behind. It was even darker here than in the foretower. There were no torches, no candles, no magical lights of any kind on the stairs, or even the landings that he presumed led to rooms he couldn't see. There were no decorations of any kind, neither tapestries nor carpets to warm the steps.

Delestrius departed the stairway on the second landing and entered a narrow hallway. A window at the far end allowed in a sliver of light, but not enough to illuminate anything near Bram and his guide. They walked, the man surefooted, Bram tentatively, in the hallway that felt as if it curved. Bram bumped into Delestrius, who had stopped before a doorway. The nobleman didn't feel the burning sensation he had the last time he touched the mage. Delestrius knocked at the unmarked door.

"Enter, Delestrius," said a voice as strong and clear as if its owner were not speaking through a thick, wooden door. It swung open without Bram's guide touching it. Bram followed Delestrius into a room that was nicely lit by a low-burning fire in the hearth against the left wall. The light radiated in warm yellow rays, striking shelves of books bound in white leather, silver runes glinting upon their spines. The golden light led Bram's eyes to a white-haired man seated behind an elaborate desk, one leg lifted casually to rest upon its cluttered surface.

"You know I would not for the world disturb you after hours, Master," Bram's guide said with an obsequiousness the young man wouldn't have thought him capable of, "if it were not of the utmost—"

"You know I trust your judgment, Delestrius," interrupted the white-haired mage. Setting down a feathered quill, he raised kindly, tired blue eyes to Bram.

It took many long seconds before Bram realized the look was a question. "I was given a faerie coin and instructed to place it only in the hands of Par-Salian," he blurted.

"A faerie coin?" repeated the old man with interest.

"Are you Par-Salian?"

Delestrius gasped and slapped the back of Bram's head. "I was told I would suffer death if I gave the coin to anyone else," Bram explained defensively, rubbing his skull.

The white-haired man behind the desk said, "Your reticence is understandable, under such circumstances. I should have introduced myself." He stood, walked around the desk, and extended a hand that winked with the facets of many precious gems. "Par-Salian, Head of the Conclave, Master of the White Robes, Keeper of the Key, and so on, and so on," he said with a self-deprecating formality.

The young man's work-reddened hand shook the mage's soft, warm one. "Bram DiThon," he said simply.

Par-Salian's eyes lit noticeably with interest at the surname, but before he could form a question, both men heard Bram's guide muttering, "Shouldn't have to introduce the greatest mage alive."

Par-Salian smoothed his snowy moustache with two fingers, hiding a slight smirk. "That will be all, Delestrius. Thank you."

Frowning, the man bobbed his head and backed through the door, leaving Bram and Par-Salian in the silence of the crackling fire.

Bram waited, red-faced, while the white-haired mage slowly shuffled to a chair by the hearth. He motioned Bram to join him. Par-Salian held out his soft, wrinkled palm, leaving no question as to what he wished. Bram rubbed the carved surface of the wafer-thin magical coin one last time, then placed it in the man's waiting hand. Par-Salian had just enough time to validate Bram's claim before the coin disappeared like snow into water.

"I'm always sorry to see them vanish so quickly," the wizard said wistfully. "I receive them with the half-decade infrequency of the three moons' eclipsing. The tuatha dundarael rarely give them away."

Par-Salian's ice-blue eyes pierced Bram for some moments. "I sense no magical training in you. What would cause the tuatha to favor you with their coin?"

he asked bluntly.

Bram shrugged. "They said I had 'high moral standards.' " He repeated Thistledown's exact words without hubris, mindful of the tuatha's admonishment about pride.

"That's interesting," remarked the wizard. He continued to study Bram's face. "I sense in you a great deal of natural talent for the Art. Is that why you've come here, to find a master with whom to apprentice?"

Bram shook his head to the question for the second time that day. "No, sir. I've come because some sort of plague, for lack of a better word, has struck my village in Northern Ergoth. I am neither doctor nor mage, but I suspect the cause may be magical in nature."

"So you're looking for a mage to find a cure," finished Par-Salian. "I appreciate your dilemma, young man, but Wayreth is the seat of magical learning, not a wizard market."

Bram frowned. "I wasn't looking for just any mage," he said. "I haven't the money to pay one anyway. I was hoping to find my uncle, whom I understand came here seeking a master nearly a decade ago."

Par-Salian's expression darkened with disapproval. "Neither are we an alumni association."

"I understand that," Bram said quickly, "but if I told you my uncle's name, maybe you'd recognize it and would know if he is even still alive. I'll leave at once, without further question, if the name is unfamiliar," he promised.

Par-Salian waved a distracted hand, signaling Bram to proceed.

"My uncle is Guerrand DiThon."

The wizard leaned back and tapped his whiskered chin. "Yes, I recognize the name," he said at length. "I also begin to understand why the faerie folk might have given you a coin."

"You know of him?" Bram exclaimed. "Then can you tell me where he is now? "

Par-Salian winced slightly. "That is a bit more complicated." He stood and walked toward the door, the hem of his white robe whispering across the stone floor. "Please wait here, while I confer with a colleague."

Bram quickly grew restless with waiting, and he began looking around the room. The bookshelves he'd spotted from the door were to his left. The white leather spines looked butter-yellow in the glow of the fire. Something about the silver-etched lettering drew his finger to trace the unreadable words. He could almost feel the magic radiating from the tomes, but when he tried to lift one, he couldn't move it from the shelf, as if it were affixed there.

He spied a plate of cookies on Par-Salian's desk and was reminded how long it had been since he'd eaten his last rubbery carrot. He lifted one from the plate. It was light as a feather between his fingers, and smelled of almond. The cookie crumbled in his mouth, tasting of butter and sugar of a quality not used in Thonvil in some time.

The door swung open abruptly, and in stepped Par-Salian. Behind him was a younger-looking, robust man in a red robe topped off by a white neck ruff. The second mage dragged his left leg in a manner that suggested it was crippled. Both regarded the young man spewing cookie crumbs with amusement.

"I'm sorry," mumbled Bram over the mouthful of half-chewed biscuit. "I was just so hungry. . . ."

"Never mind," said Par-Salian. "If I had my manners about me I would have realized you hadn't eaten for some time and offered you refreshment."

Smiling gratefully, Bram gulped down the last of the cookie and wiped his mouth on a sleeve.

Par-Salian nodded toward his red-robed companion.

"Justarius, Master of the Red Robes, this is Brom DiThon."

"Bram," the nobleman quickly corrected.

Justarius limped forward slowly, considering Bram's face. "I can see the resemblance in the hair and the cheekbones," he said at length. "Guerrand had more of the timid rabbit look about him when he first came to the Tower of High Sorcery and became my apprentice."

"Can you tell me the whereabouts of my uncle, sir?" Bram asked, feeling the weight of time press. "It's urgent that I find him right away."

Justarius lowered himself into one of the chairs by the hearth, stretching out his game leg. "What would you have your uncle do if you found him?"

"As I was telling Par-Salian," Bram began, nodding toward the venerable white-robed mage, "a strange, magical disease has struck our village. There are some who think Guerrand may be responsible for it, since he first brought magic to the village." Bram was suddenly conscious that the remark might offend the wizards. "Whatever has caused it," he added hastily, "I hope he will return with me and use his skills to cure the disease before it kills everyone I know and care about, including my family. *Guerrand's* family."

The mages exchanged looks. "So you could be spreading this disease by leaving," observed Justarius over steepled fingertips.

"I could," Bram agreed reluctantly, "but frankly I doubt it. I've been gone long enough that I would have exhibited the first symptom of a fever by now if I were carrying the sickness." Still sensing Justarius's disapproval, he added grimly, "What would you have me do, just wait there for everyone, including me, to die?"

"None of that matters here," Par-Salian interrupted dismissively. "The tower is protected from such things. The gates would have closed to prevent you from entering if you were carrying a deadly disease."

"So, will you tell me where my uncle is?"

The mages sat, very still, exchanging glances.

"It may not be important to you that a small village of people are dying while we speak," Bram said, unable to hide his frustration, "but those people mean everything to me. They're depending on me to help them; Guerrand is the only chance I have to find a cure."

Bram put a hand over his mouth briefly and willed a measure of calm. "I apologize for my bluntness," he said. "If you don't know where my uncle is, just say so, and I'll be out the front door as soon as I can find it again. But if you do know, tell me, and I'll leave just as quickly to look for him."

"You can't," Justarius said.

Bram's dark head cocked. "Is he dead?"

"I didn't say that." Justarius rubbed his face wearily. "In an odd way that would actually make him easier for you to find."

Sensing that Bram was on the brink of snapping, Justarius struggled for a less cryptic explanation. "You have put us in an odd position, Bram."

"I'm in a bit of a bind myself," the nobleman said.

Justarius pursed his lips. "We're not unsympathetic to your plight. However, your uncle holds a position of great importance to the Council of Mages, and to the future of magic, for that matter. By necessity, his location and actual duties are a closely guarded secret." Par-Salian nodded from behind his desk across the room.

"So," Bram said slowly, trying to take in the news, "am I just supposed to go on my way?"

Par-Salian stepped around his desk to close the gap between the three. "We're not sure what we expect you to do," he admitted. "Frankly, most mages are loners. We've not had a family member come looking for anyone in Guerrand's position before."

But Bram would not be so easily put off. "Well, you have now."

"This is not, however, the first time Guerrand has had problems with his family," put in Justarius. "The last such episode led to the catastrophic event that necessitated the creation of Guerrand's current position."

"I don't understand," Bram said, shaking his head.

Justarius waved the subject away. "It is a long and complicated story, and one I don't think you'd like us to take the time to explain now. But please understand that our hesitation stems only from the fact that there are many who would pay dearly for the secret of Guerrand's location."

Bram gasped. "Are you suggesting I'm a spy?"

Justarius shrugged. "You may be and not even know it. It's not inconceivable that you've been bewitched by a mage who wishes to learn the secret."

"But I haven't!" cried the young man, yet his tone was more protest than persuasive.

"There is a way for us to determine that for ourselves, if you are willing," suggested Par-Salian.

Bram's glance was hard. "Let's do it."

Par-Salian raised his arms, white sleeves fluttering like the wings of a swan, and before Bram knew what was happening, all three were gone from the study.

The nobleman blinked, and when he opened his eyes, he was with the mages in a small, dark, hexagonal room. No fire burned but the flame of a single golden candle. At the edges of his vision, Bram could make out a few long tables, an iron-bound chest, and behind him a chair.

"Where are we? Is Guerrand here?"

"Sadly, for you, no. We're in my laboratory atop the north tower." Par-Salian reached into a pocket in his gold-trimmed robe and withdrew a handful of sparkling powder. Arcing his arm, he drew a perfect circle of glowing silver onto the stone floor.

"Step into the circle, Bram," he commanded, his voice grave, eyes on the sphere.

Bram hesitated, instinctively resisting both the pull of Par-Salian's tone and the aura of the magical circle. The area of magic began to sing to him in a chorus of voices that rose from the depths of the floor it encompassed.

"Heed the song, Bram," Justarius said. "It will not lead you astray."

Bram relinquished his will and stepped slowly into the circle, hands twitching expectantly at his sides. Par-Salian opened a chest and pulled out an enormous, rough-cut crystal that he and Justarius suspended in midair between them. The two powerful mages began to swing the gem above his head in ever-widening circles.

Bram tried to shift to a more comfortable position, but found he couldn't move his legs or his arms. He tried to ask the wizards why that was so, but no sound moved his tongue or lips. He could shift his eyes, and that was all.

The mages didn't waver in their concentration. Par-Salian began to chant words Bram couldn't understand, the language of magic. Little twinkling lights, like will-o-the-wisps across the moors, danced about Bram's head and flashed like fireworks behind his eyes. The lights swayed in unison, then flew apart into a chaos of sparks and motion, then came together again to sway hypnotically once more. One after another the pinpoints of light pierced his body until they were no longer visible, but instead of pain or heat he felt only a weightlessness within himself.

Bram slumped suddenly, feeling as if all the energy had been drained from his body. Justarius caught his arm in a strong grip and pulled him from the glowing silver circle to the small room's lone chair.

"That spell searches all of the corners and crannies of your being and tends to make them sore from the intense scrutiny," the red-robed mage explained. He patted Bram's hand. "It also reads your intentions and motivations, among other things, and I am pleased to announce that your mind is clear, your cause pure," he pronounced, then sniffed at the nobleman's filthy clothing, his dark eyes twinkling with mirth, "even if you are not."

"I could have told you that and saved myself the sore muscles," the young man said.

Par-Salian smiled from where he sat perched on the edge of a table. "Justarius and I agreed that if you passed the examination, we would make an unprecedented exception in consideration of the potential repercussions of this illness, and because, as a non-mage, you present little threat to the security of this secret. We will send you to see your uncle for one day."

Bram mustered his strength to sit tall. "I don't wish to bother such important mages further. Just tell me where I may find him, and I will go there myself."

Again Par-Salian and Justarius exchanged knowing glances. "That's not possible," said the former at length. "He's beyond the normal circles of existence and can be reached only by magical means. In other words, you cannot get there from here—without our help."

"Go clean yourself up," Justarius suggested, "while I prepare a message for you to take to your uncle. Par-Salian will ask Delestrius to rustle up some food, so that some of the magical smoke we've been blowing will disappear from your brain."

Bram found himself hustled out the door, conscious only that he had won. Soon he would see his Uncle Guerrand.

# Chapter
# Eleven

Bram's eyes were shut, as Justarius directed, when the floor in Par-Salian's study seemed to slip away beneath his feet. He immediately felt as if he were quickly, steadily shrinking. In his mind's eye he saw his own small body rocketing toward a large white keyhole in the starry blackness of space. His body paused of its own will before the keyhole briefly, and in that instant Bram felt a jarring from behind, as if someone had pushed him. But then some force ahead literally sucked him through the keyhole and into a whiteness beyond so bright that it burned through his closed eyelids. The mental image ceased abruptly when the brightness was extinguished like a candle.

"Well, I'll be a bugbear! Bram, what are you doing here?" asked a voice, familiar as a distant memory.

The young nobleman heard his name through a

haze. He could feel himself swaying, yet had no idea which way to lean to stop himself from falling. Strong hands grabbed him by the shoulders and pulled him into a tight embrace.

"Dizziness is common after passing from three dimensions to two. You'll adjust faster if you open your eyes."

Bram slowly let his tightly closed lids slip open, and he got his first look at his uncle in nearly a decade. Guerrand had aged considerably since Bram had last seen him on the second-floor hallway of Castle DiThon's keep. In fairness Bram had to admit that Rand had looked older that day than the one previous to it, for if memory served, Guerrand had just buried his beloved brother Quinn that morning.

Still, Bram was not exactly prepared for the difference. Guerrand's cheek held white traces of a small fading scar. His wavy hair was much longer. Loosely bound with a red ribbon, it was past the middle of his back, and graying at the temples. The coarse red robe certainly was different than the casual, ragged tunic and trousers Guerrand had favored at Castle DiThon. The robe gave the mage an air of dignity, or at least greater seriousness.

Guerrand shook him gently, smiling hopefully. "Do I pass inspection?"

"Of course," Bram said hastily. "No one told me what to expect. I'm still a little surprised to actually have found you here"—his gaze traveled around the stark nave—"wherever here is."

The two stood alone in a soaring tower of a room with white, vaulted arches, so bright it looked like the sun itself hung from the ceiling many stories above. The snow-bright whiteness was broken by many lush, tropical-looking plants.

"This is Bastion," said Guerrand, chuckling with

disbelief and joy at Bram's presence, "and you're not the only one surprised to find you here!" The mage's hands looked soft and white against the red cloth wrapping his hips. "How did you track me down, let alone persuade the Council to send you to Bastion?"

Bram's forehead furrowed. "Didn't Justarius or Par-Salian tell you anything?"

Guerrand shook his head. "They sent a message that someone was arriving," he explained. "But I had no idea who it would be until you appeared in the nave."

A raven-haired woman walked up behind Guerrand. Arms linked behind her back, she peered around the mage at the stranger to the stronghold. "Bram," said Guerrand, stepping to the side, "let me introduce another of Bastion's guardians, Dagamier of the Black Robes." He nodded from her to the new arrival. "Dagamier, my nephew, Bram DiThon."

Bram returned the almost defiant stare of the young woman who looked no older than his Aunt Kirah. Against her onyx robe, the woman's skin was as white as the walls of the room. Her eyes were an unusual shade of dark blue, almost an indigo. Black hair, pulled into one intricate braid from forehead to shoulder blades, had the same bluish sheen as her eyes.

Unsmiling, Dagamier leaned forward at the waist and extended a pale hand. Her silk robe parted ever so slightly, revealing slim, well-muscled legs. Bram could not help but notice how cold and sensuous she looked at the same time. He jerked his eyes back to her face, where a lightless smile pulled up the corners of plum-colored lips.

"We don't get many visitors at Bastion. Or any, even," she remarked ironically. "You must be someone very special"—one dark brow raised—"or very dangerous."

Bram colored. "I'm sure I'm neither," he said awkwardly, unable to keep from fidgeting under her scrutiny. "I carry an important message for my uncle, that's all."

Dagamier finished her evaluation of him by turning on a heel. "I hope you bring welcome news," she said, disappearing into one of seven dark-colored doors that led from the central room.

"Dagamier is . . . unusual," Guerrand said diplomatically, watching her departure. He snapped his gaze away. "Let me show you around Bastion, nephew." The fifth sentinel gestured broadly with his hand to include the structure. "There's not much common area to see, but my apartments are quite spacious. We can speak privately there of what brought you, when you feel a little more oriented to the dimensional change."

Bram followed his uncle around the nave, while Guerrand recounted the history, general layout, and defensive purpose of the stronghold.

"But who would invade Bastion," asked Bram, "if no one can get here without the Council's help?"

"Nonmages would find it impossible," agreed Guerrand. "But there are wizards who would try anything to reach the Lost Citadel. There was one, not too long ago, who—" Guerrand seemed to stop this line of thought with great effort.

"Ezius is at his turn in the scrying sphere. He's a bit reclusive, but I'll make a point of introducing you later."

Guerrand directed them into his wing and down a long, wide hall, featureless except for the handful of doors that fed into it. Like a proud parent, Guerrand launched into showing Bram every cranny and compartment in the red wing.

"You seem very content here," Bram observed afterward, when they settled into the kitchen area.

"It can get a little lonely," Guerrand conceded, "but this place is a mage's dream come true." Guerrand waved Bram to a softly padded chair. "Wine?" he asked.

Nodding, Bram slipped his head through the strap of the scroll case that crossed his chest and set it by the door.

Guerrand debated over a row of prone bottles on a wrought-iron rack. Deciding on one, he gripped its narrow neck and deftly uncorked it with a flick of his thumb. A frenzy of small bubbles broke the air in a wide range of green hues and floated lazily in the draftless room.

"My own vintage," explained Guerrand. "I call it Green Ergothian." He poured two goblets of emerald green wine, drizzling amber honey into both before handing one to his nephew.

Bram accepted the glass, savoring the rich brilliance of the color. Guerrand raised his glass in a toast, moving it in small circles to make a pattern in the air with the odd green bubbles.

"Tell me why you've come," invited the mage, settling himself across from Bram.

The young nobleman reluctantly set his glass down and moved to the hearth. He warmed his hands while he contemplated how to unfold the tale of Thonvil's plague. Feeling the press of time, Bram decided on the direct approach. "Some sort of strange illness has recently struck Thonvil and is spreading rapidly." Bram watched his uncle's reaction closely and was relieved to see that Guerrand looked genuinely shocked and concerned.

"Isn't the village physicker able to help them?"

Bram shook his head. "Everyone who has contracted the sickness has suffered a hideous death. Herus and I have done what we could, which has been very little, to ease their suffering."

Guerrand's face twisted, and he gripped the arms of

his chair. "What about Kirah? Your family?"

"Mother and Father were not sick when I left, nor was Kirah," said Bram, "but I fear for them every second I'm away." He looked intently at his uncle. "I—the village needs your help, Rand."

Guerrand raised his hands helplessly. "I'm no physicker. What makes you think I can help?"

"Because there's evidence that the sickness has a magical cause. I believe only magic—your magic—can cure it."

Looking skeptical, Guerrand swallowed a mouthful of wine. "You think because a particularly virulent strain of influenza withstands your bugbane or meadowsweet that it must be magical in nature?" He looked at Bram intently. "Tell me more about this illness."

Bram rubbed his face wearily, took another deep breath, then recalled to his uncle the stages he'd witnessed old Nahamkin go through before his hideous death on the third day as a snake-limbed, black-eyed creature of stone.

Bram took a deep breath before he plunged ahead. "Before the victim dies, the snakes hiss your name, Uncle. It is no rumor, for I have heard them myself."

Guerrand paled, and he shook his head in mute disbelief. The glass he was holding shook so violently that green wine splashed over his hand. Cursing, he instinctively jerked his hand back, dropping the glass. It crashed to the marble tabletop and shattered. The mage picked up the shards and mopped up the spilled wine with a rag. "You think I'm responsible for this sickness."

"I never believed the uncle I knew could have caused it," Bram said slowly, still watching Guerrand closely. "But I think there can be no doubt that magic—that you—are somehow involved."

Guerrand nodded vaguely, his eyes focused on some

distant memory. "I knew a man once whose hand changed into a snake, but the other symptoms are not familiar. His hand was altered after being thrust through a dimensional portal, not by some contagious disease. No other limbs mutated, and he didn't die from the change."

Bram took up the glass he'd left by the chair and threw back the contents, waiting for the burn. "You'll return with me, then, to stop this pestilence?"

Lost in his own thoughts, Guerrand jumped. "It's just not that simple, Bram," he said, shaking his head sadly. "After all that you went through to find me, you must have some understanding now of my responsibilities at Bastion. I can't just come and go as I please."

"Not even for one day?" pressed Bram. "Surely your comrades could handle things here for one day," he suggested reasonably.

"Dagamier, Ezius, and I are not equals," Guerrand explained. "When I agreed to become Bastion's fifth sentinel, the Council of Three appointed me high defender. That makes me responsible for everything that happens here. It's inadvisable, if not impossible, for me to leave under any circumstances. I gave up my freedom to do so when I agreed to take this position. Abandoning my post, even briefly, could mean destruction on a scale you can't even imagine. Bastion is imbued with the magical essence of every mage on Krynn. If it fails, every one of them is diminished by it. I can't take that responsibility lightly."

Despite his words, Guerrand was obviously struggling to find some concession. He gripped Bram's hand. "I promise you, Bram, I'll use all my skills to discover what I can about this sickness. It's the best I can do."

Bram sighed heavily. He didn't like quarrels as a rule, didn't have the energy to spend on them. Still, he couldn't help saying, "I just thought that the Uncle Rand I remembered would want to know about his family and would have at least tried to return to help. But I can see he's moved beyond that now."

Bram pushed himself up by the knees. "You'll excuse my rudeness, then, but I've already wasted too much time pursuing this avenue. I'll be out of your way if you'll signal Justarius or Par-Salian and tell them I won't be needing a full day here. Do you think they'd know a way to send me back to Thonvil that's faster than walking?" Bram's last sentence was lost within a yawn, and Guerrand made him repeat it.

Looking sad and frustrated, the mage stuttered toward saying something reassuring, then gave up. "You look exhausted, Bram," he observed abruptly. "How long has it been since you've slept?"

Bram shrugged, beyond caring. "It's hard to say. My sense of time is totally twisted. Since before I left home. At any rate, it doesn't matter."

"You'll need your wits about you more than ever when you return. I insist that you stay long enough to close your eyes," said the mage, cannily adding, "I could use the time to check into a few things that may help you against this disease."

Bram only looked more resolute.

"I can arrange to have you sent directly to Thonvil," the mage offered, sweetening the pot, though his arms were crossed firmly, "but I refuse to do it until you've rested, at least briefly."

Bram shook his head, which suddenly felt heavy as stone. "I've got to get back," he mumbled, unable to keep his eyes open. He distantly wondered if he wasn't under some spell, so suddenly did the sleepiness descend. Bram hadn't the strength to resist.

Guerrand wasted no time taking his nephew's arm and leading him, droopy-eyed, through the archway to the sleeping chamber. His foot caught the strap of a scroll case Bram had set on the floor near the door when Guerrand had begun to pour the wine. Curious, Guerrand started to lift the case when Bram's eyes sparked briefly to life.

"I almost forgot," he said groggily. "The scroll in the case is for you. From Justarius."

Nodding, Guerrand toed the case to the side and helped Bram to the feather tick. The young man was asleep before his head hit Guerrand's goose-down pillow.

# Chapter Twelve

Guerrand regarded his sleeping nephew with a twinge of remorse. He'd hated to cast the spell, but Bram was in as much need of rest as Guerrand required time to think. There had to be some way to help Thonvil without abandoning his responsibilities here in Bastion. The mage snatched up the round leather tube from Justarius on his way to the library.

Guerrand settled himself behind the dark walnut desk to think. Someone was deliberately trying to connect him with the spread of Thonvil's odd plague. Guerrand had no question who that was, since he had no greater enemy than Lyim Rhistadt. The symptoms Bram had described sounded too much like Lyim's affliction to be a coincidence. This plague was revenge, pure and simple, for Guerrand's refusal to grant Lyim entrance to Bastion to cure his mutated arm.

But what an odd and evil revenge, thought Guerrand. There were too many differences between the plague and Lyim's mutation for them to be exactly the same, not to mention the convoluted way Lyim's hand was altered. The similarity reminded Guerrand too painfully of the source of the unease he'd been feeling since he'd turned Lyim away in the mercury.

Though he felt great pity for Lyim's suffering, Guerrand had no question that he had done right to forbid Lyim entrance to the stronghold. No mortal cause was worth opening the very door Bastion had been created to block. He had pledged his life to preventing a breach. He would compromise that for no one.

Still, even Guerrand's unflagging commitment to Bastion wouldn't allow him to dismiss responsibility for the plague in Thonvil. What about Kirah and the rest of his family? He couldn't stay blithely in Bastion while his nephew went back to Thonvil to suffer a hideous death. They had just found each other again. Bram had grown into a well-spoken man who reminded Guerrand not a little of himself in many respects. They held in common wavy brown hair, a slightly flattened nose, wide dark eyes, and high cheekbones. Bram seemed as determined and self-assured as Guerrand's brother Quinn had been, tempered by Guerrand's own reflective nature.

As impossible as it was for him to doom Bram, it further prayed on Guerrand's mind that the consequences of this plague reached far beyond his family and the village. What would prevent the sickness from spreading to the rest of Northern Ergoth, to the rest of the world? The end of life on Krynn simply couldn't be of lesser concern to the Council of Three than that Bastion be short a defender for a matter of days.

Guerrand had once told Kirah that he'd been wrong not to come to the family's aid, instead sending Lyim in his place. Nearly ten years later Thonvil was still paying for the misjudgment that had put Lyim on Stonecliff during Belize's attempt to enter the Lost Citadel. Guerrand could not compound the mistake by repeating it. Justarius would just have to see that stopping the spread of this magical plague was as important to the defense of magic as Guerrand's presence at Bastion. The high defender's hopes were high in that regard, considering the exception the Council had made by letting Bram into Bastion.

The thought reminded Guerrand of the scroll case from Justarius. It was unusual to receive such a formal missive from the Master of the Red Robes. He pried up the snap on the end of the tube and shook out two curled pieces of parchment inside. They fluttered to the floor. He scooped up the first and unfurled it, recognizing the large, flowing script at once.

*Guerrand,*

*Par-Salian and I have met with your nephew and find him to be of sound character. We have considered both his tale of a magical plague and your history of requests to return and help your family. Once before you were given a choice between your magic and your family, and we both know the outcome of that unfortunate incident. Therefore, Par-Salian and I have agreed to grant you a short leave-of-absence, if you will, to deal with this situation back in Northern Ergoth, if it is your judgment as high defender that Bastion is secure. Since the teleport spell does not function between planes, I have imbued this scroll with the ability to transport both you and your nephew to wherever you require on the Prime Material Plane, thus saving your spell energy for more dire events. Good luck.*

*—Justarius*

Guerrand leaned back among the cushions, stunned. Both he and Justarius had come a long way in their thinking since Guerrand's days as an apprentice in Palanthas.

The mage tossed the curled parchment onto the dark surface of his desk. He had much to do before he could depart for Thonvil. First, he must leave explicit instructions with Dagamier and Ezius. Dagamier would undoubtedly remind Guerrand she'd run the place long before he came along, but the high defender was ever careful to establish his authority with the ambitious black wizardess. Once Bastion was as secure as he could make it in his absence, Guerrand would be free to consider the components and spellbooks he should take back with him to Thonvil.

Reaching into a desk drawer, the mage snatched up quill and parchment and began to scratch a list of instructions for Dagamier and Ezius. He was on his second page when he heard the baying of the hounds. Guerrand snapped alert. The three defenders had responded in drills to the simulated sound of the hounds, to condition themselves to be ever ready against attack. But the high defender had ordered no drill today.

Guerrand jumped to his feet and raced out the door of the library. He ran into his nephew as Bram staggered into the hallway, blinking away sleep.

"What's going on?"

"Either the stronghold's guardians are fighting again, or something is trying to enter Bastion's plane." Guerrand didn't stop as he tore down the hallway, headed for the scrying sphere in the nave, Bram at his heels.

Dagamier was at her turn at the watch, standing anxiously in the small doorway of the column, which had activated the bridge to form over the moat. She was speaking agitatedly with the white-haired Ezius when Guerrand ran up to them.

"Are the gargoyles and hounds at it again?" the high defender asked hopefully.

Dagamier's expression was tight, her lips pinched. "No. Something else is just beyond the fence, stirring up the hounds."

"But how can that be?" demanded Guerrand, hands on his hips, his expression horrified. "How did something get this close to Bastion without detection in the sphere?"

Dagamier looked pointedly at Ezius. "I'm sure *I* don't know."

"I swear I didn't take my eyes from the diorama for a heartbeat!" breathed Ezius. "Nothing registered in the perimeter until the hounds started baying!"

Guerrand frowned his annoyance. "This is no time for recriminations. We'll use drill two, but this isn't a practice." Dagamier and Ezius exchanged glances. "Quickly now!" thundered Guerrand.

Dagamier seemed about to protest, since drill two dictated she remain at watch in the sphere, but she nodded reluctantly. In accordance with the strategy, Ezius raced off to the white wing to gather components before positioning himself on the watch walk outside Bastion's white wing.

"Where should I go?" Bram asked behind Guerrand, startling the mage.

"Back to my apartments," said the high defender. Saving his spell energy for what lay ahead, Guerrand didn't teleport the short distance, but instead headed on foot to the red wing to collect his own magical equipment.

Bram ran at his side to the laboratory. "You don't really expect me to go back to sleep, do you? Perhaps I can help."

"Frankly, and I mean no offense," Guerrand said distractedly while he scraped flasks and pouches directly into the sack he held to the lab's shelves, "we three defenders have practiced for defense. I don't see that there's much you can do but get in the way of that. You have no magical skill to defend yourself, and I'd have to spend my thoughts worrying about your safety."

"I'm not totally useless," his nephew said. "I managed to find you, didn't I?"

Guerrand grasped Bram by the his well-muscled shoulders and gave him five heartbeats of his attention. He had hoped to anger Bram enough to put him off, and had planned another short speech to refuse his help. But then the mage saw the determination in his nephew's eyes.

"All right," he sighed, "but stay low behind me, and do exactly as I tell you, *when* I tell you." He gave Bram a brief, bittersweet smile. "I'd rather face four seasoned mages than Rietta with the news that I'd let something happen to you."

With that, he patted Bram on the back, grabbed the sack stuffed with spell components, and bolted back down the hall. He practically kicked in the door to the storeroom, then squeezed himself sideways between the right wall and the floor-to-ceiling shelves, seeking the stairway to the red wing's watch walk.

Guerrand located the secret release, the door slid back, and he plunged up the steps. Another door flew open at the top and both men emerged into the windless, dark air outside Bastion. Guerrand stopped briefly and listened for the exact location of the hounds: they were just beyond the front gate. With Bram still at his heels, he took the left branch of the narrow widow's walk that circled the exterior of the nave.

They came to the wider balcony at the front of Bastion, above the apse and behind the facade. Guerrand reached into his sack and withdrew several rings and bracelets. He immediately slipped one of each on, then handed the same to Bram. "Get down, and stay down," he commanded his nephew. Donning the ring and bracelet without question or even knowing why, the young man reluctantly dropped to his knees, where he peered through the wrought-iron bars into the darkness.

Guerrand scanned the nearby pointed gables of the white wing and the smooth, flat ledges of the red and black sections. The hideous, winged creatures who posed as downspouts on the stronghold were in place, eyes shifting watchfully. The shadows of topiaries in the courtyard were as frightening as ever, but looked undisturbed.

All signs of intrusion still came from beyond the ornate wrought-iron fence. No longer muffled by Bastion's walls, the sounds of snarling, shrieking hounds cut both men to the core. The vicious barking and snapping changed abruptly to high-pitched squeals of pain, then nothing. The silence that followed was deafening.

Heart hammering, Guerrand looked for Ezius above the white wing to his left. He was reassured by the mage's presence, but he prayed to Lunitari that he would not have to witness Ezius's skills in battle now.

"What's happening? Where are the hounds?" whispered Bram.

"Dead." Guerrand knew it as surely as he knew anything. Only death would have silenced their howls.

Several anxious moments passed before a burst of flame cleared away a knot of brush before the fence. As the smoke and ashes parted, Guerrand saw a man riding on the back of a hell hound. The creature, obviously in torment, quivered beneath the man's cruel grip. But the shock of this sight was nothing compared to the surge of adrenalin in the high defender's system when he recognized Lyim Rhistadt on the monster's back.

Guerrand recalled the Council's edict to capture intruders for tribunal whenever possible. He fired a telepathic message to the white mage, who was already rummaging in his pack in preparation of a spell.

*Hold off firing, Ezius, until my command.* The high defender saw the pale-haired mage nod, though Ezius's expression was obviously puzzled.

"Good evening, Guerrand," Lyim said conversationally. "Or is it morning here?" He swung the beast beneath him around like a horse, though it belched flames. "It's impossible to tell."

"I see you've defied the odds and found your way here." Guerrand cursed his voice for shaking. "What is it you expect to get for your trouble, Lyim?"

"Men give up many things willingly," proclaimed Lyim. "Their fortunes, their loves, their dreams . . . Power, never. It must be taken. You gave up all those things for power, Guerrand. Your power here at Bastion robbed me of the chance to restore my hand and my life to normal. Now I've come to seize your power." The hell hound fidgeted beneath Lyim. "But then, you knew the answer to your question before you asked it."

"And you know the answer I will give," Guerrand said evenly. "I cannot and will not violate the laws of Bastion for any mage."

"Not even for an old friend who gave his hand for your life?"

"We've gone over this, Lyim," Guerrand said grimly. "To do what you ask would put every mage on Krynn at risk. I would give my hand for yours, if I could, but I cannot grant entrance to Bastion. Only the Council of Three can do that. Did you petition them as I suggested?"

"I told you before, asking those three wouldn't have

done any good." Lyim laughed bitterly. "It would only have tipped my hand, so to speak. They would have been watching me, and then I couldn't have followed the nephew who cowers behind you."

Lyim chuckled again at the sight of Guerrand's surprise. "Of course I know about Bram's presence here, Rand. I attached myself to the slipstream of the spell that sent him here. Now I find myself in the awkward position of being thankful that the Council made an exception for him that they would never have made for me."

"The Council didn't let Bram in for his sake, but for the welfare of Northern Ergoth and beyond," said Guerrand. "That's the difference between you and the Council. For the sake of one person—yourself—you spread a deadly plague in Thonvil."

"Never defend, that's always been my motto," said Lyim, idly twisting the gemstone he wore in his left earlobe. "You must seize what you want from life. If destroying everything you ever cared about was the only way to draw you out of Bastion, then it was worth it to me. Unfortunately, you seemed neither to notice, nor to care, nor to act."

Guerrand held his anger in check with great effort, unwilling to let it cloud his thinking or his judgment. He clung to the hope that Lyim would surrender. "So you intend to storm Bastion, one mage against three. That sounds like suicide."

"Whether or not we fight here has always been up to you, Rand, but beware. I am much more powerful and cunning than when we were apprentices," warned Lyim.

"You blocked detection from our scrying," observed Guerrand, just beginning to understand the measure of the other wizard's skill.

Lyim lifted the lapels of the transparent cloak that

covered his red robe. "I make it a point to plan for all possibilities and seize all chances."

He pretended to be struck with a sudden thought. "Speaking of opportunities, did Bram tell you that your sister Kirah is looking well, despite the plague?"

"You saw Kirah?" demanded Bram, standing. "When?"

Lyim pretended to tick off time mentally. "It must have been two days ago. Kirah was the one who told me you had gone to Wayreth to find your uncle," Lyim explained blithely. "She's such a trusting soul. Seems a bit smitten with me, if I'm not mistaken. You needn't worry about Kirah, though. I gave her a bottle of the antidote." He paused and tapped his chin with his only index finger. "Or was that the bottle with the plague?" He shrugged. "I guess I should have marked them better when I brought the disease to Thonvil from Mithas."

Guerrand could contain his rage no longer. "Are you trying to make me kill you?"

Lyim's friendly facade slipped away, and he looked deadly serious. "Whether I battle my way into Bastion to use the portal to the Lost Citadel or you kill me first, I'll finally be free of this hideous arm. My life is already worse than death, so I have nothing to lose. The time has come to settle this once and for all, Rand."

The hell hound beneath Lyim howled and twitched. Abruptly it transformed into the steely likeness of a bull that towered above Lyim's head as he floated easily to the ground. Its eyes glowed a fiercer red than even the hell hound's had, and when it pawed the ground, Guerrand could feel all of Bastion shudder. Foul-looking vapors blasted and curled from its nostrils with each exhalation.

*Stage two*, Guerrand mentally commanded Ezius, who stood waiting impatiently above the white wing.

Guerrand had never been face-to-face with a gorgon

before, but he recognized it from books of mythical creatures. At a gesture from the high defender, the gargoyles swooped from their perches to attack. Guerrand knew they stood little chance against this terrible beast, but perhaps they could buy some time while the mages prepared a defense. There was a chance, being living stone already, the gargoyles would not be affected by the gorgon's petrifying breath.

With deafening roars the monsters met and clashed. But Guerrand's attention was already elsewhere. With deft movements and softly muttered words he etched an intricate pattern of lights in the air before him to re-inforce Bastion's ever-present wards. The same lights, in the same pattern, redrew themselves around the exterior of Bastion. There they were suspended, puls-ing, around and above the building and its defenders.

Dagamier's spells fired from the top of the black wing would provide invaluable help, but protections on the scrying sphere prevented Guerrand from send-ing her a telepathic message. The mage turned to Bram. "Go to the scrying chamber and tell Dagamier to begin drill three. Hurry!"

Bram bolted for the trapdoor and dived through it just as a magical bolt of some sort tossed from Lyim's hand hit the facade where Bram had been sheltering, sending fragments flying past his heels.

Guerrand was in the midst of casting a protective spell on himself when chunks of the wall slammed into his legs and abdomen. He was knocked to the walk-way and bloodied. He cursed the wasted spell, only half cast.

A quick glance below revealed Lyim hovering waist-high above the ground, surrounded by shimmering bands of multicolored light. On the roof of the white wing, Ezius pointed a wand into the courtyard and mouthed several words. Even through the shielding magic of Guerrand's rings and bracers, he felt the blast of heat as three successive balls of fire exploded below. Guerrand had to turn his face away from the blinding light that flared from red to yellow to unbearable white. Three thunderclaps shook the building as blistering air seared past.

The courtyard was a swirling tumult of smoke and ashes outlined by the twisted remains of the fence, now glowing red-hot. The gorgon and several gargoyles lay blackened on the charred ground. Even before the smoke settled, Guerrand could hear the laugh he remembered so well. "Nothing is so predictable as a lawful white wizard with a wand," Lyim declared.

He counterattacked by tossing a small pouch into the air. At a wave of Lyim's hand the pouch streaked toward Ezius and burst open above the white mage, raining a fine dust down over him. A circular sweep of Ezius's hand created a shield above him that kept the flakes off. As the dust settled, the shield sizzled and popped. It was already breaking into chunks by the time Ezius flung it over the parapet and scurried away from the few remaining flecks of dust.

Out of the right corner of his vision, Guerrand saw Dagamier and Bram scramble onto the watch walk of the black wing. If Lyim hasn't noticed her, he thought, perhaps she can catch him off guard as drill three is intended to. Dagamier wasted no time in trying; one hand, small and slender, made a circling gesture. A thin, silvery ray of tremendous cold flashed from her hand across the blasted scene. Like Ezius's fireball, the attack struck the bands of scintillating color enclosing Lyim. But this time it looked like some of the spell's energy pierced Lyim's globe, as the leering red mage appeared to wince under the ray's probing fingers.

Lyim was quick to react. With practiced speed he began casting a spell to shore up his weakened defenses. The magical chant created new energy, but it had to be woven into the protective bands with Lyim's good left hand. The physical gestures were complex. As Lyim worked, the snake snapped at his left hand, biting it just behind the thumb. Reflexively Lyim's left hand jerked back, spoiling the spell.

Hoping to capitalize on what might be only a moment's advantage, Guerrand quickly created a gigantic hand, formed entirely of magical energy. The hand took shape behind Lyim. Immediately its outstretched fingers wrapped around the mage and squeezed.

At first, the hand seemed to have no affect, was unable to penetrate Lyim's colored bands. But the weak point had not been repaired, and one by one the bands burst, showering the area with a rainbow of sparks. As each band ruptured, Lyim's face grew more red and more fearful. At the last moment, the look of terror and pain on his face burned itself into Guerrand's memory. His scream rose to an inhuman pitch, then abruptly cut off.

Guerrand willed the magical hand to release Lyim's body; the other mage slumped to Bastion's dark and murky ground.

Ezius was the nearest, and so was the first to cautiously approach the fallen mage. Guerrand, and Dagamier with Bram, watched from high above on the walks. Slowly the white mage advanced across the courtyard. Pausing at a distance of several paces, Ezius withdrew a crystal lens from a fold of his robe and held it to his eye. For many moments he inspected the body. Satisfied at last, he stepped up to Lyim and nudged him with his toe, waiting for many long moments. When Ezius looked up to the high defender, no announcement was necessary.

Guerrand stumbled backward a step, a hand to his throat in disbelief. Lyim was dead. After all the drills they had performed, the defenders' three-pronged attack had worked—perhaps too well. The high defender realized now that some part of him had still hoped to take Lyim alive. Then Guerrand remembered that Lyim had fatally poisoned many without thought, and his brief feeling of loss abruptly changed to a sense of justice done. Lyim's bitterness had driven him to measures beyond redemption.

Dagamier had joined Ezius in the courtyard below. Guerrand cast a featherfall spell on both himself and Bram, and they drifted down next to the other defenders.

Ezius's face was smudged with the soot of spells. Squinting through his thick, dusty spectacles, he said, "There must be no burial ceremony for one such as he. I have some experience with coroners' techniques. If you wish, I'll attend to him."

Bram spoke up. "I think you should let him, Rand. I need you to send me back to Thonvil immediately after what this Lyim said about Kirah. How did he even know her?"

"Kirah met him once, years ago," Guerrand explained distantly, "when Lyim came to Castle DiThon in my stead. I, too, got the feeling that she was taken with him."

Bram frowned at the revelation. "The villagers all say she waits by the sea for a lover. . . ."

"If Kirah ran into Lyim again, she would have trusted him with her life," Guerrand said softly, his gaze far away and very sad.

"Do you believe he spoke truly," asked Dagamier, "or was he just trying to goad you into attacking?"

Guerrand shook his head. "I believe Lyim would have done anything to further his own ends."

Bram squared his shoulders. "Do what you must, then, to send me back immediately."

Guerrand thought of Esme, of his little sister Kirah

and the innocent villagers of Thonvil, as he watched
Ezius drag the dead body of the friend who had become his adversary up the stairs to the nave. The gem
in Lyim's ear stud caught the light from several small
fires still burning in the courtyard. It seemed somehow
fitting that Lyim's death had given Guerrand greater
freedom of mind to face disasters of Lyim's creation.

"We'll go together, Bram." The announcement of
Guerrand's earlier decision surprised his nephew. The
high defender was rewarded with a grateful smile and
a joyous pat on the back. Dagamier nodded her acceptance of his decision, with the usual mysterious light in
her eyes as she followed the two men back into Bastion.

# Chapter Thirteen

Kirah awoke at first light with an inexplicable sense of well-being she had not felt in a long time. She bounded from her feather tick, feet dancing over the cold floor, seeking her worn boots. Jamming her feet into the things, more mud than good leather now, she stoked the fire with just one small piece of wood to keep the cinders burning while she toiled in the bakery below.

Kirah had secretly done work for the baker's wife for some time. Glammis hadn't been thrilled with the idea of Cormac DiThon's crazy sister working for him, let alone living in the room above his bakery. But his wife, Deeander, had taken pity on Kirah and offered her room and board in exchange for sweeping floors, changing the rushes occasionally, and the odd bit of sewing and mending.

Kirah wasn't happy Glammis had died from the

plague, for the baker had been a kindly man, despite his prejudices. Still, she was happy that his passing had given her the opportunity for work that was more to her liking than the tedium of ordinary household chores. Today she would bake bread, until the flour ran out, that is.

Kirah shrugged on her dirt-stiffened clothing—old hose and the thin shift Deeander had given her—then gnawed off a small piece of hardtack and gulped some soured milk before skipping down the stairs to the bakery.

She bypassed the open front door and took the alleyway to avoid the patrons. Two meager, half-filled sacks of ground spelt flour were propped against the back door, left by Wilton Sivesten, the miller's son. Normally, the bakery would receive five times that amount each day, but the mill had slowed its production considerably since the death of the miller. Frankly, there were far fewer people in the village to buy the bakery's products, anyway.

Kirah asked herself why she should be feeling so light of heart when things in Thonvil seemed their grimmest. She didn't have to look far for the answer. Lyim. He had miraculously arrived in her life for the second time, bringing hope.

Once Kirah had had an endless amount of hope. Hope and two loyal brothers. But first Quinn left, then Guerrand, taking with him the last of her hope. All she'd had left was belief in herself. Even that had proved insufficient in Gwynned.

As usual, Kirah turned her mind away from that unspeakable time. There was something pleasant to ponder now. Lyim cared enough about her to travel far with the cure. She still had difficulty believing Guerrand had caused this plague, but where was he, if he was so innocent?

Kirah stepped into the stone-block baking room and looped a broad, white apron nearly twice about her narrow waist. She didn't wait for Deeander to tell her the day's tasks—they seldom varied. Besides, the baker's widow was undoubtedly busy in the front room, selling the last of yesterday's yield.

First, Kirah stoked the two brick ovens, raking out the ashes to prepare the hot floor for the loaves she would prepare next. When she was satisfied with the level of heat, Kirah went to the long marble baking table and carefully lowered the cloth-covered bowl of fermented bread starter from a high shelf. She tossed a wooden scoopful of the goopy, sour-smelling stuff into an enormous mixing bowl. To that she added coarse, brown spelt from one of the new sacks (there was no one who could afford fine white loaves, even if they could get the flour), a pinch of sea salt, and a large ladleful of warm well water from the cauldron that always hung above the fire pit. Kirah mixed it around with her bare hands, squeezing the concoction between her fingers.

Next came her favorite part. Sprinkling the marble table with a frugal amount of flour, she flung the stringy mixture onto it, pushed her sleeves past her elbows, then began to furiously knead the dough. It was the color of coarse, undyed cotton, with dark flecks of brown. Kirah counted to three hundred while she pushed and prodded the stuff around the table. When she was at last satisfied with the soft feel of it, Kirah chopped the dough into thirds with a sharp knife. Fashioning each into a perfectly round ball, she placed them one, two, three on the flat shovel end of a long, wooden peel and gently lowered them upon the hot oven floor. With a quick tug, she yanked the peel from under the bread and withdrew it from the heat before the wood could char.

Brushing the leftover flour from her hands, Kirah surveyed her work with satisfaction. Three loaves in the oven in no time at all. A wisp of hair fell across her face, and she looked at it cross-eyed before trying to blow it back. The strands stuck upon her sweaty forehead. Funny, she thought, scraping them away with the back of her hand, I don't feel hot enough to sweat. If anything, she felt a little chilly, despite her strenuous efforts at the kneading table. Must be the heat of the ovens, she decided.

Kirah was preparing to mix a batch of pie crust when Deeander pushed back the curtain to the front room.

The stout woman's face was pale with strain as she looked upon the loaves in the brick oven. "I would have stopped you had I heard you come in." She shook her head sadly. "Every day there are fewer and fewer to come and buy bread. I have yet to sell yesterday's loaves."

"People still have to eat," Kirah said.

"What people?" barked the baker's wife, her patience suddenly snapping like a lute string. "Have you looked outside today? Have you seen the bodies of stone stacked head to toe upon the green because they can't dig graves fast enough to bury the dead anymore?" Bright spots of angry red mottled her fleshy face. "Why do we make bread to sustain people who will only die horrible deaths within the week?"

"With that line of reasoning," said Kirah, "you could ask why *ever* feed someone? They will only die in forty or fifty years anyway." Her expression turned serious. "Because to *not* feed people is to ensure their deaths, that's why."

The baker woman's bosom heaved, and she wearily lowered herself into a flour-flecked chair. "It's just that I've given up hope. I see no reason nor end for this disease. Sometimes I wish it would just take me and end the waiting!"

"Don't ever say that!" Kirah gasped, looking over her shoulder to see if the woman's young son had heard her, but there was no sign of him. "You have Dilb to think about."

"It's about him that I worry endlessly," the woman confessed. "How can I keep the plague from him, when I don't know how to keep it from myself?"

Kirah massaged the woman's thick shoulder, hoping to impart strength. She wished that she could give the woman the hope she herself felt, but the town had never been trusting of mages. She would just have to wait until Lyim returned with enough antidote for everyone, then hope the townspeople would follow her example and take the cure.

"Make no more bread, and take the rest of the day off," Deeander instructed her, pushing herself up to return to the front room in hopes that someone would come to buy bread. "I'll watch the loaves you've made."

Kirah cleared the marble pastry table. Removing her apron, she hung it on a hook and wondered what she would do to fill her day. She wished Lyim would return soon, for reasons that had nothing to do with cures. He'd left two days ago to get enough antidote for the rest of the village. She missed him more than she was comfortable admitting, torn between an expectation too strong and fear of disappointment. Suddenly she could not sit still—not for a moment—leaving her in an itching agony.

She would stop by the inn. Surely Lyim would stay there when he returned with the cure. Kirah polished the bottom of a pie pan with a coarse sleeve and checked her reflection. Her face was sweaty and her hair lank. With clumsy, untrained hands, she braided the pale blond strands into one long plait that rested on her right shoulder.

Pulling on a loose, scratchy woolen cape, Kirah stepped out into the narrow, filthy alley and shivered. She hadn't remembered the air feeling so cold. Thankfully, the Red Goose Inn was only two thatched buildings and a vegetable patch down the street, across from the green. She would warm herself by the fire there before checking with the innkeeper. Kirah rounded the corner and emerged into the sunlight.

She had kept to her room and the bakery since Lyim left and was amazed at the change a few days made in the village. Never prosperous, it looked nearly deserted now. The taint of decay was everywhere, including the shabby, boarded-up shop fronts. The breeze carried the scent of burning flesh; she'd heard people were now cremating the husks of skin that victims shed on the second day of the disease, in hopes of stopping its spread. The greatest shock came from the sight of bodies piled upon the green, as Deeander had said, waiting for burial.

Without realizing it, Kirah had slowed her pace until she was barely moving. The horror of the stacked bodies was riveting. Human torsos and faces frozen in terror and pain intermixed with a mass of snakes that still seemed to writhe, in spite of being stone. She did not look closely enough at the faces to recognize anyone, but it was clear that many of the dead were children and infants. Snake bodies lay on the grass, broken off from limbs by careless or hurried handling. It was a scene from a nightmare, a charnel pit of snakes squirming over and between the corpses of the tormented dead.

Kirah yanked her gaze away from the horrid stack and covered her eyes. She had become suddenly light-headed and waited several seconds for the dizziness to pass. Her gaze went wide to the right, over a fallow vegetable patch and to the fields that surrounded Thonvil. Unharvested corn stood exposed in sodden patches, where the previous winter's steady north wind had bent the old stalks until they trailed the ground like willow branches. Kirah spied a shape trudging through the distant fields, bent almost double beneath a load. She couldn't see whether it was man, woman, or child, but she didn't hail the person, for it was enough to know there was at least one other person in the world who had not yet stopped his life for the plague.

Kirah hastened up the steps to the inn. The smell of decay seemed to vanish here, replaced by the scent of damp ashes. The hearth had just been cleaned. So much for warming myself before the fire, Kirah sighed inwardly.

No one was inside the large taproom. Kirah waited for the innkeeper at the tall counter, where the dark, pitted wood of the bar met the back wall. Feeling a little queasy of a sudden, she lowered herself upon a stool. The muscles of her shoulders, neck, and lower back had begun to ache. It was probably a good thing that Deeander had given her the day off, she decided. She'd obviously been overdoing it at the bakery.

Growing impatient, Kirah rapped her knuckles upon the hard wooden bar. Cold, despite the perspiration between her shoulder blades, Kirah shivered her thin cape closer, as if a bird rearranging its feathers.

"Hallooo?" she called toward the kitchen door when her knuckles were sore from banging.

At length a thin, shiny-pated man in his middle years pushed through the swinging door, wiping his hands on a filthy apron, a look of suspicious surprise on his face. His inn had not seen the likes of Kirah DiThon before, either as lord's daughter or crazy woman. Llewen knew her only by reputation.

"If you're here to break fast or for noon lunch, I'm afraid all we have is a few of yesterday's greasy turnips," Llewen confessed. "There's no meat to be found in the town."

"I'm not here to eat," said Kirah. "I'm looking for someone who probably stayed here recently and is expected to return any day. He's tall, with long, dark, wavy hair. He was wearing a dark brown robe."

The innkeeper raised his eyebrows at the word "he." Everyone in town believed the story of crazy Kirah waiting for the return of a lover who didn't exist. "What's his name?" Llewen asked.

Kirah saw the disapproving curiosity in the man's watery eyes. "Either you've seen the man I've described or you haven't. Which is it?"

"Haven't," he said, shaking his head. "Nobody's come to Thonvil or stayed at the inn since word of the sickness spread."

"But that's not possi—" Kirah began, then stopped. Lyim was a mage; perhaps he had magiced himself up a place to stay. "Thank you," she said weakly, turning to leave. She felt hot and limp. "Have you a cup of water, please? I'm not feeling quite right."

The man looked at her in alarm and stepped back from the bar warily.

She saw his fear through bleary eyes. "Don't worry, it's not the plague," she muttered, though the world began to spin crazily. "I can't be getting the plague, you see . . ." Kirah didn't finish the sentence, because she had slouched, unconscious, to the floor.

\* \* \* \* \*

Guerrand did one last run-through in his mind about the state of security at Bastion. He had given a hastily jotted list of instructions to Dagamier. Ezius had replaced her in the scrying sphere after removing Lyim's body from the courtyard and taking it to the white wing to prepare it for burial. She'd taken the piece of parchment reluctantly, and only after he insisted. Though she might have run things well enough before Guerrand arrived, he was responsible for Bastion now, even during his absence.

Satisfied that he had done all he could to ensure smooth running of things during his leave, Guerrand used the scroll Justarius had sent for the purpose of teleporting Bram, Zagarus, and himself back to Thonvil. The moment the words inscribed on the scroll left his lips, Guerrand felt a brief disorientation, like he was a scrap of paper in the draft of a chimney, flaming and floating, weightless. But it was only for a moment, and then his eyes were readjusting to daylight on the main street of Thonvil. He, Bram, and Zagarus stood before the open door of the bakery.

Turning, Guerrand accidently stepped on one of Zagarus's webbed feet.

The bird squawked angrily. *Watch where you're going, oaf.*

"What's eating you?" Guerrand asked him silently. "I thought you'd be happy to leave Bastion for a trip back to Thonvil. You're always complaining about living there."

*Yeah, well, I don't want to get too used to sky and earth again, since we'll be returning to that shadow box we call home too soon,* the bird huffed. The look in his beady dark eyes abruptly softened. Guerrand could see that Zag was merely covering his own trepidation with bluster.

Uncomfortable with his master's scrutiny, Zagarus told Guerrand that he was going to the cove to see if anyone from the old days was still alive.

Guerrand watched the old gull lumber into the air

and flap stiffly toward the sea. He turned in a circle, peering around with eyes that could not fathom distance or endure the sun after so long at Bastion. Before Rand could get more than a whiff of decay and an impression of Thonvil's general squalor, Bram took his hand and dragged him up the open flight of stairs next to the door embellished with a sign carved in the likeness of a steaming loaf.

"Kirah!" Bram cried, banging his fist on the door to his aunt's room. "Come on, Kirah, it's Bram. I'm back with Guerrand as I promised."

"Maybe she's not home," Guerrand suggested.

"Maybe," Bram muttered. To his surprise, the door creaked open a crack. Bram pressed his eye to it, then gave that up and gave the door a hard shove with his booted toe.

The door swung back on rusty hinges. The choking stench of sweat and vomit and rotting flesh rolled out in a cloud. Bram tore into the room ahead of Guerrand. "We're too late!" he cried.

Blood pounded at Guerrand's temples as he followed Bram into the cold, fireless room. He found his nephew on his knees at the side of a small rope bed. Unceremoniously dumped upon the dirty feather tick was someone he barely recognized.

"Bram?" she whispered, blinking in disbelief. Kirah's eyes had always looked like the sort created to house mysteries, but now they seemed no more than the soft, unseeing eyes of a cow at graze. Her once-blond hair was ash-colored and damp about her emaciated face. It looked to have been braided, but fuzzy hanks had been rubbed out of the plait in back. Her clothing was worse than a beggar woman's and beginning to rip at the sleeves.

"Yes, it's me, Kirah," Bram said, choking back a sob. "When did you get sick?"

"I . . . don't know," she said haltingly. "The last thing I remember I was at the Red Goose Inn, asking for some water. I was so cold." She shivered, remembering. "I must have had the flu because I feel much better now."

Bram looked over his shoulder. The two men exchanged worried looks.

Guerrand stepped forward into his sister's view. "Hello, Kirah." Guerrand hoped his expression held the right shade of sympathy touched by the diffidence due an estranged member of one's family.

She started, then weakly pushed herself up onto her elbows. "It *is* you. Well, well," she said caustically. "Frankly, I'm surprised you found the time for us, but I guess history *does* repeat itself. Once again, you've made it back too late to help most of Thonvil. And, once again, your old friend, Lyim, squeezed us into his schedule."

"Did you swallow the concoction he gave you?" Guerrand asked anxiously.

"Of course," she said. "Two days ago."

A cry escaped Bram's lips, a curse Guerrand's.

"Does that disappoint you, Guerrand?" asked Kirah, giving him a canny look. "That he gave me the cure to this disease you've caused?"

In the middle of her question, Guerrand had begun to shake his head in disbelief, gaining both speed and power, until his whole body shook. "Is that what Lyim told you? That I caused this plague?"

"I saw his hand," she said. "I've heard the snakes hiss your name."

A muscle twitched in Guerrand's jaw. "What would make you think I'd want to cause *anyone* to suffer such hideous deaths, let alone my family and the villagers with whom I was raised?" he demanded.

Kirah scoffed. "That question implies that I know

anything about you anymore. Lyim said you were an important mage and were trying to destroy all evidence of your humble beginnings."

Guerrand was struck dumb, and he turned away. His hands curled into fists at his side as he paced. For the first time, he was glad he'd killed Lyim. The man had poisoned his sister's body *and* mind, just to punish him. Lyim had been a master of lies.

Bram touched him on the arm, and Guerrand jumped. "From the looks of her," Bram whispered, "she had the fever yesterday." They both gave worried glances over their shoulders. Kirah was sitting up, scratching her right arm, her expression a practiced mask of carelessness.

"Are you sure she has it?" Guerrand whispered back.

Bram nodded his head reluctantly. "She's on day two, which means she's going to start shedding skin any time now. I've learned there's no point trying to stop it by tying a patient down, but it's easier on them if you can keep them on the bed." He looked at his uncle closely, then dropped his voice even more. "Do you think you'll be able to help me? It's horrifying to watch, but it's nothing compared to what will happen later."

"Of course I'll help you," Guerrand said. "That is, if she'll let me near her."

As they turned back toward Kirah, both men noticed that her casual scratching had turned to determined scraping. Her arm was covered with thick, red welts where her nails had dug into the flesh.

"Now I have this awful itch," Kirah moaned. "I really need a bath, after that fever from the flu." Her hand continued scraping back and forth on her right forearm all the while she spoke. But the scratching did nothing to relieve the itch, which only made Kirah attack the arm more ferociously.

Within moments, she was nearly frantic. "This arm, it's driving me crazy. I've never itched like this before!"

Guerrand glanced questioningly at Bram. Kirah surely must have heard the symptoms of the plague. Did she really have such faith in Lyim that she still didn't suspect his "cure"? Lyim had not been above using a magical charm on her. Or was she simply fooling herself out of fear?

"Just lie back, Kirah," Bram soothed. "We'll get a rag and some warm water. It will make you feel better."

Tears welled in Kirah's eyes and left light-colored streaks down her dirty cheeks. "Hurry, please," she pleaded, gouging ever more frantically at the raw arm.

"What's happening?" she wailed, looking down the length of her arms. Kirah's head went from side to side in shocked, old-womanish gestures.

"You have the plague, Kirah. You'll shed a layer or two of skin today," Bram explained as calmly as he was able.

"I can't have the plague!" she howled, rubbing her arms at a furious rate against the roughness of the sheets. "Lyim gave me the cure!"

"Lyim gave you the plague," Guerrand said harshly.

"I don't believe you—-I can't!" Kirah rubbed her limbs and thrashed against the bed, both men holding her to keep her on it.

"It's true," said Bram. "I heard him boast of it, Kirah."

Bram motioned Guerrand toward the wash basin for the wet rag. The older man had taken only a few steps when a piercing shriek spun him around in his tracks. Kirah was arching violently on the bed. Bram struggled to push her shoulders to the mattress. "Help me, Rand!" Bram cried. Kirah's right arm twitched horribly as she banged it over and over against the bed frame.

Guerrand dashed back to the bed and tried to grab his sister's flailing limb. "Just hold her down so she can't hurt herself worse."

Guerrand did as Bram asked and was surprised by the strength in Kirah's thin, fevered frame. Her arm struck him in the back several times, but Guerrand ignored it. A cry of anguish rent the air as the skin split along the entire length of Kirah's right forearm and hand, then slipped away in a hideous curl. She looked at the red, raw flesh beneath it with large, teary eyes. Her glance traveled to Guerrand, unable to deny the truth any longer. Kirah fell back against the soiled pillow, the need to scratch silenced for the moment. "Why?" she asked in a hollow voice. "Why would he do this? I thought he cared about me."

"He did care about you, Kirah," whispered Guerrand. "Just not as much as he hated me."

Kirah cried out again, and Bram held her tightly. He shot an anxious look over his shoulder at his uncle. "Can't you come up with some spell to lessen her pain?"

Guerrand snapped from his stupor to recall a mixture he had once given Esme when she broke her leg. He found the prerequisite herbs in his pack and hastily concocted the mixture of crushed dried peppermint leaves and cream-colored meadowsweet flowers soaked in oil of clove. He leaned in, struggling against her thrashing, and placed the tincture under Kirah's tongue. Within moments, her struggles visibly, though briefly, lessened.

"I'd like to try something else as well," Guerrand said pensively. "If this illness is magic-based, perhaps it can be dispelled."

"Do it!" urged Bram, turning back to his aunt, whose legs had begun to split now.

Guerrand reached into his pouch and withdrew a hardened leather scroll case. He popped off the lid and pulled out a heavy scroll. The spell of dispelling was a simple one to a mage of Guerrand's experience, and he had cast if from memory many times. But if this worked, he would need to cast it many more times, so he had brought along several such scrolls. Guerrand took a moment to compose himself and focus his mind, closing out Kirah's shrieks of pain. With eyes narrowed, he translated aloud the mystical symbols so precisely scribed on the parchment. As each was pronounced, it flared like a tiny wisp of paper set alight, to immediately swirl away above the scroll. Familiar magical symbols danced through his mind, organizing themselves in the proper pattern, and disappeared. Finally, Guerrand mumbled the words, "*Delu solisar*," to trigger the precisely crafted spell.

Both men held their breath as they watched. Bram's eyes darted from Kirah's legs to her face, and back to her legs again, in a nervous cycle. Guerrand sat motionless.

Finally, Bram whispered, "What's happening? Why can't I see anything?"

"Because there's nothing to see," sighed Guerrand. "If the spell had worked, it's effect would have been apparent right away. It failed."

Without a word, Bram turned back to Kirah.

When the skin was shed entirely from the first leg, she was so exhausted she lapsed into a shallow, fitful sleep. Both men knew the rest was only temporary, until her other leg began to shed. Bram joined his uncle by the cold hearth. "Is there nothing else you can try?"

Guerrand shook his head. "Despite the simplicity of the process, most magic can be dispelled. Whatever this is, it goes beyond the realm of pure magic. A multitude of forces are at work creating this disease."

"You can't even ease her pain more fully?" asked Bram, his voice far away, yet urgent.

"I can keep administering the analgesic herbs, but I'm neither a physicker nor a priest. Mine are not healing spells. I don't even understand what I'm dealing with."

"Then learn about it," charged Bram. "Walk around Thonvil and see its effects. You've got until sunset tomorrow night to come up with a cure. That's when Kirah's limbs will turn to snakes and her eyes to onyx."

Guerrand nodded. "Of course."

Bram saw the brief flash of guilt and self-doubt cloud his uncle's face. "These people will not be cured by your guilt, but by your wits and your sweat," he said. "Whatever decisions led Lyim to his actions, you are to blame for what happens here *only* if self-pity keeps you from working to cure what he caused."

Guerrand regarded his nephew with a new respect. The mage resolved to do whatever he could, leave no magical concept untried, to keep his sister from turning to stone. Her next round of pain-racked screams began as her second leg began to shed its skin, reminding the mage that he had very little time.

# Chapter Fourteen

Strangely, the sky on the afternoon of Nuindai, the twenty-ninth day of Mishamont, was clearer, warmer, brighter than Guerrand remembered for spring on the island of Northern Ergoth. Or perhaps it was because any amount of sunlight seemed glaring to the mage after the gloom of Bastion.

Still, light seemed not to reach the streets where Guerrand walked in the silence of a dying village. No blessed breeze blew away the stench of shed skins left to rot wherever they fell. Guerrand looked all ways with his eyes but had difficulty concentrating over the pain in his heart.

The mage felt certain any clue to the plague's cure lay with the symptoms themselves. He needed to see the plague and all its ramifications firsthand. His dread of witnessing such pain was lessened only by his determination to end it.

Guerrand saw a few people trudging at a distance, dirty rags wrapped around their faces and feet, as if old linen could keep the sickness from invading their skin. Their heads they kept low, fearful that a polite meeting of eyes was invitation enough to the plague. The street and stoops were littered with the leavings of life, most of the shops closed, unswept, some of them boarded over. Bram had warned him of the village's growing dereliction, that some of the closures had occurred before the plague, but the warning did little to lessen the blow of seeing Thonvil so deserted. There was not even a dog or pig or chicken in sight, where once the street had daily seemed like a small spring fair.

Three mud huts, their roofs and timbers burned, huddled at the edge of the village. Guerrand looked over them, to where a thick, black flame licked the light blue sky. He vaguely remembered Bram saying Herus had advised the burning of clothing, tools, even the homes of plague victims in a futile attempt to stop the spread of what he didn't know at the time was a magical illness.

Guerrand's head snapped left at the sound of a wagon in the street. It was a trundling green thing pulled by an old, sway-backed horse. Two people sat upon the seat: one a young boy, the other of an age with Guerrand and vaguely familiar. Both jumped to the dirt road and clambered around the wagon. Removing one side, they began to unceremoniously shove one of the heavy, stone bodies piled in the cart to the soft, greening ground of the square.

"Hey, ain't we supposed to take these to the field on the north edge of town?" posed the younger of the two, who could be no more than ten years of age. "No more room here, and no one to dig holes for 'em anyway."

The father straightened his spine above the stone-stiff bodies in the wagon and rubbed his lower back. "Who cares where they go, boy? Dead's dead," he pronounced. "The plague wouldn't a took 'em if they was good people, anyway. Not like us." He thumped his chest. "You 'n me been spared, boy, so's we get the pick of the houses they don't burn. You make sure everything valuable was off 'em?"

The boy nodded, patting a pouch at his waist.

Horrified by what he was witnessing, Guerrand tried to place the face and voice that seemed so familiar. Suddenly it came to him.

"Wint?" Guerrand called to the man, recalling him as the younger of the bullies he had chased from this very square for stoning a woman they claimed was a witch.

The man swung around in surprise at the sound of any voice. Thin lips drew back in recognition, exposing big box teeth. "You!" he gasped. Wint hooked his thumbs through his belt and cocked one scrawny hip in an effort to portray indifference. "They said you was dead, but I heard it whispered you brought this plague on us."

Guerrand looked at him levelly. "Then I'd be afraid, if I were you."

The belligerent man squinted at Guerrand, an evil grin stretching the sparse whiskers on his hawkish face. "You got no power here anymore, DiThon," he snarled. "Yer brother and sister are crazy, the whole lot up there"—he tossed his head in the direction of Castle DiThon—"they're as poor as us common folk and sealed up like mice in a tomb."

Guerrand had so little regard for the man that he couldn't bring himself to be angry.

"Got nothin' to say, without yer brother the lord to protect you, eh?" the man taunted, looking with eager pride to see if his son was impressed with his bravado.

"You're still a bully and a blowhard, I see," Guerrand observed with sigh. "Apparently you haven't the courage or brains to succeed, so you wait in shadows to feed off the work of others." Guerrand fished around in his pack of components, found his sole caterpillar cocoon, then raised his robed arms. "Perhaps it's time you saw the world through the eyes of the rat you are."

Wint's chest had puffed out indignantly, and his hands curled into fists. But when Guerrand raised his arms, the man drew back slightly, looking both confused and more than a little worried. "Whatcha doin' there? I'm warning you, stop it!"

"What's the matter, Wint? No one to protect you from the witch?" Guerrand asked. Wint's face became a mask of horror as Guerrand continued the circle he'd begun with his arms. "*Doduvas!*"

Blue and green light sparked like the hottest fire above the wagon, and where Wint had stood was now a squealing brown rat. The creature's whiskered face sniffed at the edge of the wagon, then it leaped to the ground and skittered across the road, heading for the shadows between buildings. Wint's young son took one frightened look at Guerrand, jumped from the wagon, and scrambled after his father.

The mage looked upon the faces of stone in the wagon; a youngish woman, man, and an elderly matron who resembled the man in the nose and set of the eyes. They must have been the last of a family, which was why the three were being buried by strangers.

Wint aside, so much had changed since last Guerrand was in Thonvil. He began to walk, and before long his feet led him down the twisted side streets to one in particular he had traveled many times in his youth. He tripped over something squishy. Looking down, he saw the bloated body of a dead rat. The sight propelled him on even faster.

Guerrand rounded the last corner, where the rays of the sun never reached. Wilor the silversmith's storefront came into view. Though the shutters were closed, the silversmith shop wasn't boarded up like so many of the other stores around it. Guerrand recalled briefly that his father's old adventuring crony had threatened to retire those many years ago, when Guerrand had come to retrieve a trinket for Ingrid Berwick, and to talk of his brother Quinn's casket cover.

Suddenly the mage had a nostalgic eagerness to talk to the old silversmith. Perhaps Wilor knew something about the plague that might help Guerrand.

He well remembered the metalsmith's heavy door bearing its silver unicorn; it set the stall apart from the much more practical doors of the other merchants and signified Wilor's trade. Guerrand knocked tentatively on the door, then more loudly when no one answered. When still no one came, he looked over both shoulders before tugging at the ornate door and slipping inside.

Eleven anvils were silent in the modest shop, the small furnace cold. There was none of the usual haze hanging among the exposed rafters, no glowing bits of metal anywhere. Cold, black rods lay next to many of the anvils, a testament that they had been still for some time. A crucible of tarnished silver lay clamped in a long pair of tongs, waiting for a smith's practiced hammer.

Guerrand stood remembering the last time he'd been here. It had been the second time he'd met Belize, when his life had taken such a dramatic turn. His memories of that mad wizard were not pleasant, and he turned them away. He was about to leave entirely, convinced that Wilor and his heirs had moved on, leaving everything in midproject, when he heard a low but unmistakable groaning coming from somewhere beyond the room. He followed the noise to the back of the shop, where a heavy woolen curtain hung from hooks in the ceiling.

"Hello?" Guerrand called tentatively through a crack in the curtain. "Is anyone here?"

"*Just,*" came a man's adenoidal rasp. "Who's there?"

"A . . . friend," Guerrand said, unsure if he wanted whoever was behind the curtain to know him or not.

"Come back only if you've a strong stomach."

The warning gave Guerrand pause for a moment before he pushed his way past the opening in the scratchy curtain, his lower lip clamped between his teeth expectantly. His first breath beyond it was half-choked by the stench of rotting flesh he recognized too well from Kirah's room. The mage blinked away the tears that instantly welled due to the smell.

The silversmith lay on a dirty mound of linen-covered hay in the corner of a dark room, lit in thin, muted streaks by a small window in back. The man's thick, grizzled forearms that had always reminded Guerrand of roasted meat were now six writhing snake heads. He could see that snakes also writhed beneath the blanket that covered Wilor from the waist down. The once-powerful man was shrunken and pale and crippled, and clearly would never again practice his beautiful craft.

"Guerrand DiThon, as I barely live and breath," the smith said with difficulty, surprise and pleasure evident on the pale, sunken face that the mage remembered as round and jolly. "I hadn't expected yours to be the last face I behold before Habbakuk takes me home, but I can think of none I'd rather see."

"I-I'm sorry to find you thus, Wilor," was all Guerrand could think to say. Wilor had been a short, sturdy man of immense strength from his vigorous life. His teeth were gone save one. The smith's hairline had receded even farther in the last decade and was now past the midpoint of his scalp, until only a narrow ring of salt-and-pepper hair remained.

"How is the second son of Rejik DiThon?" the smith asked, as if over shepherd's pie at the Red Goose Inn. Wilor eyed Guerrand's red robes with obvious interest.

"Well enough, Wilor," said Guerrand. What could he do but shrug his shoulders, apologizing for his healthy presence at death's grim door?

"Ah, well, *I* have been better," said the man, trying hard but not succeeding at a self-deprecating chuckle. Instead, Wilor was caught up in a choking cough that slowly subsided.

Guerrand could think of no delicate way to ask the questions that burned in his throat. "Marthe? Your sons?" he queried, looking hopefully about the dim storeroom.

Wilor didn't blink. "All dead. The boys went first, about a week ago. I wish I could have spared Marthe seeing that." His bald pate rocked from side to side. "After watching them, I considered sparing us both this, but—" He sighed from his soul. "It turns out I was too much a coward to do anything about it."

Wilor looked, unblinking, toward the window, to the sky. "Then Marthe caught the chill, and I had to stay for her." His eyes sank shut briefly, as if willing the courage for the words. "She went two nights ago. By then it was too late for me. I didn't tell Marthe, but I got the fever that afternoon and barely had the strength to bury her." Wilor bit down on his lip until it bled and a tear rolled down one wan cheek. "At least Marthe wasn't alone in the end. She got a proper laying to rest next to her sons in the field she tilled for years out back, instead of being squeezed into the green. It's all that matters now."

"I'll stay with you, Wilor."

The silversmith turned his head with great effort to

look directly at Guerrand. "You'd do that?"

Guerrand nodded heavily. "I promise to stay as long as you need me, until the Blue Phoenix comes to take you home," he vowed, invoking the Ergothian name of the god he knew the adventuring friends, Wilor and Rejik, had revered. Guerrand gained an odd sense of strength and purpose from repeating a secret promise he'd made as a seven-year-old at the deathbed of his own father.

The smith's expression contained an odd mix of gratitude and embarrassment. "The promise of Rejik DiThon's second son has always been good enough for me."

Guerrand gave him a grateful smile, then stood awkwardly, unsure what to do now, unable even to hold the dying man's hand. He ordered his reluctant feet forward to close the distance between them so that Wilor wouldn't need to strain so to speak. Suddenly the snakes hissed and snapped toward the mage. Cursing the vipers, Wilor struggled to hold them down to the bed of straw. Their tongues lashed and flickered, as if they had heard the man's sadness and were laughing. One of the heads lashed away from the rest and snatched a small, fright-eyed mouse from the shadows of the floor and swallowed the thing in one gulp.

Guerrand drew back and maintained a four-foot remove from the sick man so as not to excite the snakes again. He stared, as if mesmerized by the intricate diamond patterns behind the dark and beady eyes on their heads. Each little, slithering head recalled to Guerrand the memory of the mage who had caused this.

He circumnavigated the bed of straw to prop open both the grease-streaked window and door to let some fresher air into the sickroom. "Is there much pain, Wilor?"

Wilor seemed to realize Guerrand was not just making

idle conversation. He leaned forward and considered his bizarre new appendages. "Some, mostly when I try to control them. The change was excruciating, I'll admit, but now the snakes are more inconvenient than hurtful. I can't use my hands or feet to do anything. It's a good thing nothing itches anymore." He fell back against the straw, winded. "But it'll all be over as soon as the moons rise. There's a comfort in knowing that."

Guerrand only nodded; his repartee was not at its best today. He had often played attendant to the minor ailments of folks in Harrowdown, listening to their dilemmas and suggesting solutions both magical and not. Though this was no minor ailment, Guerrand pulled up a stool and called those long-used skills to his side.

"I'm a mage now, Wilor," Guerrand informed him softly.

"I figured that out from the robes," said the silversmith, and his glance held a covert amusement.

Guerrand reddened. "I don't know what your views on magic are," he continued somewhat hesitantly, "but I'm hoping to use my skills to find a cure. Kirah's got the plague now." Guerrand heard his own hollow voice in the quiet of the death room. "She just finished shedding the skin from her arms and legs."

Wilor bobbed his head sadly. "You've seen too much death in your life, Guerrand DiThon." The silversmith stunned Guerrand with his next words. "Use me to find the cure."

"I don't know that I can help you, Wilor," he said awkwardly.

"I'm not asking you to," Wilor nearly snapped. "Have I given you the impression I'm afraid to die?" The mage had to shake his head. "I don't wish to live without my Marthe"—he looked down at himself—"like this."

Wilor scowled when he saw Guerrand hesitate with a look of pity the mage couldn't disguise. "Don't waste time," declared the smith, looking at the slant of the light. "I'm unsure how much of that I have left."

Guerrand rummaged around in the pack he'd carried with him on his first trip from Thonvil and withdrew his much-used spellbook. Hundreds of pages had been filled with his illegible scribbling since the handful he'd painstakingly inked in secret corners of the castle and upon a potato wagon outside Wayreth.

He looked up, his lips pursed in thought. "I'm unclear about what starts the disease in some people and not others," he admitted. "Kirah said she drank something that caused the onset of the illness. Do you recall drinking anything unusual?"

Wilor creased his brow momentarily. "Just water and ale."

Guerrand scowled his frustration. "I'll bet Lyim tainted the village water, but it would help if I knew if the disease was magical in nature or simply transmitted by magic." He snapped his fingers as an easy enchantment came to mind. The mage muttered the oft-spoken words that would reveal the presence of magic in Wilor's body. He frowned when that, too, revealed no glowing emanations, nothing.

Or did it? Guerrand hastily flipped open his spellbook again, found the entry for dispelling, and traced his finger down the column of his own writing:

*Other-planar creatures are not necessarily magical. Multiple types of magic, or strong local magical emanations, may confuse or conceal weaker radiations.*

Guerrand slammed the book shut. The plague could *still* be magical in nature, despite his spell. He knew no more than he did before.

"You're getting as frustrated as some of the villagers," said Wilor. "They've come up with the craziest notions about a cure. Several tried chopping the snakes off, but they only grow back. I know of one who begged his son to poison his snake hand."

"What happened?" Guerrand asked.

"The man got violently ill from the poison," admitted Wilor, "and he still died at sunset on the third day.

"Fear is a powerful force," Wilor continued. "Shortly after the first outbreak, a group of villagers went on a rampage and killed all the snakes they could find, at Herus's suggestion. When that didn't work, they moved on to other animals."

Wilor's lips pursed with concern. "I'm afraid that those who don't die of the plague will suffer a lingering death of starvation." Abruptly, Wilor's face contorted in pain.

Guerrand shifted uneasily at the sight of Wilor's agony. "I know my spells haven't proven very impressive, but I could give you an herbal analgesic that might ease the pain."

Wilor absently nodded his approval. Guerrand quickly combined the mixture of crushed dried peppermint leaves and meadowsweet flowers soaked in oil of clove he had used to help Kirah. Resolutely ignoring the snakes, the mage quickly leaned in and placed the tincture under Wilor's tongue before the man could change his mind.

Almost immediately, Wilor's eyes took on a peaceful look, far away in time and place. "Your father would have been proud of your being a mage," he said distantly. "Rejik was more than a little interested in the art himself after he married your mother."

Guerrand's heart skipped a beat at the unexpected revelation. "I always suspected Father had more than a passing interest, from the volumes in his library."

"Zena wasn't a blue-blood like your father or his first wife," Wilor went on, as if Guerrand hadn't spoken, "but Rejik followed his heart, despite pressure to marry someone from his own class."

Guerrand knew this part of the story too well; it was the root of his conflict with his brother Cormac. Cormac's mother, of old Ergothian stock, had died of Baliforian influenza when Cormac was but eight. Ten years later, Rejik remarried a woman just two years older than his son. Zena DiThon's family had settled in Northern Ergoth just after the Cataclysm (some three hundred years before), but prejudice was rampant among the nobility. People not of the old, darker-skinned stock that had lived in Ergoth proper, before the Cataclysm split the region into two islands, were considered newcomers.

The smith's head shook. "You suffered for their union as much, if not more, than they—you and Quinn and Kirah. Especially after Rejik died. Between you and me," Wilor whispered, leaning forward conspiratorially, though no one was around to hear what had long stopped mattering to town folk anyway, "Zena was twice the woman Cormac's mother was, blue blood be damned."

Wilor fell back against the rustling straw, an odd smile lighting his face. "You get your magical skill from Zena, you know," he confided. "Her gypsy blood runs in your veins. She was a pale-skinned, sprightly miss with hair like Solinari's light, and just as enchanting. 'One with the magic of the earth,' was how Rejik described Zena. He was bewitched by her every day of their marriage."

"I . . . never knew any of that," breathed Guerrand. "Father refused to talk about Mother after she died."

Wilor managed a half-shrug. "It was the grief." He closed his eyes. "I know now what it can do to a man."

It was obvious to Guerrand that the tincture had loosened Wilor's tongue, as well as his hold on his emotions. The smith seemed to *need* to talk, as if he realized his time to do so was fast passing. Guerrand leaned back on his stool and listened patiently, arms crossed, letting the man speak his fill.

"It was Zena who noticed the oddness in Bram, you know," Wilor said faintly. Guerrand sat forward to question the statement, but the smith wasn't finished.

"Well I remember the night Rejik met me at the Red Goose, all sweaty-faced and edgy," Wilor continued, his voice picking up speed and volume. " 'Zena's certain Cormac's son Bram is a changeling,' " Wilor said in an imitation of Rejik's voice. "Your father confessed it after he'd drank more tankards of ale than I'd ever seen downed before."

Guerrand jumped to his feet. "What are you talking about?"

"I never spoke of it to anyone, nor did I seek you out now, dear boy," said Wilor, his eyes clear yet sad. "But when you arrived here today, it seemed like providence, like you were put in my path one last time for a reason. I can't let the truth die with me."

Wilor's head shook as he recalled a painful memory. "It almost killed your father, too, knowing that about his own grandson, knowing that Zena was never wrong about such things, knowing that nothing could be done about it without risking the wrath of the tuatha who'd pulled off the switch." Wilor coughed violently and spat, then asked for a drink. "The way things have been in Thonvil since then, I've had my suspicions about their meddling. . . . I've never spoken them aloud before, but what can faeries do to me that the rising of the moons won't do in mere minutes anyway?"

"Why have I never heard this before?" demanded Guerrand. "Has anyone ever told Bram they thought he might have faerie blood?" Legends were common of such baby exchanges, but Guerrand had never seen evidence of such an occurrence.

Wilor rolled his head on the straw. "Not that I've been able to see. Your father never said so, but I think Rejik shared his suspicions with Cormac, or Cormac guessed himself, because I hear tell he's always kept a distance and deferred judgment about the boy to his mother."

Guerrand couldn't deny the truth of that. His head was a tangle of questions that forced their way to the front of his tongue at the same time. All that came out was, "What am I supposed to do with this confession now? Whether it's true or not, how can I ever look at Bram the same way again, knowing my mother and father believed it?"

"Believe it or not, that is your choice. Take it to your deathbed, as I did. But remember, it makes Bram no less a man than you thought him before." Wilor's eyes traveled to the window, where the long yellow streaks of twilight stretched into the room. "I'm afraid the sun is setting." He didn't looked the least bit afraid.

"That can't be! Not now, not yet!" Scowling, Guerrand raced to the windowsill. "If only I could hold the sun in place!" he cried in frustration, but no mage was powerful enough for that. The window looked to the west. Guerrand could already see that Solinari and Lunitari had risen before sunset, faint white and red outlines in the purple sky above the Strait of Ergoth. Wilor was right—there wasn't much time.

"I fear I've left you with more questions than answers, dear boy," the silversmith said ruefully. "Life, and especially death, aren't at all neat."

Guerrand turned away from the window and back to the weakened man on the bed of straw, stopping short when the snakes rose up, hissing. "*I'm* the one who needs to apologize, Wilor. You've been a true friend."

Wilor's breath whistled two notes at once in response.

He stared blankly, and his lips moved in a word that Guerrand could not hear. Heart in his throat, the mage scorned the snakes and moved closer. They didn't writhe, but slowly settled upon the straw as softly as feathers.

"Please, not yet!" the mage gasped again as the light in the eyes of his father's oldest friend winked to black. Without thinking, Guerrand leaped to the window again, as if to question that the time had come. Though he could not see it, there scuttled across the purple-darkened sky a distant, round shadow he understood too well. The third moon, Nuitari, had risen like the gleaming onyx in Wilor's eye sockets.

Guerrand cursed the wretched soul of Lyim Rhistadt, who had made all this happen when he began following the black moonlit path of the evil god of magic.

# Chapter Fifteen

It happened every night on Krynn. Moonrise. Tonight, white Solinari rose first, a blindingly bright light that was quickly tinged a vague pink by the rising of red Lunitari. Moments afterward, the pinkish moonlight was muted further by the rising of the third moon, black Nuitari. People not of an evil disposition were never quite sure if Nuitari had risen, or if the sudden muting was caused by clouds scuttling in the nighttime sky.

Guerrand tilted his face and stood silent in the doorway for a moment, reading some pattern in the heavens. Though the night sky was partly cloudy, there were no clouds near white Solinari and red Lunitari to dim their light now. The mage recalled that Solinari and Lunitari's combined pink light had shone for many minutes while Wilor still lived. But the silversmith had turned to stone at the precise moment when

Nuitari's black light had dimmed the glow of the other two moons. Guerrand knew he had found his clue, knew it with the certainty of a seasoned mage whose experiments had met with both failure and success. Nuitari's rising was a component in the spread of the plague. Only the evil black moon no decent person could see would cause such sickness.

Why hadn't he realized before what was so obvious now? Guerrand had needed to witness the final transformation to see the answer. Everyone thought that the end came at sunset on the third day. But, not being mages, they had looked at a symptom—the setting of the sun—rather than the cause—the rising of the moons on three successive days. The villagers couldn't know the magical influence of the heavenly bodies that were the symbols of the gods of magic.

What was still unclear to Guerrand, though, was what he could do about it. It was not the sun he needed to stop, as he'd cried to Wilor, but the rising of the moons, specifically Nuitari. Guerrand sighed and ran a hand through his long, graying hair. He might as well try to split Krynn in half as keep Nuitari from rising. He doubted even the Council of Three had the power to accomplish such a feat. The mage dropped his chin upon his palm and stared out the window.

"Guerrand?"

The mage nearly jumped from his skin. He spun about, turning eyes like saucers upon the form in the straw. Wilor was still stone, still dead. The door to the silversmith's street-front shop swung open and Bram stepped through it. His brows were furrowed with anxiety, but they eased up at the sight of his uncle.

"Thank goodness," he puffed, out of breath. Bram bent over and grabbed his knees, lungs heaving. "I've practically sprinted over every inch of Thonvil in search of you."

Alarmed, Guerrand grabbed the door frame for support. "Is it Kirah?"

"The disease is . . . running its course. She's still alive, resting now." Bram broke in before Guerrand could say another word. Pausing, he tilted his head and seemed only then to sense the odd stillness in the room. Bram's gaze shifted left with a jerky motion, to the man of stone, then back to Guerrand's careworn face. He had witnessed the final transformation too many times to afford the sight of the dead silversmith more emotion than sad acceptance.

"I-I'm sorry," Bram said haltingly. "Wilor once told me that you two had been friends. That's how I thought to look here for you—after I'd covered the rest of the village, that is."

Guerrand approached the man on the bed of straw. "Wilor was alone. The rest of his family died in the last couple of days. I can scarcely spare the time, but I promised to bury him in the field out back."

"I'll help you," Bram offered. He bounded in and removed the blanket from Wilor's body.

Nodding, Guerrand hefted the smith's snake legs while Bram supported the lion's share of Wilor's stone-stiff body. Together they took him through the supply door and out into the scrubby field, where potatoes had last grown. Guerrand steered them toward three freshly dug rocky mounds of dirt, and they set Wilor down.

Bram looked around, palms up. "No shovel. Wilor must have had one to dig these other graves. I'll go look." Bram swept by Guerrand on his way back to the shop.

There was a sound of thunder above their heads. As so often happened on the windswept coast, the good weather was at an abrupt end. The mage caught his nephew's arm. "There's no need," he said, squinting skyward as the first cold drops of rain fell. Murky gray clouds covered the moons. "We haven't the time to spend on digging, anyway."

Bram whirled around and stared, slack-jawed, at his uncle. "Are you saying we should just leave Wilor in the field?"

"Of course not," Guerrand snapped, distracted from searching his memory for a helpful spell. "Just stand clear." Bram watched him curiously and stepped back as Guerrand dug around in the deep pockets of his robe until his fingers settled upon the items he sought.

The mage's hand emerged holding some miniature items. The words of the spell were simple enough, inscribed on the handle of the tiny shovel he held up in his palm, next to an equally small bucket. Guerrand lowered his head in concentration, but out of the corner of his eye he could see Bram was about to question him, then thought better of it.

*"Blay tongris."* Instantly, the top layer of mud, then drier dirt began to fly from the ground in a steady stream as if under the paws of some invisible, burrowing creature. Although the hole was wide enough, Guerrand mentally directed the crater to lengthen to accommodate Wilor's height. When he determined it to be of sufficient size, the mage simply stopped the spell by breaking his concentration. The bucket and shovel remained, the mage knew, because the duration of the spell had not yet expired.

Bram looked impressed. Guerrand's face was flushed with success, his lower lip red because he'd been biting down on it as a focus. Together, as the rain turned from drizzle to torrent, the two men lowered the smith into the ground. Turning his attention to the newest mound of earth, Guerrand reactivated the spell and commanded a hole be dug there. The loose earth flew again and landed atop the stone body of the silversmith. When all the dirt had been replaced in the grave, Guerrand cut his concentration again and the digging stopped. None too early, either, because this time the tiny bucket and shovel disappeared from Guerrand's soft, white palm.

Guerrand regarded his nephew, blinking against the drops of rain that splashed his face. "I've discovered the plague's final component that causes victims to turn to stone."

Bram pushed wet ropes of hair back from his face. "You know how to stop it then?"

Guerrand shook his head. "I didn't say that. Come inside where it's warm and I'll tell you what I've learned." The mage gave Wilor's grave a final, farewell pat, then trudged back toward the smith's shop, Bram clumping along eagerly beside him. Mud gathered upon their boots until their feet felt as heavy as blocks of wood.

Guerrand seized the handle of a bucket full of rainwater sitting by the door, then removed his muddy boots before stepping inside. Next he stoked a fire in the hearth of the storeroom, and made two double-strength cups of Wilor's tea from the rainwater. He felt a jitteriness inside that crawled up into his throat, telling him to run all ways at once, seeking an instant solution. But he had too much to consider and no time to get the answer wrong. Kirah had less than twenty-four hours left before she, too, would turn to stone, before she, too, would be placed in the ground. Guerrand forced himself to sip the tea.

Bram took the steaming mug his uncle offered, then sat back on his haunches before the fire. He wrapped a blanket around his shoulders and over his head, watching the mage with thready patience. If Bram had learned nothing else about this stranger of an uncle in the last days, it was that Guerrand would not be rushed.

Guerrand pulled up a child's chair by the warmth of the flames. He wasted no time, revealing to his nephew his theory of Nuitari's damaging light.

Bram's lips were pursed in thought above his mug. "I don't understand why this black light is so important. It's not the cause, but just a trigger, isn't it?"

"I believe it's a trigger for the initial infection and all three stages and days of the plague," said Guerrand. "Exposure to Nuitari's light triggers the fever, and so on, until the final exposure turns the victims to stone."

Bram was still shaking his head. "Then why can't we just shield everyone from the black moon's light— lower the shutters, put them underground, cover their eyes, that sort of thing?"

"I doubt seriously whether that would have any effect," said Guerrand, with a long, slow, sorry shake of his head. "Magic just doesn't function that way. Moonlight, especially, is insidious. Where magic depends on its effect, you rarely need to actually see it in order for it to work. You can even bottle it, if you know what you're doing." He shrugged, adding, "Moonlight shines on our world whether we see it or not."

Guerrand felt the need to pace while he pondered, thumbs hooked in his waist. "I'm going to have to think of a way to actually prevent the black moon from shining here."

"Can't you ask the Council of Three for help?"

Guerrand grimaced. "I've considered it. But you told them about the plague and they didn't offer to come."

"How can they turn their backs on the decimation of an entire village?"

"They're too powerful and important to concern themselves directly with anything but the welfare of the whole world." Guerrand saw Bram's continued confusion. "In their own way, they have helped Thonvil more than I would have expected, first by letting you speak with me in Bastion, and second by allowing me to return here to do what I could to save the village."

Bram nodded his understanding at last.

"It's funny," said Guerrand, struck with a new thought. "This wouldn't even be happening at Bastion. No moons shine there." The mage's expression shifted from vague musing to recognition. He snapped his fingers. "Bastion is on a two-dimensional plane and not part of Krynn, or subject to its moons."

Bram could see his uncle's face light up as his mind went to work. "So? You're not contemplating some really strange idea, like transporting everyone to Bastion, are you?"

Guerrand obviously was, because his face fell when he admitted, "I couldn't manage that magically, even if it weren't a violation of my vow to keep intruders from entering Bastion." He squinted at his nephew. "You still haven't told me what you said to persuade Par-Salian and Justarius to send you there."

"I know it may sound strange, but some magical creatures called 'tuatha dundarael' have apparently been helping me restore the gardens at the castle for some time. They gave me a coin and set me off on a path they called a faerie road." He looked far away. "It feels so long ago I can scarcely believe it myself, but it apparently impressed your Justarius and Par-Salian enough to bend the rules for me."

For a brief moment, Wilor's dying words came into Guerrand's mind, and he found himself scrutinizing Bram's face to assign hereditary features.

"What are you staring at?" Bram asked, coloring to the roots of his hair. "Did I say something wrong?"

Guerrand jerked his eyes away awkwardly. There were no answers to be found in his young nephew's face. It wouldn't do for Bram to further question the scrutiny. "I—No, you didn't say anything wrong,

Bram," he hastily assured his nephew. "As a matter of fact, your thoughts are helping me a great deal."

Bram beamed. "What about sending victims someplace else on Krynn to avoid the moonlight?"

Guerrand shook his head. "Aside from being impractical to accomplish, Nuitari's light would find them eventually. No, I've got to figure out a way to prevent Nuitari from rising."

He scratched the pink scalp beneath his brown hair. "The only mages I know who've even come close to disrupting the course of the moons are the Council of Three. I believe I told you that after the conclave of twenty-one mages completed Bastion here on Krynn, Par-Salian, Justarius, and LaDonna combined magical energies to send the behemoth from the Prime Material Plane and compress its three dimensions to two while not altering its function. . . ."

Guerrand's voice trailed off as an idea began to blossom behind his eyes. When Bastion was completed, the Council had to prepare it for transit to the two-dimensional demiplane where it now resided. In effect, they had to strip away one dimension. That alteration was unnoticeable, because it seemed normal in the fortress's new location.

The exterior of Bastion was covered by mystic runes, scribed by Par-Salian, LaDonna, and Justarius as the final step in the building's construction. Though he had not witnessed their inscribing, Guerrand had studied the runes often in the long months of solitude as high defender. He found their intricacies fascinating. As far as he could determine, the runes themselves provided most of the impetus for the change from three dimensions to two. It had taken the combined power of all three council members to move the structure from one plane to another, but almost any mage could have triggered the dimensional collapse, with the runes to back him up.

Guerrand was pacing in Wilor's small back room, his demeanor growing more and more excited with each new realization. Finally, Bram had to interrupt his uncle. "What is it, Rand? You're on to something, aren't you?"

Guerrand paused for a moment with his head down, collecting the rush of thoughts before they disappeared. "Bram, you probably won't understand this, but we can make Nuitari two-dimensional—actually turn it on it's side—by transcribing the runes from Bastion to the moon. The runes are the key. We have a lot of work to do before the next moonrise, but by the grace of Lunitari we'll get it done."

"You're right," agreed Bram, his brow crinkling. "I don't understand. I didn't see any runes at Bastion, and even if they are there, how do we get them to the moon?"

"Of course you didn't see them," Guerrand said. "They're magical. Half the trick of reading magic is just being able to see it. What I'm proposing here is ambitious. I'm going to need your help," he continued. "Will you do whatever I ask, no matter how strange it might sound at the time?"

"Of course," his nephew replied, "but I still don't understand what you're going to do."

"That's not your concern now," Guerrand said. "I'm going to need as many sheets of parchment, pots of ink, and good goose quills as you can find. While you're at it, tell everyone you meet to avoid the village well and drink only freshly collected rainwater. I'm guessing Lyim passed the disease through the communal source of water. If—*when* I succeed, the absence of Nuitari should cleanse the water of the plague." He left the stench and darkness of the death room and went back into the silversmith's shop at the front of the store.

Bram followed him, staring transfixed.

But the mage scarcely noticed him, his mind racing ahead. He spotted Wilor's large worktable. In one quick motion, Guerrand swept Wilor's tools to the floor and dragged up a stool. "This will do perfectly," he announced. "Bring everything here; this will be my work area." The mage dumped the contents of his shoulder bag onto the desk and began sorting out the few sheets of vellum and quills he carried. He looked up then and noticed Bram's gaping inactivity. "Hurry now. You have important work to do before you can get back to tending Kirah."

As if he'd snapped from a trance, Bram jolted, then jogged out the door into the darkness and rain. Guerrand shouted his name, and Bram stopped in the puddled street to peer back inside, squinting against the raindrops.

"Bring candles, too!"

Bram sprinted away down the street, splashing as he went.

\* \* \* \* \*

Guerrand was still hunched over the table, completely absorbed in scribing illegible characters onto a sheet of parchment, when Bram returned for the fourth time with supplies. Other sheets were scattered across the workbench, mostly covered with drawings and arcane writing. Zagarus was perched on an opposite corner of the table, snoozing peacefully. Bram struggled through the doorway and plunked his heavy basket on the floor.

The noise attracted Guerrand's attention. "Oh, thank goodness you've returned," he expounded, "I was nearly out of parchment, and I've carved at least six new points on this quill." Immediately the mage began rummaging through the package, and his face brightened tenfold. He held aloft a sheaf of new parchment and a bundle of beeswax candles. "This is marvelous, Bram! Where did you find all this?"

Bram stepped to the fire to warm his hands and dry his cloak. "Leinster the scribe died three days ago, and his wife and children fled town. They left most of his things behind. I got the candles from a . . . a friend. I helped make them a few days ago, although it feels like months, with all that's happened."

Guerrand was already shifting fresh supplies to his worktable. "I will probably need even more parchment than this, if you can find it," he called over his shoulder. He lined up three stone vials of ink from the basket and, one by one, unstoppered them, smeared a bit of their contents between his fingers, smelled it, and even tasted one batch. His face wrinkled up in distaste.

"This ink, unfortunately, won't do," Guerrand announced sadly.

Bram cast a worried look away from the fire. "I don't know where I can find any more. Leinster made that ink himself, and anyone in the village who needed ink bought it from Leinster."

"What about at the castle?"

"The castle is closed off," Bram said, obviously embarrassed by the admission. "My mother thinks that if she bars her door securely enough, none of this will affect her. She as much as told me that if I left the safety of Castle DiThon to find you, even I would not be allowed in again."

"The mountain dwarves did the same thing to their own during the Cataclysm," said Guerrand. "I can't help thinking there must be a message in the parallel somewhere."

The mage sat upon his stool and stared at the substance on his fingers. "This ink was made from dogwood bark. It doesn't have sufficient richness—it isn't substantial enough to carry magic." The mage sat for several moments, rubbing his fingertips thoughtfully. "We'll just have to make it work. Do you have any oak gall in your herb stocks?"

"I don't, even if I could get to it," Bram said. "But I'm sure I could find some in the same place I got the candles. Nahamkin has—*had*—an exhaustive collection."

Guerrand scooped up the three ink bottles. "Dump all this ink together. Then mix in a good, strong infusion of oak gall and some sulfate of iron." He fished in a fold of his robe and tossed a vial to Bram. "This ink doesn't have to stay black forever, but it does have to make a trip to the moon." Guerrand flashed a smile of encouragement at his perplexed nephew, then turned back to his work on the table.

Bram picked up his damp cloak and was nearly out the door when Guerrand's voice stopped him again. "Did you check on Kirah?"

Shivering against its cold wetness, the young man pulled his clammy cloak around his shoulders. "She was sleeping in fits a while ago. I gave her honeyed tea for energy and a fresh blanket." He grimaced. "I don't like leaving her alone. In the morning she'll begin to—" He neither needed to nor could finish the sentence.

Whittling pensively at his quill tip, Guerrand gave a grim nod. "Fetch that gall, then go sit with her. I'll be at this for the rest of the night and the better part of tomorrow's light, anyway."

Bram was surprised. "That long?"

Guerrand looked up from his work. "I told you magic was a complicated and time-consuming business, and not all lighting fires with your finger." He looked back with great concentration to his tracings. "Now be off, or I'll miss my sunset deadline."

Properly chastised, Bram disappeared once more into the darkness, a shadow in rain-shrouded moonlight.

* * * * *

The moons, at least the ones Guerrand could see as he hurried from the silversmith's to Kirah's, rose before sunset. In the still-bright sky, pale Solinari looked like the bleached bones of some great beast, sucked dry of their marrow.

Guerrand tried not to dwell on the fleeting day. His task of transcribing Bastion's runes from memory had been more taxing than even he'd expected it to be; the demands on his memory were extreme as he reconstructed the intricate patterns, making subtle changes as necessary. He believed—and hoped—that he had enough time remaining to put his magical plan into operation.

*Tell me again how this works,* requested Zagarus, swooping low across Guerrand's path. *Do you seriously expect me to carry something to the moon?*

"No, Zag," replied Guerrand, "at least not all the way." The mage paused at the rear door to the bakery. Bram was upstairs with Kirah, had been through her third terrible morning of the plague. By now her limbs would be a writhing mass of snakes. Guerrand steeled himself against the shock of seeing her like that.

As Guerrand climbed the stairs, everything that had happened in the past few days seemed to focus on Kirah's life. He was the only person who could save her. If this spell worked, she would live; if it failed, she would die. His hand trembled as he reached for the door handle.

As his uncle entered the room, Bram stood, weary eyes searching for a sign of hope. Guerrand was tremendously relieved to see that his nephew had pulled sacks over Kirah's limbs, although the way they bulged and twitched nearly brought up Guerrand's meager lunch.

Kirah turned, too, and watched Guerrand enter. Like Wilor, she appeared perfectly lucid, but the fever had been much harder on her than on the stout silversmith. Her cheeks were beyond sunken, her eyes hollow and dark. She opened cracked lips to utter a barely audible, "Hello, Rand." A flicker of his old, scrappy kid sister came into her pale eyes. "You'll have to excuse me for not dressing for visitors. I'm feeling all thumbs today," she managed with a weak grin, then lay still.

Guerrand's own smile held affection and sadness and a thousand other things. More than anything, though, he wanted to pick up his sister and carry her away from all this horror. He wanted to play fox and hound over heather and creeks the way they had as children. He wanted to be anywhere but in this town filled with death, pinning Kirah's life on a basketful of scribbled runes and an untried spell.

Bram cut into Guerrand's thoughts. "We haven't much time. What can I do to help?"

Guerrand quickly focused his mind. "I'll need to be outside."

"Take me along." Kirah's whisper-weak voice caught both men by surprise. She could barely raise her head from the pillow. "I don't want to be alone in here when—" Her eyes were pleading.

Bram looked to Guerrand, who motioned him toward the bed. Together they picked up the straw mattress with Kirah on it and carried it outside to beneath a tree on the edge of the green. Bram ran back to the room and fetched Guerrand's basket of papers.

The wizard picked up a sheaf of them, weighed it thoughtfully in his hands, added another sheet, then rolled and tied them with a bit of twine. To Bram he said, "Help me bundle these parchments, seven sheets at a time. Be sure to keep them in the proper order."

Bram dropped to his knees and set to work, rolling parchments.

Guerrand looked to his familiar, perched on the roof of the bakery. "You're on, Zag." The gull swooped to his master's side. Guerrand held toward him the first parchment roll, letting the gull grab the twine in his beak. "Fly this up as high as you can go. When you can't possibly get any higher and we just look like tiny dots on the ground, give the roll a toss. Then return as fast as you can for the next one."

*Give it a toss?* wondered the bird. *You think I can throw this all the way to the moon? While I am a hooded, black-backed Ergothian gull, the—*

Guerrand squeezed Zag until his breath squeaked out his beak, cutting off the gull's trademark reply. "Of course you can't throw it that far. The scroll will know where to go, and the rest of the trip will take care of itself."

With a stifled, slightly indignant "Kyeow!" Zagarus lifted off. Three pairs of eyes watched his progress as he climbed, circling round and round. The bird was nearly lost from view when a flash of orange light drew two surprised gasps. Flaming runes etched themselves across the sky, flashing until all were complete, then raced away eastward toward the darkening blue, finally disappearing behind the horizon.

Zagarus folded his wings and plummeted like a rock, arriving with a tremendous flapping tumult just moments after the last flaming sigil dissipated. He snatched another bundle without pausing and was off again, spiraling skyward.

Rolling parchments next to Bram, Guerrand explained the process: "The symbols and runes on these parchments are etching themselves on Nuitari. When that's complete, I'll trigger the spell and the moon will become two-dimensional, with its edge turned toward Krynn, like a coin on its side."

Squinting, Guerrand's gaze shifted. "Here comes Zag for the last bundle."

By now, Zagarus did not land so much as he simply slammed into the ground. *I . . . don't know . . . how much longer I can do this*, panted Zagarus, staggering to his feet.

Guerrand held out the bundle. "Just one more, old friend, and then you can rest for a year and eat all the fish you want."

*It's a good, thing, too . . . because I think Nuitari is about to rise*. The gull took the bundle in his mouth, stumbled down the street with wings flapping, and took off.

After watching the final batch of sigils head skyward, Bram turned back to Guerrand. "What about the moon's edge? Won't that still provide a tiny bit of light?"

Guerrand had already rolled back his sleeves and closed his eyes in concentration. "Not if the spell works properly. If Nuitari becomes truly two-dimensional, its edge will not exist in this world. If you want to worry about something, worry that the spell won't work at all; that's far more likely.

"I don't know how long I can maintain it," the mage continued, "so I'm going to cast the spell at the last possible moment, just as the sun disappears. I have to prepare now." He pressed his hands to his ears briefly, clueing Bram to stay back quietly.

As the sunlight waned, Guerrand silently repeated the words of the spell over and over with great concentration, until he felt himself no more than a black hollowness, like the length of a flute through which the invisible sound passed. He repeated the spell like a mantra the entire length of his mind's body, opening passages to the power and stopping the interference of others. He dared not open his eyes, lest he lose concentration. He would know without seeing if the spell worked. The mage squeezed his eyes shut more tightly, and with every clenched and tingling muscle in his body, he willed the spell to work. He'd done everything he knew how to make it happen.

Guerrand felt the mental presence of Zagarus at his side, telling him that all the scrolls had been dispatched. Guerrand pronounced the words he had been rehearsing.

*"Ine jutera, Ine swobokla, jehth Ine laeranma."*

A tremendous clap of thunder rattled doors and shook the ground beneath their feet like an earthquake for many moments. Guerrand's eyes flew open in alarm as he stumbled about, crashing into Bram, who was already on his knees.

"What's happening?" cried Bram, struggling to keep Kirah on her straw mattress.

But Guerrand could only shake his head mutely. What had he done with his rearranging of ancient symbols? A bolt of lightning cracked the dusky sky and zagged a path above the buildings of the village, straight to Guerrand. The bolt struck the mage full in the chest in the very instant he realized it would. To his greater surprise, there came only a slight tingling pain.

Guerrand reached up a hand to the wound, but the earth dropped away beneath him, throwing him off balance. Yet he did not tumble down but flew forward, as if all the wind in the world were at the small of his back, arching him like a bow until he thought he might snap. The skin of his face drew back from the incredible speed of his passage, exposing the outline of every tooth and bone in his head. His ears rang, and his head felt stuffed with wool.

Strangest of all, Guerrand seemed to be going somewhere in a great hurry. He was hurtling through a vast expanse of blackness broken only by tiny pinpoints of distant light. One of those points loomed larger than the rest, until its impossibly bright, blinding light was all that was ahead, choking out the blackness, burning Guerrand's eyes.

And then the breakneck ride stopped. Instantly. Guerrand was thrown to his knees, and his head snapped forward painfully. He kept his eyes shut as he crawled to his feet, one hand rubbing his neck. He was afraid to open his eyes, but curiosity won out, and he spared a glance around him.

The mage was in a room defined so only by the four crystal-clear glass walls that separated him from the vastness of blue-black space. Even the floor beneath his feet was transparent, cold glass, the view broken only by winking stars. The feeling was disorienting, as if a surface as thin as a soap bubble were all that kept him from tumbling through the heavens.

Slow-paced footsteps abruptly hammered against the glass. Guerrand's head jerked up, eyes wide. A youngish man stepped into view from the blackness of space. His jet-black hair and long black robe seemed to form from the darkness beyond the glass. Pinpoints of starlight twinkled in his eyes, set slant-wise and sly and entirely ringed with shadows. He radiated a sense of majesty, cool and unreachable. Guerrand would have dropped to his knees in supplication if he weren't already kneeling.

The aristocratic man stepped to the middle of the room, a curious smile playing about his mouth. He bent at the waist, and a chair grew beneath him, rising out of the floor like stretched, heated glass. He casually crossed his legs and raised an arm, and a table grew similarly beneath it. He appraised Guerrand with a serene visage, his eyes alighting with brief interest upon Guerrand's red robe. If not for his venerable aura, the man looked at a distance like any intelligent listener sitting at a table in an inn, with fried root vegetables and a cup of lily wine on the table before him.

"Why are you scribbling on my moon?" he asked coolly.

"*Your* moon?" Guerrand gasped. With a small jerk of his head, he looked all around the glass walls and noticed the dark, circular shadow that loomed taller than a cliff face. He could almost make out smaller shadows of familiar magical runes scratched upon the darker shape. Guerrand's head snapped back to the man at the table. The red-robed mage grew paler than a mushroom, when, with simple, terrible understanding, he realized he was looking at the god of dark magic himself, Nuitari.

"Did you think I wouldn't notice?"

"I-I didn't think—"

"Always dangerous for a mage," broke in Nuitari, his lips pursed in displeasure.

"I had good reason," Guerrand began again feebly.

The god smothered a yawn. "You earthbound mages always do."

"I'm not some ordinary mage playing at spellcasting," Guerrand managed. "I am one of the wizards who was chosen to man Bastion, the stronghold that defends against entrance into your Lost Citadel."

The mage dispatched Bastion with a flick of his long, tapered nails. "Do you truly believe I need your help to protect anything?"

"N-No," stuttered Guerrand. "I just thought—"

"That a position I did not bestow should grant you favor?"

"No!" exclaimed Guerrand. "I just thought it would not displease you if I prevented another mage from continuing to use the power of your moon without your leave."

Nuitari's dark-ringed eyes narrowed. "Explain."

Guerrand quickly complied, taking heart from the fact that Nuitari, drumming his nails on the glass table, seemed to seriously consider his story about Lyim.

"I knew of it, of course. But why should I care about this other mage's purpose," he posed at last, "as long as it increases the presence of my dark magic in your world?"

"But this mage was not even of the Black Robes!" exclaimed Guerrand.

The god frowned, reconsidering again. "It *is* somewhat distressing to have power drained without devotion paid to the proper god." He shrugged. "Still, the end result is the same." His slyly slanted eyes narrowed still further. "At least he was not scribbling on my moon."

"The inscriptions are only temporary," revealed Guerrand in his most conciliatory tone.

"You think that mitigates the fact that they are there at all, and without my permission?"

Desperate, Guerrand dropped to one knee and bowed his head. "Then I humbly ask your leave now."

"Too little, too late, don't you think?"

Guerrand looked into the god's sparkling star eyes and said gravely, "I know only that it grows late for my sister and the others whose very lives depend on me hiding the rays of your moon for this one night."

"We are between times here," Nuitari said dismissively. "It will not pass for those you left behind until— if—you return." Again he drummed his dark nails, considering some point. After staring at Guerrand's red robe briefly, he seemed to come to a conclusion.

"Perhaps it's not too late for both of us to benefit from this unfortunate episode," he said in a soft, gray voice. "Never let it be said that I let anger cloud my vision from opportunity."

Guerrand shook his head slowly, fearfully. "I don't understand."

Nuitari gave a patronizing roll of his shadowed eyes. "What I'm saying is, cast your little spell to change my moon to two dimensions—temporarily, that is," he said. "I will even advise you, free of obligation, that you would be better served to rearrange the final two symbols. Doing so will lengthen the duration of the dimensional change, to last until the rising of the sun."

"That's it?" Guerrand asked, incredulous. "You're going to let me return to Thonvil and finish the spell?"

The god looked amused. "Nothing is ever that easy, mage of the Red Robes."

Guerrand jumped as if electrically shocked when Nuitari reached out with black, manicured nails and gently fingered the cloth of his red robe. "I ask only one thing: Remember this favor I have granted you."

Every muscle in Guerrand's body froze. He played the god's words through his mind again in disbelief, then shifted just one eye up to Nuitari's pale face. "Are you asking me to change . . . ?"

"I'm asking you nothing," interrupted the god of dark magic. "I have no use for another minor suppliant at this moment. Later?" Nuitari shrugged. "Who can say? For now, simply remember the favor I have granted you. I will."

Guerrand bowed his head and said nothing. When he looked up, for a brief moment the features of Rannoch, the black wizard who haunted his dreams, played across the face of the god of dark magic. Guerrand blinked in disbelief and the illusion was gone, some trick of his overtaxed mind, he supposed.

Nuitari's laughter rang in Guerrand's ears as the glass floor sagged beneath his feet. There was a loud *ping!* as if a large bubble had burst, and then Guerrand dropped into the darkness of the heavens. He plummeted head over heels, past bright Solinari, past the red glow of Lunitari, past a thousand unnamed stars. He didn't know whether he would live or die, whether Nuitari had already reneged on their unspoken deal, only that he was falling.

And then, in the blink of an eye, he stopped. Like a teleport spell, one moment he was tumbling through space, and the next he stood in the exact place and position, arm gestures and all, as before he'd been thrust into the heavens by Nuitari. The moment had held.

"Guerrand? Uncle Rand!" The last was a bark from Bram's mouth.

The mage's vision finally sighted the face of his nephew. Guerrand's gaze traveled to his sister lying beneath the lone tree, looking wan and hopeless in the moment before her death, and he well and truly came back from wherever he had been.

Except in one regard. Guerrand silenced Bram with a stinging glance. He snatched up one last piece of parchment, hastily scrawled the rearrangement of the final two symbols he had placed upon the black moon, and sent Zagarus skyward one more time.

Guerrand waited for some earth-shattering, cosmos-shifting sign. But white Solinari and red Lunitari drifted without concern across the dusky sky as before. There could be no question that the sun had set, for no last orangy beams stretched eastward from the west. Guerrand refused to look at Kirah, to even turn his head slightly to see if she still moved. Neither he, nor Bram, nor Kirah seemed to draw breath. A few dead leaves skipped over the cobbles in the breeze, and still the three waited, as still as statues, for the end to come or the beginning to start.

Bram blinked in wonder at the sky. "The night seems brighter than usual, as if daylight's wick has been turned down just one notch."

"Nuitari's black light," Guerrand began to explain, his voice thin but growing, "usually mutes the intensity of Solinari and Lunitari's rays. Without it, the moonlight is much brighter."

"And that's not all," Bram fairly shouted. "Look, near the crown constellation!"

Guerrand scanned the sky looking for the familiar crown-and-veil arrangement of stars. It was obscured, not by clouds or night mist but by dark, fleeting shapes. The sky seemed suddenly crowded with them in the area where the crown of stars usually twinkled. Guerrand saw nothing obscuring the nearby constellations: the graceful double ellipses of Mishakal and the massive bison zodiacal symbol of Kiri-Jolith were clear. To the far side of the bison, where the constellations should have portrayed a broken scale and a dragon's skull, the stars were again obscured by darting bits of darkness.

"What does it mean?" Bram wondered aloud, turning in a circle to view the odd sky.

"I can only guess," Guerrand replied. "Those constellations that are obscured tonight must usually reflect the light of evil Nuitari, now absent. It is a good sign, I think."

Guerrand's musing was cut short when Kirah's snakes suddenly became agitated. Her limbs thrashed wildly beyond her control, upsetting the blanket she had insisted upon covering herself with out of an uncharacteristic sense of vanity.

At first Guerrand and Bram were worried that the fighting was some new manifestation of the disease, until they noticed that the snakes appeared to be in great pain. Then the creatures began to attack and bite each other, those conjoined on the same limb, as well as from one limb to the next. Kirah struggled in vain to get as far from her warring reptiles as possible. She had to settle for turning her head and squeezing her eyes shut, though she couldn't silence the sound of their violent hissing and thrashing. She began to scream, a long, low wail of pain that gave the snakes only a brief pause. Finally Kirah fell still, unconscious, either from shock or as an escape, or both.

Guerrand and Bram watched helplessly, both wondering if they should stop the snakes from killing each other, but not knowing how to go about it. Bram made a move toward the thrashing black creatures, but Guerrand stayed him by grasping his arm.

"For better or worse—for Kirah's sake—we've got to let the malady reverse itself," he said softly.

Then Bram emitted a gasp and pointed down the street. "Look, Guerrand—snakes!"

Guerrand followed Bram's pointing finger until he, too, saw them. Knots of thrashing snakes were clearly visible in the bright moonlight. They had emerged from their hiding places all around town and, like the snakes on Kirah's limbs, were fighting to the death in squirming knots. Bram picked his way carefully down the street to the village green. When he returned, he reported that hundreds of snakes were attacking each other all over the town, seemingly driven mad by the light.

The last snake on Kirah's body, vibrant colors now dull, died of its wounds just before sunrise. Kirah was unconscious until that very moment, when her eyes flew open wide, hopeful, and instantly alert. As the first rays of the fourth day's sun cut across her face, the lifeless snakes simply slipped away with the last traces of moonlight, replaced with fully formed arms and legs the pinkish hue of a newborn babe.

Face shining with joy, Kirah planted her new legs beneath her with the awkward gait of a colt. Bram stumbled forward to help his aunt, while Guerrand stood back and watched with joyous amusement, recalling Kirah's first toddling steps as a child. They could hear the jubilant shouts that began ringing all over the village that, just yesterday, had been as silent as the tomb it had become.

Kirah's pale eyes welled up as she looked at her brother. "I'm sorry I doubted you, Rand. Ever."

Guerrand sank to his knees with relief at the sound of her voice. He struggled to control the flood of emotions coursing through him, to find something uplifting to say, but no clear thought would settle upon his lips. His nephew squeezed his shoulder encouragingly.

The mage felt utterly empty of magic, could sense the void where his power should be. He was certain it would take some time before it returned, at least a night's sleep. What he had done to turn the moon had drained more from him than any act of magic ever had. Yet, seeing his sister restored, hearing the villagers' happy shouts, Guerrand thought all the strain had been worth it.

The mage found himself raising his eyes to the heavens in silent tribute. But the smile upon his face froze, and his heart skipped a beat. Clear to his view for the first time, next to the white and pink bones of Solinari and Lunitari in the lavender morning sky, was the darker shape of Nuitari.

The moon no decent person could see.

# Chapter Sixteen

The celebration was brief, considering Kirah's weakened condition. She, of course, wanted to dance in the streets, but a few coltish steps proved the young woman was a long way from doing a jig. At last Kirah agreed to let Bram carry her, frail but with restored limbs, across the road and up the stairway to her room, where she could rest in comfort.

Seated upon the bottom step near the entrance to the bakery, which was still dark, silent, and scentless, Guerrand waited for him to return. The mage scarcely noticed the street around him; he stared at it, without really seeing.

What did it mean, seeing the black moon? Was he disposed toward Evil now? Guerrand didn't feel any different. Maybe that was the point. Perhaps evil people weren't all the same, or even as different on the inside as he'd believed. Hadn't Justarius said that same thing after Guerrand's Test?

Bram slipped down the staircase and joined his uncle. "Kirah's as scrappy as ever," the young man said fondly. "Tried to talk me into taking her for a walk in the sunlight, but I finally got her settled. She fell asleep before I could get to the door."

Guerrand nodded his head to acknowledge the comment. One by one the limbs of plague-stricken villagers had returned to normal, reassuring them that the plague's spell had been broken. Just yesterday Thonvil had looked and sounded like a ghost town, the deadly stillness that had pervaded broken only by a groaning spring wind. This sunny morning a handful of people walked the streets, stirring up the noises of living, though where any of them were going when no shops were yet open was anyone's guess.

But the greatest sign that fear had passed was that folks would meet each other's eyes again.

"They don't even know you're the one who saved their lives," Bram said when a young girl and her mother, both with head shawls lowered to feel the heat of the sun on their chocolate-brown hair, nodded in greeting.

"It's better that they don't," Guerrand said soberly.

The men fell into a dull silence, watching the village slowly come back to life.

"I should get home—I mean to the castle, to see how everyone there has fared," Bram said after a while. The young nobleman stood reluctantly, turning the gesture into a long, slow stretch. His eyes traveled south, over the buildings of Thonvil, to the distant, dark fortress that rose up between blue sea and green earth like a mountain of cold stone.

Bram didn't look at his uncle as he said, "You should come with me."

Guerrand thought the centuries-old fortress appeared more foreboding and entrapping than the Tower of High Sorcery at Wayreth, which had been designed to look that way. "I . . . don't think that's a good idea, do you?"

"Perhaps not," Bram agreed soberly.

"Besides," Guerrand said, standing also, "I should be getting back to Bastion."

Bram's head swung around, his eyes wild. "So soon? You arrived just days ago."

"Is that all it's been?" Guerrand shook his head in amazement. "It feels like years since . . ." He stopped himself short of mentioning Lyim's death. So much had happened in so short a time.

"I know what you mean," Bram agreed, plucking at his filthy clothing. "I've worn this same tunic and trousers for so long they're stiff."

Bram's observation left a thoughtful silence. His expression grew sober. "Strange, but it feels like only hours since I found you." The young man looked away and said softly, "I'm just not willing to say good-bye again yet. Didn't Justarius's note say you could take as much time as you needed?"

"Yes," acknowledged Guerrand, "but my work here is done."

Bram's adam's apple rose and fell slowly. "I was hoping you'd welcome the chance to get to know your nephew again."

Guerrand felt his throat thicken. Meeting his nephew's gaze, the mage wondered what growing up at Castle DiThon had been like for Bram. Probably as frustrating and fatherless, considering Cormac's state of mind, as it had been for Guerrand. From all accounts, life at the castle had gotten steadily worse in the last decade. Rank poverty didn't usually improve things. Bram's mother, Rietta, was . . . well, Rietta. As for his father,

Cormac had always seemed distant from his only son, and now he was crazy, gone even when he was present. Guerrand was reminded again of Wilor's dying words.

Bram could see his uncle weakening. "One afternoon, that's all I ask," he pressed. "One calm afternoon, where I can learn what lifepath took you to Bastion, what interests or irritates you and what doesn't." Bram gave his most persuasive smile. "I know a place where nothing intrudes except the rodents in the thatch overhead."

"Truth to tell," said Guerrand, "I'm not in *that* great a hurry to return to where there is no grass or sky or trees." He looked sidelong at Bram. "This place you know, is it one where a man can put up his feet and have a decent cup of tea?"

"The best!" Bram was already three steps down the street, forcing Guerrand to hurry to fall in stride with him. Rounding the corner on the far edge of town, they came into sight of a run-down shack.

"I sat with Nahamkin through the plague just before I left to find you," Bram explained. "I was more than a little surprised this morning to find that the villagers hadn't burned down his cottage."

At first glance, Guerrand thought it wouldn't have hurt the look of the village if the shack were gone. The thatch was old and black all over. The walls were of rocky mud, crumbling in places. And yet, as he got nearer, Guerrand couldn't help but see the comfortable, lived-in and well-loved look about the place. The garden appeared to be struggling against neglect and the season to renew itself.

The cottage reminded him of a run-down version of the one he'd shared with Esme in Harrowdown. There came that familiar tight feeling in his chest, as of the apprehended return of pain that always came with thoughts of Esme, especially now. He resolved to try to contact her before he returned to Bastion, when his magical strength returned.

"Nahamkin," Guerrand repeated. "Wasn't there a farmer who lived in the surrounds by that name?"

"One and the same," Bram said. "Nahamkin's family more or less abandoned him once the plague struck. I was his only friend, and he mine." He said the words matter-of-factly.

Bram stopped and stooped before the oddly tilting wooden door, as if recalling some pleasant memory, then stepped inside and waved Guerrand in.

Pots and tins and wooden buckets were on every available surface, but no drips fell from the rotted roof today. Hanging from the rafters was a year's supply of butter-colored candles in a variety of shapes and sizes. The place smelled of moss and worms and long-dead ashes.

Bram returned from the well with a pail full of water that he set by the hearth. The young man dropped to his knees with a sigh. "Damnation," he cursed softly. "I didn't even think to grab flint and stone to start a fire." He stood and looked around with a frown on his face, hands on his hips. "There must be something around here I . . . "

Guerrand knelt next to Bram, nonchalantly lit the logs with a simple cantrip, then dropped into a caned ladder-back chair by the hearth.

Bram regarded his uncle with obvious admiration before moving to Nahamkin's dry sink. Underneath he shifted around crocks until he found the one he sought. Standing again, he shook his head. "I'm embarrassed to admit that I've always thought my herbal skills were pretty useful," he said, sifting two pinches of dried rose hips into Nahamkin's best pewter mugs. "Now they seem pretty inconsequential compared to your magic."

He gave a self-deprecating snort while he added hot water to the mugs.

Guerrand shifted uncomfortably under Bram's admiring glance. "You'd be surprised to hear, then, that there are mages whose range and knowledge are greater than mine. You met two of them at the Tower of High Sorcery."

Bram sighed wistfully. "What I wouldn't give to cast even one of your spells."

The room was still dark. As the young nobleman reached for a candle atop an empty, narrow-necked bottle and held it to the new flame in the hearth, he appeared struck with a sudden thought. "Perhaps you could teach me a few spells! That fire one would certainly come in handy."

"Magic is not something to be learned piecemeal," Guerrand said, "like knot tying or scrimshaw carving."

Bram reddened and drew back in surprise. "I'm sorry, it was just a thought. I didn't mean to imply—"

"Unless you're talking simple cantrips," Guerrand said, "true magic demands that you renounce everything you've ever cared about. Are you prepared to do that and devote all your energies to the study of the Art?"

"I don't know." Bram was obviously flustered, but strangely unafraid. "I've always suspected I had a feel for magic. But I had neither books nor a mentor nor hope of either until now."

Holding his mug, Bram strode over to a small window that overlooked a weedy garden patch and stared out. "I don't spend much time pondering impossibilities. That's partly why I've thrown myself into restoring Castle DiThon. I can feel the progress with my hands, see it with my eyes. It's real to me. Still," he muttered again, more to himself than Guerrand. "I just can't shake the feeling that my life, though obviously not charmed, is somehow . . . magical."

Guerrand held very still, recalling when he'd had the exact same thought about Bram in the hallway of Castle DiThon on the day he'd left to become a mage himself. He found himself remembering as well Wilor's dying words about Bram's possible heritage.

"You have more than enough ability to achieve whatever is your goal, Bram, be it magic or otherwise," he managed after he had sorted through the briar patch of his thoughts. "But know, too, that every desire comes at a price. Only you can decide if the gain is worth the cost."

"Has it been worth it for you?" Bram asked.

"I thought so." The mage's answer was abrupt, involuntary, and it shocked him. He set his mug down more forcefully than he'd meant on the rotted wood floor.

"Thank you for this afternoon, Bram," Guerrand said briskly. "It's meant more to me than you can know. But now it's time for me to pay my respects to your aunt and return to Bastion."

Expecting Bram to protest, Guerrand avoided his nephew's gaze and jumped up from the chair by the fire. Strangely, he found his feet would not settle beneath him. His head reeled. He looked questioningly at Bram; his nephew's head was slumped upon his chest. Guerrand could only fall back into the unyielding chair as darkness descended in a wave.

\* \* \* \* \*

Guerrand knew before he opened his eyes that something was wrong. A chill breeze, damp and green, blew across his face, very likely the cause of his awakening. But he couldn't recall where he'd been so that he could determine what was so different now. Wherever he was, he was certain he'd not been lying down before. He heard no conversation or other movement to indicate anyone's presence, and yet the air fairly tingled with expectation, with waiting.

Guerrand cracked his eyes enough to see, but not enough to alert anyone nearby of his wakefulness. Something small and warm began prying his eyelids open painfully. "Hey!" he cried, slapping reflexively at whatever it was. His eyes burned madly, and he blinked away a rush of tears.

"He's awake, all right?" Guerrand heard Bram say. "For pity's sake, just leave him alone before you blind him."

Guerrand sat up and dug his fists into his eyes until the watering stopped and he could nearly see again. Two short beings with big blue eyes in pale little faces stood staring back. Their rich brown hair was feather-fine and supported jaunty hats of wool, one grass-green, the other flawless white. Pouches and tools dangled from their shoulders and waist belts.

"Who are you?" Guerrand asked. The two creatures merely blinked their eyes at him like silent, watchful owls. "Well?" he fairly howled.

"These are the tuatha I told you about meeting before," explained Bram, dropping to his knees by his uncle. "Not these two in particular. They're very like the faeries of wives' tales, secretly performing household functions for food, but don't make the mistake of calling them brownies."

"I've heard of them," Guerrand interrupted, propping himself up on his elbows. "They must have put a sleep spell on us."

Bram nodded. "I guess they wanted to get us into Nahamkin's garden," he suggested. "Though what they want with us here is a puzzle. Still, they're benevolent little creatures. They're probably the only reason

I'm speaking to you now. I never would have made it to Wayreth in time to find you without their help."

"I've heard the tales about the tuatha dundarael, of course," said Guerrand as he walked around both tuatha, peering closely at the small, soft-featured beings. "But I've never met any before." The creatures looked back at him impassively. "They vaguely resemble a sylph I once met."

"Probably another kind of faerie-folk," Bram concluded. "I'm surprised a speaker wasn't sent. I got the idea they always traveled in threes." He peered expectantly into the taller weeds at the edge of the garden. "Maybe these two just want a mug of milk or a bit of bread for some past debt," he muttered, though his tone indicated he doubted the thought himself.

Suddenly the air began to sparkle around them. Frolicking hues of gold and red and green danced just above the brown, withered remains of last year's garden. Everywhere the sparkling touched, the plants became slightly greener and stood a little straighter. The effect was startling yet beautiful.

While the humans and tuatha watched, the twinkling, colorful lights slowly gathered into the recognizable form of a third tuatha. The two mute tuatha dropped to their knees and bowed their heads.

Bram recognized the newly arrived child-sized being, wearing a slate-blue mantle and wool cap. "Thistledown!" he exclaimed, then cocked his head, his expression clouding with concern. "Your face looks pale and drawn. Are you unwell?"

"All will be explained to you," the blue-mantled tuatha said. "Bow before King Weador."

Guerrand and Bram exchanged surprised looks. Some force, like a great hand, pressed down on their shoulders, dropping them hard to their knees.

A rain of light fell on the garden then, illuminating

everything with rainbow hues, running off Bram's and Guerrand's backs in multicolored waterfalls. The light puddled on flat surfaces, only to evaporate away in an instant. Then, in a most unmagical fashion, the weeds parted and between them strode a sight that was incongruously majestic in the tangled garden patch.

The tuatha, who from his obvious wealth and regal stature must be King Weador, approached them in slow, measured steps, as if ceremonial music played that only he could hear. Supporting himself with a walking stick, he stopped between two fragrant rosemary topiary plants. The noble tuatha's eyes sank shut as he inhaled languorously, then opened slowly so that he could consider the two humans who were considering him.

The tuatha king's hair was white as new snow and hung down his back to within a hand span of the ground. His face didn't look old or wrinkled exactly, though it was etched with straight, parallel, deep brown crevices. The effect reminded Guerrand of a lady's perfectly folded, oiled parchment fan.

Weador's clothing looked far richer than the serviceable wool garments of his servants. His mantle, draping him to the thighs, was made of carefully stitched mouse pelts, decorated with the subtle underfeathers of a pheasant, and was held closed with a shiny gold brooch. Fine-spun spider-silk garments dyed in the muted tones of the earth completed his stately appearance.

Every one of Weador's ten fingers, short, thick, and fringed with downy white hairs, carried a ring of a natural substance: several of carved, creamy scrimshaw, ivory, stone, and wood. In his right hand was the scepter he had used as a walking stick. Its tip was a bleached-white turtle skull. The eye sockets had been replaced with pure, shining gold.

Guerrand noticed all these things and was properly impressed. Yet the feature that caught his attention and held it was the king's frosty blue eyes. King Weador's eyes were the saddest Guerrand had ever seen.

"Rise." In that one word, the king's voice was like the sound of fog rolling over the Strait of Ergoth, like wind through willow leaves, like raindrops on a thatch roof, like all of the sounds defined by words. "I apologize for my methods, but the sleep spell seemed the gentlest way to keep you here when you seemed determined to leave.

"I must also apologize for my delay," King Weador continued, lowering himself upon a throne that grew before their eyes from a small toadstool. "I have not traveled with a destination in mind recently and did not properly gauge the time needed in human terms."

All manner of responses came to mind at once, but none came to Guerrand's lips.

"I will waste no more time," continued King Weador, "since there will be little left for us here unless we three reach some manner of understanding. I feel compelled to seek it before commanding an exodus."

"With all due respect," Guerrand began, "why should we listen to you after the way we've been treated? Honorable wizards who seek the cooperation of strangers don't usually get it by casting spells upon those strangers."

The king bowed his head with good grace. "Forgive me, but I could not risk your leaving before we spoke. The presence of my people—and yours—in Northern Ergoth depends upon it."

Guerrand was intrigued, as Weador had intended. "Go on," he said softly.

Weador's blue eyes blinked. "Though most of you are unaware of our existence," he began, "humans and tuatha have a symbiotic relationship. That is, when the humans thrive, we tuatha thrive, and vice versa. We secretly clean your houses, tend your gardens and fields, turn your mills, and perform myriad other daily tasks that make humans happy and fruitful. In turn, we flourish, both from the increased production and the positive energy stimulated by all aspects of a thriving economy.

"We have been in Ergoth since the beginning of time, since the construction of the magical pillars at Stonecliff. We survived the Cataclysm here, when Ergoth was divided into two islands, and the subsequent droughts, floods, and famines. But never, in all that time, has the decay here been as severe as it is now. This plague has affected even the tuatha, as young Bram noticed in our Thistledown's face."

"But the plague is over," Bram exclaimed. "Guerrand made the moon two-dimensional so—"

"I am aware of what occurred," the king cut in gently. "But you are shortsighted if you think curing the cause of the plague will instantly erase all of its aftereffects."

"What do you mean?" Bram asked.

"Most of the animals have been slaughtered," the king explained. "Crops have yet to be planted, nor are they likely to be, since tuatha scouts report that many of the grain stores were destroyed by Thonvil's hayward in the hysteria over the source of the plague. With the seed stores gone, how will the already low food supply be replenished?"

"I have some seeds at Castle DiThon," said Bram. "If they aren't enough, I'll buy or beg what I can from villages that weren't affected by the plague."

The king's snow-white head shook imperceptibly. "I hope that will be enough, for we tuatha can only augment what exists. If little or nothing exists to embellish, then we are forced to move on to survive."

"And if you move on," prompted Guerrand, catching the king's direction at last, "then Thonvil, in its already fragile state, will very likely perish."

The king snapped his thick fingers. "Exactly."

"So what are you telling us to do?" asked Bram.

"Humans are not subject to my rulership," the king reminded him placidly. "I'm merely suggesting options. If you care about the survival of the village or the presence of the tuatha, then you must work immediately to restore the lands."

"You know, of course," began Bram, "that I've been trying to do just that for many years. The tuatha have been helping me."

"That might have been enough," conceded the tuatha king, "if not for this plague. However, time is critical now. The village will survive only if someone provides direction and leadership that has long been lacking here."

Bram fidgeted. "Thonvil already has a lord in my father."

"Yes, I know." The pause that followed spoke volumes about the king's opinion of Cormac DiThon. "A little more than two of your decades ago, I predicted this decline and took what steps I could to stave it off. We increased intervention in your fields and homes," the king continued. "I daresay our efforts made the difference, in the last decade, between eating and not for many of your villagers. I know it did for us tuatha."

"You're suggesting I seize my father's authority," said Bram.

Guerrand had no love for Cormac. There was no doubt his brother should have relinquished his authority to Bram years ago. "Haven't you all but done that anyway?" he asked his nephew.

"I had hoped to spare my father some measure of dignity," conceded Bram, "though he has done nothing toward that himself."

"We," said the king, speaking royally, "have taken other, more severe, measures to prevent Thonvil from perishing." His intense blue eyes held Guerrand's meaningfully before settling upon Bram. "But they have yet to yield fruit. I am not without hope; however, I don't think Thonvil can wait."

Guerrand felt a precognitive shiver run through his body.

"Let us assume, for the sake of argument," said Bram, "that I'm willing to oust my lord and father. Just how am I supposed to lead the people to salvation?"

"You are a human of high intellect and moral character," the king remarked, "not unlike the previous lord, Rejik DiThon. He was a strong and virtuous leader."

"I was very young when my grandfather died," reflected Bram. "I'm afraid I remember precious little about him, and certainly not enough to emulate his behavior."

"But your uncle does." Though his words were directed at Bram, the king's frosty eyes held Guerrand's. "Can you envision what your father could have accomplished during his reign if he'd had an able mage at his side?"

The question strummed a sharp memory chord, and Guerrand nodded vaguely. Even his small magics had brought new life to the small village of Harrowdown-on-the-Schallsea.

"Then imagine how Bram's compassionate rule and your magic could restore this land," prompted the king.

Guerrand recalled, too well, a discussion with Cormac on the very subject. He'd tried to convince his brother to conquer his fear of magic and see the good it could do in Thonvil. But, of course, Cormac had flatly refused to consider that magic was anything but evil.

Guerrand thought it ironic that, ten years later, he was being given the chance to prove he'd been right.

King Weador watched the play of emotions across the mage's face. "You will have a wise advisor and powerful magical ally in your uncle," the king said confidently to Bram.

Guerrand came back from his thoughts and held his palms up. "Slow down, there. I already have a job."

The king's white eyebrows turned down. "Ah, yes. Bastion."

"You know of it?"

"That question indicates an inadequate understanding of tuatha dundarael," King Weador observed. "Remember, we made it possible for Bram to reach Wayreth in a matter of moments, instead of a fortnight. There is almost no corner of the cosmos our faerie roads do not reach. In fact, there is very little in the magical world of which I am not at least peripherally aware."

Weador's intense blue eyes abruptly penetrated Guerrand's in a most disconcerting way. The king said nothing at first. Instead, he reached out a stubby, beringed hand to the front of Guerrand's robe and brushed away the sooty black smudges there. All but one magically disappeared under the king's fingers. Expression grave, Weador gave that side of the robe a tug so that Guerrand could better see the mark.

Perplexed into silence, Guerrand squinted down his chin to regard the dark smudge that so interested King Weador. On closer inspection, the soot appeared to have a pattern, like the whorls and lines of a thumbprint. A black thumbprint.

Guerrand's head jerked up, and his eyes met Weador's knowing gaze. He gasped as the memory of who had last touched the front of his robe sprang to mind: Nuitari.

"It's a thumbprint. So what? What does it mean?" demanded Bram.

"I have sensed you were in grave danger from the moment we met," King Weador admitted to Guerrand, ignoring Bram's question. "But that feeling intensified when we spoke of Bastion." The king's eyes commanded Guerrand's in a manner the mage couldn't resist. "Beware there, Guerrand DiThon."

That said, the king of the tuatha pushed himself up from his toadstool throne. "Our business is concluded." Before their eyes, the white-haired tuatha king and his silent minions faded from view like a bittersweet dream upon waking.

And, like a dream, Guerrand could not call Weador back for questions.

"I've got to get to Bastion," Guerrand declared, his voice breathy with anxiety. He fished around in the pouch whose strap still crisscrossed his chest.

Bram grabbed his arm. "Stop and think, Rand," he pleaded. "Weador said there was danger for you there. What better reason do you need to stay here in Thonvil?"

Guerrand stopped rummaging briefly to gape in disbelief at his nephew. "You can't mean that—you're no more a coward than I am, Bram. Bastion is my responsibility."

Bram rubbed his face. "No, I didn't mean that. I'm just worried, is all. I haven't gone through all this to lose you to some threat I don't even understand."

Frowning his preoccupation, Guerrand didn't hear Bram. His fingertips at last met with the object he sought. "Got it!" he cried, holding the fragment of magical mirror aloft.

Bram looked at the shard in that accepting way he'd come to view strange things of magic, took a deep breath, and stood up straight. "Well, then, let's get going."

Guerrand lowered the mirror slowly. "You can't come with me, Bram."

"Why not?"

"I'll list some of the countless reasons, in no particular order," Guerrand said. "Bastion is my responsibility, not yours. You haven't permission to return there. You're needed here to begin bringing Thonvil back to life."

"That can wait one day," Bram countered.

"Can it?" Guerrand's tone suggested he thought otherwise. "Besides," he added, "you have to stay here and keep my mirror safe."

Bram looked perplexed.

"I can't teleport between planes," Guerrand explained. "Instead, I'm going to step into this magical mirror and exit through one in the red wing of Bastion. But that means I have to leave the mirror behind. Although only someone who has seen the inside of Bastion could use it to follow me there, it's still too powerful a device to let fall into the wrong hands."

Bram's nostrils flared in anger. "So I'm to stay here and protect a piece of glass while you're in who-knows-what manner of danger." Guerrand's expression told Bram he wouldn't budge on this issue. "I don't like this one bit," the younger man said, but he bowed his head in resignation.

"I *must* go now, Bram," Guerrand said as gently as he could. Turning back to the cottage where Zagarus rested on the roof, he yelled, "Come on, Zag." The familiar spread his wings with a dolorous flap, apparently resigned to never getting any rest, and flew directly into the tiny piece of glass and disappeared.

Guerrand raised a foot, but turned to Bram. "I'll

send word, either in person or by missive, so don't fear." He touched his nephew's sleeve, then bent his head to the shard. "Be of strong heart, Bram."

"Have a care!" Bram cried, but his uncle had already disappeared into the impossibly small mirror. All the nobleman could see now was his own fretful expression reflected in the shiny glass. He snatched up the mirror, placed it in a pocket, and strode off to face his own problems at Castle DiThon.

* * * * *

Guerrand fairly flew through one of the reflective mirrors in the seascape room, trying to look all ways at once. He stopped and shook his head at his behavior. As if whatever danger Weador predicted would be lurking in his seascape where Zagarus was perched at water's edge.

The first thing Guerrand did was race to his dressing area and remove his red robe, more tarnished than soiled. He wrenched it from his shoulders and flung it to the ground, unable to resist the temptation to grind the thumb-printed thing under his feet as he reached for one of the clean red garments that hung in his clothespress. He shrugged that one on and cinched it tight about the waist. As if to confirm that he had removed Nuitari's mark and was safe, he checked himself in a glass. Before his horrified eyes, the mark reappeared in the same spot on the new garment, and on each of the three others he frantically donned. Devastated, Guerrand gave in to the inevitability of the mark and slid down the wall to the floor to think.

Did the ever-present black thumbprint mean the danger Weador said awaited him at Bastion was somehow linked to Nuitari? The god had a representative here at Bastion: Dagamier.

Guerrand's eyes narrowed with suspicion. Ezius was too quiet and befuddled to ever be a threat. But Dagamier . . . She obviously coveted the position of high defender; the black wizardess had fought against Guerrand's authority from the first moment they'd met. She'd made it easier for Guerrand to take his leave from Bastion by assuming his responsibilities. Had she spent the time arranging his downfall?

He turned back to his shoulder bag, now lying on the floor, and donned the bracelets and rings that carried his protective spells and were capable of shielding him against both physical blows and magical forces. Checking the scrying schedule, he determined that it was Dagamier's shift in the sphere.

Guerrand covered the distance to the nave in a matter of heartbeats. He passed through the door and approached the white column that housed the scrying diorama, willing himself to remain calm. Still, he didn't hesitate to briskly call her name across the moat from where he knew the door to be. "Dagamier! It's Guerrand. Open the sphere, please."

After a brief pause, the door slid open as requested. Dagamier stepped up to stand in the small archway, her cheeks dimpled in a smile that set her green eyes slantwise. Her body looked slim and salamander-smooth in the snug-fitting black silk robe that clung to every curve.

"You're back." The smile gave way to her usual studied mask of indifference. "I trust things are well again in Thonberg with Bertram?"

A muscle leaped in Guerrand's jaw. "*Bram* has things under control again in *Thonvil*."

"Fine." Dagamier made to return to the scrying sphere.

"Form the bridge, Dagamier," Guerrand commanded. "I would have a report of events since I left."

She frowned at the unusual request. "Can't it wait until Ezius's turn at the sphere? There's too little room, as you must realize—"

"No."

Dagamier searched his face and must have seen that he would brook no defiance today. Shrugging, as if Guerrand's authority still meant little to her, Dagamier touched a tapered finger to the button that activated the bridge, calling it forth.

Guerrand crossed the crystal bridge and joined her in the narrow column. The darkened room, the real heart of Bastion, was austere and functional. Dagamier was already seated again before the faintly glowing diorama of Bastion and its perimeter.

Guerrand pressed his back to the wall away from Dagamier, to keep from touching the black-robed wizardess. "Please tell me of your activities, both unusual and mundane, since I left."

Dagamier kept her eyes fixed on the model. "That's an odd request. I took my turns at the sphere, which were doubled, I might add, by your absence. I slept, studied, drilled for defense, and conducted experiments in my apartments. The usual things."

"Nothing else of interest occurred, either inside or outside Bastion?"

She gave him a fleeting glance, her lips pursed. "That depends on if you consider conversing with Ezius interesting," she said coolly, returning her glance to the diorama. "However, the demiplane has been as quiet as a tomb since you left."

The younger woman abruptly leaned away from the subject of her gaze and crossed her arms. "Why don't you just tell me what's got you so edgy?"

Guerrand watched Dagamier's reaction closely as he said, "Someone I have reason to trust said that great danger awaited me at Bastion."

"So naturally you thought of me." She returned her gaze to the model, betraying neither concern nor offense.

He watched her expression. "I'm thinking of invoking my right as high defender to search both yours and Ezius's apartments, Dagamier."

To Guerrand's great surprise, the black wizard gave her trademark shrug. "Go ahead and check my apartments if you must. That is your right. While you're in the white wing," she continued, nonplused, "please remind Ezius to arrive on time for his next shift. Maybe it was the change in schedule while you were gone that threw him off, but he forgot to show up for a few of his turns here."

"Did he?" asked Guerrand. "That's unusual. Ezius is usually very punctual and reliable."

Dagamier looked unconcerned. "He came immediately when I reminded him. If you ask me, he forgot because he's become preoccupied with the body of that wizard friend of yours who 'dropped by' just before you left with your nephew."

"Ezius told me he was going to arrange for proper disposal of the body," said Guerrand, frowning. "I thought he would have done so by now."

Dagamier could only look at Guerrand.

The high defender's mouth drew into a pinched, worried line. "Have you noticed anything else odd about Ezius since I've been gone?"

The black wizard returned her gaze to the model. "He's kept to his apartments when he wasn't scrying." She chuckled suddenly. "There is *one* thing, though it's more funny than odd. You remember how long it took you to keep him from calling you Rind, after that cobbler he once knew?" Guerrand nodded. "Well, Ezius may have got your name straight now, but he's taken to mixing mine up. He keeps calling me Esme," Dagamier said, her eyes still on the sphere. "I've never even known anyone by that name."

Guerrand's blood froze in his veins. He slowly lifted his head to stare at her pale, chiseled profile before whispering hoarsely, "Are you sure about that name?"

"Yes," she said. "It was unusual enough to remember." Dagamier shifted her eyes to look at him quizzically.

Without speaking, Guerrand whirled on his heel in the small chamber, meant only for one. The door raised, the bridge formed across the small moat, and he walked across it, oblivious to the plant fronds in his path. His heels pounded across the cold marble floor on his way to the white wing.

The door to the wing was closed, as usual. Guerrand grasped the heavy brass ring that hung from the griffon's-head knocker and slammed it against the door. When no response came, Guerrand tried again, waiting with increasing impatience.

"Ezius!" he howled to the roof, legs spread, arms and fists stiff at his sides. "I demand that you open this door at once!"

The white door remained closed.

Guerrand didn't hesitate to call forth the spell given only to the high defender. He placed his right hand against the door. With his fingers arranged very precisely, he muttered, *"Lenithis kor."* The air around his hand flared bright yellow, and the door shuddered beneath an ear-numbing boom.

But still it did not open.

No legitimate power in Bastion could have prevented the spell from giving the high defender access to any area in the stronghold. Undaunted, Guerrand prepared to break down the door to the white wing.

* * * * *

The white-robed mage's head shot up. Loud banging at the far end of the wide-open wing briefly broke his concentration. Recognizing Rand's voice, he willed himself not to panic. So, the high defender had returned. . . . What did it matter? The mage had prepared for this possibility and put up protections to prevent, or at the very least significantly slow, anyone who tried to enter the white wing. It would take some time for Guerrand to break through the door, and there were still additional safeguards beyond it.

The thought considerably calmed the mage. He stood next to a white marble table that held the corpse of Lyim Rhistadt. The table was part of a small work space in the section designated as the wing's laboratory. Though there were no walls to delineate rooms here, the purpose and boundaries of each area were clear, designated by function: bookshelves plainly marked off the library, thick carpets lent warmth to the small living space, tables and countertops in neat rows filled the work area.

Since bringing the body into the wing, the mage had maintained a spell that also prevented scrying or other magical methods of direct observation. Because of the spell, even the high defender was virtually powerless to know what was happening inside the white wing. Whether Guerrand was merely seeking a report upon his return to Bastion, or was already suspicious of Ezius's behavior, it mattered little. The mage in the white robe had worked too long and hard toward the goal that was moments from being realized to be turned back now.

To further protect himself against interruption, the stooped, pale-haired mage quickly prepared to cast two more spells in a sequence that would cause the second to protect the duration of the first. Withdrawing a small crystal bead from a deep pocket in his robe, he

muttered the arcane word, *"Pilif."* The globe of invul-
nerability appeared as a faintly shimmering sphere
around the mage and the entire marble lab table before
him. He set the crystal bead on the table by the corpse.

The second spell would prevent anyone from dispelling the magic of the globe. For it, the white-robed
mage removed another gem from his robe, a large diamond. Placing it gingerly in a marble mortar, he drove
the pestle into it like a hammer again and again, until
he had shattered the precious stone. He ground the
diamond into coarse dust and sprinkled both himself
and the red mage's body with the glittering shards.
Though there was no visible effect to indicate the
.spell's discharge, the mage instinctively felt that he had
successfully made them immune to most spells. For a
short time, anyway.

The mage prided himself on his good planning. But
he was also dependent upon a measure of luck for having gotten this far. It had been the greatest good fortune that the high defender's nephew had taken him
away, giving the mage time to prepare his spells before
anyone questioned his activities with the red-robed
corpse.

Dead? Hah! The mage in the white robe pressed two
fingers to the death-cool left wrist of the body that lay
beneath him upon the cold marble slab. A reedy pulse,
slowed to a tenth its normal rate, was barely detectible
against the warm index and third digits of his right
hand. What a delicious sensation was feeling a pulse
through fingers, thought the mage, though it had taken
some time to readjust to having a right hand at all.

But not as long as it had taken to get accustomed to
looking at one's own body through the eyes of another.
Lyim had never noticed the small ring of moles at the
nape of his own neck, or that his chin in profile receded
slightly. Maybe he'd just been too consumed in recent

years with the monstrosity at the end of his right arm to notice anything else. Unconsciously, Ezius's dark eyes were turned by Lyim's darker mind to the diamond stone piercing Lyim's left lobe.

The magic jar spell that made all this possible could not have worked more flawlessly. In Villa Nova, before his final attack upon Bastion, Lyim had chosen the diamond ear stud to be the receptacle, briefly, for his life-force, because he felt certain a small earring was likely to remain with his body, unlike a larger, more ostentatious piece of jewelry. Besides, he doubted the mages at Bastion were looters.

It had been a relatively simple thing, then—a matter of timing in the heat of the battle Lyim had forced—to transfer his essence to the diamond ear stud. His body had collapsed as if slain, while his life-force went into the gem.

It had been Ezius's bad luck that brought him first to inspect Lyim's body. Seizing the moment, Lyim jumped his life-force from the gem into Ezius's body, simultaneously forcing Ezius's body into imprisonment in the diamond. The spell had been instantaneous and seamless; no one else could have detected the process.

That was why there had been no reason to question the white mage's offer to carry the body of the "slain" red mage into the white wing of Bastion for burial. As Lyim had hoped, Guerrand had been too overwrought by the battle to question Ezius's offer. The Black Robe obviously hadn't cared to deal with the body of a mage not from her order, which was just as well, from Lyim's perspective, though it might have been interesting to inhabit the body of a woman.

It had all worked so smoothly that Lyim had struggled to keep from smiling when, with the Black Robe and Rand, he had carried his own body up the stairs and into the sacred halls of Bastion. As Ezius, he fought against gaping in wonder, since none of it would have seemed new to the White Robe. Fortunately, they'd left him at the door to his wing, which allowed him to familiarize himself in private. Lyim's first task had been to place protections on the door.

Only later had Lyim learned from Dagamier that Rand had left Bastion to battle the medusa plague. Rand's absence had been the greatest gift, giving Lyim precious time to lay the groundwork for recreating the events that had mutated his hand. He had hoped to be done with the preparations sooner, but of course everything took longer when you were working in someone else's laboratory, not to mention body.

The magic jar gave Lyim the option of keeping Ezius's body, with its two good hands, but he had no interest in living very long in anyone's body but his own. Ezius's was stiffened with age and a level of inactivity to which Lyim was unused, and his eyesight was good only through the use of thick lenses. Still, Lyim needed to keep himself locked within Ezius's form now for one very important reason: two hands were needed to make the complex motions required by the spell that would cure his hand.

Soon, he told himself, the hideous snake would be gone, and he would have his own form again. Lyim used the thoughts to give himself energy for the tasks that still lay ahead.

There were no moons at Bastion to worry about aligning, nor did he need to anchor a cross-dimensional bridge. Thanks to the meddling of the Conclave of Wizards, Bastion was at a dimensional crossroads, the only one that gave access to the Lost Citadel. But, unlike his master before him, Lyim had no intention of entering the Lost Citadel; he wished only to open exactly the same sequence of pathways unlocked by Belize, then insert his arm so that it crossed the snake-creature's plane. Only upon seeing its home would the reptile flee from Lyim's body, allowing the limb to return to its natural form.

Lyim thought he heard Guerrand howl Ezius's name outside the wing's entrance. He turned his mind to casting the most important spell of his life.

Ezius's hands summoned a swirling sphere of flame. The ball writhed between his fingers, twisting, flickering, contained only by Lyim's will. With intense concentration the mage turned and extended his arms so that the ball of energy hovered over his physical body on the marble slab.

The flickering globe flared angrily and swelled to twice its previous size. Its eerie light shimmered on the clean surfaces in the all-white laboratory.

Next, Lyim drew a succession of vials and containers he had placed for this purpose upon the shelves. He tossed each into the swirling inferno, just as Belize had done those years ago next to the stone plinths. He muttered arcane phrases and completed the specified hand gestures—one short slice with the right hand, both hands slowly circling thrice. The fiery globe grew steadily larger until its shape began to change, to flatten and stretch into an oval. The swirling mass yawned open with an unbearable, purplish light.

Lyim looked through Ezius's bespectacled eyes at the hated appendage covered in scales of brown, red, and gold, patterned symmetrically in rings and swirls. Without hesitation, he commanded Ezius's hand to raise the silent snake arm and plunge it toward the wall of whirling hues.

There was no soul within Lyim's body to scream this time, or to writhe in pain. But through Ezius's hands Lyim could feel the limb thrashing, could sense the unworldly energy blazing through it. The memory of the flood of agony, undimmed by the intervening decade, surged to life again. But now he was steeled by years of striving, and he would let no scream pass his lips.

Lyim recalled his master's words as if they'd been spoken just yesterday: "These portals frequently contain the undead remains of centuries' worth of unsuccessful adventurers. They jump like starving fleas upon the first fresh traveler they meet."

Lyim knew there would be no new creatures waiting in the passage, since Bastion had blocked this dimensional portal almost since the disaster at Stonecliff. A decade of curiosity about what happened beyond prompted Lyim to bring Ezius's head nearer the opening he'd created in the plane.

The mage was astonished when the incandescent curtain of swirling light parted for him like an opening eye. Beyond it lay a passage, a tunnel bored through the dimensions. The walls, floor, and ceiling pulsed with electrical energy and twisted and writhed like a living thing.

A creature thrashed below him. Lyim immediately recognized the snakelike head next to a pale, limp arm. But the snake's thick, fur-covered body supported by thousands of red-veined fingers made Lyim gasp. It was impossible to tell how long the creature was, with its coils lapped one atop another in thoughtless loops. Rather than slithering, the monster wound its bulk sideways as if rolling down an incline, and disappeared through the tunnel wall into whatever unknown dimension lay outside, leaving behind a faintly glowing trail.

Lyim was watching the glow recede when the undulating tunnel erupted in brightness more blinding than a thousand candles. He clamped his eyes shut, but the light burned through his lids. Without moving, Lyim was physically drawn through the portal. Next to him he could feel his own, unconscious body being lifted off the marble slab and dragged into the maelstrom by the restored arm, as if some power were drawn by the mages' magical emanations. The pull was overwhelming. Though he had not come for this, Lyim, once exposed to the citadel's power, didn't even want to resist. The bodies of both mages glided through the pulsating confines of the tunnel toward the distance source of the brilliance.

Though Lyim's eyes were still closed, the light etched upon his lids a multisensory image. He witnessed the birth of the world, the origins of the races, the calamities and triumphs that marked thousands of years of Krynn's history. He saw magical forces being molded and applied in ways he had never dreamt possible, as well as magical disasters that altered the shape of the world.

The force that pulled the mages' bodies stopped as abruptly as it began. Lyim commanded Ezius's eyes to open.

Radiant gates of spider-spun gold rose up from a knee-high fog. A jagged range of polished minerals and semiprecious rock encircled the citadel. Three immense diamond spires sliced through the billowing fog and gold and silver foothills to penetrate the blackness of space. The triangle of glittering spires was set upon a pentagon of polished gold, the source of the yellow radiance that sent blinding light up through the faceted diamond spires. The whole effect reminded Lyim of an enormous jeweled pendant.

No windows or balconies marred the crystalline surface of the spires, nor doors the gold base, to mark it as a habitable place. Yet the citadel pulsed with magical energy, with the essence of life. The contrast of stark, cold minerals and hot golden light seemed to symbolize the complexities of magic itself.

An understanding of what he saw came unbidden to Lyim, as if any mage who looked upon the forbidden Lost Citadel could not but realize these things about the most magical of places. The faceted surfaces reflected the foundation upon which all earthly things were built—a mirror held to the universe to reveal a skeleton complex beyond compare. The citadel's mineraled walls had risen naturally millennia ago from the mire of Krynn to house three novice mages. When those first wizards unleashed far more magic than they could control, setting off floods and fires and earthquakes, they were transported in their tower to a place beyond the circles of the universe. Ever after, the tower was known as the Lost Citadel. The mages became the founders of the Orders of High Sorcery.

Ezius's old fingers curled around the delicate gold filigree of the gate. As he did so, the craggy, cold foothills surrounding the citadel began to quake, sending boulders of gold and silver tumbling toward the gate. The quake continued, unabated, until the tunnel beneath Ezius's sandaled feet and Lyim's prone, true body trembled. Lyim grasped the gate tighter to steady himself, but the move only increased the intensity of the tremors. Lyim felt himself thrown to Ezius's knees.

The power of the collapsing portal began to drag both mages back through the tunnel in much the same way as they'd been pulled toward the gate. Ezius's hands futilely stretched toward the gates of the citadel, even as Lyim's mind reached out to the wonders beyond them. Ezius's body slipped from the tunnel, through the portal's purple whorl, heartbeats after Lyim's. He fell upon his own unconscious body, slumped on the marble slab, then tumbled like a fish to the cold floor of Bastion's white wing.

Lyim was only barely aware that above the slab, the portal spiraled slowly inward and began to darken and shrink. The vibrant colors that had been almost too bright to look at quickly faded to dark red-orange, then disappeared.

Lyim was dazed and incredulous. He had looked upon the source of all magic, witnessed the wrath of the gods. Almost everything he had ever done seemed trivial compared to that.

Except for one thing. Lyim's gaze traveled up to his own body, beautifully restored and dangling from the slab above him. There was no need for loathing anymore. Lyim examined all five fingers of his right hand with a child's joy.

It came to him in a flash that he had no more need for Ezius's old and tired frame. He quickly closed Ezius's eyes to concentrate on the gem in his own ear. Instantly his entire consciousness was altered. His senses were completely stripped away; he was suspended, numb, in a blackness that no light, sound, or heat could penetrate. Instinctively he homed in on the slow, thin pulse of his own body. Slowly, like fog slipping over the sea, his essence drifted from the gem. Lyim found himself draped across the marble table, staring at the vaulted ceiling far above. He had been out of his body for perhaps two days, but still it felt strange to Lyim. In moments the feeling passed, and a thrill ran through him as he realized he was whole again.

Lyim gathered up his red robe and rolled stiffly into a sitting position atop the cold white slab. His body felt strong and right, as if he'd slipped on a familiar, buttersoft glove. The mage flexed the fingers of his right hand before wide, disbelieving eyes, until he couldn't contain his elation. He leaped from the slab into the air. Coming down, he crashed into Ezius, slumped against the marble base.

Lyim blinked at the white-robed mage. Ezius raised

a trembling hand, as if about to cast a spell. At least that's what Lyim presumed when he reached out with his own right hand and touched Ezius's temple. The older man's face went slack, and all comprehension left his eyes. Ezius stared around the room like an idiot child, bewildered by everything he saw. Lyim reached out his hand once more, poising it above the mage's head. "Take a little rest, Ezius. You've earned it." Fine amber dust drifted down from Lyim's hand. The dust clouded Ezius's already vague eyes, and then his head slipped gently to the porcelain floor.

"Lyim!"

The mage looked up at the sound of a familiar voice cursing his name. Lyim spun about to face his most hated foe, his handsome face spread in a wolfish smile of anticipation.

# Chapter Eighteen

Bastion's high defender stared at the pulsing, writhing, purple glow around the door, and the meaning of King Weador's warning came clear to him. Guerrand had witnessed light like that only once before: during the triple eclipse on Stonecliff. Lyim Rhistadt had lost his hand that night. There could be no mistaking the danger now.

Guerrand called Dagamier from the scrying sphere and sent her to collect all the wands, cloaks, and components she could lay her hands on. He sized up the magical protections on the door and settled upon the likeliest spell to break them. From his ever-present pack, the mage pulled a stringed chime—a small, silvery tube—and waited impatiently for the black wizard to return.

The radiance beneath the door flared up, streaming

through the cracks so that Guerrand was bathed in an ultraviolet glow. The high defender knew he could wait no longer.

Setting aside the chime momentarily, Guerrand searched through his pouch again and withdrew a small glass bead. As he whispered an incantation, he used the bead to trace magical symbols on his forehead, the backs of his hands and arms, his chest, and finally, in the air surrounding him. With the final phrase of the spell, Guerrand released the bead. It shattered like a fine crystal glass, and the mage was surrounded in soft, shimmering light. As long as it lasted, he would be protected against all but the most powerful magic.

Guerrand retrieved the chime and held it up by the string. He struck it slowly once, twice, thrice with a small, rubber-tipped mallet. With the third tone, the double doors burst inward. Guerrand leaped one step inside the door, discarding the chime.

The high defender had been inside Bastion's white wing only on those few occasions when Ezius had invited him. The area near the door was dim with murky blue-violet light. But the purple, incandescent portal throbbed and swirled with energy at the far right corner of the wing's vast, open room. It glowed so brightly at its center that Guerrand could not bear to look directly at it.

The mage glanced away, eyes burning as if he'd stared at the sun. A pair of luminescent eyes, unblinking and motionless, rose before him. They were feline in shape, but far too large to belong to any cat Guerrand had ever seen.

With a wave of his hand and a muttered word, Guerrand filled his end of the vast chamber with light. There was no sign of Ezius or Lyim, dead or alive, anywhere in the wing. But he found the source of the odd, luminous eyes. No past experience could keep him from starting backward. The creature that blocked his path to the portal resembled a snake or an eel in form, but its proportions were monstrous. It was coiled into a loop, but Guerrand guessed the creature's body must have been at least twice as long as his own frame, possibly more. The body appeared black, but where light reflected from the tiny, glossy scales, they flashed a dark, subterranean blue.

Most unsettling was the creature's human-shaped head. The dark, slanted eyes had vertical irises, like a cat's. The ears were pointed and too far back on the head to look human, though, and its teeth resembled needles.

At the other end of the body, held straight up in the air with great menace, was a bony stinger as long as Guerrand's forearm. Venom glistened on its tip. Guerrand shuddered; Lyim had chosen his guardian with irony.

The two adversaries eyed each other warily. Guerrand had heard about nagas, fiendish and intelligent monsters with a hunger for magical knowledge. They were known to offer their services to powerful mages in exchange for spell formulae. Even when Guerrand was an apprentice, Justarius had warned him against dealing with such beings. If Belize had done the same for his apprentice, Lyim had obviously ignored him.

The wizard was greatly relieved to hear Dagamier's footsteps as she returned across the nave. The black-robed mage stepped into the white wing and slung a heavy cloak across Guerrand's shoulders that would protect the wearer like a suit of armor.

The naga's eyes followed Dagamier, the first movement Guerrand had seen the monster make. He raised his hands before him. Sparks raced across Guerrand's flesh, ready to leap forward as a bolt of lightning.

Nagas were highly susceptible to bribes, so before attacking, Guerrand thought to offer one. "We want your master, and have no quarrel with you," he began, searching his memory of Bastion's collected magical items for an artifact of use to a limbless creature. "Stand aside, and I will give you a magical circlet after I'm assured we've passed freely."

"My master is not here," the naga replied in a dark voice that held no trace of an accent. "He has entered the portal. I will accept your offer and let you pass." With silken grace the naga's coils slid off one another. The creature backed away warily, but its unblinking eyes remained riveted on Guerrand.

Dagamier tossed a disbelieving glance at Guerrand. He, too, was surprised at the monster's easy acquiescence, and did not entirely trust it. With the spell still ready to cast, he advanced into the white wing, balancing caution against the immediate imperative of drawing Lyim from the portal. Dagamier followed three steps behind him.

A scream set Guerrand's heart hammering. Looking back over his shoulder he cursed. Silhouetted by the doorway, Dagamier had her arms thrown wide, and a look of horror and pain was frozen on her death-pale face. With great effort, as if pulling against a harness, she tipped her dark head back to peer up into the rafters above.

But Guerrand had already seen what Dagamier could not. Dangling heavily from an overhead beam, just inside the door, was a second naga. Its serpentine tail hung down and disappeared behind Dagamier. The naga quivered its tail, making Dagamier twitch like a marionette. Slowly her eyes rolled back and her head slumped. The black wizard's entire body went limp. Yet she remained standing until, with a flick of its tail, the naga snapped its poisoned stinger out from her back.

Dagamier collapsed sideways and lay motionless.

Before the woman's body hit the floor, two bolts of lightning ripped from Guerrand's hands to smash into the monstrous snake-thing above the door. The air crackled and buzzed as the twin arcs twitched in a fantastic dance across the open room, rooted at one end to Guerrand and at the other to the naga.

The blast constricted the rippling muscles in the creature's body. The glistening stinger thrashed and jerked through the air, which quickly filled with the stink of burning flesh. The shriek that erupted from the second naga's lips was nothing like the smooth tones of its accomplice. The naga was blown from the rafter amidst a whirlwind of smoke and wood splinters. It landed next to Dagamier, a mess of burned flesh and smoldering blood.

The first naga launched a spell of its own. The nagas' magic was unique to their species, because their spells had to be triggered with no material ingredients. The first naga's humanlike lips curled back across its needle teeth, and a ball of blue flame rolled down the length of its forked tongue. The naga caught the roiling pellet on the tip of its stinger and then hurled it, with a snap of its tail, straight at Guerrand's back.

The ball expanded as it flew, until it smashed into the protective globe surrounding Guerrand. It flattened itself against the magical field and groped with tendrils of blue flame across the softly glowing surface, searching for any weakness. The blue flame continued growing in size and intensity until it appeared it might engulf Guerrand inside his invulnerable globe.

The high defender could feel the heat against his skin even through the magical shield and cloak. Still, he was confident that the blue flames could not penetrate his defenses. Within moments the flames began to flicker and fade.

Guerrand's vision was obscured by the naga's spell for brief seconds, time the beast used to rush forward, stinger-tipped tail slashing at the wizard. Drawing a small rod from his waist belt, Guerrand leaped toward the thing's tail and struck it. Crimson light flowed out from the rod to encircle the naga, constricting and crushing it. The monster thrashed in a frenzy and stiffened momentarily. But the unearthly glow returned to its eyes as it shook off the rod's effect.

The naga screeched its rage until Guerrand thought his ears would burst. It stopped only to stare at him warily, malevolent intelligence shining in its cruel eyes.

*I'll distract it,* came the thought into Guerrand's mind, *so that you can kill it.*

Startled, Guerrand scanned the room, spotting Zagarus perched atop a bookcase against the far left wall. *No,* he thought. *The naga's too dangerous, Zag. I can handle it. Go back to our quarters.*

But the sea gull was not so easily put off. *I'm sure I can peck a snake without getting hurt.* Zagarus spread his wings and launched himself into a slow glide across the vast, open room.

The naga was weaving back and forth, looking for an opening for its poisoned tail. Zagarus swooped low across the creature's back, slashing at the tiny blue-black scales with his beak. The naga's howl was more pique than pain. The snake-thing whipped its body around like a club so quickly that the sea gull was knocked to the floor.

Dazed by the blow, Zagarus scrambled on the hard tiles to get away from the naga. But he had hardly moved before a stream of smoking ichor sprayed from the naga's mouth and splashed on the gull's back. "Kyeow!" The bird thrashed on the floor as the feathers and flesh on his back bubbled away in sizzling gobs.

"Zag!"

A horrible, burning pain seared Guerrand's spine. He stumbled slightly from the shock, but his mind clung tenaciously to the magical formula he was reciting. In the time the monster had spent responding to Zagarus's unsuspected attack, Guerrand had prepared a spell. Through his and his familiar's shared pain, he recited the magical words before the naga could turn back to him. The floor beneath the thing turned to rippling white liquid. The enormous snake-creature let out another shriek of shock and pain as three-fourths of its length was abruptly rooted to the liquid floor. It fought madly to tear itself away, but without success.

Sensing its doom, the naga flailed in a berserk frenzy to break free. Slowly the last of its head sank, screaming, into the swells of the floor. The porcelain surface immediately returned to its original state, smooth and undisturbed.

Three quick steps brought Guerrand to where Zagarus had fallen. The faithful familiar was lying still, except for his breathing. *It doesn't hurt so bad anymore*, came the bird's thought, labored and slow. *My body is so numb . . . I can hardly . . . feel anything . . .*

Guerrand stroked the gull's dark, feathered head tenderly, his throat thick. *I'm not ready to release you as my familiar, Zag.*

*Of course you aren't, Rand.* Zagarus's thoughts came hard and broken, the effort nearly too much. *I'm a hooded, black-backed Ergothian sea gull—*

"The most strikingly beautiful of all seabirds." With a catch in his voice, Guerrand finished the sea gull's favorite description of himself. Zagarus's dark little eyes sank shut, and his labored breathing stopped. Crimson spears of pain pierced Guerrand's body, twisting upward through him to explode in his head. For several unendurable moments he felt as if he had been ripped in half, front and back, by talons of flame.

The mage fell to the floor. Then the pain fled, leaving only a heavy ache in its wash.

Lying on his side next to Zagarus's still form, Guerrand tasted blood in his mouth. The death of his familiar had caused the terrible reaction in his own body. Guerrand felt mentally weakened, and knew, too, that Zag's passing had drained him of magic that he could never regain. Whatever the cost to himself, Guerrand thought fiercely, Zag had been worth it. He reached out and ran a finger along the bird's white-tipped wings, his ebony back one last time. *Rest well, friend.* There was a hollowness inside Guerrand when, for the first time in more than a decade, there came no echoing response in his head.

Guerrand swallowed his grief and struggled to his feet. He half walked, half hobbled to where Dagamier lay near the door. Expecting that she, too, would be dead, Guerrand was surprised to find her breathing. The wound in her back was ugly. The flesh had blackened and shriveled away from the poison, but the wound wasn't terribly deep. He called Dagamier's name while patting her cheeks, but she responded groggily, as if drugged. Guerrand recalled the nagas' glistening bodies and realized they must have been armed with a paralytic or sleeping poison. He briefly considered running back to his own storeroom for a potion that would neutralize the poison, when a noise behind him in the depths of the white wing made him turn back to the portal.

But the blazing purple opening to the Lost Citadel was gone. Beneath where it had hovered, a much-changed Lyim sat upon a marble slab. Ezius was slumped at his feet, reaching feebly toward the reborn mage. Before Guerrand could do more than take in the scene, Lyim gestured with his hands, and the white-robed mage's head dropped to the floor.

"Lyim!"

Guerrand's old nemesis spun around with a look of joyous anticipation on his face.

"What have you done?" Even as he asked the question, Guerrand knew the answer.

Lyim stood above Ezius's body, smiling malevolently. His once-solid red robe was streaked in shades of bleached and baked red, and his jet-black hair was veined with white. His skin, however, was burned a deep red, with creases so deep they looked like sun-baked cracks. "You can't even imagine where I've been, or the things I've seen, Rand."

"Oh, but I can," Guerrand said, matching Lyim's glare. "I, too, saw the citadel, but I had the strength to turn back. The gods will not let your trespass go unpunished—for any of us." He unconsciously made the warding sign against evil.

Lyim's eyes narrowed. He was silent for a long time, his hands quiet at his sides. Then, unexpectedly, he grinned. It was like a flash of raw light. "Even after all that has happened between us, I can't quite bring myself to hate you, Rand."

A nerve leaped in Guerrand's jaw. "Strange, I have no trouble hating you." His brown eyes narrowed with unconcealed loathing, and he advanced on Lyim.

With a quickness that belied the pain still shooting through his body, Guerrand launched a spell of petrification, hoping to capture Lyim by turning him to stone. Gray dust materialized and swirled around the renegade mage.

Lyim watched it in amusement until, with a wave of his hand, he dispelled it. "We both know I have always been the better mage."

Guerrand bristled under the taunt. He wanted to unleash every bit of magic under his command, but was bound by the Council's directive to take intruders alive to face a tribunal.

He laced his fingers together into a lattice while shouting, "*Dattiva, meshuot, lathrey dattivasum!*"

Thin bars of pure force sprang from the floor to encircle Lyim. Spreading outward and upward from a single point on Lyim's left, they threatened to enclose him. Lyim sprang toward the opening and leaped through before the cage could close. But the bars were quicker than he'd anticipated. They closed on his waist, trapping him partially in and partially out of the cage.

Lyim cast a spell on himself. His body began to swell. His muscles bulged and his chest expanded, straining against the shimmering bars. Massive hands gripped the bars and pushed, bending them outward. The cage of force twisted apart and Lyim stepped out, once again resuming his normal size. But the strain showed on his face.

"All I ever wanted was to heal my hand," he said fiercely, his breath a loose rattling sound.

"No matter the price to others," Guerrand said evenly. He looked at the slumped white-robed mage. "How'd you do it, Lyim? Did you feign death in the courtyard, then overtake poor Ezius once you were inside the white wing?"

Lyim shrugged his muscular shoulders. "Never explain, never defend, that's always been my motto." His smile was anything but apologetic.

"We can see how that's held you in good stead," Guerrand said caustically, "by the success you've made of your life. Lyim Rhistadt, brave slayer of innocent women, children, and old men!"

Eyes narrowed, Lyim rolled his fingers, exposing a sharp-tipped metal dart. Flicking his wrist, he expertly fired the barb at Guerrand. The dart shattered Guerrand's protective shell with a loud *ping!* on its path to the mage's chest. Guerrand dodged to the side in the last heartbeat, and the magical dart's acid tip caught in the flowing right sleeve of his cloak of protection.

Guerrand's hatred flared to new heights. He released the stored-up spell that would magically compel the other mage, then formally declared, "Your actions have made you a renegade, Lyim. Surrender to me and the Conclave will fairly judge your actions."

"I'd end up like Belize." Lyim's eyes shifted as he sensed Guerrand's spell. His anger exploded. "You'll never control me with a geas, Rand, particularly to face the Council. Who are they to judge my actions?"

"They're the peers whose rulings you agreed to uphold when you declared your allegiance to the Red Robes."

"Not anymore," vowed Lyim, his bitterness obvious in the pinched line of his mouth. "Now that I've spent time in both a red and a white robe, I must confess I find both of them confining." He paused, head tilted in thought. "I have pursued magic according to the Council's rules for nearly a decade," Lyim said slowly, as though the truth of that had just occurred to him. "Magic, in all its machinations, has consumed nearly two thirds of my life. And it has failed me at almost every turn."

"You chose your own path, Lyim. Everything," said Guerrand, repeating Lyim's own words, "is a question of choice."

Lyim's eyes narrowed, and he seemed about to speak when the floor shuddered faintly. The quaking was weak at first, then it stopped entirely. Both mages looked at each other suspiciously. Moments later the quaking returned, stronger and of longer duration than before. With the third occurrence, beakers and other glass and ceramic containers on Ezius's shelves rattled.

Lyim reached for the marble slab to steady himself.

"It's not me," he said, a look of concern crossing his face for the first time since he'd emerged from the portal.

The tremors had grown so strong that it was difficult to stand. Guerrand's first thought was to check the scrying diorama for disturbances on Bastion's plane. He stumbled toward the doorway to the nave, collapsing to his knees when he reached the spot where Dagamier still lay unconscious. Looking out into the nave, he saw that the quakes passed through Bastion like a wave, shaking each wing of the building as they passed and returned.

Books crashed off the shelves, followed by glassware. Looking back toward Ezius's laboratory, Guerrand saw vials, spell components, scrolls, and untold other mystical ingredients smashing together on the floor. Jars were exploding on the shelves, sending smoking fragments of glass and pottery through the air.

Guerrand was unsure whether the white wizard was alive or dead, but while there was a chance to save him Guerrand could not give Ezius up. He dashed back into the wing to save the mage. "No one's safe in here, Lyim," Guerrand said to the wizard. "Help me get Ezius and Dagamier into the nave." Without waiting for an answer, Guerrand grabbed Ezius's robe and dragged the white mage's body toward the doorway.

Lyim, looking about in stunned disbelief, seemed barely to hear him. "What's happening, Rand?"

Guerrand came to the doorway and stopped briefly. "As I feared, the gods of magic are not letting your trespass into the Lost Citadel go unpunished. They're destroying Bastion. We've got to get out into the courtyard before we're crushed."

Energized by adrenalin, the high defender grabbed Dagamier's robe with his free hand and dragged her along with Ezius out into the nave, away from a rapidly building cloud of vapor that choked the white wing. Another tremor drove the struggling Guerrand to his knees as chunks of masonry rained down from the dome roof. With a tremendous crash, the scrying chamber collapsed in a boiling cloud of dust. Rays of white light pierced the rubble, searing outward in every direction. Mercury and sulfur spilled out from under the pile to drain into the tiny moat.

The trembling now was continuous, with no discernable pattern. Guerrand heard explosions in each of the wings. Through the open doorway, he saw flashes of lightning zigzagging crazily about the white wing.

"Come on, Lyim, before it's too late!"

Lyim's response was a piercing scream. His tortured howl rose above the tumult, then was lost again in chaos.

Guerrand's attention was drawn away from Lyim's fate as swirling shapes, like speeding, mother-of-pearl clouds, formed from the magical mortar between blocks in the nave. The choking, dust-filled air there filled quickly with these energized clouds, streaking in from all three wings and swooping around like malefic birds. Two rushed at Guerrand, eyes blazing and gaping jaws full of razor teeth. The dust-streaked mage hadn't time to dodge when the first shape crashed into him. The entity of coalesced energy knocked Guerrand sprawling to the floor with a bad gash in his arm. Others surged forward behind the first, but Guerrand dived out of their way as they swooped past to smash holes in the dome and knock out massive sections of wall. The odd, dim light of the courtyard cut through the dusty air in slants.

The stored magical energy of a thousand mages was being unleashed with instruction to destroy. Guerrand had to get the defenders out of the stronghold and into the courtyard, where at least they would stand a chance.

Guerrand looked toward the apse, a tumbled heap of shifting rubble. The high defender crouched between the still forms of the other two sentinels and formed the words of a spell in his mind. It was a dangerous gamble. Safe teleportation required perfect knowledge of the destination, and Guerrand had no idea what sort of changes might have occurred outside from the devastation. He willed total concentration until, once again, he experienced the familiar sensation of momentary unreality.

Guerrand nearly cried his relief when he opened his eyes and saw the shadows of the topiaries, though half of them were ripped out by the roots. Blocks from the facade had fallen here, too, but not nearly as many as inside. He chanted and motioned again, and a clear shell, like half of a hollow crystal orb, formed above their heads. It grew into a perfect semicircle and sealed itself against the ground. The shell wasn't high enough for Guerrand to do more than sit, particularly with the prone forms of Ezius and Dagamier, but it was welcome sanctuary. Guerrand turned his attention to the wounds of his fallen comrades.

Four multicolored shapes, ravenous creatures of coalesced smoke and ash, dashed themselves against the barrier. They slashed and gnawed at the clear surface with talons and teeth that grew longer as the entities' fury mounted.

But the creatures scattered when they heard the dome of the nave crash down inside the stronghold. The hammer blow resounded like a huge bass drum even in the courtyard. Guerrand watched as the entire roof of Bastion collapsed. Tons upon tons of elemental-forged stone and masonry rained down inside the walls and outside upon Guerrand's protective sphere. Summoning the very dregs of his magical energy, he strained to maintain the spell and hold up the shield, fearing the pounding would never stop.

When the last block in the last wall fell, Bastion's magical essence turned on itself, as if one last battle between the orders of magic remained. The mortar fiends sank their razor-sharp teeth into each other in a hideous feeding frenzy until all but one were devoured.

Inside the protective shell, Guerrand waited to emerge until after that last bloated fiend exploded from its gorging. Only a handful of whole red blocks of granite remained in his wing. Numb, Bastion's high defender stared at the rubble for many moments. A hollow wind sounded in the distant corners of this plane that had known no breeze. Guerrand raised a feeble, dust- and blood-covered hand in a spell.

*Dimu sagistara.*

One of the blocks jerked from the rubble and rose shakily above the others. His muscles shook from the effort, but Guerrand held the block aloft by sheer dint of will until his failing energy couldn't be denied. Acknowledging the futility of the gesture, Bastion's high defender directed the block to fall again. The stronghold built with the energy of a thousand mages could not be rebuilt by one.

\* \* \* \* \*

The full Conclave of twenty-one mages never failed to inspire reverence among its members. They gathered only rarely in the cold and cheerless Hall of Mages, the vast chamber in the base of Wayreth's south tower. Par-Salian of the White Robes, Head of the Conclave of Wizards, sat upon a great carved throne in a semicircle of stone chairs. To his right, as always, sat LaDonna, Mistress of the Black Robes. The six stone chairs next to her were filled with wizards clothed all in black, their hoods pulled low over their faces. To

Par-Salian's left sat Justarius of the Red Robes, his six red members of the Conclave beside him. The remaining white representatives finished the circle.

Never a lighthearted affair, the gathering this day was unusually grim. All twenty-one members were feeling the effects of the magical essence they'd lost with Bastion's destruction. The stronghold they had united to create was rubble on a distant plane. Bastion had collapsed under the wrathful hands of the gods of magic.

Par-Salian spoke from his chair in the center of the dais. "Fellow mages," the venerable white-haired wizard said, "we gather again under dark circumstances. However, I submit to you that while Bastion was destroyed, it did not fail."

Par-Salian's announcement fell like drops of water into a still pond, causing ripples of movement and sound through the vast and shadowed chamber.

"We—not just the guardians, but all twenty-one of us—failed Bastion and the mages we represent." Par-Salian's icy blue gaze swept over the wizards on either side of him.

The heads of the three defenders of Bastion—Guerrand of the Red Robes, Dagamier of the Black Robes, and Ezius of the White Robes—dipped noticeably lower. Noting that, Par-Salian held up a pale, wrinkled hand to silence the restless gathering.

"Bastion's collapse was caused not by incompetence," he insisted, his voice sharp, "but by arrogance." There were more angry murmurs, and a number of the Black Robes threw back their hoods and raised up in their stone seats. Sadness was reflected in the faces of most of the red and white-robed mages.

"I would finish!" Par-Salian snapped. His anger rolled around the hall like thunder. After a moment, the Black Robes reluctantly dropped back in their seats, still frowning. "This fractious meeting proves my point. All of us had more pride in our orders than in the thing that unites us: our Art. Magic is our first loyalty, no matter who we serve or what color robes we wear." His white head shook ruefully. "We forgot that when designing Bastion in three distinct and separate wings." The head of the Conclave was disrupted anew by voices.

Dark-haired LaDonna rose from her seat and waved an arm like an ominous raven's wing. "Silence!" The head of the black order spoke so seldom during the Conclave that everyone fell quiet in surprise. LaDonna's black eyes pierced those of her order. "We Black Robes were the greatest culprits in this," she said bitterly. "Our own wing was a model of disunity. While that reflects our natures, it worked in opposition to the purpose of Bastion."

"We share the blame equally," insisted Justarius, with a firm shake of his salt-and-pepper head. "And from it shall we learn equally."

"*That* is the point of this Conclave," Par-Salian interrupted with a relieved sigh. "It was not enough to give a part of our magic to Bastion's mortar." Par-Salian paused deliberately, letting his words penetrate the disparate temperaments of the Conclave.

Then, very slowly, the Head of the Conclave let a hopeful smile spread across his lined face, to encourage the healing of Krynn's wizards. "All is not lost, brother mages," he said at length. "The Council of Three has decided to rebuild Bastion. This time, however, it shall truly represent the cooperative effort of all three orders of magic. One structure designed by all three, inhabited by a representative of all three. Next to the entry of our failure, Astinus the historian will record a new spirit of cooperation between our orders."

A silence descended while the Conclave absorbed

the decree.

"Are you seeking new candidates for the defender positions?" asked a member of the Red Robes.

Justarius cleared his throat. "I can't speak for the white and black orders, but—"

"If it pleases the Council," Ezius of the White Robes said anxiously, "I would like to keep the post I have held since Bastion was first raised." He touched a hand to his bandaged head. "These will be off shortly, and I'm told I'll be fully recovered."

"Duly noted," said Par-Salian with a nod.

"As for the Red Robes . . ." Justarius turned his thick, raised eyebrows to face Bastion's high defender. "What say you, Guerrand DiThon?"

Guerrand stood self-consciously and bowed to the Conclave as custom dictated. He spoke without guilt or guile. "Acting as Bastion's high defender has been the greatest experience and honor of my life," he said. "That is why I must relinquish the position. There is another more deserving and desirous of the post." His gaze crossed the room to the young mage of the Black Robes. Dagamier's face spread into a grateful smile that few there recalled ever having seen from her.

Justarius leaned forward in his chair, wincing at the pressure on his game leg. "You would not be saying this out of a feeling of failure?"

"No, Justarius." Guerrand's denial was genuine. "You have made me see the error of that thinking. In truth, I believe my magical skills are needed more in my homeland." He bowed his head in respect. "Of course, I submit myself to the will of the Council of Three in this decision."

The Council briefly conferred quietly. All three heads nodded as they leaned apart. "Your request to be replaced is approved," announced Justarius.

LaDonna's gaze fell upon Dagamier, though she

spoke to Guerrand. "Your suggestion for replacement is well taken, but it requires further discussion." The young wizardess's head bowed respectfully to the mistress of her order.

"What of the renegade who set in motion the destruction of Bastion?" demanded a black wizard from the depths of his drawn hood.

"Lyim Rhistadt is dead," exclaimed Ezius of the White Robes. "No one could have survived the destruction inside Bastion."

"No body was found," Dagamier pointed out softly.

Par-Salian frowned. "If he is alive, Lyim Rhistadt will be dealt with in the manner of all renegades." The head of the Conclave pushed himself up from his stone throne. "This special Conclave is adjourned. We will gather again at the usual time in a fortnight, when Solinari is in High Sanction. Until then, I counsel you all to consider your part in the construction of the new Bastion."

The Council of Three stayed behind while the White Robes filed out first according to custom. They were followed by the Black Robes, in deference to LaDonna's secondary seat on the Council of Three. Justarius's Red Robes were the last to vacate their seats among the dark shadows of the Hall of Mages.

It had also become custom among the Council of Three to conclude each Conclave with a reflective bottle of elven wine. Justarius did the honors this time, producing from thin air a dusty red bottle and three delicate crystal goblets.

Par-Salian swirled the rosy liquid in his glass, then sipped gingerly at the rim. Just as he liked it: dry. "Lyim Rhistadt does present a dilemma," he said almost without voice.

LaDonna lifted a plucked black brow, slender fingers twirling the fragile stem of her glass. "That depends on whether you feel compelled to obey the letter of our laws."

The wine was too acrid for Justarius's taste. He set the goblet down after one sip. "I agree with LaDonna in this, Par-Salian. *If* he is alive, Lyim is too dangerous to round up in the usual manner for tribunal. We all know what must be done to insure the survival of our Art."

Par-Salian bowed his balding pate briefly. "The survival of magic alone must guide our actions," he agreed. "Very well, then." The Head of the Conclave swallowed the last of his ruby wine before waving a white-robed arm. Three heavily cloaked figures appeared from the shadows. Though the colors of their robes identified their different magical orders, they held one thing in common: the assassin's scimitars slung across their backs.